ALMA
THE YOUNGER

OTHER BOOKS AND AUDIO BOOKS
BY H.B. MOORE:

Out of Jerusalem: Of Goodly Parents

Out of Jerusalem: A Light in the Wilderness

Out of Jerusalem: Towards the Promised Land

Out of Jerusalem: Land of Inheritance

Abinadi

Alma

OTHER BOOKS PUBLISHED UNDER
HEATHER B. MOORE:

Women of the Book of Mormon: Insights and Inspirations

a novel by

H.B. MOORE

Covenant Communications, Inc.

Cover image, *The Conversion of Alma and the Sons of Mosiah* © Gary Kapp.

Cover design copyrighted 2010 by Covenant Communications, Inc.

Published by Covenant Communications, Inc.
American Fork, Utah

Printed in The United States of America
First Printing: June 2010

15 14 13 12 11 10   10 9 8 7 6 5 4 3 2 1

ISBN: 978-1-60861-020-4

Praise for H.B. Moore's Books

"*Alma* has it all: vibrant characters, danger, spiritual challenges, and bittersweet joy. Moore has created an epic tale that's simply impossible to put down."

—Jason F. Wright
New York Times Bestselling Author

". . . an exciting and faith-promoting tale—the Book of Mormon in 3-D and Technicolor."

—Richard Cracroft
BYU Magazine

"In a pattern that has become warmly familiar, H.B. Moore crafts a page-turning yet well-researched story of the challenges that a Book of Mormon personality faces when trying to lead a colony of believers to safety, not once but twice. Alma the Elder, who begins his life in debauchery, becomes the respected adviser to a king and the leader of his church, and more. On a personal level, this man becomes the model for all of us who seek to arrest a wasted life and turn it into something grand and meaningful."

—S. Kent Brown
Assistant Director, BYU Jerusalem Center

"[*Alma*] is an exciting and interesting exploration of the followers and enemies of Alma and how they might have been involved in and affected by what happened. Not only do they struggle to survive, but the characters love and mourn and laugh and misunderstand and grow together, or apart, as the case may be. Moore is true to what is known about that time and place, and this book offers worthy speculations of what surrounded those events."

—Kathleen Dalton-Woodbury
Mormon Times

"H.B. Moore takes the reader on an incredible journey of a man who makes the ultimate sacrifice. *Abinadi* is a historically rich, well researched, poignant account of one of the most influential prophets in the Book of Mormon. Moore's creativity, mixed with the heart of Mesoamerican culture, brings new insights to the influence that the prophet Abinadi had on generations to come."

—Dian Thomas
#1 New York Times Bestselling Author

"This book is a delightful combination of careful research and getting inside an inspiring character. Although H.B. Moore disclaims being a scholar, her Abinadi not only lives and breathes but is authentic to the time and place in which he lived. While she paints a fuller picture of a fascinating Book of Mormon character, she stays close to the facts, as presented in that book."

—Ann Madsen
Professor of Ancient Scripture, BYU

"[Moore] is adept at building suspense even in such a well-known story. Those who like scriptural stories dramatized will enjoy this one whether young or older. Even those who prefer to not mix scriptural stories with fiction will find this story will draw them in with vivid details of the life and culture of this historical era in Mesoamerica and Moore's careful adherence to the facts of the story."

—Jennie Hansen
Meridian Magazine

"In the first three volumes of her [Out of Jerusalem] series, H.B. Moore showed that she could create a view of an ancient world that combines the best scholarship with a lively imagination. She does a fine job of walking the tricky line of faithfulness to the scripture and creative storytelling. She opened up the hearts of her characters in ways both remarkably touching and authentic. In [the] fourth and final volume she does all of that, as well as writing one of the most exciting adventure tales that I have read in a while."

—Andrew Hall, *Association of Mormon Letters*

For my son, Kaelin
A mother's prayer is always heard.

GULF OF MEXICO
Bay of Campeche
Narrow Neck of Land
MEXICO
Wilderness of Hermounts
Valley of Gideon
Chiapa de Corzo
Hill Amnih
Land of Zarahemla
R. Sidon
GULF OF TEHUANTEPEC

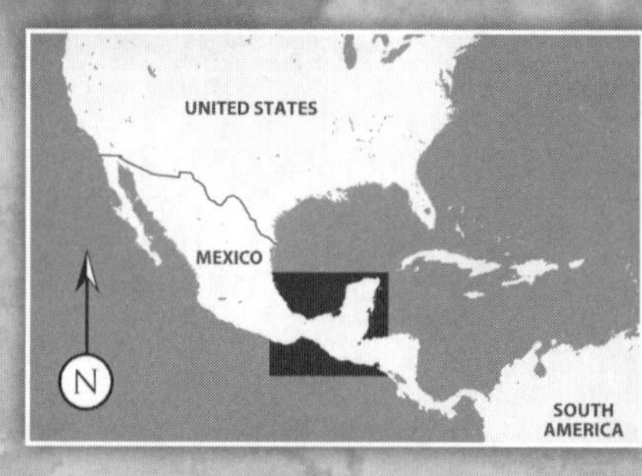

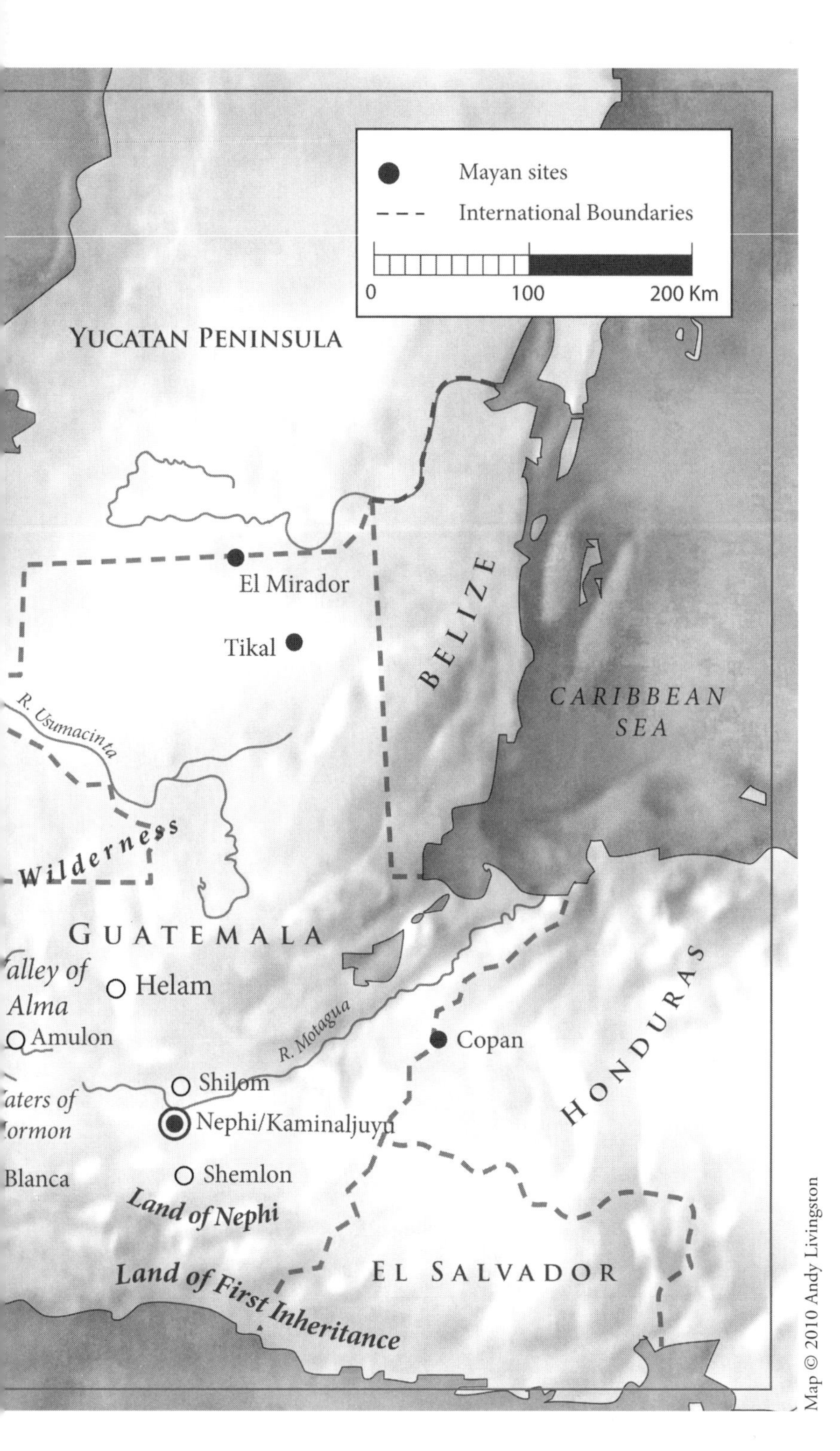

Mayan sites
International Boundaries
0
100
200 Km
YUCATAN PENINSULA
El Mirador
Tikal
BELIZE
CARIBBEAN SEA
R. Usumacinta
Wilderness
GUATEMALA
alley of Alma
Helam
Amulon
R. Motagua
Copan
HONDURAS
Shilom
aters of ormon
Nephi/Kaminaljuyu
Blanca
Shemlon
Land of Nephi
Land of First Inheritance
EL SALVADOR

Acknowledgments

The brainstorming of plot and character are essential ingredients before a word is typed onto a page. Preparing to write Alma the Younger's story was no exception. Part of the challenge was creating a protagonist who was also the antagonist of the story. Thanks to my parents, Kent and Gayle Brown, who answered endless questions and read early drafts of the manuscript.

Gratitude goes to my various alpha readers who were fastidious as always, yet encouraging at the same time: Annette Lyon, Lu Ann Staheli, Robison Wells, Jeff Savage, Michele Holmes, and GG Vandagriff.

I deeply appreciate my network of support: my father-in-law, Lester Moore; webmaster Phill Babbitt; and map designer Andy Livingston. Special thanks to all those at my publishing house, Covenant Communications, who have a hand in the final product: Eliza Nevin, editor; Kathy Jenkins, managing editor; Margaret Weber, designer; Robby Nichols, marketing; and Kelly Smurthwaite, publicity. I also belong to two writing communities, the LDStorymakers and the League of Utah Writers, who have been an excellent resource in many areas.

Also, many thanks to my readers and the reviewers who continue to support my work and spread the word.

Last, but never least, thanks to my husband, Chris, and my children for supporting me when their wife/mom spent many years writing and "hoping" to get a book published.

Preface

In the book of Mosiah, we learn that Alma the Elder has been made high priest over all of the land of Zarahemla (Mosiah 26:7–8). When he and his band of believers, who had escaped the wicked leader Amulon, had arrived in Zarahemla, King Mosiah was there to greet them (Mosiah 24:25), just as he welcomed Limhi, former king of the land of Nephi, and his people (Mosiah 22:14). A fantastic reunion must have taken place among friends and possibly family members.

Life for Alma and his people must have been bliss compared to the previous years of near slavery in the land of Helam. Alma and his followers are finally able to worship the Lord openly and establish His Church throughout the land with the blessing of King Mosiah. The years pass in relative peace, except for some persecution from the nonbelievers toward the members of the Church.

In spite of King Mosiah's decree against religious persecution, his sons, along with one of Alma's sons, choose to join the unbelievers and become a threat to the stability of the Church of God. Alma discovers that his son, Alma the Younger, has turned into a "very wicked and an idolatrous man . . . therefore he led many of the people to do after the manner of his iniquities" (Mosiah 27:8). If there was ever a time for a father to pray for his son, this was it.

The question is whether Alma the Younger knew that what he was doing was wrong. Or had he been so carefully led by Satan down the path of idolatry, and an anti-Christ pattern of belief, that he truly believed he was in the right?

Another question we might entertain is how Alma the Younger could exert so much influence over people as to lead them astray from the Church. The record tells us that he did "speak much flattery to the people" (Mosiah 27:8). He must have been a natural leader, charismatic and easily loved by people, with the power to persuade. His influence nearly toppled the Church in Zarahemla as he stole "away the hearts of the people; causing much dissension" (v 9), so his preaching was no small thing.

In studying Mosiah 26–28, I was struck with the idea that Alma the Younger was no rebellious teenager, playing pranks or skipping Sabbath meetings to go fishing or hunting. He must have been intelligent and well educated. If he was so intellectual, could this have contributed to his lack of faith or to a lack of humility to turn to the Lord like a little child? This led me to a study of the classic analogy of an anti-Christ.

Robert L. Millet gave an exemplary description of an anti-Christ: "they deny the need for Jesus Christ"; "they use flattery to win disciples"; "they accuse the brethren of teaching false doctrine"; "they have a limited view of reality"; "they have a disposition to misread and thereby misrepresent the scriptures"; and "they are sign seekers." (See Robert L. Millet, *The Book of Mormon: Jacob Through Words of Mormon, To Learn with Joy,* "Sherem the Anti-Christ," 176–182.)

"They are sign seekers" is a powerful consideration. In discussion with several colleagues who've had family members and friends stray from the Church, there was a resounding theme. Their loved ones wanted "proof" or a "sign" that the Lord was real and that His Church was true. They desired intellectual and physical manifestation or they refused to believe. Also, these doubters had "all or nothing" types of personalities. I can very well see that when Alma the Younger doubted, he went to the extreme and led souls down with him. When he believed, he did just the opposite and spent the rest of his life preaching and sharing his testimony. This does not make his story one that was "happily ever after," however. In fact, Hugh Nibley clarified that Alma the Younger and the sons of Mosiah "suffered the rest of their lives because of what they had done" (*Teachings of the Book of Mormon—Semester Two,* 153).

A final question we might ask is why the Lord saw fit to send an angel to intervene in Alma the Younger's behalf. Yes, his father and many others had been praying and fasting for him to have a change of heart. But there are many parents who pray for their errant children and angels aren't sent. This led me to believe that what Alma the Younger was doing had such grave consequences and the potential to devastate an entire nation—thus thwarting the Lord's plan—that extreme action was needed. Nibley pointed out that "throughout the Book of Mormon . . . angels only appear in times of great crisis to reverse the course of history. They turn it around" (*Teachings of the Book of Mormon—Semester Two,* 151).

Alma the Younger is a story of hope and redemption. It's my hope that we can learn from Alma's journey and fully embrace the Atonement in our own lives—just as Alma did.

Character Chart

Alma the Elder—High Priest in Zarahemla
Married to Maia*
Sons: Alma the Younger
Cephas*
Daughters: Bethany*
Dana*

King Mosiah—King of Zarahemla
Married to Naomi*
Sons: Ammon
Aaron
Omner
Himni
Daughter: Cassia*

Limhi—Former king of the land of Nephi
Married to Miriam*
Son: Nehem*
Daughter: Ilana*

Gideon—Legion Commander

Priests in Zarahemla
Helam
Jachin*, father of Maia*
Ben*
Abe*, son of Abinadi

Future missionaries who will serve with the sons of Mosiah
Muloki
Ammah

*Denotes fictional names/characters created by the author

CHAPTER 1

A foolish son is a grief to his father, and bitterness to her that bare him.
—Proverbs17:25

94 BC

Alma the Elder

The pulsing of the drums vibrated the walls as Alma the Elder entered his home, frantically searching for his wife and children. "Maia!" he yelled, alarm in his voice betraying the fear in his heart. Something moved in the cooking room to his left, and he spun around. "Maia?"

She stepped out of the late afternoon shadow that stretched across the room, her trembling hands gripping the arms of their girls, Bethany and Dana. "Is it the Lamanites?" she whispered, her eyes wide with fright.

"No," Alma almost shouted, crossing to her in three steps and enveloping his family in his arms. He buried his face against his wife's hair, breathing deeply, trying to calm himself. "A mob has broken into the temple."

"What?" Maia gasped and clung to him, shuddering.

But Alma drew away, staring into his wife's dark gray eyes. "Listen to me carefully. Rebels have threatened to destroy the temple before, but now it's happened."

"Who is it, Alma?" Maia breathed. "Who's leading this mob?"

"We don't know. King Mosiah thinks it might be a former Church member or maybe a former palace guard, someone with just enough knowledge of the temple to find the weak spots in our security." His wife nodded, but Alma hadn't delivered all the news yet. "Threats have reached the king's ears—threats against his family . . . and ours. We need to evacuate our property immediately."

Maia stiffened, a horrible understanding dawning on her face. "They've threatened *us?*"

The girls seemed to melt behind their mother, their expressions anxious.

"Yes," he said, trying to keep panic out of his voice. "We are to take cover at the king's hunting lodge. Until Commander Gideon and his soldiers who are stationed at the borders arrive to offer additional defense, we are in great danger. Some of the king's own soldiers have defected—we don't know who to trust anymore. There's no telling how many have switched loyalties. Two guards are outside waiting to lead us to safety. The royal family has already fled. We need to move quickly. Bring what we can carry."

His wife's gaze faltered, and she looked around the cooking room. "All right. Then we'll put together some food, and the rest will be left behind," she said as she released Alma and turned to the girls. "Go get two tunics each, one extra robe, and one favorite item."

The girls broke from their mother and hurried to their room.

"Cephas is napping in our bed." Maia pushed past Alma and entered the bedchamber. Alma followed, trading his indigo and silver embroidered high priest robes for a plain brown one that hung on a peg by the door.

He crossed to the platform bed where the copper curls of Cephas's head peeked from beneath the rug that covered him. Alma pulled back the rug and touched his six-year-old son's shoulder. "Wake up."

Cephas's eyes flew open. "Father!" His small arms wrapped around Alma's neck. For a second Alma allowed himself to cradle the child's head against his shoulder. His heart swelled, thinking of the sweet innocence of this boy, and how his older brother used to be just like this.

"Come on, son, we're going on a hike," Alma said.

"Can Mother come too?" Cephas asked.

Alma smiled and pulled his son close again. "Yes, Mother will come too." He looked over at Maia, who was rifling through a small wooden chest, pulling out pieces of jewelry. "Just take the box, Maia."

Her hands paused as she looked up at him. "I don't need it all—just some things to pass down to the girls in case—" Her voice cut off as her mouth trembled. She bit her lower lip, turning away again.

"What's wrong with Mother?" Cephas asked.

Alma turned to him. "Go help your sisters get ready for the hike."

Cephas looked from his mother to his father, then nodded and scurried from the room.

Alma pulled the rug from their platform bed and spread it on the floor. "Just pile things on this. I'll carry it." She nodded without speaking, and Alma left the room in search of weapons. He hesitated outside of his oldest son's room. His namesake, Alma the Younger, had left months before, after a heated argument—he was old enough to be married and living on his own but had never taken responsibility seriously. His son's last rebellion—at least, as far as Alma knew—had been to quit his position as a temple scribe. Soon after deserting the temple position, his son had moved out of the home, leaving no word of his whereabouts.

Alma walked through his son's doorway, seeing the bow and sheaf of arrows propped in the corner of the room. The bow had been one of his son's prized possessions, left behind in a flurry of anger. Alma gathered up the bow and sheaf, then from a high shelf, he took down a knife with an elaborately decorated hilt—a gift from Ammon, the eldest son of King Mosiah. Ammon had a fascination with weapon-making, and Alma the Younger was the finest hunter in the land of Zarahemla.

And tonight these decorative weapons may save my family, Alma thought. He hid the knife in his waistband and hoisted the bow and quiver over his shoulder. He took a final glance about his son's room before leaving. It felt empty—as if the room had never been occupied by a vibrant, brilliant young man—a young man who refused to believe that a Church member could rely on faith alone, a young man whose intellect was so vast he could not humble himself to ask the Lord a simple question.

Alma turned from the emptiness and left the room, dreading the position that he was in tonight with his family. When he had arrived at Zarahemla more than twenty years before, he had thought he'd never have to gather up his loved ones and run from hatred again. And now it was within the city that the hatred had festered.

"We're ready," Maia called out.

He walked into the front room, where his family stood holding separate bundles. At their feet lay a larger bundle for him to carry. Even Cephas carried a rolled up bundle. Ten-year-old Dana's angelic face was paler than usual, her gray eyes—so much like her mother's—blinking back tears. Bethany, at fourteen, had a protective arm about Dana's shoulders.

Alma's gaze moved to his wife, and emotion rocked through him. Maia knew that the bow he carried was their son's. If the rebels invaded their home, it might also be the last remaining item they'd have to remember their son by.

"What if he returns and we're gone? How will he find us?" Bethany asked, the boldness of her words hidden by her dark eyelashes that fluttered nervously.

"Your older brother has had plenty of chances to return," Maia said in a dejected tone. "He'll certainly hear of what might happen to our home, wherever he is." Her gaze met Alma's again over the head of their daughter.

"Can we leave him a scroll with a message?" Bethany asked, her eyes hopeful.

Alma shook his head. "It could fall into the wrong hands." The unending pulsing of the drums from the city brought back the sense of foreboding, and a new urgency filled him. "We must go." He reached for the bundle and swung it onto his back with a grunt. His days of hard labor were long over. Although he still spent many hours overseeing his crop workers and fields, the majority of his time was spent in the temple. This trek would be physically hard, yet he hoped it wasn't a permanent sign of things to come.

He grasped his wife's hand as they followed the girls out the door. Cephas ran ahead, only to be called back to wait for the rest. The drums were louder now, vibrating through the warm afternoon. The thudding echoed the sick feeling in Alma's stomach. From their property they could just see the roof of the temple over the trees.

In his mind, he pictured the edifice perched on top of a western hill above King Mosiah's elegant palace. It was as if the building were set in its own grove of beauty—luxurious gardens surrounded the temple, flowers blooming along the edges of the stairs, creating a heavenly scent that reached down the hillside. But he suspected that tonight the gardens would be trampled. He hoped the priests had been able to get most of the records out of the archive. A single flaming torch could destroy the stories of their people forever.

The two guards waited by the gate of the courtyard. They nodded a silent greeting, then led the way, avoiding the wide road that led into the heart of the city. The center plaza at the foot of the palace would certainly be crowded with the mob. The guards guided them along a narrower side path that was used mostly for leading animals to market.

Suddenly Dana broke away from them. "My goat. Eli!"

Maia handed her bundle to Alma and hurried after their daughter. She reached Dana before she could get very far. "We'll be back," she said, putting her arms around Dana.

But she shook her head, the tears coming fast. "Who will feed Eli in the morning?"

Alma would have chuckled if his daughter didn't look so pitiful. Her favorite goat would have no trouble finding something to nibble on.

Reluctantly, she returned to the family, and they continued following the guards along the bumpy trail. Just before the path joined the main road that led into the city, the guards stopped. "We'll cut through the trees until we have circled the palace," one said. "There will be a lot of hill climbing once we reach the king's preserve. But we should arrive at the lodge before it's too dark for traveling."

Cephas still ran and skipped, his energy far from depleted, but the girls looked exhausted, so Alma redistributed their bundles and put more weight into his. Dana's eyes were bright with unshed tears; Bethany's lips were pursed with determination. His wife cast him a grateful glance, and they set off through the trees.

As the trees thinned, the temple came into view. It stood on the opposite side of the grand plaza, a centerpiece to the orange sun to the west. The brilliant architecture rose from the escarpment, seeming to touch the sky. Alma stopped, and the guards paused. He stared at the people who had gathered in the plaza. At least a dozen drummers had set up in front of the temple steps, pounding on their instruments in powerful unison. All three tiers of the steps were occupied by various groups, and others hovered by the sacrificial altars on the platform that surrounded the temple mount. His gaze moved to the tower that had been erected by King Benjamin at the side of the temple. Just beyond the tower was a smaller building, used to archive the priestly records—where his son had once served as a scribe.

At least the door to the records room remained shut. For now.

Northeast of the temple stood the palace, surrounded by King Mosiah's royal soldiers—at least the ones who had remained loyal. The palace seemed well protected, but the king's soldiers made no move to scatter the temple intruders—there were just too many of them. Alma knew they were waiting for Gideon and his border soldiers to arrive and offer reinforcements. The king's soldiers kept an eye on the mob in the plaza below and those above at the temple but didn't attempt to intervene or control the crowd. Alma shook his head in disbelief at the number of rebels mixed with defected soldiers milling in the plaza. There were more than he could have ever anticipated.

Maia's hand rested on his arm, pointing toward the temple. "What are they doing?"

His stomach knotted as he spied men running through the carved stone archway leading to the temple entrance, their bare heads and torsos painted with dark crimson marks—as if they were ready for war. Then his heart jolted as a man was dragged out of the temple. He was clearly a priest, wearing the indigo robes trimmed in silver embroidery that marked his temple office.

"Ben," he whispered. Ben was a master blacksmith and newly ordained priest.

Maia grabbed Cephas's hand and drew her daughters closer as they watched Ben fight fiercely against his captors, but he was outnumbered. The unbelievers forced Ben to his knees, and one of them struck the priest on the side of his head, finally bringing him into submission.

"No," Alma said, jerking forward. His mind raced. There was one of him, and hundreds of unbelievers—but something had to be done. Maybe he could urge the palace soldiers into action. Ben was struck again, and this time the force sent him sprawling.

Maia put a hand over Cephas's eyes, and Bethany and Dana cried out and clung to their mother.

Alma turned to the guards. "Take them to the king's lodge. I'll meet you there."

"No, Alma," Maia said, and Dana started to cry.

He met his wife's gaze, feeling her fear pierce him straight through.

"Hurry," he said, then looked at the guards. "Keep them safe."

Maia backed away, pulling Cephas and the girls with her. "Please Alma, come with us."

"I can't," he said in a pained voice, watching his family leave with the guards. When they had disappeared into the thick of the trees, he tore his gaze from the last glimpse of his family to look at the temple mount.

Ben had rolled over, and one of the men kicked him in the side.

For an instant Alma couldn't move, his gaze locked on the horror before him. His head throbbed as the drums seemed to grow louder, faster, matching the rhythm of his pounding heart. No man deserved this treatment, especially Ben. He was no criminal facing his fate. Ben was a man who had been orphaned as a child, stood up to a wicked king, suffered wrongful imprisonment, traveled the length of a country with Alma, been forced into servitude by the enemy, and . . .

Now several men were on top of Ben. *They're tying him up.*

Memories flashed through Alma's mind—prisoners tied up, prisoners killed for little more than a small infraction, prisoners beaten to death with flaming sticks . . . burned alive.

Like Abinadi.

Not again . . . Something snapped in Alma's mind. It didn't matter that he was armed with only a knife and a few arrows. He was not a soldier commissioned to protect an empty palace, but the protector of his people as the leader who delivered them from the hands of King Noah and Amulon.

Alma started running toward the plaza.

Withdrawing the knife at his waistband, he pushed through the last of the brush, his eyes focused on the limestone platform at the top of the temple steps.

His feet hit the hard earth of the plaza, and he jostled his way through the crowd. It parted, letting him through, as if the men were curious to see what this madman would do.

Alma kept the knife low and angled downward; he didn't want anyone to know his plan before he reached Ben. He sidestepped the rebels on the steps leading to the temple. His legs burned as he leapt up the stairs, but he ignored the deep ache, focusing on the laughing men who had started to kick Ben again.

A man moved in front of him, and a fist slammed into Alma's stomach. He reeled back. Losing his balance, he stumbled backwards, his hip then shoulder crashing against the stairs. He slid down to the base. In the fall, he'd lost hold of his knife. The rebels buzzed around him, but it was difficult to understand what anyone was talking about. Alma rolled over and moved to his knees. His shoulder pulsed with pain, and his left hand was badly scraped.

He scrambled to his feet again, scouring the ground for the fallen knife. He wiped at his nose, coming away with blood on his hand. He turned, scanning the stairs to see if the knife had tumbled down, but the moving feet made it impossible to see much. A few men gave him curious looks, yet no one asked him questions.

Alma took a deep breath and turned toward the steps. As he started to climb, he noticed stone idols perched on the top platform. They were in the form of a woman, a warrior woman. Before he could guess which pagan goddess the statue was, a hand clamped down on his shoulder, and a large man moved in front of him. "You didn't learn your lesson the first time? Where's your armband?"

Alma looked the man over, noticing the red leather armband with the imprint of a half-moon. Was this their leader? He certainly looked ferocious enough. The man's dark hair was long and filthy, and his skin and robe reeked of spoiled wine.

"No armband, no access to the temple," the man growled.

The increasing weight of the man's hand on his shoulder caused Alma to stagger down a step. "I want to free that man up there—the man wearing the blue robes."

"The king's priest?" The man's eyes narrowed. "You know him?"

"He's done nothing to you. I'll give you whatever you want."

The man threw his head back and laughed. Then he sobered and glared at Alma. "I don't want your silver, old man. I'm afraid it's too late to help him. Maybe you'd like to join him, though?" His grip tightened on Alma's shoulder, and he leaned forward. "You can stay in the plaza and watch the ceremony, but if you try to step on temple steps again, I won't be so kind."

Alma took another step down, reaching ground level. His gaze swept upward, seeing the red leather bands worn by the men surrounding the temple. They no longer seemed to be a random crowd milling about looking for trouble, but were organized in groups of twelve. Each group formed two lines, some stationary, watching over the crowd, others walking in unison along the limestone platform. The men surrounding Ben were also an even twelve. He had stopped moving. Alma's stomach tightened, and bile rose in his throat. He had to get past these men and reach Ben before it was too late.

The crowd quieted, and the drums dimmed to a soft rumble. Alma looked around him, then followed their upturned gazes. Someone walked out of the temple toward the tower. He wore a deep scarlet robe with a hood, and the unified hush that had fallen over the crowd told Alma that this tall man was their leader. His mere presence seemed to command attention without a word.

The leader climbed the ladder, and eleven other robed men, all wearing matching scarlet hoods, exited the temple and formed a line in front of the tower. The sun had sunk behind the temple mount, casting its brilliant orange and yellow across the gardens, turning them from green to golden. Darkness would quickly follow, and Alma knew he was not safe among these rebels, but still he could not move.

This is the leader of the opposition, he realized. *The man who has incited this rebellion and those all over the city over the past few weeks.* Alma's throat constricted as the leader reached the top of the tower. This man dared to preach from the very place that King Benjamin, beloved former king of Zarahemla, had uttered his final blessings upon the people of the Church. This man defiled the tower with his very presence. He raised a hand and the drums silenced at last, creating an eerie quiet.

"Greetings," the leader's voice bellowed out over the crowd. "Tonight is the first step we take in reclaiming what we have lost!" His voice carried well across the plaza.

An unexpected chill spread through Alma's entire body as he shuffled against the crowd to get a better look at the man at the top of the tower. He recognized that voice. *It can't be.*

A shout went up among the crowd, then the leader raised both hands for silence, and the noise abruptly died. "Tonight marks a new beginning—one that allows every man to choose for himself!"

The crowd responded with shouts and cheers again, but Alma had stilled, his eyes locked on the red figure above. He knew that voice, had heard it every day for twenty-one years, each inflection and tone etched into his soul.

No! It's impossible.

The crowd cheered wildly at something the leader had shouted. The man raised his arms again, and his hood slipped from his head.

Alma froze. *My son.*

Even as the realization tumbled into his mind, Alma couldn't grasp it. His own son . . . the leader of the revolt to bring down the Lord's Church. His mind argued with his heart, but there was no doubt as he gazed at the man at the top of the tower. His son had shorn his thick wavy hair, but the chiseled face was the same. Nausea rocked through Alma. His heart felt as if it would explode. But he kept his eyes focused as dread flooded his soul, his hands clenching into fists until his fingernails broke the skin of his palms.

His son was grinning, basking in the mob's ecstatic yelling. The yelling formed into a chant until hundreds of people were chanting the same words. "Save us! Save us!"

Alma spun, looking about wildly. What did they mean? He turned back to the tower; his son had his hands clasped together, head bowed.

Then his son raised his head and held up a single hand. The crowd's shouting faded. "Your cries have been heard. Tonight we will sacrifice the old church upon the altar of the new church—*our* church—the Church of Liberty." He pointed to the steps as the crowd hushed further.

Alma looked to where the men surrounding Ben had moved aside, and the scarlet-robed men started to walk toward the prostrate figure. Four of the men lifted Ben, then carried him toward the tower. The drums started up again as the crowd chanted, "Save us! Save us!"

With horror, Alma watched the robed men carry Ben to the sacrificial altar.

Alma's knees buckled as he gasped for breath. *They can't. They won't.*

"No!" Alma cried out, pushing through the frenzied crowd. The drums kept beating, drowning out his voice, and the robed men continued tying Ben to the altar as Alma plowed his way to the temple steps. He leapt up them, and no one tried to stop him this time. He was almost to the top when he was sure his son had spotted him. They locked gazes, and for an instant, Alma thought his son would come to his senses and abandon the sacrifice, but his eyes were cold, dead.

Then a man in a scarlet robe blocked Alma's way. He wore the crimson hood, his face shadowed.

But Alma recognized him. *The king's oldest son—what is he doing here? Why isn't he with his family at the hunting lodge?* "Ammon?"

"Sorry, old man," Ammon said, then shoved Alma backward down the stairs.

CHAPTER 2

Honor thy father and thy mother:
that thy days may be long upon the land which the
Lord thy God giveth thee.
—Exodus 20:12

Three Months Earlier

Alma the Younger

The leaves above Alma shuddered as if in anticipation of the death of the deer that stood three dozen paces down the ridge.

"You'll lose control if you take the downhill shot," Aaron whispered.

"Shh! If anyone can hit it, Alma the *Younger* can," Ammon said in a hushed, teasing voice.

A smile pulled at Alma's face, but he kept his aim steady as he slowly pulled back on the already taut string of the steel bow. Every chance Ammon had, he made fun of Alma's "younger" title. He'd been called that since birth, since his own father was named Alma too, but only adults referred to him as the younger one.

The surge of adrenaline in Alma's chest told him that he'd pinpointed the target and it was time to release. He spent another two breaths rechecking the measure, then fired the arrow. The soft twang of the bow sounded in his ear and seemed to alert the animal. The deer moved a fraction before the arrow hit, but instead of piercing its heart, the arrow bedded into the upper chest, and the deer bolted.

Alma leapt to his feet and burst out of the line of trees.

"Ha!" Aaron called after him. "I knew you'd miss!"

At a half-run, half-stumble, Alma ignored the jibe and made his way down the steep ridge, trying to keep from tumbling.

The brothers plunged after him. Alma could hear their bickering as he ran ahead, trying to keep the deer in sight.

"It wasn't his aim, it was the bow," Ammon said with frustration. "Not finely crafted. I knew that merchant was telling us a story—"

"Alma missed the other two deer we saw earlier too," came Aaron's panting voice.

"Because you couldn't keep quiet . . ." Ammon started to say.

Alma tuned out the brothers. He had a deer to track. Ahead, the animal disappeared into the thick foliage. He was losing ground already. When he reached the spot where the deer had been hit, Alma was out of breath, but he smiled. Dark spots of blood colored the ground, creating a scant but readable trail. Now it was just a matter of time before the deer collapsed. By the position of the sun, Alma still had a good hour of daylight left in which to follow. No longer worried about startling beasts, he called back to his friends, "You better keep up, or you'll miss your supper!"

A whooping shout answered; the brothers ran faster and caught up with Alma, shoving each other in the process. Alma shook his head—they never seemed to stop, probably even fought in their sleep. "Let's go!" he said and started running again, balancing the bow in one hand.

Ammon, the oldest brother, kept pace with Alma quite easily. At twenty-three Ammon was two years older and was also the more logical of the two brothers—having been trained for the kingship since birth—although he let his unruly temper get the best of him sometimes. His stride matched Alma's as they wove in and out of trees pursuing the deer.

Aaron lagged behind but not due to lack of strength. He was tall and lanky and, compared to the other two, not as tough of a fighter, yet he made up for it in intelligence and determination.

Alma glanced over at Ammon, seeing the perspiration soaking his close-cropped hair and the band of red-dyed leather he always wore around his head. "Tired?"

"Never," Ammon said with a huff and pushed a little faster. Soon he pulled ahead.

"Wait for me," Alma said, "or you'll lose the trail."

"You're not the only one who can track a deer," Ammon said. "Besides, that long hair of yours is getting in my way."

"You better watch out, or you'll trip and fall on those thirty knives you're carrying—"

"Two! I only have two with me," Ammon called back.

Alma laughed. He knew Ammon was just envious since he had to keep his own hair short—as princes, the brothers had to conform to even stricter rules than Alma. His hair was just to his shoulders, falling in dark waves, yet it was "too wild," according to his father. But that was the least of his and his father's differences.

The men came to a meadow, and all three slowed. "The blood trail is heavier here," Alma said, pointing at the ground. They started walking the tree line, looking for more signs of blood.

"Six knives," Aaron said in a mocking voice. "He carries at least six at all times, just like a little boy with his collection of rocks and sticks."

Ammon's face was dark red. "Tell my brother to shut his mouth before I use one of my knives on him."

Alma glared at Aaron, who raised his hands in frustration. "What?" Aaron said. "Why do I always have to be the one to back down first? You're older than me."

"He's right," Alma wheezed, nodding to Ammon. "Both of you need to cool down. We're already in trouble for stealing the turkeys last week." The three of them had traded a couple of the king's turkeys for some pulque, a very potent agave wine. "And now we're hunting illegally on the king's grounds."

"Well, I say these are *my* grounds," Ammon said. "I'm heir to the throne, after all." He threw his brother a superior look.

"That is, if I don't put a snake in your bed some night, *Your Majesty,*" Aaron said, his voice a sneer. "The people like me better anyway."

Ammon stopped and blocked his brother, crossing his thick arms over his chest. "Is that a threat?"

Aaron stepped closer and narrowed his eyes. "Do you want it to be?"

Alma put a hand on both brothers' shoulders. "That's enough," he growled. "If you don't stop now, both of you will be sorry. Next time, I'm bringing your younger brothers. At least Omner and Himni know how to stay quiet." He turned away with a disgusted shake of his head. "Come on." Settling into a brisk walk along the edge of the meadow, he kept his eyes trained to the ground. A moment later, he heard the unmistakable tread of footsteps behind him. Their voices had fallen silent—blessed silence.

Alma had grown up in Zarahemla with the sons of King Mosiah. The two oldest, Ammon and Aaron, were as close as brothers to him, even closer than his own siblings. But some days, like today, they grated on his nerves. Today's hunt had taken much longer than it should have because the brothers, with their incessant arguing, had scared away the first two deer. *Spoiled* is what they were. They'd never had to work for their food, so hunting was a game to them.

Not that I've really ever had to go hungry either, Alma thought, but shook the idea away before it could fester. He hadn't gone hungry as long as he never stepped out of line. His parents gave him plenty of hard-labor chores during his youth and even sent him to work in the fields with the commoners. He could hear his father's rebuke right now: "Don't call them commoners. All men are equal in God's eyes."

Casting a quick glance behind at the princes, Alma knew that all men weren't equal, so how could his father make that claim? If God viewed all men as equal, then why were there so many divisions in society?

Not all men lived in a palace like the royalty with servants preparing food and the best masters brought in for lessons and discussions on politics, art, law, and commerce.

All men didn't wake up in beds of luxurious fur like the aristocrats, surrounded by sturdy stone walls. All men didn't wear jewels at their throats and on their fingers or carry daggers made of the finest obsidian like the successful merchants.

No, his father was wrong. There were commoners, and there were aristocrats, and they were not the least bit equal. A child born into a poor family had no choice but to remain poor. A woman could only marry a man her own rank. The classes in society stayed separate no matter how much the Church leaders preached equality.

The problem was that he had no one to discuss it with—except for his friends, who were locked into a confining lifestyle just as he was. *Don't question,* Alma had been told. A good debate about a religious concept ignited the fire in his father's eyes more quickly than a single flame held against a dried maize stalk.

The blood trail thickened, and Alma turned to alert the brothers. They both nodded, their expressions saying they understood. The men moved into the trees, and Alma held up his hand for silence. The sound of snapping twigs reached them, and about a dozen paces away at the edge of the meadow, the deer staggered out. Its legs crumpled beneath its weight, and the animal sank to the ground, its ribcage heaving up and down.

"It's still alive," Ammon whispered.

The men waited a few more minutes, making sure the animal didn't try to get up to flee or to defend itself. Alma pulled his knife from his waistband and crept to the brown, shuddering creature. In a single swift action, he slit the deer's throat and put an end to its suffering.

"Bravo!" Ammon clapped. "Supper!"

Aaron snorted as he looked down on the bleeding animal. "There's a whole spread of delicacies waiting for us at the palace."

Both Alma and Ammon started laughing.

"What fun is that? Why would you trade the wild for the tame?" Alma said. "How will you lead a whole city of commoners when you don't even know what it's like to be one?"

"That's what my advisers will be for," Aaron said.

"Hmm," Ammon said. "I guess you'll have to kill off *me* and *my* advisers before you can achieve your precious destiny." Ammon turned to Alma. "And you call *me* spoiled? At least I can get my hands dirty." He held them up to prove his point.

Ammon grinned and started stripping off his outer robe. From his waistband he withdrew not one, but two knives, each with jeweled hilts. Another benefit of being royalty. "I made them myself."

Alma was impressed. "Let me see them." He took both knives and turned one over in his hand. The steel hilt was smooth and elegantly curved. The obsidian blades were thinner and sharper than he'd ever seen.

"I put the steel through a second smelting process. That made the hilt smoother and the blades thinner without breaking them," Ammon said.

"Quiet!" Aaron said.

"You're just envious," Ammon said, anger in his voice. "The only thing you can do with your pretty hands is—"

"Shh!" Alma said, hearing a low growl coming from just beyond the deer. Unless the deer's spirit sounded like a jaguar, they had some competition for their supper.

Ammon's eyes widened, and he yanked one of the knives from Alma's hands. "To the trees," he hissed.

The three men moved as a cohesive unit to the tree line and crouched to watch. Another low growl filled the clearing. Alma could almost feel the excitement emanating from Ammon. "We can't let it get the deer," Ammon whispered.

Aaron shushed his brother again.

"Let's wait to see how big it is first," Alma said. He'd killed jaguars before, but with an arrow from a distance, not one that could see him before an attack.

A black speckled head appeared through the trees on the other side of the meadow, close to the deer. It looked young, maybe two years old. Alma reached for his bow, then carefully nocked an arrow. The jaguar moved toward the deer, looking around as if he were confused at the various scents. Alma kept his arrow trained on the large cat's neck. It would be harder to kill a moving target, but he wanted to hit the beast before it touched the deer.

He glanced at Ammon who was gripping a knife in his hand. One signal and the prince would probably try to single-handedly wrestle the cat to the ground.

The jaguar walked past the deer, then turned around, sniffing the air. *It knows we're here,* Alma thought, his pulse hammering. He made the adjustment with his bow. Then he noticed the cat's sagging belly.

A nursing female. As he held his position, sweat began to bead along his forehead, and he relaxed his hands.

"Take it," Ammon whispered.

The jaguar turned its head toward their hiding place.

"Now!" Ammon whispered louder. "It's either him or us."

"Her," Alma corrected, lowering the bow. Ammon was at his side instantly, jerking the bow from him and taking aim. The movement warned the cat, and it retreated a few steps until it was standing behind the deer. Ammon released the arrow—too fast, without careful precision as Alma would have done. The arrow hit the deer, and the jaguar bolted.

Ammon turned to Alma and stared at him in disbelief. "Why did you let it go? You had him."

"Her," Alma repeated. "A nursing female. Did you see how her belly sagged with milk?" He looked to Aaron for support. The prince just shook his head and started for the clearing.

Ammon threw the bow to the ground at Alma's feet. "This thing is nothing but bad luck." He turned his back to Alma and followed after his brother. Over his shoulder he called out, "I can't believe you were afraid to shoot it. Could have had a nice fur cape to impress the women with."

"I don't need a jaguar coat to impress women with," Alma retorted. But inside he was embarrassed. He'd gone soft over a female cat. If this story got back to their other friends . . . he had to make up for it somehow. He left the shade of the trees and hurried to catch the brothers. "I'll clean the deer, and you both get the fire ready."

Aaron turned, squinting at him in the fading light. "The smoke will attract too much attention. Someone will spot us."

"What? Are you scared now?" Alma said. "I thought this was *your* land. We shot it, and we should be able to cook it where and when we want to. Just because this is the king's land doesn't mean he should get a share. He had nothing to do with the hunt." He hesitated, looking from Aaron to Ammon. "We're still together on this, right?"

Ammon gave a half-nod. "I'm just glad we're fast runners."

Alma grinned. "Get the wood." He borrowed one of Ammon's knives, then set to work cleaning the deer. He ignored the proper order of preserving the best parts for the temple priests—there were no priests hovering over him here. He'd dry and preserve those parts for himself, later. He didn't want to beg food from the princes or return to his parents' home. Besides, he'd eaten without following all of the rules many times and nothing had happened to him yet. That was one of the questions his father didn't seem to be able to answer, other than it was God's will. What did God's will have to do with preparing supper?

When the fire was laid, Ammon helped Alma finish cleaning the deer. Alma filleted several pieces to be cooked over the fire. Aaron paced nervously, as if watching for a king's guard to appear at any moment.

Alma placed the filets on the rocks next to the fire. "I'm going to find a place to wash," he said.

"I'll come too," Ammon said.

The two of them left Aaron behind to watch the fire, and they set off downhill. "Let's go to the pond just below here," Ammon said, shaking his head. "I still can't believe you let that jaguar go. Since when do you care whether it's male or female?"

Alma shrugged. "It was a mother, and we want her babies to grow up, right? More coats for us later."

Ammon laughed, slapping Alma's back. "You're right. You should have been born a prince. You're far smarter than both of us—just don't tell *Aaron* that."

"Don't tell my father, either," Alma said in a quiet voice. "I'm just a lowly scribe to him."

"Have you talked to him lately?"

"Not for a couple of weeks," Alma said. "Every time I show up, he has a long list of complaints. He wants me to work from sun up to sun down copying manuscripts in a cell-like room. I'll be gray and bent over with age before I'm able to make my living. The only one I really feel sorry for is my mother, but she's obviously taken my father's side."

"At least you have a choice," Ammon said.

"A choice? How? My father told me that I had to live by his rules if I stay in his house. There's no choice in that. So I left. Hunting feeds me and brings a little extra income to improve my hut."

"You can stay with me if you want," Ammon said.

"Sure. How are you going to sneak the vagrant son of the high priest into the palace?"

"You wouldn't be the first person I've sneaked in," Ammon said.

"I enjoy living in a village of idol-worshippers. Life is much more interesting. Besides, it's the last place my father would look."

Ammon shook his head.

Alma smiled, then stopped walking, listening. "Did you hear something?"

"Is it back?" Ammon asked, reaching for his knife.

"No—not a jaguar—someone's laughing."

"Maybe it's Aaron."

The high-pitched laughter sounded again.

"Unless Aaron's laughing to himself like a girl, there's someone else at the pond."

They slowed their pace to stay quiet. Within minutes, they could see the pond, the low moon reflecting off the dark water.

"Oh!" Alma said, too surprised to whisper. Two girls . . . women . . . were wading along the shoreline, their robes hiked up to their knees. He felt a quick stab of warmth as he recognized the taller one.

"Hey," Ammon said. "What's my sister doing here?"

Cassia. Alma started to backtrack, his heart pounding even harder than when he'd faced the jaguar. "Don't let them see us like this—we're covered in blood."

"Good idea," Ammon said as they crept to a group of trees.

Laughter floated in their direction again.

"Who's the other one?" Alma asked.

"Aaron's betrothed, Ilana. The daughter of Limhi," Ammon said.

Alma peered at both the women. Ilana was shorter and looked quite a bit softer and more shapely than Cassia—but then again, Cassia was practically still a girl. Practically. They'd been friends until about two years before. Around the time Cassia turned sixteen, her father forbade her from spending time with him—another wrongful injustice. They'd grown up as playmates, all four of them: the brothers, Cassia, and Alma.

"Is Ilana the one who broke down and cried when she found out she was to marry you?" Alma asked, trying to hold back a laugh.

Ammon punched him in the arm. "It wasn't like that. She thought Aaron was the oldest, and when she discovered I was, she was confused . . . and quite emotional."

"So, the second brother gets married before the crown prince? I'm surprised your father, the supreme rule-maker, would allow any sort of error," Alma said.

"There was already an agreement for Ilana to marry me. So when she requested to marry Aaron instead, my parents couldn't very well back out and maintain their good relationship with her father."

Alma shook his head. "But what woman in Zarahemla doesn't know the difference between you and Aaron? Yes, you are both annoying, but you don't look much alike."

"Is that a compliment?" Ammon asked, his eyes glinting in the dark.

"Not really," Alma said. "But you can take it as one."

"Only if you admit I am the more handsome one."

"Oh no. I'll admit nothing. I'll let the poor sap of a girl who has to marry you pay the compliments. Hopefully she won't be a crier like Ilana."

Ammon elbowed Alma in the ribs, and Alma sprawled on the ground with a moan. "That really hurt!"

"Try seeing your 'used-to-be-betrothed' around the palace every day. Ilana came a whole month before the wedding to live in the palace," Ammon said, shaking his head in disgust. "Aaron isn't supposed to officially spend time with her until the welcoming ceremony tomorrow night."

"And has he?" Alma said.

"What do you think?"

Alma chuckled quietly. Aaron's sense of entitlement to everything and anything in Zarahemla would have propelled him to arrange secret meetings with his wife-to-be. Especially one who had chosen him over the crown prince. "So what does he think of her?"

"Oh, he likes her well enough," Ammon said. "He's keeps hinting that he's glad he is marrying before me. I don't know why. He won't be able to spend as much time with us anymore—he'll have to spend time with his *wife.*" He started laughing.

Alma nodded absently, no longer paying attention to Ammon. He watched the two women leave the shoreline and walk along a path that led back to the palace. They had linked arms and conversation and laughter seemed to flow easily between them. Cassia was definitely extending the warm welcome to her new sister-in-law. A deep jab of loneliness flooded through Alma, but he shook it off as he stood. He'd grown up; Cassia had grown up. Things had changed. He couldn't very well show up at her palace door and ask her to have an archery contest like they used to.

"We'd better clean up and hurry back to eat—assuming Aaron hasn't absconded with supper."

CHAPTER 3

And I, the Lord God, said . . . that it was not good that the man should be alone . . .
—Moses 3:18

Alma the Younger

Alma watched the flames dwindle to their last orange coals. He was tired and was reluctant to douse the fire. "Let's just sleep here," he said with a big yawn.

Next to him, Ammon stirred, his eyes glazed over. "Did you say something?"

"Yeah—look at Aaron," Alma said.

Ammon looked over at his brother. "Sleeping like a babe." He chuckled quietly. "Should we leave him?"

"Not if we want him to ever do anything with us again," Alma said, stifling another yawn. The night had grown cool, and he moved slightly closer to the dying fire. "You two can return to the palace—I'm staying here tonight."

"When are you going to let us see your hut?" Ammon said.

"As soon as I get it fixed up."

"I wish I had my own place," Ammon said in a quiet voice.

Alma rubbed his eyes. "You have a whole palace."

"Yes, and I never get a moment alone," Ammon said. "Tomorrow morning at dawn, my mother will be in my room—my private quarters that is—telling me to get dressed for the ordination."

"You're going through with it?"

Ammon shrugged. "It's all to present an image to the city. I don't know anything about being a priest—you know more than I do. I still don't know how you got out of your ordination."

Alma waved his hands toward the fire. "That's why I'm out here, eating over a fire. Do you think my father would allow me to exist beneath his roof for very long—one who embarrassed him at every turn?" He pulled his knees to his chest and stared at the glowing wood. "It's your duty. You'll be king someday."

"But you don't seem to care about duty. You're out here, free, doing what you want."

Alma grinned. "There are some benefits to being cast out of your home."

"You are the bravest man I know," Ammon said, his tone reverent.

"Who's the bravest man?" a voice chimed in. Aaron pushed up on his elbow, staring at the two with bleary eyes.

"Alma," Ammon said. He turned back to Alma. "You've stood up to one of the most powerful leaders in Zarahemla—what's more, your father may be more powerful than mine. The king goes to your father for many of his questions."

"The king has given my father too much power, in my opinion," Alma said. "My father not only oversees the Church, but hands down civic judgements to the people."

"Some of the other priests do that as well," Ammon said. "It gives my father more time to attend to other matters."

"Agreed. But the line between religion and government is too thin. Why should an unbeliever be judged by a Church leader?" Alma said in a bitter voice. "Although I suppose it gives my father something more to do, and he *loves* to stay busy. When he's not preaching or condemning those who aren't in church each Sabbath, he can preach to your father. Sometimes I think my father believes he *is* the Christ he's always preaching about, and one of these days, he'll say to the people: *Surprise, it's really me. Now bow down and worship me.*"

Ammon laughed. "That sounds like blasphemy."

"Yeah," Aaron said, sitting up and scratching his head. "Blasphemy."

"It's not blasphemy if there's no Christ," Alma said.

The brothers were quiet for a moment.

"Do you think there's no Christ?" Ammon finally asked.

"Have either of *you* ever seen God?" Alma said.

Both brothers shook their heads.

"So how can you blaspheme against someone who's not real?" Alma picked up a few twigs lying next to him and tossed them into the fire. "All my life, I've listened to my parents preach—done what they have told me to—"

"Blasphemy again and definitely lying," Ammon cut in with a laugh.

"All right," Alma said. "But until recently, I've done things their way. And I've never seen any proof that what they are saying is true. I'm a reasonable man, and I know the value of a good deer carcass. It's straightforward. You bring deer meat to the market, and you sell it for a certain price. You can see the meat, and you can see the silver onties." Alma picked up a nearby stick and held it in the air, as if illustrating his point. "Preaching of Christ, a god who hasn't even been born, and the necessity to follow all of these laws is a ploy parents use on their children to get them to do what they want." He paused, snapping the stick. "Show me Christ, and I'll believe."

"Has your father said he's seen Christ?" Aaron asked, fully alert now.

Alma lifted a shoulder. "Some of the old stories are filled with claims that he heard God's voice. I guess that keeps King Mosiah coming to him, but *I've* never heard God say anything."

"Neither have I," Aaron said. "I think God ignores most of us."

"*All* of us," Alma said. "Isn't it strange that those who have the most power claim some special relationship with God? Maybe that's how they get their power in the first place."

"But why would so many people believe in the Church?" Ammon asked, his eyes bright.

"People want to believe in something, and they want someone to tell them what to do," Alma said. "It takes away the responsibility of making their own decisions. They are like little children, too frightened to go out on their own and ask questions." He looked from one brother to the next. "But I'm not afraid." His eyes narrowed as he focused on Ammon. "Tomorrow they'll ordain you a priest. Can you honestly tell me you believe that what they are doing is right for you? Are you ready to be a priest in the temple? Talk in hushed whispers all day long, wear those long, stifling robes, and give up all of this freedom?" He waved he arms at the trees above them.

Ammon's gaze dropped, and he scraped his foot in the dirt. "No," he said in a quiet voice.

"What did you say?" Alma asked.

"No!" Ammon looked straight at Alma. "I don't want to be a priest. I don't want to be who they want me to be. I want to make my own decisions."

Alma folded his arms, nodding, then looked over at Aaron. "What about you? Are you ready to marry Ilana because your parents want you to?"

Aaron looked from Ammon to Alma, his gaze wary. "What does that have to do with Ammon becoming a priest?"

Alma burst out laughing. "I'm teasing. If you're happy with Ilana, that's all that matters."

A look of relief crossed Aaron's face. "Good tidings, because I wouldn't mind being married to her. But even if the two of you didn't approve, I wouldn't care."

"Am I supposed to believe that?" Alma said, exchanging a knowing grin with Ammon.

Aaron's face reddened and he leapt to his feet, pouncing on his brother, wrestling him to the ground.

Alma leaned back on his elbows, laughing as the two brothers scrabbled together, and the dwindling fire sent a few last sparks shooting into the dark sky.

Life is good out here, he thought. In fact, he wondered if it had ever been better.

* * *

Cassia

Cassia hugged Ilana at the doorway of her bedchamber. *It is going to be wonderful to have a sister.* Not that she could complain about her childhood, but having four brothers, especially ones like hers, was not always the sweet side of honey.

"Thank you for showing me the pond," Ilana said, blinking her long, dark lashes.

Normally Cassia might have felt a pang of envy at Ilana's natural beauty, but there was not a mean thought in Ilana's whole body, and Cassia could never hold anything against the woman.

"You're welcome," Cassia said. "Tomorrow I'll show you the cooking rooms. They've been renovated."

Ilana arched a fine brow. "That would be wonderful."

"Until tomorrow then." She bade goodnight and left her soon-to-be sister. She knew Ilana wasn't interested in cooking like Cassia was, but Ilana was just the type of person to be gracious no matter what she was doing. Cassia hummed as she walked the corridor to her own room, thinking of how fortunate she was to have such a pleasing sister-in-law—one with a ready laugh and a mild temper—nothing like her rambunctious brothers. She only wished her new sister could share some of her beauty. Cassia's own lashes were short and stubby, her hair too curly, taking forever to grow, and her body was mostly angles like her brother Aaron's. *If only I had a few more curves like Ilana.*

She cracked the door open to her bedchamber. An oil lamp had already been lit, and she closed the door with a soft sigh, welcoming the quiet. Now that she was alone, exhaustion hit her hard. It had been continual entertainment for the past week as she'd served as Ilana's official escort. Pulling off her outer robe, Cassia settled onto her bed with her day tunic still on. She was suddenly too tired to change her clothing, wash her face, or even blow out the lamp.

Tomorrow, she thought, *tomorrow I'll impress Ilana with one of my honeyed creations.* Then her sister-in-law would be delighted. Cassia's stomach did a small tumble when she remembered that Ilana's brother was arriving the next evening as well. As sleep claimed Cassia, she wondered what Ilana's brother was like and whether he favored women on the thin side.

* * *

The morning meal is taking forever, Cassia thought, but she smiled politely at the conversation surrounding the women. Her mother, Naomi—the queen of Zarahemla—sat on Cassia's right. To her left was Ilana. Then across from her was Alma's mother, Maia, and her two daughters. The women sat together in a circle, eating sweet cornmeal tamales. They were in the queen's day room, where she hosted her good friends when they came to visit.

The younger girls, Bethany and Dana, had finished first and were trying hard not to wiggle around too much. Finally, their mother excused them to go walk in the gardens. Cassia looked after them longingly. Although she was eighteen now, she wished she didn't have to be included in all of the grown-up occasions. Maybe she could offer to walk with the girls, but then she also wanted to be with Ilana and find out more about her brother. Yet Cassia could hardly ask those kinds of questions in front of everyone.

"I don't know when they returned last night," Naomi was saying when Cassia focused back on the conversation.

Maia's face paled. "Have you spoken to Aaron yet today?"

"Only briefly," Naomi said. "My husband took him into a conference early this morning."

"What about Ammon?" Maia's voice sounded subdued.

"He's probably still sleeping."

Cassia wasn't sure what they were speaking about, but tension was thick in the air. If Ilana hadn't been in the room, there might've been a lot more information shared.

But Maia didn't seem to mind the presence of the bride-to-be. "Do you think they were with Alma?"

"I'm not sure," Naomi said. "I'm sorry I don't have more information for you about your son. I know you miss him."

Cassia's head came up sharply. She knew Alma had left home several weeks before—some argument with his father. But Alma was so easygoing she'd assumed he was back, though from Maia's strained expression, she could see he hadn't returned. If he had been with her brothers the night before, surely they'd talk him into restoring favor with his father.

Cassia knew there was more to the story, and she burned with curiosity to know it, but she decided to do her mother a favor. "Are you ready to tour the cooking room, Ilana?"

Ilana patted her mouth with a square of cloth and smiled. "Certainly."

The two linked arms and walked together down the corridor to the back wing of the palace. Cassia couldn't help but grin at the surprise she'd show her sister-in-law.

"What's your favorite sweet?" Cassia asked.

Ilana turned her dark eyes to her. "Cacao."

Cassia clapped her hands. "I love that drink. I enjoy it with delicacies such as amaranth seeds and honey—it makes a delicious combination."

Ilana's brows drew together. "I don't think I've ever tried that."

"I'll show you how to make it, then we can take it with us on our walk this afternoon."

"Your mother allows you to prepare food?"

Cassia smiled and squeezed Ilana's arm. "Not very often. But the servants are good at keeping my secret."

"Then I'll keep your secret too," Ilana said with a laugh.

They stepped through the arched doorway that opened into a high-ceilinged room. Several low tables lined the walls, and baskets of drying herbs hung to one side. The newly laid stone floor seemed to gleam in the morning light. This was Cassia's pride—she'd made the suggestion to add a stone floor to the cooking room so that less dust would be kicked up during the warmer months.

Already, with less dust, there had been an improvement in cleanliness and the presentation of the food, even noticeable to the king. Two women looked up from a basket of beans they were snapping. Their eyes widened with surprise when they saw Ilana. Cassia motioned to her new sister. "This is Aaron's betrothed. I want to show her how to make a treat."

The women bobbed their heads and retreated to the second cooking room, where dried slabs of meat hung and a large stone pit was laid for an additional cooking fire.

Ilana rotated slowly around, taking in everything. "This room is almost as large as my home."

Cassia laughed, knowing that Ilana's home was plenty large. After all, her father had been a Nephite king before coming to Zarahemla. "The palace is your home now. Here," she said, showing Ilana a tightly woven, leather-lined basket that contained the tiny amaranth seeds. "We need a couple of handfuls to put into the clay bowl, but first we have to grease it."

Ilana grimaced as Cassia dipped her fingers into a small jar of animal tallow. The smell wasn't too pleasant, so she used just enough so that the honey wouldn't stick to the sides.

"Do you want to try?" Cassia asked.

Ilana shook her head. "I'll just watch."

"All right," Cassia said as she scooped two handfuls of the amaranth seeds into the bowl. "Now for the honey. The trick is not to use too much or too little." She reached for a dark brown jar and lifted the lid, peering inside. "Oh. The jar is empty." She didn't want her plans to be ruined. "We'll just have to go to the beehives behind the garden and see if any honey has been collected." She moved to the outer door and took the leather mitts and a veil from a hook. She turned—her sister-in-law was absolutely pale."What's wrong?"

"I—I don't think I want to go near the beehives," Ilana said. "Perhaps we can let the servants do it."

Cassia looked from Ilana's worried expression to the second room where the women had disappeared. She didn't think either of them collected the honey. It was usually a man's job, but she'd seen it done before.

"Don't worry, we'll probably find a servant in the bee yard who can bring the honey back for us." She held up the leather mitts. "These will protect us just in case no one is there."

Ilana shook her head, looking even paler. "I don't think you should try that. We should wait."

Cassia felt deflated, and she replaced the mitts and veil on their hook. She hoped that they'd have something more in common—at least a little sense of adventure. And now . . .

Squeals sailed into the cooking room from the garden just beyond the doorway. Cassia turned to see Alma's two sisters chasing each other. She smiled, then made her face serious as she turned again to Ilana.

"Why don't you visit with the younger girls while I walk down to the beehives and see if any honey is ready? Since we found the jar empty, the servants may have already put in a request."

Ilana nodded but still seemed hesitant.

Cassia leaned out of the doorway and called to Alma's sisters. "Come over here, girls. Ilana wants to see you." The two girls stopped, then Dana rushed to Cassia, throwing her arms around her. The older girl laughed and pulled away. The sisters stared at Ilana. Cassia didn't blame them; Ilana was beautiful.

"Can you show me your favorite part of the garden?" Ilana asked.

Inwardly, Cassia sighed with relief. Ilana was so kind, diplomatic, and . . . well, accommodating. She was certainly the perfect match for Aaron. Cassia watched the three of them walk off, then slipped back into the cooking room and snatched the leather mitts and veil. She might as well be prepared.

It didn't take long to walk through the gardens to the beehives. They were somewhat secluded behind a short stone wall, with high bushes running along the edges, adding to the concealment. In the quiet of the morning, the buzzing reached Cassia's ears before she could see the hives. She reached the narrow opening in the stone wall. "Anyone working here?" she called out before venturing farther.

No one answered, and she hadn't seen any servants on her walk to the bee yard. She searched for clay jars next to the stone wall, hoping to find one filled with honey, but there was nothing. She knew the keepers used a smoking stick to make the bees drowsy, so she looked for the basket with the fire-lighting tools. It was near the first hive, and she crept to grab it without alerting any bees. There were about twelve hives, all with a few slow-circling bees outside.

Cassia's stomach tightened, but she remained determined as she struck two pieces of chert together to create a spark. After a few tries she was able to light a long, thick stick. She propped it against the basket carefully, so as not to ignite anything, then drew on the mitts and put on the veil. She picked up the burning stick and continued toward the first hive. Right before she reached it, she blew on the stick to extinguish the fire and create a smoking end. The small flame flickered out, and Cassia thrust the smoking end into the hive opening. Immediately, at least a dozen bees flew out.

She jerked back with a yelp. She'd forgotten to wait until more smoke had filled the hive before moving the stick inside. Holding still, she kept the stick steady as the bees circled the hive and a few reentered. Cassia moved toward the opening again, but this time held the stick at the entrance for several minutes.

But more bees flew out, and she felt a sharp pinch on her upper arm. "Ow!" she cried out. Then another pinch on her neck. This one hurt more, causing her eyes to smart. She panicked and started waving the stick at the bees. She knew she shouldn't make a sound, but after another bite, she started screaming and waving her arms frantically, ripping her veil off to swat at them. "Get off! Get off!"

More bees came out of the hive, heading directly at her, and Cassia turned and ran toward the wall opening. But before she could reach it, she tripped and fell, landing on the smoking stick.

CHAPTER 4

. . . choose you this day whom ye will serve; . . .
as for me and my house, we will serve the Lord.
—Joshua 24:15

Alma the Younger

A scream echoed through Alma's head, and he tried to shake the bad dream away. Then he opened his eyes and realized it was no dream. He staggered to his feet and grabbed his bow and arrow. Maybe the jaguar had caught some helpless victim in its claws. Another scream sounded, although this one was faint. He ran in the direction of the sound, adrenaline replacing the sleepiness and aches in his body from spending the night on the ground. As he ran, he realized exactly where the sound had come from: the hives on the north side of the palace gardens. He'd played on these grounds enough as a youth to know every bush and tree.

He sprinted up the ridge and climbed the stone wall at the farthest end of the preserve. What he saw on the ground drew him up short. A woman lay on the ground fighting off a swarm of bees with a stick. It wasn't much more effective than his bow and arrow would have been. Alma lunged toward her and grabbed both of her arms, dragging her to her feet. Then he pulled her through the front entrance. "Run!" he said as he urged her along.

His eyes widened when he realized who it was. *Cassia.*

They ran to the far end of the garden, away from the bee swarm, Alma swatting away the bees that clung to her body. Once at a safe distance, he came to a halt and turned to check on her.

She looked up at him, her face streaked with tears. "Alma?"

"You're safe now—the bees are gone," Alma said, catching his breath. "Are you bitten badly?"

"A few times," she said, her voice nearly a whisper. She wiped her eyes with trembling hands, then held out her arms, examining the red welts.

"Ouch," Alma said.

She looked up him, her gaze filled with disbelief. "I can't believe you're here—it's really you?"

Now he understood the disbelief. He brought a hand to his stubbly beard, then ran his hand through his unkempt hair. "Yes, it's me."

Cassia took a step back, hesitation in her eyes—or dismay.

Alma's heart dropped. Not that he expected her reaction to be any different than maybe his parents', but hers cut deeper than he expected. "What were you doing with the bees?"

Cassia looked down at her swollen arms. Alma noticed how she was shaking and wished he could do something about that, but he didn't want to scare her more.

"I—I was trying to get honey."

Alma stared at her for a moment, then chuckled.

She looked up at him, narrowing her eyes. "Is that funny?"

He sobered, but his eyes still gleamed. "When I saw you on the ground screaming, it looked like you'd decided to fight off the whole bee population of Zarahemla at once."

A corner of her mouth twitched, and Alma grinned. Then her eyes filled with tears.

Assuming she was in pain, he stepped closer to look for bites. "You need to get a salve for those." He took one hand and tried to lift her arm to get a better look.

She pulled away as if she'd been bitten again. "I—I'll be fine." She examined her arms, then glanced up. "Your mother's worried about you," she said in a quiet voice.

Alma sighed and shook his head. So word had reached even Cassia. *Of course.* He watched her press on a growing welt on her hand. He wanted to explain, but it was too complicated, and he hadn't been friends with this girl—this *woman*—for a long time. His face felt warm and his beard itchy as he noticed more and more that she really had grown into a beautiful woman. Her dark curls had fallen out of the plaits in her hair, and her cheeks colored with exertion. Her eyes had always been nicely shaped, but they seemed luminous as she stared at him. He took a step backward. "Tell my mother I'm fine."

The flush in her cheeks spread. "Is that your only message? Your parents are heartbroken. They have no idea where you've been or what you've been doing—"

"My father knows exactly why I left, and I don't know what he's shared with my mother," he said. "But you can't understand what it's been like living with them."

"They're good people. You need to talk to them."

"You can't pretend to know anything about me, Cass. Not anymore."

She recoiled and shook her head. "I know you better than you think. Just because we're grown up now and don't swim in the pond or have archery contests doesn't mean I can't tell when you're acting spoiled and selfish."

He folded his arms, his heart pounding with barely contained anger. "That's a big accusation coming from the daughter of a king, one who's never had to work a day in her life."

"Oh, and you have? You've suffered?" Her flushed face deepened to dark red. "You've gone hungry? You've been driven out of your homeland like your father was? You've had to fight for something you believe in at the cost of your life?"

"My life might not be in danger, but I am standing up for what *I* believe in," Alma said, clenching his hands into fists.

Cassia stared at him, and he stared back. Finally she broke her gaze. "And what do you believe in, Alma? Dishonoring your parents?"

"It's too late for that," he spat out. "If I returned, all I'd be is one long strand of disappointments to them."

"You don't have to be," she said, her eyes filling with tears. "I know your father forgives you completely. He'll accept you whatever your choices may be."

Something inside Alma softened for just a moment, but then it hardened again. "My father can't separate religion from anything else I might or might not accomplish. To him, I could never be successful unless I worshiped his way. Tell my mother not to worry. I can take care of myself, and I don't need my father's charity." He took one more lingering gaze at Cassia's doubtful expression, then turned to leave. "You should get a salve on those bites right away," he said over his shoulder. She didn't call him back.

He hurried back through the gardens, careful to stay near the outer path. He could be cited for trespassing, and he couldn't bear to see his father's pitying eyes if he were to be brought for judgment. He wondered what, or how much, Cassia would tell his mother—or her parents, for that matter. He'd find out soon enough from Ammon, who never missed any bit of information.

Alma returned to where he had stored the deer meat from the previous night. He wrapped the prepared meat into the cloth he'd brought the day before. Then he loaded it into his back sling.

With anger still fueling him, he made good time through the king's hunting preserve until he reached the edge of the road that took him to the Isidro village. Ironically, this village was one of the poorest in the land, although it was adjacent to the main city. The Isidro villagers were crop farmers, relying wholly on their labor and the weather for their well-being. Yes, the people were idol-worshippers, but they were hard-working people who cared deeply about their families. Isidro was the perfect place to live and hide.

The morning was hot by the time he climbed the final hill leading to the village. His hut was one of the first, sitting off to the side of the main path, secluded nicely by an overgrowth of trees.

The hut was crude but serviceable. He'd almost saved enough silver to purchase new timbers to buoy the walls. Alma walked around the hut and kicked at a rolled-up tarp in the back courtyard. He deposited the deer meat on the heavy tarp, then dragged it into the shade. After spreading out the pieces of meat to dry, he entered his hut, scrounging for something to eat on the mostly bare shelves. A stale heel of bread would have to do. He'd only been back a few minutes when a knock sounded on the door.

He crossed the small space and opened the door wide to reveal Kaman, a local villager.

"I thought that was you," Kaman said, his bearded grin lighting up his face. "Out all night, eh?"

Alma laughed and slapped the man on the shoulder. He was the Isidro village watchdog and always knew the comings and goings of everyone. The man was short, with a wiry build—able to move in and out of shadows quite effectively. "Know anyone who wants to buy some meat?" Alma asked.

"What did you get?" Kaman asked, pushing past Alma without an invitation. The back door of the hut opened into the courtyard where Alma had spread the meat out to dry. "Ah, a small one."

"About average in size. There's plenty to feed a family for at least a fortnight."

Kaman nodded, scratching his neck. "I'll ask around."

"Thanks," Alma said as Kaman turned to go.

Then Kaman stopped. "Did you hunt that jaguar?"

Alma followed his gaze to the frame that held the skin of a jaguar. "I caught it about a week ago."

Kaman let out a low whistle as he examined the fur. "You are skilled—I see no flaws in the pelt. I've never seen such a clean job." He straightened, eyeing Alma. "Why don't you come with me? I'm going to the tavern—to meet my friends. Might be someone there who's interested in the deer meat as well as the jaguar—if you think you can bring in more."

"Always," Alma said, noticing the excitement in Kaman's eyes. He stifled a yawn. "Is the tavern busy in the middle of the day?" He was tired, but if it would get him a customer, a couple more hours wouldn't hurt.

With a grin, Kaman said, "Pleasure never sleeps."

Alma followed Kaman through the quiet village. Most of the men were in the fields, and the women stayed inside their huts to avoid the heat. The past year had been hard on these people, and Alma could see it in the hungry eyes of the children as he passed. Today he had nothing to share with them, but tonight that would change, he decided. The king was hosting Limhi and his family for a banquet.

There would be plenty of leftover food and drink, which Alma planned to confiscate. The royals would never miss it.

The tavern sat just off the main village square. The front looked like an ordinary home, but Alma knew that inside was anything but ordinary. Various rooms had been divided off to house men and their female company, while the main public enjoyed pulque, a drink made of fermented agave juice, in the front room.

A guard dressed in civilian clothing sat on a stool by the door. It was his job to alert the people inside if any unwelcome guests arrived, which sometimes came in the form of a wife. Alma nodded as the man rose to greet them. He didn't wholeheartedly approve of the activities here, but he certainly understood the desperation and stress that led a man to places like this. They had cropped up with more popularity in almost every village surrounding Zarahemla.

With a nod of approval from the guard, Alma followed Kaman inside. The interior was gloomy at first, and Alma blinked against the dimness until his eyes adjusted. A low murmur just barely covered the soft melody being played on a flute by a woman sitting in the corner. She wore a bright scarlet tunic cut generously at the neck so that one sleeve had slipped to reveal a tawny shoulder. Several jade bracelets decorated her arms, and she looked as if she'd dyed her lips a dark red. The first time Alma had visited, he'd been surprised at the casual intermingling of men and women. But with women present, the men were better tempered and more likely to spend their silver onties on drinks, keeping the atmosphere lively.

Alma had only been here during the nighttime hours previously, so he was surprised to see how many men were there—at least a half dozen. He wondered who worked in their place in the fields today.

"Some wine, my friend?" Kaman said, putting a warm hand on Alma's shoulder.

"Yes, that would be nice."

"Have a seat. I'll bring some."

Alma looked around again. Cushions were piled against the walls of the room, accentuating the colorful rugs. A few low tables were scattered around, but most of the patrons held cups in their hands. For a brief instant he met the eyes of the woman playing the music.

She smiled, a sort of hazy smile, as if she didn't really see him. He was just another customer.

Alma found several empty cushions and settled on one of them. A couple of the men greeted him—Alma recognized them but wasn't sure of their names.

Before he knew it, Kaman was back with a surprisingly large cup—more like a bowl. Alma accepted the wine and took a sip. It was strong—as strong as the agave wine he and the sons of Mosiah had purchased the other day.

"How much do I owe you?" Alma asked.

"We'll worry about that when we leave."

Alma said, "Is there anyone here you think I should meet?"

Kaman nodded, stalling for a bit. "People are curious about you. They want to know where you come from."

"I told you my past is not something I care to talk about."

"I know," Kaman said, studying Alma. "You're a skilled hunter with the finest weapons. Your clothing is high quality, although I can see you don't know how to take care of it much." He laughed. "It seems to me you've been quite pampered."

"Ha." Alma scoffed. "I could out-wrestle any man in this room."

Kaman gave him a knowing look. "I don't doubt that, my friend. I suppose I'm just curious—I've always been that way."

"Does it really matter where I used to live?"

"I suppose not," Kaman said with a shrug. He waved over a stocky man with a crooked nose and introduced him as Jacob. The man looked very interested when Kaman told him about the deer and the jaguar.

"What else do you hunt?" Jacob asked.

"Nearly anything," Alma said, leaning forward. "Once I sell the deer meat, I can take a personal request."

"He's one of the finest hunters I've seen in Zarahemla," Kaman said.

Alma flushed at Kaman's praise but couldn't help feeling pleased. He looked around. Others had ambled over and were listening with interest. "I had a good shot at another jaguar last night, but I let her go."

"Why did you let her go?" Kaman asked, looking satisfied that they'd garnered so much attention.

Alma lifted his shoulder. "Already have one pelt. Didn't know if I could sell a second one."

The men around him grinned. "Sure you can—Kaman here is looking for a jaguar coat to impress his new woman friend."

Kaman flamed red, and the other men laughed.

Alma smiled. "Well, then, who wants to buy a fresh deer?"

Two men raised their hands.

"Let's talk prices," Alma said.

* * *

Cassia

Cassia stared at her image in the polished metal. She was wearing a new tunic, one that had been edged with colored threads of green, red, and turquoise in intricate embroidery. She slowly plaited her hair as she thought about her encounter with Alma that morning. She'd hardly recognized him, but she knew that beneath all that wild hair and his dirty clothing, he was still the friend she remembered. Somewhere. He had been practically like a brother to her, until that fateful evening when her parents had told her she was about to be betrothed. To a virtual stranger—an older man she barely knew, who had been widowed with several children.

In a desperate attempt at avoiding the betrothal, she'd confessed to her father that she wanted to marry Alma someday. She had allowed herself to imagine marrying Alma but never dared speak of it aloud to anyone. At fifteen, she hadn't expected the impact her careless words would have on her father. It wasn't but a few days later that her parents took her aside and informed her that her carefree days with Alma were over. From that point on, she had to spend her time focusing on improving her feminine skills.

Picking up a red ribbon, Cassia threaded it through one braid. She hadn't meant to talk to her father about marriage to Alma, nor did she realize how serious her comment might be taken, but it was really Alma's fault for putting the idea into her head.

She closed her eyes briefly, transposing the grown-up unruly man who'd saved her from the bees today with the young man she used to spend hours with swimming in the pond and trapping frogs. He was always teasing her, always laughing, always seeming to have the entire world at his fingertips. He had dozens of friends who surrounded him constantly, and he was a natural leader. If he asked someone to move a log out of his path or to fetch him a drink, they'd do it without question.

But as they grew older, their relationship started to slowly change, and they were no longer two friends jumping from rock to rock or climbing hills to watch the herons flying overheard. Cassia hadn't been sure if it was just in her mind or if it was because she'd started feeling different around him.

"Have you ever wanted to leave Zarahemla?" Alma asked.

Cassia looked over at him, where he had perched on a low branch of a cypress tree. She sat on a nearby rock, grateful to let her tired shoulders rest. They'd spent most of the afternoon shooting targets with a bow and arrow. Well, Alma had been shooting the targets, and she'd been missing them. His fingers were stained black at the tips—evidence of the long hours he spent as an apprentice to the temple scribes. The days they spent together were few and far between now.

"I don't think I can very well leave," Cassia said. "I don't see my parents letting me go—since I'm their only daughter." She studied him, surprised at his sudden melancholy.

His gaze seemed to bore into hers, and the intensity made her nervous for some reason. "What's wrong?" she asked.

"Nothing," Alma said, peeling off a few leaves from the branch and letting them drop to the ground.

Cassia shook her head. His usual optimistic disposition was subdued today. "Even if I did want to leave, where would I go? We're surrounded by Lamanite territory." She'd heard the stories of the city of Nephi and the land of Helam over and over. There were too many enemies out there. Alma's father had made a narrow escape from that wicked Nephite-turned-Lamanite, Amulon. Sure, she was curious to see other lands and people, but not if it put her life in danger.

Alma was silent for several minutes, then he hopped down from the branch. "Sometimes I wonder about life outside of Zarahemla—outside of our fathers' control. We've lived here our whole lives, and nothing ever changes."

Cassia put her elbows on her knees, smiling at him. "You're getting taller."

With a short laugh, Alma leaned against the trunk of the tree and put his hands behind his head. "I guess I get tired of being the high priest's son. Everyone looks at me to follow my father and to be just like him. Talk like him . . . act like him . . ." He looked at Cassia. "Don't you get weary of being a king's daughter?"

She lifted a shoulder. "I do feel restricted when I can't go out like the other girls, and I always have to have one of my brothers with me or another escort."

"Or me," Alma said with a fleeting smile.

"Or you," she said, looking away from him. She felt achy inside. Maybe it was the heat. The day had grown hotter, even under the shade. Perspiration started to form on Cassia's neck, making her uncomfortable. Or maybe it was the fact that she knew he was studying her. They sat in silence for a couple more minutes.

"Maybe we could leave together," Alma said in a quiet voice.

Cassia glanced at him. "You mean go with the traders?"

"No . . ." His voice was slow and thoughtful. "We could find a section of land and build our own homestead—away from everyone."

Cassia looked down at her twisting hands, feeling her face and neck flush.

"We would have to get married first, of course, but that wouldn't be a hindrance, would it?" he said.

Cassia felt him staring at her. Waiting. Her heart was now pounding so fast, she didn't dare meet his eyes. Surely he could hear it. She brought a hand to her moist neck, wishing she could dive into a cool pond right now.

Then suddenly, he left the tree and crossed to her, crouching so that he was right next to her, eye level.

"Cass?"

She was forced to look at him. The intensity of his gaze told her that he hadn't been teasing.

"I—I don't think I want to leave home," she whispered.

He grabbed her hand and threaded his fingers through hers, something he'd done plenty of times in the past, but this time it made her whole body feel hot. His hands were large like a man's—he was *a man now, she reminded herself.*

"We don't have to leave if you don't want to," he said in an almost-whisper.

Cassia nodded, not sure if she was still sitting on the rock or perhaps floating above it. "All right," she barely managed to say.

A whistle sounded in the distance.

"It's probably Ammon looking for us," Alma said, but he didn't release her hand. Instead, he stood and pulled her to her feet, still clasping her hand in his strong one. They walked together in the direction of the palace, and just before Ammon came into view, Alma let go of her hand.

Cassia opened her eyes, imagining that she could still feel the touch of Alma's hand heating her palm, even after all this time. She stared at her glimmering image in the polished metal, remembering how after she'd pronounced that she wouldn't become betrothed to a stranger, she'd foolishly told her parents about what Alma had said to her. Then her father forbade her from spending time with "the boys." No more excursions with her brothers and Alma. That same night, she'd sneaked out of the palace and fled to Alma's house to tell him. He was angry that she'd told her parents, yet more so that she'd almost been betrothed against her will.

But it was Alma's fierce embrace on that night which she still remembered so well. She'd never felt so safe—so connected—with another person. With Alma's arms around her, she knew she never wanted to marry anyone else. But that was their first and last embrace. Alma obeyed her father's command implicitly.

After that, they'd only seen each other in social settings—always formal, always with other adults around, and never comfortable. And he'd never touched her again.

Cassia brushed at her stinging eyes. She shouldn't think about the past now, but seeing Alma that afternoon had brought it all back. He'd never renewed his sentiments about marriage, and sometimes she wondered if she'd imagined their conversation. Or perhaps he *had* been teasing her, and she'd destroyed their friendship and ended her childhood for nothing.

She finished threading the final ribbon through her hair, then applied another layer of salve to the bites on her arms. Her shawl would keep the red bumps hidden. Music wafted through the hallways, and Cassia suddenly felt anxious about an evening of entertainment and dancing. She peered closely at her metal reflection to see if there was any trace of redness in her eyes. Satisfied, she took a deep breath and opened the door to her chamber.

CHAPTER 5

And ye shall seek me, and find me, when ye shall search for me with all your heart.
—Jeremiah 29:13

Alma the Elder

Alma sat on the pole-platform bed, watching his wife, Maia, plait her hair. She did so expertly, having spent years in captivity as a servant to a Lamanite princess though Maia herself was the widow of a Nephite king.

In the early evening light, Alma still remembered the night he'd been reunited with her in the city of Helam. She'd been abducted along with twenty-four daughters of the Lamanites and had been forced to live under the malicious rule of Amulon. She'd come so close to being forced to marry the vile man. But the Lord had spared her, and only He could have brought Maia back into Alma's life. Each day he thanked the Lord for this remarkable woman.

More than twenty years had passed since they'd escaped the traitor Amulon and fled to freedom. After Maia had borne their son, Alma the Younger, on their treacherous flight to Zarahemla, two daughters had followed—Bethany and Dana. They each had their mother's dark gray eyes and copper hair. Then Cephas, the youngest, came, and they named him after Alma's father. The young boy resembled Maia as well. Only Alma the Younger took after Alma—and reminded him of his younger days.

In fact, his son reminded Alma too much of himself. Unfortunately. He sighed, exhaustion invading every part of his body.

Maia turned to look at him, as if she could read his thoughts. "Tired?"

Alma nodded as she crossed to him and placed her gentle hand on his shoulder. She rubbed his shoulders for a moment as he stretched his neck forward. She had been so melancholy as of late. He missed her singing, even her humming. The house had seemed so quiet since their son had left on that terrible night months before.

It was the next day that Alma noticed his wife had stopped singing to herself as she worked. Her voice had been legendary in her youth—in fact, her singing had earned her the title of queen when King Noah fell in love with the sixteen-year-old beauty and her melodic voice.

Maia's hands pressed a stiff muscle in Alma's neck, and he flinched at the sudden pain. She softened her touch, and he bowed his head as she worked on his neck. There was a time when Alma had closed his heart to this woman. She had married the king on the promise that her parents would be well cared for throughout the rest of their lives. But she had sacrificed everything for them.

King Noah had beaten his young wife into compliance, then when he grew tired of her, he took another woman to wife, adding yet another innocent to his collection of wives and concubines. Alma couldn't remember what number of wife Maia had been, but he'd seen the physical change in her over the months and years as King Noah snuffed out her light from within. And then her infant son had died at birth, and King Noah had threatened to kill her for it.

As one of the king's priests, Alma had risked his life to defend her in court, and it was then that he knew he was in love with the woman—a love that could earn both of them death by fire. He'd buried his heart to preserve them both.

And then everything had changed.

Abinadi came to preach in the city, and Alma's childhood haunted his dreams each night. Abinadi's words echoed that of Alma's father's, and Alma could not forget them.

Alma finally took courage the morning Abinadi was sentenced to death. But by then it was too late. Abinadi died in a wall of flames and smoke, and Alma fled from the city—away from his diabolical life. Away from his king. Away from even Maia.

He only returned to teach in secret and hundreds of believers joined him at the waters of Mormon, then followed him on to the land of Helam. He was unexpectedly reunited with Maia, by then a widow, and they married. When he finally led his people away from the city of Helam and their cruel taskmaster, Amulon, Alma vowed to protect his new wife with his own life—to never allow her to suffer, go hungry, be a slave to anyone, or to cry herself to sleep one more night.

But now their son was gone. Their beloved son—whose heart had turned cold, whose eyes had grown dark, and whose spirit had dimmed.

It was a moment before Alma realized his wife had stopped rubbing his neck and was sitting on the bed next to him. She stared ahead, silent and rigid.

Alma put his arm around her, feeling her soften a little. He kissed the top of her head as she burrowed against his chest and wrapped her arms around his waist.

"Do you think he'll ever return?" Maia whispered.

Alma stroked her arm. "He knows we love him. He'll come back."

She sighed against his chest. "I can't imagine what he must be doing or must be thinking right now. Where is he living? What if he's hungry?"

Alma wrapped both arms around her. "Our son could charm a beggar out of his last morsel. I don't think he'll be hungry."

"But what if he has no place to sleep?" Maia pressed. She leaned back a little and raised her eyes to gaze at him.

It hurt him more to see her pain than it did to think of his son's disobedience. Anger burned someplace deep inside as he thought of their son hurting Maia by his careless actions.

If only his son weren't so stubborn, so set on having things proved to him. Faith wasn't like that, and neither was the Lord. Following the commandments brought blessings, which reinforced the faith. His son claimed he'd done everything right for long enough—but that he still felt no confirmation, no answers.

"You claim to have heard the Lord's voice. Why haven't I?" his son asked. "I've been a scribe in the temple for three years—I've read every word of every so-called prophet. They were no different than I, no better than I, yet why does the Lord choose to speak to them?"

It was the same argument every day. There was nothing he could do to prove the Lord's existence. Understanding and realization came by faith, not by proof.

"Faith is believing in what you can't see or hear," Alma had explained as patiently as he could. The girls had long been in bed, and Maia had retreated when the argument began. This was no new argument, and Maia knew this had to be dealt with between father and son.

His son had folded his arms, his eyes dull with disbelief. "You use the Church to control the people."

"No," Alma said. "Belonging to the Church is the Lord's way. The right way."

"You mean your *way. King Mosiah's way."*

Alma couldn't explain it, but he just never had enough patience when his son argued this way. His anger never stayed buried for long when his son spoke like that. "You blaspheme against the very God who delivered your mother from the grasp of evil men! You blaspheme against the hand of God that preserved our lives so you and your sisters and brother could enjoy a life free from oppression and servitude."

His son had smiled at that—but it was a cruel smile. "You call living in this house, following your rules, working at your precious temple, a life free of oppression? I say you traded one oppressive life for another!"

Alma was on his feet now, his face hot with his frustration. He stood face to face with his son, who now exceeded him in height and strength.

"You think this *is oppression? You have no idea . . . You claim to have read the accounts of our people—yet you are like a spoiled child who won't share one piece of sugarcane out of a pile with his sister. You've never known hunger, nor thirst, nor nakedness. You've never had to pray over a sick wife or watch a friend being attacked by the brutal Lamanites. You've never watched a true prophet of God being beaten with flaming sticks until his clothing caught fire and his flesh was consumed in a hellish inferno."*

"Enough!" his son had shouted. "Save your ranting for your Sabbath congregation. Save your fear and damnation for them. *The king has given you too much power to wield over the people—just because I don't want to worship as you do doesn't mean that I am* wrong. *I will no longer listen to you—Wo unto me who does not listen to the almighty high priest." He spread his hands wide and looked up at the roof. "May the Lord strike me dead if I am wrong!" He waited a breath, then threw a triumphant look at the man he was named for. "Nothing."*

"Son," Alma pled in a hoarse voice. "If you would only ask the Lord for yourself, like Nephi of old. His brothers, Laman and Lemuel, refused to find out for themselves, and their hearts were forever—"

"Hardened. And they never forgave their brother for stealing them from their homeland. I know the story. You'll never let me forget their wickedness." His eyes bored into his father's. "And I'm sure Nephi never tired of putting them in their places as well. He told them they were selfish for wanting to return and claim their inheritance for their wives and children. No wonder their hearts were hard. I wonder if Nephi ever apologized for taking away his brothers' birthright."

Alma stared at him, stunned.

His son turned away and grabbed a robe that hung by the door. "I guess we'll never know—it doesn't say in all those records at the temple." He glanced over his shoulder, his face red with fierce determination. "I'm resigning my position as a scribe. I'm sure you'll be able to find someone who doesn't ask questions." He tugged the door open, then said without looking at Alma, "Tell Mother good-bye."

"I thought he'd be back after he calmed down. He always came back before," Alma whispered.

Maia's arms tightened around him. "If only I had intervened that night."

"No," Alma said. "He was too angry—more so than I'd ever seen before. He seemed determined to trip me up—find something to accuse me of. If he would have turned his verbal assault on you, there's no telling what action I might have taken against my own son."

Maia shuddered, and Alma pulled her closer. "We should be leaving soon. The girls will be waiting, and Lael is probably already here to watch after Cephas."

Maia nodded against his chest. "I don't want to face a crowd of people tonight. I couldn't eat a thing. Maybe I'll just stay here with my mother. "

Alma drew back and cupped her chin, seeing that her eyes were bright with unshed tears. She'd had no appetite since their son's departure. Alma knew she felt the same as he—sick with worry. "We'll stay together, and if you need to depart early, let me know. I hope to ask King Mosiah if any of his sons have mentioned seeing Alma."

Maia's expression brightened. "He was such good friends with Ammon and Aaron. Maybe they can find out where he's living."

Alma stood from the bed, pulling up Maia by the hand. Looking into her sad eyes, he wished he could clear away the pain for her. He knew it would be hard for her to be around a family who was celebrating a betrothal—it was something that he and Maia had hoped for their own son. But over the years, he'd refused to consider any of the eligible women his parents had suggested.

"If only it were our son," Maia said as if she were reading Alma's thoughts.

"If only he weren't so stubborn, it might well be."

She touched his arm and leaned against him. "I think he's had his heart set on someone for a long time."

"Who?"

"The king's daughter."

Alma exhaled, considering the likelihood of Cassia and his son getting married. He'd watched her grow up, and she and her brothers had been playmates with his son throughout their youth. He shook his head. "The king would never allow it."

"That's what I assumed," Maia said in a soft voice. "And I think our son knew it as well." She turned from him and grabbed her cloak from a peg on the wall. "King Mosiah has always seemed to frown on our son."

"What do you mean?" Alma asked.

"He holds him to a higher standard—even more so than his own sons," she said, her voice surprisingly harsh.

Alma waited for her to turn around. "Our son should be held to a higher standard. He's been taught correct principles all his life."

"I know," Maia said, with a sigh of frustration. "But the king should expect his own sons to behave just as much as he expects ours to."

"I didn't realize—"

"It's probably something only a mother notices. I just have the feeling the king blames our son for any mishaps committed by his sons, as if ours has been the bad influence, and his have no willpower of their own."

Alma ran a hand through his hair. Maia might be right, but it was difficult for him to look at the king that way. He knew the man as a thoughtful and careful leader. In fact, Mosiah often came to Alma for advice, especially on spiritual matters. It was hard to imagine the king holding a grudge without having said anything over the years.

Feeling disheartened once again, Alma followed his wife from their bedchamber. There was no defense he or his wife could come up with for their son now anyway. He'd left the family and his position as a temple scribe. Mosiah knew about it right away, and he'd probably guessed the reason. Everyone, including Alma, had hoped his son would outgrow his wild youth, but it hadn't happened. He'd gone from a mischievous and wildly popular young man to closing himself off from the family, his mentors, and things of the Spirit.

His son's whole demeanor had changed, Alma realized. The light-heartedness had changed to bitterness.

Dana and Bethany rushed into the room, arguing over a scarf, nearly bumping into Alma.

"Mother," Dana said, "Bethany promised I could wear it this time."

Lael, Maia's mother, was close behind, her hands outstretched as if she'd given up. Maia cast a stern look at Bethany. "Did you promise your sister?"

Bethany's eyes shifted, giving just enough evidence needed by her mother. Reluctantly, she handed over the scarf to Dana, who promptly smiled and ran to the front door.

Maia kissed her mother. "Thank you for coming."

Lael's wrinkled face shifted into a smile. Cephas came from out of the cooking room, a honeyed treat in his hand and a grin on his face. "We'll have a wonderful time together, won't we Cephas?"

The boy nodded, his mouth full.

Maia kissed Cephas's sticky cheek. "Behave yourself for Grandmama."

Once outside, Maia linked an arm through Bethany's as the family made the short walk to the palace. "She always gets her way," Bethany grumbled. "Just because she's the youngest."

"Next week we can visit Cassia and have her teach us how to weave that pattern. I think Helam's wife taught it to her."

Bethany's countenance immediately lightened. "Raquel? All right." Within a few minutes, she'd joined her sister, and the two of them talked excitedly about the banquet.

Alma moved to his wife's side and took her hand. If only every complaint in their family were so easily solved. He pictured Alma as a youth and wished he could return to those seemingly carefree days. Parenting had seemed much easier then.

Maia's fingers pressed against his, and he squeezed back. "Are you ready for this?" she asked in a quiet voice as they neared the palace.

The front entrance was surrounded by flaming torches in the near dark, making the palace look even more regal. Though Mosiah and his family lived simply, the palace was still an impressive sight. Two guards acknowledged them and stepped aside so the family could enter. "The banquet is in the back courtyard," one guard said. The second guard escorted them.

Laughter and animated conversation reached into the gleaming halls as Alma passed through them with his family. The palace was beautiful, and having his wife and daughters by his side should have fulfilled Alma. But his oldest son had left a hole that seemed to grow deeper each day.

The pressure of his wife's hand increased as they stepped outside into the colorful courtyard.

* * *

Cassia

The music from the flutes in the garden courtyard seemed to float through the whole palace. When Cassia came into view of the back entrance, she realized she was one of the last to arrive, made more apparent when an expression of relief covered the queen's face. Cassia's mother and father stood at the gate of the garden courtyard, speaking with Alma the Elder and his wife.

Cassia immediately stiffened. Had someone seen her talking to Alma that morning? Cassia stepped into the garden, and her mother rushed over to her.

"Why are you so late?"

Cassia smoothed her braids, looking anywhere but at her mother, although she could feel her mother scanning her features. "You look beautiful, dear. Ilana has been waiting to introduce you to her brother."

Cassia nodded, though first she wanted to know what Alma's parents had been discussing with hers. The bites on her arms were still itching, a constant reminder of Alma. "Has Maia received news of her son?"

A flash of surprise crossed her mother's face, but she recovered quickly. "No, they've asked to speak to your brothers about it, but your father's worried that it will make Alma retreat even further."

Relief spread through Cassia. So they hadn't been discussing her and the bees, and it seemed they didn't know about Alma's sudden appearance. As her mother led her gently by the arm to where Ilana stood, Cassia glanced over at Alma's parents again. The concern on Maia's and Alma's faces made Cassia wonder if she should confess that she'd seen him this afternoon. *No,* she thought, *they'll learn plenty from Aaron and Ammon, even more than I know about Alma.*

"Cassia, this is my brother, Nehem," Ilana said.

Cassia focused her gaze on the man standing before her. He was about her height, and stocky—his build reminded her of her brother Ammon, yet without the definition. But Nehem probably didn't spend all of his time sparring, hunting, or building weapons like her brother did.

Nehem bowed, straightened, and grinned. His dark hair was cropped short, and he wore a necklace of quetzal feathers. He wore a single ring on his finger, and his feathered cape was of high quality. And he had a nice smile. His lively eyes held hers, as if he found something amusing.

"Welcome," Cassia said, matching his smile. "I hope you'll enjoy your evening."

"I'm enjoying it very much now," he said, smoothing the feathers against his neck. "Especially now that I've met the beautiful sister I've heard so much about."

"Oh, Nehem," Ilana said. She shook her head at Cassia. "He can be so comical."

Cassia laughed, then keeping up the pretense said, "Well, thank you very much, sir. It's a privilege to meet Ilana's fine brother."

"Call me Nehem, please," he said with an overemphasized wink.

"All right, then," Cassia said, looking from Nehem to Ilana. "Have you tried the cacao drink? I tested it this afternoon, and I must say, it's delicious. I even added a few extra spices that will surprise you. You also might try the avocado paste; it's excellent with the roasted turkey."

Nehem raised both of his brows. "A woman who knows her food and drink. How refreshing." He held out his arm. "Lead the way. I'll eat whatever you recommend."

"Nehem!" Ilana said with mock horror. But Cassia saw her sister-in-law flush with pleasure. She must have a wonderful relationship with her brother.

Cassia stepped to Nehem's side and took his arm. She wanted to laugh at his silliness, but instead she kept a demure expression as she led him to the low tables bursting with food. "You must try the baked squash—I asked the cooks to glaze it with honey. Also the fried chili and mushroom mixture goes nicely with the maize cakes. The cooks dice the vegetables and simmer them together so their flavors blend."

"I wouldn't think a king's daughter would spend much time in the cooking rooms," Nehem said.

His question might have sounded demeaning to another girl, but Cassia heard admiration in his voice. "I don't think my parents know how much time I spend in there," she said. "But I do have plenty of free time, and that's how I usually choose to spend it."

"The servants must really appreciate your help."

Cassia pulled a face. "They are more my friends than servants."

"But of course," Nehem said with a generous smile.

Cassia could see the similarity between Nehem and his sister—both were so agreeable.

Nehem folded his arms, his gaze completely focused on Cassia. She felt her skin grow a bit warm with all of the attention. She wondered if he told every girl he met she was beautiful. "Tell me about your friends, then."

It was Cassia's turn to be surprised. No one had ever taken so much interest in how she spent her time. She told him about the ladies in the cooking room and their families. "Shuah is very good with herbs. She's teaching me about all the different spices. The men usually collect the honey, but they've let me watch a few times." She nearly clapped her hand over her mouth, then remembered that no one knew about the bee attack.

"What else do you like to do?" Nehem asked, his warm eyes intent on her face.

Cassia shrugged. "I suppose embroidery is all right. It just takes so long to get one design ready. When you cook, you can have a delicious meal within hours."

Nehem laughed and brushed her arm with his hand. "I can see why Ilana likes you so much. She has been talking about you ever since I arrived."

"Oh? Not about her betrothed?"

"Perhaps a *little* about Aaron," Nehem said in a sly voice.

Cassia surprised herself by laughing aloud. She quieted quickly, not wanting to draw too much attention to herself. She glanced around at the milling guests, but no one seemed to be watching them. Turning her attention back to Nehem, she said, "Tell me, what do you do with your days?"

His eyes lit with amusement, and he offered her another bow. "So inquisitive," he murmured. "I spend my days sitting on various councils throughout the city. Rather tedious compared to your activities, I must say."

She cocked her head. "Which councils?"

Nehem tapped a finger to his chin, exaggerating the time it took him to respond. "Nothing very interesting. Just the tax collecting council."

"You can't be very popular then," Cassia said.

"I get a lot of closed doors in my face. And a few curses."

She laughed.

Nehem laughed with her, his hand touching her arm again. "Someone has to be the enforcer." He lifted a shoulder. "I'd do anything to help your father, no matter how unpleasant."

His gaze was so endearing that Cassia felt a flutter in her chest. Before she could analyze it, he continued, "Another council I sit on is made up of men trying to establish peace between the unbelievers and the members of the Church."

"Oh. That sounds very interesting, and . . . challenging."

"Yes and yes," Nehem said, his eyes bright. "It's a problem that seems to have no solution as of yet. Many of the unbelievers choose to ignore the king's edict of peace. They can be a stubborn lot. We've created a guard that visits the leaders of each community and surrounding villages to explain the laws as established by the king. But the visits don't always run smoothly, so the members of the council sometimes have to get more involved."

Cassia nodded. "You must know my brothers quite well, then."

"Oh yes, Ammon and Aaron are on that particular council as well." He continued to explain one of their latest policies, but Cassia could only be distracted for so long, no matter how lively Nehem seemed to make his council work.

Her gaze kept straying to Alma's parents. For the most part it appeared that they were enjoying themselves. They moved from person to person, greeting and entering into brief conversations. From time to time, someone would pull Alma aside and ask a more serious question—she could tell by the man's furrowed brow and concentrated expression. As the high priest over all of Zarahemla, he was often in demand as much as the king himself.

Ilana and Aaron eventually drifted together. Cassia couldn't help but smile when she watched the two of them together. She could tell that they were maintaining formality in public, but there was a tangible tenderness between the two of them. A burst of laughter erupted through the gathering. Ammon's laugh was unmistakable, and Cassia turned to see what was happening.

Ammon stood with Alma the Younger's sisters, helping them catch fireflies. Cassia was about to cross to them and introduce Nehem when the shell trumpet sounded. The opening socializing was over. Time for formalities.

As everyone quieted to listen, Nehem leaned over and whispered, "I thought if Aaron was a brute around women, I'd steal my sister back. But even if he was, I think she'd stay just because of *you.*"

Cassia felt her face go red. "You *are* too comical!"

He chuckled quietly.

Mosiah began his welcoming speech, and Cassia looked over to where her father stood, flanked by all four of her brothers. Ammon and Aaron were staring at her, and neither of them looked pleased to see Nehem at her side.

CHAPTER 6

Take heed unto yourselves, lest ye forget the covenant of the Lord your God. . . .
—Deuteronomy 4:23

Alma the Younger

Not a dozen paces from where Cassia stood, Alma hid behind a large, drooping cypress tree. He'd seen everything. And heard almost every word. Watching Cassia and Nehem talk, he felt a hard knot in his stomach tighten with each passing moment. The man was sweet-talking her, and she was falling for it. Hard.

Alma exhaled with frustration. She had been protected all of her life; the only men she'd spent time with had been relatives, unless he counted himself. And now she was practically sinking to her knees in acceptance before the first man to pay attention to her and tell her she was beautiful.

Alma leaned against the tree, ignoring the scratching of the trunk against his bare arm. Regret entered his heart for the first moment in a long time. Regret for the falling out between him and his father. For if there'd been no disagreement, Alma would have been a guest at this event tonight—an *invited* guest.

Cassia's laughter caused him to tense. Shaking his head, he realized that the evening might have turned out the same way, even if he'd been visible. Cassia would have still been introduced to Nehem, and would a glowering Alma the Younger have been able to dissuade Nehem from speaking his honeyed words?

She smiled at something Nehem said, and he started to fawn over her even more. Alma's neck itched with irritation, and he kept flexing his hands open, then closing them. If only he had his bow to create a diversion . . .

Then his mother caught his eye.

His heart caught at his mother's soulful expression. He knew her well enough to see that she was trying to appear cheerful. He acknowledged that he'd hurt her deeply, and that's what caused the trickle of doubt to enter his mind. But it was too late to turn back now. He'd left his scribe position for good with no desire to return. Not even if it would bring a genuine smile to his mother's face.

As usual, she wore a relatively plain tunic compared to that of the queen's. His father was plenty wealthy, yet his mother practically dressed like a commoner, looking out of place among her friends. If it weren't for her natural beauty, she'd be outshone by the number of jewels in the courtyard. But that was his mother—never assuming.

Alma wasn't surprised to see Cephas absent. He was probably with one of the grandparents receiving a stomachful of sweets. Alma was relieved—he didn't know if he could stay away from his younger brother if he saw the boy's impish smile. He ached just to think about how much he missed the little fellow. The only thing that brought ease to his heart was watching his two sisters play with Ammon. They seemed unaffected, and the prince was like a child himself most of the time. Dana wore a multi-colored scarf he'd never seen before, and Alma could almost bet that it was a gift from Cassia. The girls looked to her like an older sister. Like family.

Yet Alma knew his anger at seeing Cassia with Nehem was something much more than protective, brotherly concern. Much more. But he pushed that deep inside, as far away from his heart as possible. King Mosiah had made his feelings about Alma clear more than two years ago. And the king hadn't likely changed his mind. Especially now. Alma could just imagine the king's reaction to the tale of his sudden departure. Enough Sabbaths had passed that the priests in the temple had certainly realized he wasn't returning.

Alma's gaze strayed to the royal couple. The king and his wife stood together, speaking to what looked like Ilana's parents. They looked so proud, so regal, so elegant in their fine clothing. Alma knew they worked hard to serve the people, but that didn't excuse the squalor that a portion of the citizens of Zarahemla were forced to live in.

Alma eyed the food, most of which would go to waste. His real purpose for coming tonight was to confiscate the leftovers. He'd secretly deliver it to the most needy families of the Isidro village. He couldn't believe Isidro was filled with children who were hungry! And his father had accused him of never going without. Well, Alma hadn't been hungry, but there were people living within the land who were. It was inexcusable. The poor people of the village were in more need of the king's food tonight than the aristocratic guests.

His gaze moved from the meal to Cassia again just as Nehem leaned close to her and whispered in her ear. Her face went red, and Alma felt his face redden as well, but his with anger.

Everyone had fallen quiet, and it appeared King Mosiah was about to make an announcement. His sisters hurried to his mother, where they nestled against her. Then he saw Aaron and Ammon. By their expressions, it appeared they weren't too pleased with Nehem's undying attentions either. *Good. At least I'm not alone,* Alma thought. He knew the brothers were affiliated with Nehem in various councils, and neither liked his pompous attitude—which was ironic, given Aaron's own tendencies.

With everyone quiet, Alma heard Mosiah's words clearly. "We are pleased to welcome Ilana and her family to our home tonight."

You mean to your palace, Alma thought.

"When Limhi arrived in Zarahemla, I had no idea how important his family would eventually become," the king continued. "I didn't know then that our families would be joined in the sacred union of marriage."

Alma couldn't listen anymore. Couldn't watch the formalities, the politeness, the grandeur. He was happy for Aaron, though he knew that his friend would rarely spend time with him and Ammon once the marriage took place.

Alma turned away from the festivities; away from Cassia and those eyes that were drinking in every word that Nehem uttered.

Alma would find a way to make her not forget who she was. Who *he* was. He made his way quietly through the garden, listening for any potential servants scurrying around on one errand or another. When he arrived at the beehive yard, he knew exactly what he had to do.

In the newly descended dark, the bees were quiet. Not taking any chances, Alma found the basket of chert and long, dried sticks. He struck two pieces of chert together, igniting a spark big enough to light the end of a stick. After blowing on it until the stick was sufficiently smoking, he put on the leather mitts. He approached the first hive, the one closest to the garden entrance in case he needed to make a quick escape. Trying to remember how he'd seen the beekeepers do it, he held the stick just below the opening, allowing the smoke's natural course to take it into the hive. After a couple of minutes, he reached in and removed a honeycomb. As he pulled it out, a lone bee flew out and perched on his forearm. Before Alma could shoo it away, it bit him.

"Ow," he muttered, then he quickly reached in and retrieved a second honeycomb.

Two should be enough, he decided. He extinguished the smoking stick and put the mitts back into the basket, then left the grove. On his way out of the garden, he pulled off some leaves from a nearby sassafras tree to wrap the honeycomb in.

Alma took his usual route around the palace. The music and feasting continued, but he had grown weary of watching the guests, especially Nehem and Cassia. The next time he saw Aaron and Ammon, he hoped they'd be able to tell him that they'd scared Nehem off.

He moved around the perimeter of the palace, careful to avoid the guards, who were as predictable as ever. He found the bedchamber window belonging to Ammon and tucked the leaf-wrapped honeycomb into his waistband so he could scale the climbing bush.

He hesitated before poking his head up to look through the window. There was an oil lamp glowing in the room, but it appeared empty, and Ammon would be absent until the end of the evening. Alma hoisted himself onto the ledge then dropped softly into the room.

His heart was pounding, but his mission was only half complete. He opened Ammon's door leading into the hallways. Alma assumed Cassia's room would be the same as it had been in her youth. He crept down the corridor, stopping often to listen. Everything was quiet—a good sign.

He halted, catching his nervous breath in front of Cassia's bedchamber. No light glowed beneath her door—she was still at the banquet. He opened the door, careful to keep quiet in case anyone happened down the hall. Peering through the darkness, he looked for a place to leave the honeycomb.

Alma quickly crossed the room and placed the wrapped honeycomb on a stool near the window. He unwrapped them, satisfied that neither had broken, and she'd be able to remove plenty of honey from them. As he turned away, he hesitated as voices sounded in the hallway. The banquet was far from over. Maybe they were servants, but one thing was certain—the voices were female.

He looked around frantically. The window was too small to escape through and the bed too low to hide under. He noticed an upright wooden screen—probably the place where she changed her clothing. In a few strides, he'd stepped behind it and crouched low, just as the door swung open to the room.

"Thanks for walking with me. I'll rejoin you in a moment," Cassia's voice drifted in.

A giggle followed, and a sing-song voice replied, "I'm sure my brother is mourning your absence right now."

Cassia laughed.

Alma cringed.

Then the door shut. Alma held his breath. He'd wait until she left again, then make his escape. Cassia let out a loud sigh, and Alma's muscles stiffened. Was it a sigh of frustration, tiredness, or joy? He wished he could see her expression, but he didn't dare move.

Her footsteps seemed to echo as she crossed the room. Then they stopped, and she let out a small gasp. *The honeycomb.* She'd seen the gift.

Alma waited to hear her next movements, but there were no more sounds. Sweat prickled against his neck. What was she doing? Had she fallen asleep standing up?

Then she breathed in sharply. "Alma?"

He flinched at the sound of his name.

"I know you're in here," her voice floated over him. "You couldn't possibly fit through my window."

He moved from his crouched position. Every stretch of muscle and creak of bone seemed to be amplified in the silent room. He stepped out from behind the divider.

Cassia stood facing him, her arms folded. He could just make out her curious gaze in the moonlight.

"Sorry," he said in a quiet voice. "I didn't think you'd come back so soon."

She continued to stare at him. "What are you doing here?" She walked to her bed and picked up a shawl, pulling it around her shoulders.

He lifted his shoulders, but then her gaze fell back to the honeycomb. She looked at them for several seconds, then said, "Thank you."

Nodding, he crossed to the door.

"Wait," Cassia said. She walked toward him, clutching at the shawl around her shoulders. The moonlight streamed behind her, making her look as if she were the moon goddess crossing the room.

Alma moved back a little as she came to a stop right in front of him, looking up at him. "Why did you bring them?"

He fought a smile. "I—thought you could use some."

She shook her head, sadness coming to her eyes. "I knew it."

Now what have I done? "Knew what?"

She placed a hand on his chest, right over his heart. He thought it might pound out of his chest.

"I knew you were still good," she whispered.

The pounding slowed and was drowned by a flood of anger. "What are you talking about?"

Cassia let her hand drop. "They—our fathers—have been discussing you tonight. Speculating about things that I could hardly believe of you." Her eyes were wide again, as if she were part afraid, part curious.

"What is it you can't believe?" he asked.

"That you'd want to hurt your parents."

"Why does it have to be about hurting them? Why can't they accept that I believe differently? Why does a difference in opinion have to make me wrong?"

Her face faltered. "I—I don't know."

"Just because I'm considering other possibilities in life doesn't mean I want to hurt my parents. There are plenty of good people out there, and not all of them are members of the Church."

"I didn't mean that . . ." She met his eyes. "You know how important religion is to your parents and how much they fought to be free. They only want you to be happy."

He moved a fraction closer to her, pleased that she didn't move away. "I'm happy when I'm with you."

A smile touched her lips, but she shook her head. "Then why did you leave?"

"It was impossible for me to stay in my parents' home," Alma said, studying her in the dim light. A lock of her hair had escaped her plaits, and he wanted to reach out and smooth them. "It's good for them to miss me, let tempers cool." He paused. "Do you miss me?"

When she met his eyes again, he could see moisture in them. "Oh Alma, how can you ask that?" She turned away.

He stared at her, stunned. "Are you crying? What's wrong?"

"Why did you have to ask that? Of course I miss you." She turned to look at him, tears on her cheeks. "I miss everything about you, and that's why I can't stand you living out in the wild somewhere. I worry about you—everyone worries. Your poor mother . . ."

He touched her hand lightly, then drew back. "Then why can't they accept me for who I am?"

She wiped the moisture from her cheeks. "It's their lives, Alma. It's *my* life. Our belief in God and the Church is everything. It's in every breath we take, in every thought we think."

Alma looked away; he couldn't stand to see her pleading eyes, the tears. "I didn't know that not attending Sabbath services was such a crime. And maybe instead of your father warning you about me, he should be warning you about Nehem."

Cassia sobered, and her eyes flashed. "What about Nehem? You don't even know him."

"I don't have to," Alma said. "Any man could see his intentions—"

"What do you mean?"

"His words are empty, Cassia. He spends his days coercing and bullying villagers into signing laws they can't even read themselves. How could you be impressed by him?"

She folded her arms, her expression defiant. "Who said I was impressed?"

"I can see it."

"I barely met Nehem—you don't know anything. You weren't even at the party."

"I saw the two of you together when I passed by."

"Well," Cassia said, straightening. "Nehem is a nice man, and he seems sincere." Her gaze held his as she slowly said, "Why are you concerned about him? Why do you even care what he says to me?"

He knew why he cared, but he couldn't tell her, not now. Her gaze challenged him to be bold. But two years before her father had made it clear what his feelings were about a marriage between the two of them. Alma took a deep breath. "Just trust me. He wouldn't be a good match for you."

"He's not asking me to marry him, Alma." Cassia's face reddened, and she broke her gaze and looked down. "We both know my parents have been patient long enough. I know what my duty is, and one of these days, I'll have to fulfill it."

Alma's chest tightened as he wondered how she could truly believe that. "You shouldn't marry out of duty."

"Why not?" Her tone was hard, but the uncertainty was plain in her eyes. "Most people do—look at Aaron," she said, as if she were trying to convince herself.

"Ilana is in love with him, and he seems to like her," he said. "It's not much of a sacrifice on his part."

Cassia lifted her gaze to study him, and for a tense moment they stared at each other.

"No, it's not," she said, breaking her gaze. "But we aren't all that fortunate."

"No . . . we aren't," he said, the words hanging heavy in the air. He couldn't stand it any longer, and he reached out and brushed back the lock of hair that had escaped her braids.

Cassia inhaled sharply, though she didn't move. His fingers lingered near her neck as he leaned toward her, dropping his voice to a whisper. "Do you ever wonder what might have happened if—"

Voices filled the corridor on the other side of the door. He straightened and let his hand fall.

Cassia put her finger to her lips until the hallway was silent again, her gaze holding his.

Alma's heart pounded as he looked at her. It was almost enough to make him want to make peace with his parents.

"I'd better return to the banquet before someone comes looking for me," she said, breaking the tension of the moment.

Alma nodded, reluctant to move aside.

She hesitated, then touched his arm. "Don't do this, Alma," she whispered. "Come back to your family, to those who love you. Even if you don't know for yourself, trust in those who *do.*" She reached up and kissed his cheek. "Please."

He stared at her, then opened his mouth to answer, but she disappeared through the door.

* * *

Alma waited until his heart rate slowed before exiting Cassia's room. She made returning to his family sound so simple, but she didn't understand. He was a full-grown man now and needed to find his own way in life, not live in his father's shadow. He didn't want to spend the rest of his life as a scribe. But seeing Cassia again had tempted him to return to the mundane—could he settle into his old routine just to be with her? He shook his head—the king had made it clear years earlier—and that was when Alma was living at home and being mostly obedient. He hadn't been good enough for the king's daughter then, and he certainly wouldn't be now.

Alma left Cassia's room and crept down the hall. Once in Ammon's room, he let himself relax as he thought of his options.

If the transaction earlier that day in the tavern was any sign of his future, he might become a successful merchant. He could hunt each day and perhaps hire someone to sell the meat for him. Meat, fur—it was all free as long as one knew how to get around the hunting laws and be in the right locations at the right time.

He crossed the room and climbed out of the window, landing with a thud on the other side.

"What are you doing?"

Startled, Alma looked up to see Ammon watching him.

"I, uh—"

Ammon laughed. "I don't even want to know about it." He extended a hand. "Come on."

Alma reached for his friend's hand and stood. He looked around. "Party over?"

"Not yet. It's the dancing part. Nothing I'm much interested in."

"You don't want to dance with Aaron's bride-to-be?" Alma said with a grin.

"Hardly. She smells like lemons."

"That doesn't sound too bad."

"Rotten lemons."

"Ah. I can see how that would be a deterrent."

Ammon punched Alma in the arm. "What are you doing? Taking me up on my offer to stay with me?"

"No," Alma said. "I was just looking around . . . and thinking."

Ammon crossed his arms with a quick shake of the head. "Never a good thing for you. Thinking gets you into too much trouble."

Alma grinned. "You might be able to help me."

"How?"

"First I need to know how strong you are," Alma said.

Ammon narrowed his eyes. "Do you want to find out?"

"Easy," Alma said. "Can you help me carry some food to the Isidro village?"

"Why?" Ammon said, his expression curious.

Alma looked around at the still night, lowering his voice. "The place where I live—the village of Isidro to the west—has farmers who are poorer than I've ever seen. The kids eat boiled cornstalks. Today,

I gave away half of the deer we killed last night, then sold the other half."

Ammon's eyes widened. "You *gave* it away?"

"I can shoot another," Alma said, lifting his shoulder. "But what I really want to do is deliver all that extra food from your father's banquet to those villagers. We'll go in disguise; they'll never know it's us."

"Why can't they know who it is?"

"Do you think your father would approve?" Alma asked.

"Maybe, but—"

"But he'd have to think about it for three days, then come up with some sort of law so that there's equality among all the villagers and any handouts," Alma said, finding it difficult to keep the bitterness out of his voice.

"I see what you mean," Ammon said slowly. "All right. I'll help you. What do you need me to do?"

"Can you find us four alpacas?"

"No problem," Ammon said, his eyes amused. "Follow me."

CHAPTER 7

. . . a virtuous woman . . . her price is far above rubies.
—Proverbs 31:10

Alma the Younger

A couple of hours later, Alma and Ammon, along with Omner and Himni, led four alpaca laden with food through the palace gates. The men also wore heavy packs on their back with additional food. Ammon had secured official-looking capes for the four of them. Anyone passing would think they were on the king's business.

"When we leave the city, we'll need to get rid of these," Alma said. He looked at the ominous sky. A bank of clouds had developed in the west, blocking out the stars.

Omner was the most nervous about transporting the food. The seventeen-year-old, who was nearly as tall as Alma, kept looking behind him. At least Omner wouldn't be asking pesky questions like Himni.

Alma hadn't wanted to involve too many people, but Omner and Himni had caught them while they were loading the food, and Alma's first instinct was to invite the younger brothers along. They were even more reckless than their older brothers. They came and went as they pleased. But King Mosiah's attention was mostly focused on Ammon, and then Aaron, since they were the older sons and would one day advance to the throne. Omner and Himni would live off the royal name for the rest of their lives, always in the shadows of their older brothers. Alma had seen no evidence that either of them had any ambition, which meant they were more than happy to go along with any plans set by Alma.

Breathing hard, Himni had trouble keeping up. "Do you want to return to the palace?" Alma offered.

But Himni hefted the pack on his shoulders more securely and pushed out his thick chin. "No, I can do it. Are we going to do this every night?"

"No," Alma said. "And we need to keep as quiet as possible." At fifteen, Himni was the youngest prince, and perhaps the most spoiled if one was to judge by his girth. This was caused by two things—too many sweets and a lack of an opportunity for adventure. Himni had practically salivated when Alma invited him on their trek.

The next question from Himni was whispered. "How long is this going to take?"

Ammon hushed him.

The men entered the plaza just below the palace. Merchant trading took place here during the day, and lines of people congregated to request an audience with the king. They crossed the empty plaza—it was well past dark now, and no one was milling about. The clouds hadn't covered the moon yet, so it remained bright enough to light the way. As long as they wore the soldier capes, they could follow the main road. But they'd ditch the capes once they exited the city to cool their trail.

To the west of the palace, the temple stood on a hill. It was the place his father spent the better part of his days administering to those in need and offering sacrifices for people's sins. It was all very well and good if one believed in a God who played favorites. Even as a young boy, Alma was astounded when he'd seen a stooped, elderly man, dressed in nothing but rags, carrying a sickly looking pigeon for sacrifice. Then right behind him came a wealthy merchant, flashing jewels from head to toe, toting a fat goat for his sacrifice. The merchant likely had a herd of goats at a large homestead somewhere, and the elderly man was sacrificing his only decent meal of the week.

Which one did God accept as the true sacrifice? And how could there be such a wide discrepancy? Wouldn't the elderly man be blessed for giving nearly all that he had? If so, why did that same man return week after week, looking just as miserable as the week before? Where were those promised blessings? When Alma questioned his father, he had said, "It's not for us to question God's commandments to men, or to judge whom the Lord sees fit to bless with wealth. The law is the same for the poor and the wealthy. No one is exempt."

Alma passed the temple without another look at it. Even in the moonlight, he could point out every line, every angle, and he could recite the history of the Nephites, which had been drummed into him as a child. How the people of Limhi fled to the land of Zarahemla and were joined later by his father and his followers. How Limhi and his people were baptized into the Church—the same one that King Mosiah endorsed. Seven congregations were set up throughout the land of Zarahemla, and a mass baptism took place. It was a fever raging among the people to scramble and join together—like animals blindly following after each other.

Alma had been but a baby when his parents had come to Zarahemla, so he'd known nothing else. He'd shared in none of the stories, the battles, or the adventures that the other Nephites had in common. He had done nothing. He was the son of a man who'd saved hundreds of lives and, upon arrival at Zarahemla, was given the power to lead the entire Church.

Alma shook his head at the irony. His father was saving people's souls while he was sneaking through the streets to give stolen food to some farmers.

At the next turn in the road, Alma slowed his pace. "Let's get off the main road here." The brothers veered off the path with him and cut around a collection of homes. They were almost out of the city, and Himni was panting heavily now.

"You can return if you need to," Alma suggested.

But Himni's eyes were determined. Too out of breath to speak, he just shook his head.

The city faded as they walked, the homes turning into homesteads spread farther and farther apart, with fields extending behind them.

The Isidro village was uphill from there, just beyond the grove of trees. As they crested the hill, Alma turned onto a path that led to a small hut. "There's my home," Alma said.

"It's . . . nice," Ammon said.

Himni and Omner stopped and stared at the crude hut. "Do you really live in that?" Himni asked.

"It's not so bad inside," Alma said. "Let's tie the alpacas out back. We'll return for these loads of food later."

Alma was surprised that Kaman wasn't waiting for him inside—as he so often was. But Alma wouldn't be surprised if he appeared any moment asking to help with the food delivery. Clouds moved in front of the moon as the four men moved silently through the village streets, placing wrapped bundles of food—everything from prepared squash and maize cakes to honeyed delicacies—on doorsteps.

"It will be like a holiday when the villagers awake," Ammon said, grinning a boyish grin.

"What if the villagers wake up now?" Himni asked.

"No one will wake up if we are quiet," Alma said, trying to hide a smile.

"If someone sees us, will we get in trouble?" Himni continued.

"Let's ask questions later," Alma said. "We need to hurry."

Working together, the task went quickly, and soon they returned for the food the alpacas carried. By then the first drops of rain had begun to fall. They hurried to complete the deliveries, then returned to Alma's hut, where he offered the brothers a place to sleep the rest of the night—an offer he assumed they'd refuse. There weren't any extra mats to sleep on, but at least the hut would keep them dry.

Ammon looked around. "I think sleeping outside in the rain would be preferable."

"Can we stay inside?" Himni and Omner said at the same time.

"Don't you think your mother will miss you?" Alma asked with a knowing smile.

Himni opened his mouth to respond, but Ammon cut them off with a firm look. "We're heading back."

Alma went with them to the main path and watched the brothers walk down the hill, Himni asking whispered questions of Ammon. For a moment, he wished he had a nice home to go to, but then his stubbornness kicked in. He would create his own home and someday find a woman to share it with. But for now, being alone was exactly what he wanted.

* * *

Alma cursed as his arrow narrowly missed the deer. It was his second missed target that afternoon. He'd had to practically peel Kaman off him to go hunting alone. Today of all days, he didn't feel like talking to anyone. After the night at the banquet and seeing Cassia smile at Nehem, and reliving the experience in his dreams, he didn't want to be around anyone. He could still hear her pleading voice. *Don't do this Alma.* Don't do what? Live his own life? Forge his own path? He shook his head, trying to quiet her persistent voice. He'd packed no food for the day but carried a water skin filled with wine. It was a better companion anyway.

Trudging through the undergrowth, Alma walked to one of his favorite waterfalls. But instead of walking all the way to the falls, he stopped short, remembering that he'd been here with Cassia several times. He turned away before the path grew steep. A deer was crossing the trail below. Alma soundlessly crouched and pulled out an arrow, nocking it within seconds. He released the arrow with precision, and the instant it hit the deer's upper shoulder, Alma was on his feet giving chase.

He ran hard, barely keeping up with the fleeing animal. Putting all of his pent-up anger into his sprint, Alma finally overtook the deer as it slowed from loss of blood. He wrestled the animal to the ground and slit its throat. He took a long drink of wine from the water skin, then in one swift motion, he hoisted the deer onto his back. It was a younger deer, and Alma carried it through the rough terrain with only minimal difficulty.

The sun was just setting as he turned toward the village. His back ached and his head was fuzzy from wine, but his energy held. He rarely traveled by the main road anymore, but had his own path to the village. It prevented him from running into someone who might know him or his family.

He traveled quickly, pushing away exhaustion. The sun was gone now, but the moon displayed the path before him as he trudged on, his breath coming in short, even breaths as he paced himself. He slowed as he reached the path leading to his hut. A strange glow seemed to be coming from within it. Instinctively, he reached for his knife—one made by Ammon—and the jewels on the hilt glinted in the moonlight.

A burst of raucous laughter came from the hut as Alma neared. The hairs on the back of his neck stood up, and he gripped the knife tighter in his moist hand. *There must be a whole band of robbers,* he decided. But what were they stealing?

Alma had hardly any belongings and very little food in the hut. He left the carcass outside. Then, heart pounding, he walked to the back of the hut and peeked through the window. *Kaman.* Plus several men he recognized from the tavern. But they weren't destroying anything, just sitting around drinking and casting lots.

Alma pushed open the back door, and all heads turned.

"You're back!" Kaman cried out, and the rest joined in a chorus of greeting. His eyes strayed to the knife Alma held.

"I'm sorry," Kaman said. "We waited outside as long as we could, but it started getting cold. We decided you wouldn't mind us coming in." He looked around the nearly empty hut with an amused smile. "I hope we didn't damage anything."

Alma laughed and returned his knife to its sheath. It was hardly cold outside, and there was nothing to damage. "I don't think that's possible." Everyone laughed along with him, then one by one they fell silent, staring at him. "What's the occasion?" Alma finally asked.

"My friend," Kaman said. He rose and walked over to Alma, seeming to be a bit unsteady on his legs. "I'm afraid I broke my word to you."

Alma narrowed his eyes, studying the man. "What do you mean?"

"I told the men how you delivered food to their homes the other night."

Alma drew in a breath, his gaze traveling to the silent men. He hadn't wanted any attention for this, but what he saw was admiration in their eyes.

A couple of them set aside their wine jugs and stood. "Thank you," one man said in a quiet voice.

The room erupted with combined thank-yous.

Alma spread his hands. "I didn't do that much. The food would have gone to waste."

Kaman nodded vigorously and wiped his flushed face. "We want to thank you in person. Tonight the wine with our compliments."

"And the women!" one of the men called out, and everyone hooted.

Alma laughed nervously along with them. There were no women in the room, and he knew most of the men were married anyway. Kaman thrust a wine jug in his hand, and Alma settled among the men, taking a quick swig. He'd had plenty of wine that day while hunting, but this wine tasted quite fresh. Plus it felt good to forget about Cassia for a while and be among people who really appreciated him.

Then Kaman handed him a maize cake. Alma bit in with relish, enjoying his first decent food of the day. "Why are you casting lots?"

"To see who gets to escort Belicia home," Kaman said.

"Belicia?" Alma took a second look around the gathering. Unless there was a very masculine woman in the group, it was just men in his hut.

"You'll meet her very shortly," Kaman said with a grin. "Jacob went to fetch her. I think you'll find her pleasing—we picked her especially for you."

A woman is coming to my house, Alma thought. He knew he should feel apprehensive about these men's intentions, but he felt strangely relaxed. It might have something to do with the refreshing wine.

As if on cue, the back door opened and Jacob walked in, leading a woman wearing a veil. The men in the room whistled and a few called out greetings.

"Enough!" Kaman said in a stern voice. "She's here tonight for Alma, not any of you monkeys."

The men snickered, then quieted for the most part.

The woman scanned the room, then her head turned to Alma. Through the veil, Alma imagined her smiling at him. He could just make out her features. Large eyes, prominent nose, lips painted blood red. Hanging from her neck was a jade half-moon. Alma had seen other women wear the symbol before, but on Belicia, it set off her pale skin and made it shimmer. But it was her hands, long and elegant, that drew his attention.

Jacob had carried in a small drum. He moved to the corner and started playing a steady, sultry beat.

The men moved out of the center of the room and leaned against the walls. Alma scooted back as well, but Kaman put a hand on his shoulder. "Stay where you are. Her performance is for you." He lowered his voice. "She's going to perform the moon goddess dance."

Alma looked back at Belicia, who had indeed started to dance. Something pressed against the back of his mind—a fleeting thought of foreboding, but he decided to ignore it. There was no harm in watching a beautiful woman dance. No one was being hurt. He took several more swallows of wine, letting the warmth of the potent liquid soften any resistance by his mind. Besides, just watching the moon goddess dance wasn't harmful. It wasn't as if he were praying to a statue.

As Belicia moved in time with the soft drumming, Alma was amazed at her skill. It exceeded that of any dancer he'd ever seen. She moved with little flair, but the beat and her slight movements flowed together.

Alma drank more of the wine and ate the food that Kaman had offered, all the while watching the woman, unable to take his eyes off of her long elegant fingers and the swaying of her hips. The drum rhythm increased in tempo, and the woman moved faster, keeping pace. She swayed closer to Alma, then came to a halt in front of him and extended her hand. Alma looked over at Kaman.

"Take her hand," Kaman urged. "You are the sun god tonight, and she is the moon goddess."

"What am I supposed to do?" Alma whispered.

"Stand up and dance with her," Kaman said, not bothering to whisper. The men in the room chuckled and several of them started to clap to the rhythm. Kaman put a hand on Alma's back and pushed him forward.

On his feet, Alma towered over the petite woman. He wiped his sweaty palms on his robe, and held out his hands. Her fingers flitted against his. *It's like holding onto a butterfly,* Alma thought.

He'd seen more dancing than he'd participated in, and he'd never seen anything like this moon dance, but Belicia didn't seem to notice his awkwardness. She merely slowed down her movements until it was easy for him to follow. When Alma was finally feeling confident in his dancing, she let go of his hands and started to circle him, letting her hand trail along his body. He flushed red, and the men roared with laughter, which made Alma's face burn even hotter. Just like the sun.

Belicia stopped and crouched to the ground, holding her arms overhead.

Alma looked frantically over at Kaman. "Now what?" he mouthed.

"The moon is setting, and the sun is rising to heat the day," Kaman said. "Keep dancing until the moon rises."

I guess I'm the sun. Alma turned a few times, unsteady on his feet. The men all stared at him, wearing broad smiles. He just hoped the wine would make them all forget his awkward dancing in the morning. Then Belicia rose slowly from her cocoon-like stance, and the men cheered again. Alma almost applauded with relief.

She moved toward him, sliding her arms up his chest and around his neck. Her hands felt like silk against his skin, and he closed his eyes, wondering why he'd never indulged in this type of dancing before.

The pulsing music faded into the background, and all Alma seemed to hear was Belicia's steady breathing against his neck. The men's laughter and clapping diminished until Alma wondered where everyone had gone. Belicia hugged him a little tighter, and he felt his body relax against hers. Nothing else seemed to matter for the moment, and he wondered why he ever thought it did. Cassia was out of his life, his parents were a distant memory, his scribe profession was forgotten . . . A new life was ahead—one with people who respected him and celebrated his simplest contributions.

One by one the men left, ushered out by Kaman, but Alma barely noticed their departure. The music had stopped, yet still Alma swayed with the moon goddess.

When the silence was complete, Alma pulled away, his vision hazy in the dim light. All but one oil lamp had been put out. Belicia's eyes sparkled through the sheer cloth covering her face.

"Remove your veil," he whispered.

Belicia obeyed. Her eyes were luminous in the light of the single oil lamp. Her dark red lips were so close to his. For an instant, he wondered about a woman who seemed to accept him for who he was and had no desire to reprimand his actions. A woman who had no fear of him and who was open with her emotions. Her hands snaked around his neck again, and she lightly tugged him closer, and he followed, lowering his head toward hers.

Then her lips touched his.

* * *

Light moved back and forth against Alma's eyelids. Something in the back of his mind told him it was morning, but he was too tired to open his eyes. Then a foreign sound reached his ears. Someone was quietly singing, or chanting, but he didn't recognize the song. He turned over on the hard floor, groaning at the queasiness in his stomach. *Why am I on the floor?* He dragged his eyes open; he was indeed on the floor in the front room of his hut. The next thing he noticed was that his robe was gone, replaced by a thick rug.

Slowly, he moved to his elbows, wincing at the pounding in his head.

"You're awake," a soft voice said.

He looked to see a woman standing in front of him, clad only in a sleeping tunic.

Memories flooded into Alma's head as he stared at her. *Belicia. We danced. We kissed . . .* She smiled knowingly, and for a panicked second, he wanted to dart out the door. But as she knelt by his side and touched his face with her silky hands, he returned her smile.

"You had quite a night," Belicia said.

He nodded, grateful he remembered her name, though many things were still quite hazy. But by the way she was closing in on him, he guessed there were many things he was about to recall. She kissed him slowly, then pulled back, laughing. "You don't remember anything, do you?"

Alma tried to sit up more, but it was hard with her leaning against him. It was then he noticed he had Belicia's half moon necklace tied around his neck. He touched the jade, lifting it from his chest. "I recall the dancing."

"And?"

"And we . . ." He remembered Kaman and the men leaving, and Belicia removing her veil, then . . . "We kissed."

Belicia laughed, caressing the back of his head, running her fingers through his hair. "You are a very sweet man," she said, her hand moving along his shoulder, then clasping his hand that held the necklace. "Don't worry. Your memory of last night will come back. Keep the necklace." She stared at him thoughtfully for a moment. "You must be hungry."

His face flushed as he nodded. She peeled herself away from his side and rose to her feet. When she disappeared to the cooking room, he rubbed the back of his neck, raking his memory for what had happened after that kiss, but his pounding head made it impossible to organize a cohesive thought. He grabbed his robe that was lying not far from him, then stood and walked out the back door into the fresh air of the morning. The sun was well above the horizon, and his trained eye told him he'd missed the best hunting for the morning. He'd have to wait until late afternoon if he were to have any success.

He turned back to the hut just as Belicia came out. She was fully dressed now, a basket of fruit in her hand. "I thought you might enjoy these."

Avoiding her gaze, he took a guava and bit into it.

"You looked tired," she said in a soft voice.

He nodded. "Probably too much wine."

"You have many troubles on your shoulders." Her voice was sympathetic. "How old are you?"

"Twenty-one."

She smiled. "Just a year older than I." She shook her head. "You are too young to have troubles. I saw it the moment I came into the room last night. That's why I decided to stay even though it wasn't required of me."

"Required?"

"Usually, my appointments are much shorter."

Alma narrowed his eyes, trying to understand what she meant. "I was an . . . appointment?"

Belicia laughed. "My sweet. Don't worry, your friends have taken care of me. You owe me nothing. After what you did for our village, I consider this more than a pleasure." She reached up on tiptoe and kissed his cheek, her hand lingering on his shoulder. "I have another appointment tonight, but tomorrow night I'm available. I can come by after dark." Her hand trailed down his arm, touching his hand briefly.

"I—I won't be here," Alma said, reaching up to untie the necklace. "I can't keep this," he said, putting the half-moon of jade into her hands. He tried to smile naturally, but inside, anger stirred.

She accepted the necklace with a shrug, and he watched her walk out of his yard and disappear around the corner. He crushed the fruit in his hand and threw it into the trees.

She's a harlot. His faced flushed again, but this time it was with self-loathing.

He kicked open the door to his hut and crossed to the front room. He surveyed the clutter, evidence of the previous night. In a few minutes, he'd folded the rug and cleaned up the empty wine jugs littered about the room. All of the men who were in his home the night before knew what Belicia was. She was more than entertainment, more than a dancer. She was a seductress. And he'd fallen for it.

His chest tightened as he thought how he'd been deceived by her, thought maybe she was really interested in him. He'd believed she was a woman who didn't judge him based on what church he attended. A woman who cared about him—*just him.* While dancing with her in his arms the night before, he'd felt powerful, even loved.

His face burned with embarrassment. He'd been such a fool. Alma filled a pack with the fruit Belicia had left, along with several pieces of smoked meat, then grabbed his bow and arrows. Before the sun hit the center of the sky, he left his hut, leaving the memories of the previous night far behind as he trudged through the hillsides to his favorite hunting spot.

CHAPTER 8

. . . discern between the righteous and the wicked,
between him that serveth God and him that serveth him not.
—Malachi 3:18

Alma the Elder

The new day brought fresh hope. Alma's heart was light as he kissed his wife and children good-bye and left for a day's service at the temple. Several nights ago at the banquet, Ammon and Aaron had admitted to seeing his son. They wouldn't reveal much, but at least he was able to tell his wife that their son had a roof to sleep under.

The plaza was empty in the early morning, the sun having just crested the temple mount, throwing everything into a gleaming yellow-gold glow. From the opposite side of the plaza, coming from the main road, was Ben. Alma smiled as the man rushed to greet him. Ben's new robes glistened in the early light—he had been made a priest the week before and proudly wore the long, indigo robe edged in silver embroidery. Already Ben had made it a habit to arrive as early as Alma. As a priest, he was expected to carry on with his regular job, in addition to fulfilling his new calling in the Church.

"Good morning," Alma said.

"Good morning," Ben said as he gripped Alma's hand with his own, calloused with years of hard work as a blacksmith. He had gained a fine reputation in the city of Zarahemla and citizens from neighboring villages often sought his services.

"Any news from your son?" Ben asked.

"Nothing since Ammon told me he saw him about a week ago."

Ben nodded, his expression sober. "We pray for him morning and night."

"Thank you," Alma said. No matter how many times someone expressed their concerns over his son, gratitude flooded through him. He turned toward the temple and started to walk, Ben following. "Are you ready to inspect the archives this morning?" he asked, trying to make things light again.

Ben smiled, rubbing his hands together and brushing them against his robe. "I can smelt almost anything with my hands, but I don't know how well I'll do as a scribe."

Alma's heart pinged as he thought of his son vacating the position that Ben now held. But Alma hid his anguish and returned Ben's smile. "You'll do fine, my friend. We'll start you out slowly."

They scaled the temple steps together, moving in companionable silence. At the platform, Alma paused just a moment to inhale the fragrant air. The gardens surrounding the temple mount were in full bloom, and it was an incredible sight to behold. Ben continued walking, and Alma followed him into the temple. The interior was cool, and immediately Alma felt a rush of calm pass through him. The familiar temple walls always had the power to soothe even during his most grievous moments.

He was surprised to see King Mosiah already inside, standing near the Holy of Holies. Alma and Ben crossed to him, but by the expression on the king's face, Alma knew immediately that Mosiah wasn't there to prayerfully meditate. He'd been waiting for them.

"I need to discuss something with you, Alma," Mosiah said without preamble.

Ben immediately bowed and left the two men alone, moving back toward the entrance of the temple.

Alma lowered his voice, dread touching him. "What is it?"

"There have been more uprisings in the outer villages. My soldiers have been there all night. One of our churches was set to fire last night. Gratefully it was quickly put out and no one was injured."

"I don't understand why the rebellion continues," Alma said, shaking his head. The increasing acts of vandalism and violence were what they had feared the most, the unbelievers retaliating against the new laws established by the king. A proclamation had been sent out months before, which stated that there should be no persecutions among the members of the Church and that no unbeliever could persecute a member of the Church of God.

According to the king's soldiers, the proclamation had met with some resistance, but persecutions had mellowed for a time. And now this—another infraction.

"Have the perpetrators been found?" Alma asked.

"We have caught two men so far, but there are likely more. They too will be arriving shortly and you must judge them according to the commandments of God."

Alma furrowed his brow. "You mean they are Church members?"

"Yes," Mosiah said with a heavy sigh. "Both are on the records of the Church, but I don't know what their commitment level has been lately."

Alma exhaled, feeling the weight of judgment land on his shoulders. The lightheartedness and new hope of this morning quickly dissolved. "Do we know anything more about them?"

"No," Mosiah said. "You and Ben will have to look up their records."

"Names and ages?"

Mosiah gave the names and offered his best estimate on the ages.

Alma nodded, then crossed the length of the temple quickly, meeting Ben just outside. "Your orientation will be much quicker than we thought."

Even though Ben hadn't overheard the conversation, his face was solemn as if he had.

Alma led the new priest to the small building just beyond the tower at the side of the temple. From his waistband he withdrew a key and unlocked the heavy wooden door. The musty air greeted the men as they entered, and Alma inhaled sharply, remembering one of the first times he'd been in this room.

His son regularly insisted on going to work with his father. Alma chuckled as the eight-year-old boy followed him like a shadow. Today was no different, and they accompanied King Mosiah into the archives.

While the king explained to Alma about a record that needed updating, his son spied the thick box that contained the brass plates.

"Father, what's in here? A treasure?" his son asked, interrupting the old king.

Fortunately, King Mosiah was more than patient with the young boy, having several children of his own.

Before Alma could reply, King Mosiah crouched next to the boy, and said, "There is indeed a treasure inside the box."

His son's eyes widened and his fingers were instantly touching the edges. "Can we open it?"

King Mosiah smiled. "Before we open it, try to guess what the treasure might be."

The boy sat back on his haunches. "Gold!"

"No," the king said with a laugh. "Try again."

"Jewels and quetzal feathers?"

"No," the king said. "Something more valuable than all of the jewels and feathers in the whole land."

"Really?" Alma's son had nearly shouted. He leaned toward the box and put his ear against it, then turned his face and smelled it.

Alma tried to hide a smile.

King Mosiah's eyes twinkled as he put a hand on the young boy's shoulder. "There is nothing to hear and nothing to smell." He removed a small dagger from his waistband and inserted it below the overhanging lid. "Only to read."

The boy's forehead wrinkled as he spoke. "Read? What do you mean?"

The lid lifted, and Mosiah carefully slid it off.

Alma's son peered into the box then turned to look at the king. "You said it wasn't gold."

"It's not. They are plates made from brass." The king lifted them from the box with a grunt. He carried them to the low table in the center of the room. "Come here, son, let me show you one of the greatest treasures on earth."

The image of King Mosiah's dark head bent next to his son's smaller one faded when Ben spoke.

"This place is amazing." He stood, eyeing the rows of shelves stacked high with records on metal plates and neatly arranged scrolls.

"Look here," Alma said, moving along the first wall of shelving. "Carved in the edge of the shelf is the year of baptism. The king has asked us to locate some records. We'll collect three years' worth to start."

Alma told Ben the names and approximate ages of the men, then Ben ventured a question. "Why are we looking up these men?"

"They've broken the commandments as well as the laws of the land. We need to locate their names in case they do not choose to repent. We may have to blot their names from the records."

"They'll be excommunicated?" Ben mused, his eyes wide. With Alma, he carried the scrolls to the center table, where they carefully smoothed them out.

The first scroll contained one of the names, and the third scroll they looked at contained the second name.

"Let's go," Alma said, replacing the extra scroll on its shelf. "Bring the two scrolls with you and the vial of dye with its brush."

By the time they exited the archives, a crowd had gathered at the base of the temple. Several soldiers stood on the bottom steps, preventing unbelievers from ascending. They were there to support their accused friends and appeared calm for the most part, but that could change at any moment. Out of habit, Alma scanned the crowd, looking for the face of his son. He didn't think his son would go so far as to join the unbelievers formally, but he knew he had friendships among them.

Regardless, Alma was relieved not to see his son among the crowd. The fact added another measure of hope that he would spend a bit of time away from his family and church, then come to the realization of what was really important.

He and Ben turned back toward the temple and entered. The priests had arrived; most traveled from within the city of Zarahemla, although a few lived in the outlying villages. Alma greeted his friends one by one—Limhi and his brother; his father-in-law, Jachin; and Helam and his stepson, Abe. They were sober this morning—their business serious and grim.

The prisoners had been delivered, and the two men stood in the center of the temple, their hands bound behind their back. One hung his head. The other, a bearded man who was wiry and darker-haired, held his head up, staring in the direction of the king with a defiant expression.

Alma's heart sank. This would be no easy task.

The Church court was called to order, and Alma took his place next to the king. As the king opened the formal proceedings, Alma found his gaze straying to the two men. The wiry one was introduced as Kaman and the other as Jacob, who was of a stocky build. It was obvious that he'd been in a fight at some point—his nose was about as crooked as Alma had ever seen.

Kaman held Alma's gaze defiantly. Alma was the first to look away as the king had finished speaking. Alma sat next to Ben, allowing the prisoners a chance to speak in their own defense.

"I have done nothing wrong," Kaman started immediately. "You say I broke the law. I say I redeemed the law." He looked from the king to Alma, his gaze bold.

Alma had heard this type of plea before—it was nothing new. The criminal acted as if he knew nothing about the new proclamation by the king. But setting a church afire was more severe than the persecution cases usually brought to the court, such as minor disputes over lower or higher market prices given to a Church member versus an unbeliever. Outright persecution of Church members would be tried as a crime, and the criminal would be sent to prison. There were no more warnings allowed. The final warning had come in the form of the king's proclamation.

The man next to Kaman eyed the king, then quickly looked down again. He was less bold but seemed a staunch ally of Kaman.

"Two months ago, my widowed mother was taken ill while I was away on a hunting trip," Kaman continued. "She'd spent her whole life dedicating her services to this Church, giving of her last morsels of food, of housing to anyone who had fallen on hard times, even letting her own health worsen when she stayed up all night with a sick neighbor."

Kaman cleared his throat and said, "I was gone only a few days. She fell ill, and no one thought to check on her. No one missed her or wondered what had happened to her. When I returned"—he paused, his voice growing harsh—"she was lying in her own filth, her skin dried and cracked from a fever that had raged through her. No one brought her relief in *her* time of need, to clean her or feed her in her misery." He looked directly at Alma. "She was dead. The Church failed her—the church she'd dedicated her life to."

Alma let out a breath, feeling the pain and betrayal this man felt. He slowly stood, gathering his thoughts. "I'm sorry about your mother."

Kaman folded his arms across his chest. "You are the first to say so."

Alma dipped his head. "I lost both of my parents in my youth. For years I blamed others for their deaths, including the Church, and even God."

Kaman stared at him, his eyes riveted.

Alma could tell that this was not the response the man had expected. "I turned away from God. I cursed Him for many years. Perhaps if I'd been given the opportunity, I would have burned down a church or two."

The space within the temple was quiet. "Fortunately," Alma said, "the Lord is merciful. In all His infinite knowledge and power, He saw fit to forgive me of my trespasses. He asked only that I would repent." He looked from Kaman to Jacob, then back to Kaman. "I repented. Yet my losses still grieve me, and I continue to miss my mother and father. But they are bearable now. Through the Lord, all things are bearable. We must seek His help and not turn away in anger. We must not destroy His work in this land."

Kaman's face was pale, his eyes searching Alma's face. He seemed unable to reply, so Alma said in a gentle voice, "Do you repent of your wrongdoings, Kaman? Do you confess your sins?"

Kaman's head dropped for a moment, and his hands fell to his side, gripped tight. Alma waited, praying silently that this son of God would soften his heart, recognize and take responsibility. Then Kaman raised his head, his face reddened with emotion.

"I do not," he said in a low growl. "I have *not* sinned. I have nothing to confess. My mother's death has been redeemed by my hand, and I am not sorry."

The breath went out of Alma, and he held the man's gaze for a long moment. But Kaman's eyes were dark, hard, and unrepentant. Alma knew he'd lost the battle.

He turned to Ben. "Please blot the name of Kaman, son of Dedan, from the records of the Church. Let it be written that he will be imprisoned for one year."

In the silence, Ben's actions were magnified as he uncorked the vial of dye and dipped the brush into the dark liquid. The sound of the light scratching could be heard in the silent temple, as if it were magnified a hundred times over.

When Ben replaced the cork and set down the brush, Alma turned back to the prisoners, his watery gaze sliding over Kaman to Jacob.

"Jacob, son of Meshech, what is your defense?"

CHAPTER 9

The Lord . . . heareth the prayer of the righteous.
—Proverbs15:29

Cassia

Cassia entered the cooking room a short time after the midday meal had been cleaned up. She smiled at one of the serving ladies, then proceeded to check on the straining honey. She was pleased to see that the honeycombs were quite bare, and there was enough honey in the jar to make a few desserts. The servant knew not to touch the honey, that it was Cassia's project.

The past few days had been a blur. Spending so much time with Ilana and her brother, Nehem, helped Cassia forget about Alma the Younger. But not completely. Each time she remembered his visit to her room, her breath caught. Though the light had temporarily faded from his eyes, she knew her former best friend was still inside that man somewhere. She'd found herself praying more than once that he'd see the error of his ways, he'd return to his family, and all would be well again.

And what had he been about to ask her? The fact that he went back into the beehive yard and risked getting bitten to retrieve the honeycomb proved he still cared for her. Didn't it?

It had been years since her father's initial rejection of her suggestion of marrying Alma. Perhaps enough time had passed that her father might change his mind. Cassia's heart felt even heavier—with Alma's recent actions, she doubted her father would be any more lenient.

Besides, she'd seen her father's reaction to Nehem—they seemed to be very compatible. Of course it was easy for the king to be fond of Nehem; it seemed everyone was. He was all heart and was very vocal about his faith and his support of the king. A great deal of his time was spent mediating between Church members and the unbelievers.

Nehem also declared his feelings without reservation, almost as soon as he thought them. His sister, Ilana, tried to keep him subdued as much as possible, but Nehem was not to be deterred. Cassia found it quite amazing, but in truth, she was growing a little suspicious of his motives. Alma had warned her, and now her older brothers, Ammon and Aaron, seemed aloof around Nehem. But they had given her no reason why.

She poured amaranth seeds from a grain sack into a bowl coated with animal fat. Then she stirred the honey in until it reached a sticky consistency. She quickly poured the mixture onto a tray, wet her hands, and patted it flat. Within an hour, she could cut the treat into squares.

"There you are!"

Cassia looked up to see Ilana and her brother standing at the back entrance that led to the gardens.

"We were looking for someone to walk with us," Ilana said.

Nehem gave a short bow, a broad grin on his pale face.

"Let me clean my hands."

"Cooking?" Nehem said.

"I made a honey treat, but it has to sit for a while."

She washed her hands in the basin of water that had been changed out after the dishes were done. Stepping into the sunshine, she noticed Nehem move deliberately to her side. Ilana linked arms with her immediately.

"Show us where the beehives are," Nehem said. "We employ a few beekeepers at our home as well." He moved closer to Cassia and put his arm through her other one.

She didn't know what to think at first. She glanced over at Ilana, but her sister-in-law kept her eyes focused ahead. "How many hives do you have?"

Nehem answered. "Six. One of them has been failing, though."

"Oh?" Cassia said. She half-listened to Nehem's description of what the beekeepers had done to encourage more bees to populate the hives. When they approached the bee yard, anxiety rose in her chest. She didn't know whether it was from the attack or because the memories of arguing with Alma came flooding back.

"Cassia?" Nehem said.

She shook her thoughts away and focused once again on him, giving him a small smile.

"I'd love to show you around my home some time," he said.

She nodded, recalling what she knew of Ilana and Nehem's home. It was an elegant structure, though not as large as the palace, of course. But their father, Limhi, was a former king. In Zarahemla, he was a member of her father's cabinet, and he served as a priest. In fact, he had been Alma the Younger's mentor when he first learned to become a scribe. There. She was thinking about Alma again. No, worrying about him.

She hesitated at the gate leading to the bee yard.

"Let's not go in," Ilana said, pulling back a little.

My thoughts as well, Cassia realized.

"We don't have to go in," Nehem said with a chuckle.

Ilana released Cassia's arm and walked away from her and Nehem. "I'm going to fetch my shawl," Ilana said.

Cassia watched her go, and suddenly she was alone with Nehem—and feeling nervous. She casually withdrew from his arm and wandered over to a low bench near where she and Alma had argued.

Nehem was right behind her. "What do you think, Cassia?"

She turned to face him. "About what?"

"About coming to my home?"

His skin seemed especially fair this morning, she thought. She couldn't help but compare him to Alma. Nehem was light, where Alma was dark. "To see the bees?" she asked.

A smile touched Nehem's face. "Yes, and anything else you want to see as well."

"Perhaps, if my parents allow it."

The amusement in his eyes fled, and he looked serious. Taking her hand, he said, "I'm sure they will be more than pleased."

He raised her hand to his lips, but before he could kiss her hand, Cassia pulled it away. Her heart was pounding, worried about what exactly Nehem meant. Would going to see his home turn out to be more than a social visit?

Then his hand brushed her cheek, and she jerked back.

"Sorry," Nehem said, his eyes intent on hers. "It's just that you're so beautiful." He shook his head, and his expression softened. "Do you realize how beautiful you are, Cassia?"

She stared at him, wondering if he was speaking only to flatter, or if he really meant his words. "I—I don't know."

He laughed. "Of course you don't. That's what makes you even more exquisite."

Cassia reddened, wishing Ilana would come back—and quickly. "I'm not very good at this sort of thing . . ." She looked away and took another step back.

"What sort of thing?" Nehem moved slightly closer, watching her.

"I—you speaking such flattering words."

"I'm not trying to flatter or impress you," Nehem said, his eyes widening slightly. "I'm only speaking the truth of what I feel inside . . . here." His hand went to his chest as if to emphasize his words.

"I can't believe I'm really as beautiful as you claim I am." She clasped her hands together, keeping her eyes adverted.

Nehem took another step forward. "One thing I'd never do is tell a lie," he said, his voice low and serious. "You *are* beautiful, though I suppose there are many pretty faces around Zarahemla. But you are much more than that. You are kind and charming. You've been a friend to my sister, and you welcomed me with no reserve. You have many talents . . ."

Cassia found herself being drawn in, swept up in his compliments. She didn't know Nehem very well, but he was the son of a former king, the brother of her future sister-in-law whom she'd come to be such dear friends with.

"You don't know the effect you have on me," Nehem continued in a quiet voice. "And I plan to make that known soon."

"What do you mean?" Cassia asked, feeling her face heat up.

Nehem reached for her hand just as Ilana came into view. Cassia moved away as Ilana approached, a knowing smile on her face.

"Should we see if the honeyed treats are ready?" Ilana asked.

Cassia nodded, grateful for Ilana's distraction. Her heart still pounded to think of what Nehem was about to say. It wasn't that she didn't like him. He was very nice, and of course, flattering. He certainly seemed to like her. But she knew very little of men outside her family.

The three of them walked back to the palace and entered the cooking room. Ilana and Nehem chatted about what was growing in the garden while Cassia cut up the amaranth bars. She hid a smile, wondering what other man besides Nehem would have so much to say about a garden. Certainly not Alma.

"Try one and see if you like them," Cassia said, holding a bar out to Nehem and Ilana.

They bit in and exclaimed that they were excellent. "The honey is very sweet," Nehem said. "Your keepers have raised healthy bees."

Cassia shrugged at the compliment. "I'll prepare the rest then join both of you later."

Nehem furrowed his brow slightly, but his good humor remained, and he offered a bow. "Until later then."

With the brother and sister gone, Cassia felt relieved. She couldn't really explain why. They were both friends now—entertaining as well. But it was as if they were guiding her to think the way they thought and do the things they enjoyed. She didn't think she'd ever spent so much time in the gardens, just walking and talking, as she had until Ilana arrived. Cassia had neglected her cooking far too long.

As she finished cutting and wrapping the bars in thin sassafras leaves, she started thinking of Alma again, wondering if her brothers might know where he was staying. She decided that if she had the chance to speak with him again, she might be able to convince him to return to his family. And it wouldn't hurt to bring him some honeyed treats either.

She hurried out of the cooking room, several wrapped bars in her hands, and made her way to the side courtyard. She was sure to find Ammon somewhere in the vicinity. He spent any free time he had shooting targets.

She was disappointed to see Himni and Omner at the targets. "Where's Ammon?"

They both turned, and Cassia was surprised to see how unkempt they looked—as if they'd been awake all night. A guilty glance between them told her they were hiding something.

Omner shrugged and turned away, aiming his bow again at the tied bundle of maize stalks a couple of dozen paces away.

"Himni?" Cassia challenged. "What's going on?"

"He—he didn't come home last night," he said, then ducked his head.

"Don't tell her anything else," Omner whispered to Himni, keeping his back to her.

"Tell me—or I'll tell Father you were both out all night too."

Omner whipped around. "How did you know?"

Cassia kept a straight face. "I know a lot of things that might surprise you."

Another guilty glance between the brothers, then Omner said, "He's with Alma."

"And Aaron?"

"Aaron didn't come home either," Himni blurted out. "Maybe he was with Ilana."

Omner laughed, then immediately looked contrite.

"Where does Alma live?" Cassia asked.

Silence.

"You'll be in more trouble if you don't tell me."

"He lives at the top of the first hill outside of the city. It's the ugliest hut I've ever seen," Omner said.

"Yeah," Himni echoed. "You can't miss the place. The door looks like it was burned off, then reattached."

Cassia wrinkled her nose. "Thank you. Anything else I need to know?"

They started to elbow each other, but both shook their heads adamantly.

Cassia turned away from them, her pulse drumming. Did she dare? She didn't. But as she walked back to the cooking room, she realized how easy it would be to leave while everyone was busy. She could wear one of the servants' mantles and put on some old sandals. Maybe away from everything—from the palace and the temple—

Alma would tell her what was really going on, and she could convince him to return.

"Oh, my dear, there you are," a voice said as soon as she entered the cooking room.

Her mother stood in the doorway. "Ilana said we might find you here."

We? No one else was with her mother, but for some inexplicable reason, Cassia's hands started to sweat. She set the wrapped bars on a high shelf, hoping her mother wouldn't question why she'd been carrying them around. Then she turned to face the queen.

Her mother was smiling like she had wonderful news that she could barely hold back. "Father wants an audience with you. He's just finished with court, and now he'd like to see you."

Cassia wiped her moist hands on her robe. "What's it about?'

"Oh, you will have to wait," her mother said. "Come with me. Quickly."

Well, at least the news was good, Cassia thought, which meant that her father didn't know Ammon had spent the night away with Alma. And whatever secrets her younger brothers were keeping from her were still hidden.

Cassia half expected to be led to the throne room, but her mother turned down the corridor just before, and they stopped in front of the king's private quarters. So it was not a public announcement, Cassia thought, which made her even more curious, although a bit anxious.

The guard posted in the hallway nodded at the queen and opened the door to let them inside.

Cassia never got used to the interior decoration of her father's quarters. He had gifts displayed from all over the land, from the highest mountain to the deepest stream that had been given to him by his people. Carved jade figures, lustrous shells from as far away as the high seas, exotic furs from animals she'd never seen, painted pottery, and more lined the room.

The fur of a huge jaguar had been made into a rug and covered a good portion of the floor. The king sat with two scribes who rose as soon as the women entered.

"You may go," Mosiah said to the scribes. They scurried out of the room.

Cassia turned to greet her father, who was all smiles. His beard had recently been cut short, making it look grayer than usual. He crossed the room and kissed her cheek. "Did you find her in the cooking room, Naomi?"

"Yes," her mother said with a laugh.

Despite the lightness of the conversation, Cassia noticed faint shadows beneath her father's eyes. His usually striking face looked drawn and aged, and frown lines pulled at his mouth where Cassia thought she'd only noticed smile lines before.

Mosiah rubbed his hands together, excitement plain in his eyes as he reached for his wife's hand. She took it and stepped close to her husband so they both faced Cassia, both of their eyes bright.

Cassia felt she might burst out of her skin with anticipation. Maybe Alma *had* returned to his family and made amends. That's what Ammon had been doing with him all night—convincing him to come back. And that's why Omner and Himni were so tired. They were helping Ammon, and now her father wanted to thank her for helping to convince Alma. She was about ready to ask, but her father spoke first.

"We had a surprise visitor this morning," Mosiah said, his eyes gleaming.

Alma was back!

Her mother broke in, her voice breathless with enthusiasm. "He made it very clear how he felt about you."

Was it possible?

"Of course, we told him we'd have to get your consent first," her father said with a soft chuckle. "He understood immediately. It seems he knows our Cassia quite well already."

What did her father mean? She'd known Alma forever.

Mosiah cleared his throat. "I'm happy to give my blessing to a union between you and Nehem."

Nehem? She looked from her father to her mother, who nodded encouragingly. "I—Nehem?"

"Why yes, dear, who did you think?"

"I—" Cassia said, feeling her heart twist. She tried to speak calmly through her shaking voice. "I thought it might be him."

Her mother crossed to her and put an arm around her shoulders. "What do you think, Cassia? He's a very nice young man. He cares for you."

Cassia nodded, her eyes burning. She didn't want to cry in front of her parents, and more importantly, she didn't want to say anything she'd regret.

"He'll make a fine husband," her father said, coming to her other side. He squeezed her hand. "He even suggested a double wedding with Aaron and Ilana."

Cassia's eyes blurred. *A double wedding.* "I'll have to think about this. Tell him . . . tell him I'll think about it." She backed away, trying to keep her forced smile in place. Then she turned and left the room before her parents could see her tears.

She ran. Past the guard and down the corridor. Fortunately, she passed only one person on the way—a servant who wouldn't question her flight. In her room, she shut the door and leaned against it. Her head was spinning, her heart bursting.

Nehem had asked for her hand in marriage. *Not Alma.*

She brought her hands to her head and groaned. *Not Alma.*

Then she sank to the floor, sobbing.

CHAPTER 10

For, from the days of Cain, there was a secret combination,
and their works were in the dark, and they knew every man his brother.
—Moses 5:51

Alma the Younger

Two days passed before Alma saw Kaman again. One morning he just appeared outside, as if he'd never been gone. "I knew it was you," Kaman said as he leaned against the wall of Alma's hut.

Alma blinked in the bright sun as he stepped through the door and smiled. It was good to see his friend again.

"What do you know?" Alma said, stifling a yawn. He peered closer at his friend. The man's eyes were red with exhaustion, his clothing torn, and he had ash on them.

"What happened to you? Are you all right?" Alma asked.

Kaman ignored the questions. "You brought more food to the village, didn't you? Two more deer and several tapir as well."

On instinct he shook his head but saw that Kaman had that knowing look in his eyes. "Is there something wrong?" Alma said with a shrug.

"Where are you hunting?" Kaman asked. "It's rare that a man can catch more than one beast in a day, let alone several. And wild tapirs? Very hard to hunt."

Alma stretched his neck. Sleeping on the mat was somehow more uncomfortable than sleeping in the wilds. He'd be paying for it all day. "I couldn't very well reveal that, now could I?" He sneaked a smile. "I might be thrown into prison if I did, and if I tell you, you'll be sent there too."

Kaman threw back his head and laughed. After a few seconds he sobered. "Nothing that I haven't encountered before."

Narrowing his eyes, Alma sized him up. "Where have *you* been, Kaman?"

Kaman let his gaze drop, then he spoke in a quiet voice. "I was at the Church court in the temple."

Alma stared at him, waiting for him to continue. He tried to imagine all sorts of scenarios as to why Kaman could have been at the Church court. "You're a member of the Church?"

"*Was* a member," Kaman said, lifting his face. His expression was angry. "They blotted my name from the records."

Alma exhaled, relieved he hadn't told Kaman who his family was. It was most likely his own father who'd handed down the judgment.

"No loss to me though. I could never quite accept the Church like my mother did. I guess I took after my father too much." Kaman paused, then said, "I need you to help me with something. I managed to escape my prison time and need to hide out for a little while." He withdrew a dagger from his waistband. "Can you shave my head? It would be better if my appearance changed."

Alma looked from Kaman to the blade. "What did you do?"

"Can you keep a confidence?"

Alma nodded, then Kaman told him about burning the church in the village of Piedra a week or so before as a restitution for his neglected mother.

"I didn't know about your mother. I'm sorry about her death," Alma said.

Kaman grunted, a faraway look in his eyes. "If only she'd stayed away from those Church members in the first place. She'd be heart-broken if she knew my name had been blotted out, but I'm the better for it." He focused back on Alma. "I escaped and had to hide for a couple of days. Now I'm putting together a few men to get Jacob out of there too."

Alma tried not to show his surprise that Kaman could escape from the king's guards. "Have you done this sort of thing before?"

Kaman slapped Alma on the shoulder with a laugh, nearly knocking him off balance. "All the time, my friend. It's part of protecting our own against the tyranny of the king's church."

Kaman's words struck a chord within Alma. The two might come from different backgrounds, but their ideals were the same. "All right then, let's go behind the hut and get that head shaved." He strapped on the sandals he'd left near the front door. "Then you should probably get some rest—you look terrible."

"No time for sleeping. My business is with you today. With my disguise, I'm not worried about the king's guards spotting me. Hairy Kaman is gone forever." Kaman spread his hands. "I've decided to retire from burning churches for a more noble cause. I'm at the service of the savior of our village."

"You can't mean that," Alma said, leading Kaman around the side of the hut. "I just delivered a little food to tide a few families over for a short time."

"You should have seen my children when I showed up this morning. They didn't care that I'd escaped prison or been gone two days," Kaman said, lowering his voice. His eyes brimmed with sudden moisture. "It was the food you brought. They couldn't stop talking about it. My wife thought the maize god had just walked into our home and blessed us with eternal prosperity."

Alma stared at Kaman. "That's a lot of credit to give the maize god. Isn't your wife a member of the Church?"

"No. My mother was really the only one who believed in the king's church. My father just went along with it to please her. But he never gave up his idols, just had to keep them out of the house. I sneaked them away after his death." Kaman leaned close to Alma, his voice breaking with emotion. "The strangest thing is that a couple of nights ago my wife and children made a special offering to the maize god. And the next morning when they woke up—surprise!"

"Your children will be disappointed to discover that I'm no god." Alma shook his head, surprised that an act of service could be attributed to a fictitious god. Idol worshipping had gone on ever since he could remember in Zarahemla, but he had never been friends with someone who believed in the power of the idols.

"Forget the maize god. You're more powerful than the maize god. I'm calling you the savior of our village."

Alma laughed off the suggestion.

"What?" Kaman said. "You've done more for this village—"

Alma punched Kaman's shoulder lightly. "Maybe you're worshipping the wrong god."

Kaman's face twisted. "Don't tell me you are a member of the king's church."

Alma let his hand drop, realizing he'd given too much away. He didn't want to offend his new friend either. "I—I grew up in that church, but I haven't been a part of it for some time."

The man's face relaxed. "I didn't think so, or you wouldn't have come to the tavern with me. Or spent so much time with Belicia." He smirked. "Did you know those church people have burned down taverns in almost every village surrounding Zarahemla?"

"Really?" Alma said. "Like you set their church on fire?"

Kaman drew his brows together, not understanding the irony. "That was different—restitution for my mother is justifiable. Burning down a tavern just because they don't agree with the activities is plain hypocritical. Of course they'd never admit it, religious zealots that they are. Always preaching and judging us. They should focus on helping their own neighbors, I say. Ask themselves how they let a good woman like my mother die alone."

"I'm sorry about your mother," Alma said again.

"That's what the high priest said," Kaman said in a quiet voice. "He wasn't what I expected—not that I know any of the other priests."

Alma stiffened at the mention of his father, wondering what Kaman would think if he discovered the connection.

But Kaman plowed on. "Except I know the high priest is no different from the king, forcing his beliefs on us . . . It's contemptible." He perched on a large boulder at the edge of the back courtyard and handed his dagger to Alma. Then he bent his head forward. "Just start at the back. Take it all off."

Alma lopped off the longer sections of hair first, then using water from a goatskin, he started to shave near the scalp. When he finished, he was surprised how different Kaman looked. It gave him an idea. He returned the knife to Kaman. "Will you shave my head too?"

Kaman chuckled, taking the dagger and trading Alma places. "I guess we both have something to hide from."

* * *

Alma and Kaman wasted no time in putting a plan together to free Jacob from prison. They would strike tonight, while the surprise over Kaman's escape was still fresh.

Fortunately, Alma had already planned to meet Ammon and Aaron at the old hunting lodge on the king's preserve.

Kaman kept up with Alma as they climbed the hilly countryside on the way to the lodge. Kaman had sworn an oath not to reveal the location of the king's lodge, and Alma was satisfied with that. As they approached, Alma gave his customary bird call. Within seconds it was returned. Ammon stepped into view on the right side of the lodge.

"Wait here," Alma told Kaman. "I'll let you know if you're clear."

Alma hiked up the final hill to the lodge. Aaron was now standing next to his brother. The two eyed him with curiosity, obviously wondering why he'd shaved his head.

"Anyone else with you?" Alma asked when he reached them.

"Omner and Himni are inside, looking for something to drink," Ammon said. "What happened to your hair?"

"I'll explain in a minute," Alma said. "Let's go inside."

"Look what we found," Omner said as the men entered the lodge. He held up a large waterskin. "Leftover wine from a royal hunt." Next to him Himni grabbed for it and soon the brothers were wrestling each other.

"Enough, you two!" Ammon called out, "Alma has something to tell us."

The scuffle ended, and Himni stood, rubbing his head. "What happened to your hair?"

"I needed some disguise." Alma looked at the others. "I have a request to make of you. We could get into some trouble for this—possibly even thrown into prison. But before I tell you, I want to know if you're willing to keep what I am about to say a secret."

Ammon and Aaron both nodded. Omner and Himni looked at each other, then back at Alma, grins on their faces. "We're in," Omner said.

"Especially if it means we might be in danger of getting thrown into prison," Himni said.

"All right," Alma said. "This is very serious and requires a blood oath."

The brothers' eyes all widened, but no one protested. "First I want you to meet someone. He is completely trustworthy."

Alma moved to the door and signaled for Kaman to come to the lodge. When Kaman stepped inside, Ammon reached out to shake the man's hand. Kaman returned it with a look of surprise on his face. "You—You're the—"

"Do not reveal their names outside this circle," Alma interrupted. "Everyone, this is my friend who was wrongfully excommunicated from the Church." He explained Kaman's court trial and subsequent escape. Then he continued, "Now we need to free his friend from prison."

Alma held out his right hand, a dagger in his left. He slid the dagger across his right palm, wincing at the sting and saying, "With my blood I pledge never to reveal the members of our circle or any of our secrets." Then he passed the dagger to Ammon, who repeated Alma's words and sliced his palm. One by one they clasped each other's hands and repeated the pledge in unison.

When every man had made the blood oath, Himni asked, "Do we have to shave our heads too?"

Alma laughed. "No. Kaman just doesn't want to be easily recognized, and I don't need people reporting my whereabouts."

Kaman pulled a square of cloth from his waistband and tore it into shreds. He handed one strip to each of the men so that they could wrap their bleeding hands. After he finished binding his own hand, he said, "The people of my village want to start a new church, and we want you to lead it." He turned to Alma as he finished.

Alma looked at Kaman in surprise. "A new church?"

"You can be our church leader, help our village get the food it needs, then protect us from the king's soldiers who enforce unfair laws against the unbelievers."

Alma's mind spun, but he shook his head. "I am no leader of any church."

Kaman's eyes were filled with fire. "You would make us proud of something."

Placing a hand on Kaman's shoulder, Alma said, "You are kind. But let's focus on the present task and free our friend."

Alma's gaze swept across the lodge. "Let's prepare now; it will be dark soon."

Less than an hour later, the men crept along the ridge that overlooked the city prison. It had been built into the side of a hill west of the market square.

The sky was nearly black, all touches of twilight faded. Alma looked at his companions. Each of them had smeared black charcoal on their faces. If it weren't for their clothing, he wouldn't be able to tell them apart.

Omner and Himni couldn't wipe the grins off of their faces. They were full of energy, and Alma worried they'd make too much noise. So he stationed them along the ridge. "If you see anyone coming, give the signal," Alma told them.

The two brothers nodded vigorously, gripping their knives tightly.

Aaron took his post on the hillside just above the roofline of the prison. The other three men made their way silently down the hill until they were parallel with the prison entrance.

"Two guards," Ammon whispered. "We'll have to take both down and give one of us enough time to release Jacob."

"How many prisoners are inside?" Alma asked Kaman.

"Maybe three or four when I was thrown in—all in different cells."

"Do you think you can find Jacob without disturbing the others?"

"Yes."

Alma turned to Ammon. "You and I will have to silence the guards before they can raise the alarm. We'll have to attack at the same time."

Ammon nodded, and the three moved closer to the prison, keeping their bodies crouched as low as possible. The closer they got, the more Alma realized the prison entrance was too much in the open. There were no nearby trees or brush to give them cover. His gaze moved across the prison, studying the roof.

He motioned for Ammon and Kaman to look upward. Ammon's brow furrowed as he understood what Alma wanted to do, but then he nodded and followed Alma up the slope a little farther.

The two scaled the side of the prison, moving quietly and quickly. Alma's cut hand throbbed as he gripped the outer stone wall to pull himself upward. He reached the roof first, then held his hand out to help Ammon up the last few paces.

Both men caught their breath, then Alma looked for the others to make sure they were still in position. The narrow gleam of the moonlight provided just enough light for Alma to spot the men—although it would have been nearly impossible for another to do so if they weren't looking for figures in the dark.

Below, the guards' voices rose into the night. They were discussing some women they'd met in the marketplace that morning. One guard yawned and moved away, walking back to his post. Each guard had a crude stone bench to sit on, but mostly they paced back and forth in front of the prison entrance, exchanging stories.

With Ammon by his side, Alma watched and listened to the guards, looking for any weaknesses. His heart pounded as he thought about actually fighting someone. He'd wrestled with his friends and trained in fighting with the king's sons, but these guards were trained to kill. His fist closed around the knife at his waist, gripping it, then releasing it.

Finally he leaned over to Ammon and whispered, "We'll wait until they are at opposite ends of the prison, then we'll both make the jump."

Ammon nodded and slowly scooted to the closest edge of the roof. Alma made his way to the far side and perched near the edge. From this corner, he could see Kaman crouched and waiting. Alma alternated watching Ammon and the guards below, then finally he signaled, holding up three fingers, then two, then one.

With a sharp inhale, Alma leapt to his feet and jumped off the roof, his arms outstretched. The guard looked up just as Alma made contact, his cry cut off as he was driven to the ground. Alma shook off the pain from the impact and straddled the guard, reaching for his neck. With one arm pinning the guard down, he swung at the man's face with his right fist. The guard's nose cracked under the blow, and the guard cried out, then his body went limp.

Alma withdrew his knife, holding it against the guard's neck, waiting for him to wake up. But the guard didn't move. At the other end of the prison, Ammon was making fast work of the second guard. Alma removed the set of keys hanging on a cord around the man's neck, then held them up for the dark figure rushing toward him. Kaman snatched the keys and hurried past Alma, then into the prison.

He removed the length of rope hidden in his waistband and proceeded to tie the guard's hands and feet, then he shoved a piece of cloth into the man's mouth. It wouldn't hold for long once the guard woke up, but it might buy them a few more minutes.

A scuffling sound reached Alma's ears, and he looked up. Ammon had dragged over his bound and gagged guard. Together, they dragged both guards from the prison to the hillside, leaving them among the brush.

Then screaming came from the prison—it was so loud that he feared it might be heard to the residential areas. Alma's skin went cold. Ammon's gaze met his, and the two of them ran for the prison entrance.

It was even darker inside, and Alma bumped into Ammon. There was a long row of cells, most occupied by men pressed against the bars. They were all yelling, screaming, or cheering—Alma wasn't sure yet. Then he saw the reason.

Another guard had been inside the prison, and he had Kaman by the throat. The two men were on the ground, struggling viciously, but Kaman was getting the worst of it. Without another thought, Alma threw himself on the back of the guard, wrapping his arm around the man's neck and pulling him off Kaman. The guard reared up and slammed against Alma's chest. They toppled to the ground together. Above the screaming, Ammon was yelling something. Alma avoided a blow from the guard and turned his head toward Ammon.

"Which one is he?" Ammon yelled again.

Alma jerked back, avoiding another swing from the guard. The blow went wild, catching his forearm. He looked for Kaman, who was prostrate on the ground, then he looked at the screaming prisoners, waving their hands through the bars. Seeing Jacob in the mix, Alma shouted, "The second from the end!"

A fist made contact with the side of his face, and he fell back to the ground. His mind clouded for an instant, then the pain cleared it again. The guard gripped his neck, pressing with all his strength. The man's eyes were bulging with anger, and Alma knew he wouldn't offer any mercy. His chest heaved as the air was cut off. He tried to push against the guard, but the man had the advantage. In a desperate attempt, he reached for the knife at his waistband, and his hand closed around the hilt.

The guard's eyes rolled back in his head, and he collapsed onto Alma.

The breath left Alma, and he flailed beneath the guard's weight. The pressure released, and Alma looked up to see Kaman dragging the unconscious guard off him.

With a groan, Alma sat up, his head pounding.

"Let's get out of here," Kaman said as he deposited the guard in the corner. He hurried over and pulled Alma to his feet. Jacob was out of the cell, next to Ammon. Beyond them, the guard was still motionless. Alma didn't want to consider whether the man was alive or dead.

They fled the prison, away from the pleading prisoners, and started climbing the hill. As they cleared the prison, Aaron was at their side, asking if everyone was all right.

Alma could only nod. His throat felt as if the guard were still squeezing the life out of it. But they couldn't stop to rest. The noise from the prisoners would draw attention soon enough.

They scurried up the hill where Omner and Himni stood guard, and Jacob made the rounds, embracing each man and thanking him over and over.

"You said you would do it, Kaman. I should have had more faith in you. I owe you my life." Jacob's eyes gleamed with emotion. "I didn't even recognize you at first with your face blackened." He looked at the others. "Who are your new friends?"

"We'll make introductions later," Kaman said, his voice gruff with exhaustion and emotion.

The shouting continued from the prison, and Alma knew it wouldn't be long now until the break-in was discovered. The men hurried along the ridge then down the other side. It would take them the better part of the night to return to the Isidro village.

When they had made sufficient progress, Alma stopped the brothers. "We must separate here so your father is not suspicious of your absence."

Jacob embraced the brothers again. "Whoever you are, I owe you my life. If you need anything, I am your servant."

Ammon pulled away from Jacob. "It has been an adventure."

Jacob peered at him. "Will you tell me your name so that I can thank you properly?"

"A friend of Alma's is a friend of ours," Ammon said and held out his palm, still wrapped with a bandage. Aaron and the other brothers did the same, along with Alma.

Kaman joined in, and understanding dawned in Jacob's eyes. Kaman handed him a knife, and Jacob cut his own palm with a sharp intake of breath. "With my blood, I pledge to keep everyone's identity a secret and never reveal what happened on this night." He gripped each man's hand in turn, his blood soaking into their bandages. Then he turned and allowed Kaman to wrap his hand with cloth.

Ammon stepped forward and introduced himself, followed by each brother.

Jacob's mouth hung open as he stared at the royal princes. "You are the king's own sons? *You* broke me out of prison? Why?"

"Alma asked us to help you," Ammon said. The other princes nodded.

Jacob shook his head, disbelief etched across his face. "I am most honored, your highnesses. I am forever in your debt." He knelt to the ground, his head bowed.

"Stand up, my friend," Ammon said, touching Jacob's shoulder. "We are all equal in this circle. No one pays subservience to anyone else."

Jacob rose, speaking in a trembling voice. "I have never felt such honor in all my days."

Alma moved forward, looking at the brothers. "You must go quickly—be sure to clean your faces before anyone can see you."

Ammon nodded and clasped Alma's hand. "Be careful."

The brothers left amidst more platitudes from Jacob.

As Alma started out again toward the village, he noticed Kaman lagging behind, limping badly. He moved back to his friend, but Kaman waved him off. "I'll be fine. It's just a knife wound."

Alma made him sit on a rock, and he and Jacob inspected the man's injuries. He had a deep gash in his upper thigh. Alma tore a strip of cloth from his own tunic and wrapped Kaman's leg wound. "This will hold until we can get you more help at the village."

Kaman grimaced as he stood again but refused anyone's help. He moved a bit easier now, but it was obvious he was in quite a bit of pain.

Just as dawn softened the dark sky, they reached the road leading to the village. "One more hill to climb," Alma said. "Both of you can stay in my hut, and I'll go fetch the healer."

Halfway up the hill, Alma paused. The air seemed heavy, the silence too deep. No birds or roosters made a sound in the early dawn.

That's when they saw the smoke.

CHAPTER 11

For the morning is to them even as the shadow of death. . . .
—Job 24:17

Alma the Younger

"Run!" Kaman shouted, hobbling up the hill to the village where the smoke billowed.

The sight of smoke sent fear into Alma's heart, and he tore after Kaman. Somewhere behind, Jacob was running as well. Alma's heart pounded as the column of smoke thickened, growing darker against the lightening sky.

Their steps slowed when they crested the hill, affording them a view of the village. The smoke came from somewhere near the center. They ran along the main path, passing others who had just stepped out of their huts, expressions turning from confusion to panic.

Alma hoped it was a field or some bordering trees, but the smoke was clearly coming from the center of the village, which could only mean one thing.

"It's the tavern!" Kaman cried out.

As they ran past the last grouping of houses before the main plaza, Alma saw a line of men passing along jugs of water, throwing jug after jug onto the blaze, although by the appearance of their tired, ash-stained faces, it looked as if they'd already given up. Only a few paces from the tavern was the judgment hall. Flames threatened to leap across the gap.

Other men stood around, shaking their heads. *Why didn't they jump in to help?* Alma wondered. His gaze moved to a group of women standing in a cluster, their scant clothing revealing their professions. They were clutching each other, wailing.

Kaman's hand gripped Alma's arm. "Someone could have died in the fire!" He ran toward the women near the head of the water line, Alma following. "What happened?" Kaman shouted.

One of the women turned, tears streaking her cheeks. "Belicia didn't come out!" She fell against Kaman, who encircled her with his arms. "There's nothing we could do."

Alma stared at the grieving women and the passive villagers, who seemed to move in suspended motion as they passed the jugs to each other. It was as if they expected this to happen and bowed down when it did. They were allowing Belicia to become victim to the flames.

Without another thought, Alma headed toward the blazing inferno. The front entrance was a deathtrap, so Alma sprinted around the back to the rear entrance. Smoke billowed from the narrow cracks of the reed door, and Alma kicked it in just as Kaman reached his side.

"No," Kaman said, grabbing Alma's arm. "No one should go in. It's too dangerous."

"I have to find her," Alma yelled, his throat already raw from the heat and smoke. But Kaman wouldn't release him.

Alma shoved the man to the ground and plunged through the smoke. Instinctively he dove to the ground, keeping lower than the smoke trapped by the roof. He knew he only had seconds before the thatch collapsed, sending fiery pieces everywhere. He pushed open door after door in the long corridor, shouting for Belicia, his voice growing weaker with every cry. The smoldering air was acrid, stifling, causing him to gag. His eyes burned, but still he pressed on. The front room was engulfed in flames, and it was too late if she had been caught there. The heat was intense, singeing the hair on the back of his arms and hands.

Something, someone, called above the roar of the fire. He pivoted and crawled toward the sound. Then he saw movement. A hand reaching out of the gray toward him. He grabbed the hand, and the fingers moved, clutching his. Alma scrambled to his feet, trying to hold his breath as the smoke threatened to overcome him. He reached blindly for the flailing figure, lifting her in his arms and rushing to the door. Once outside, his knees buckled, and the woman slipped from his arms.

He tried to see her, to find out if she was all right, but his eyes stung fiercely and his body gave in to wracking coughs. "Belicia," he whispered, although he could no longer hear his own voice. Someone grabbed his arms and dragged him along the ground.

Get Belicia, he wanted to say, but his voice was silent.

* * *

Hours later Alma awoke in a darkened room. A moan reached his ears, and he wasn't sure if it was his, until he turned his head and saw a woman lying next to him. Her dark hair was tousled, different from the smooth shininess he remembered. But it was Belicia, alive.

Someone entered the room. "You're awake," a woman's voice said.

He moved slowly to look at the woman, Kaman's wife, Eden.

"My husband will be so grateful," Eden said. "You frightened the whole village, going into the burning tavern like that."

"How . . . how is she?" Alma rasped.

"I don't know yet—she has only minor burns, but she's very ill with smoke sickness," Eden said. She knelt by Alma's side and dipped a cloth into a bowl she carried. She gently wiped his face and neck, then moved the soothing cloth along his bare torso. Alma hadn't noticed until now that his old clothing had been replaced with a clean kilt. While Eden worked on Alma's arms, he looked over at Belicia again.

"Has she woken?"

"Not yet, but by all her moaning, I assume she'll wake soon." Eden looked at him, her eyes bright with reverence. "You are like a god in our village. The children are making up songs about your heroism."

Alma flushed with the praise. "I only did what others would."

"No," Eden said as she dipped the cloth back into the sweet-scented water. "No one else had the courage. Kaman said you knocked him to the ground."

His lips turned up in a smile, but the effort sent him coughing again.

"There you go," Eden said with a nod. "Get the smoke out of your chest."

Belicia moaned, but her eyes remained closed. Eden turned to her and used the cloth on the woman.

When Eden finished, she looked again at Alma. "I'll leave you to rest. In a little while I'll bring some soup so you can recover your strength. The village has a special ceremony planned for when you're well."

"Have they caught the arsonists?"

"We already know who they are—the king's guards have tried to purge taverns before."

Alma furrowed his brow, and Eden swished out of the room. With her gone, he moved to sit up, panting as he did so. The smoke had robbed him of his steady breath, but he wanted to get a good look at Belicia. Her smooth complexion was nearly colorless, making her look much younger than her twenty years, and her dark hair contrasted deeply against her skin. She looked so delicate, so helpless. He reached for her hand and found it cool to the touch.

He brought her hand to his lips, blowing warmth onto it. She stirred, and another moan escaped her pale lips. Her eyes fluttered open, and she gazed at him for a moment.

"Belicia," Alma whispered. "Can you hear me?"

Her eyes closed, but her fingers wrapped around his hand, and he held on, watching her carefully. *Is she in great pain?* he wondered. The smoke had nearly suffocated him, and he'd only been inside the tavern for a few moments. How long had she inhaled the vapors?

"Alma," she said, her lips moving in a barely audible whisper. Her eyes had opened again, her gaze lucid.

"How are you feeling?" He scooted closer.

Her other hand reached for his face, trembling slightly, and she touched his cheek. "You saved me," she said. "You are my savior."

Alma clasped her other hand in his. "I could not bear to leave you in the burning building."

A faint smile appeared on her face, and color rose in her cheeks. "Take my necklace—as a token of my gratitude. It will remind you of our first dance together. Please." She raised her delicate hands to her neck, but Alma stopped her.

"Let me do it," he said and gently untied the cord. He put it around his neck, and she nodded with satisfaction, but her breathing was still shallow. Her hands moved to his neck, and she pulled him down to her, placing his head against her shoulder.

Alma heard her heart gently pulsing, but her breathing rattled in her chest. He tried to lift his head, afraid of causing her more pain, but she said, "Stay here. I want to be near you in my last moments."

His hand went to her waist as he moved even closer until he was against the length of her fragile body. "You'll have many more moments, Belicia, a *lifetime* of moments. Rest, and you'll recover soon."

She shivered, then inhaled sharply. Her whole body seized as she coughed.

When the coughing subsided, Alma reached for the nearby cup and helped her take a sip. Tears had appeared beneath her lashes. He brushed them away, and she gazed at him, pain in her eyes. "Hold me, Alma," she whispered. "It hurts so much, as if the fire is inside me."

"I know," he said, although what he felt was probably minimal to what had happened to her body. "Try to sleep."

A slight nod of her head, and her eyes slipped shut again. Alma adjusted the rug over the both of them, remembering the first time he'd seen this woman. She'd been so exotic, so enchanting, and lying next to her brought back the feel of the softness of her skin beneath his touch. Back then, he hadn't known she'd been a harlot; in fact, he'd been dismayed that he'd fallen for her attention and thought she'd returned his interest. But now he understood that she was just like him, just like anyone else—with fears, emotions, pain, and the desire to be loved.

"Kiss me one last time," she said, her voice so faint that he wondered if he'd heard right. But then she spoke again. "Please, Alma, kiss me before I pass from this world."

Alma hesitated, fear for her life coursing through him. Was she really dying? He was about to call for Eden, but then Belicia's eyes opened, and he saw the burning desire in them—desire for *him.*

"You are a man I could have stayed home for," she said.

His throat thickened at her words. Harlots never stayed home and settled their hearts on one man. She had chosen him after all. Bending over her, he kissed her softly, and she responded, lighter than a butterfly. But he didn't linger, not wanting to hurt her or steal any breath from her fragile body. When he pulled back, she was smiling.

Then her breathing deepened, and panic lit her eyes. Her body flinched as she violently coughed. Blood appeared on her lips, then dribbled down her chin.

Fear jolted through Alma, and he reached for the cloth left by Eden to wipe the blood away. "Eden!" he called out. Belicia kept her eyes on him as he yelled, but her face remained calm and resigned. "Eden, I need help!" he shouted again.

Belicia's hand moved to Alma's shoulder. "It's no use," she whispered. "There's nothing she can do." Her eyes had darkened, the panic fading, replaced by an emptiness.

"No, Belicia," Alma cried out, his voice breaking. "You're not going to die. Please—please don't leave me."

He looked toward the door where Kaman's wife had disappeared earlier. "Eden!" he yelled again. Then he turned back as Belicia's hand dropped from his shoulder and her eyelids closed.

* * *

The next day passed in a haze for Alma. He was still weak but demanded that a search be started for those who had set the tavern fire. The death of Belicia had set the village into action like he'd never seen before. Although his chest burned with the pain of smoke, his heart burned more. Still, by late afternoon he insisted on leaving the sickroom and speaking to the villagers.

Someone brought a stool and put it on a platform that had been set up in front of the judgment hall. Alma noticed that the building had incurred some damage, but it was nothing like the charred tavern next to it. The acrid smell of smoke still hung in the air, and thin wisps of white curled from the black remains of the building.

Kaman and Jacob came to his aid and helped him up the platform. Alma tried to wave them away, but when he broke into a coughing spasm, he was grateful for their help.

He sat on the stool, flanked by his friends, and touched the jade necklace at his throat, thinking of those last few precious moments with Belicia. He may have once been angry that he'd allowed himself to be misled by a harlot, but now, as he thought of the helpless woman who had accepted her fate with such grace, anger drummed through him.

Someone within the Church, the king's church, had deliberately set fire to a building that was occupied by people. And that someone had to pay.

As the crowd gathered and quieted, all eyes on him in anticipation, Alma bent his head forward and untied the necklace. With one hand, he raised the jade carving for all to see. The group of women near the front of the crowd gasped, and one identified it as Belicia's.

"Yes," Alma said, his gaze landing on one of the harlots—a petite, raven-haired woman. Her pale skin reminded him of Belicia, but this woman had a narrower face and rounder physique. "Belicia gave this to me before she passed from this life. I did not have time to make her this promise—but I make it to you now." He gazed at the eager faces before him. "We will avenge our dear woman's death—we will discover who set the tavern on fire and bring them to justice!"

The crowd shouted their agreement, and Alma smiled, still holding up the necklace. "In order to never forget Belicia, each person in the village will wear one of these necklaces—in the shape of a half-moon."

"She danced like the moon goddess!" someone shouted.

"Nay," the petite harlot said, standing and turning. "She *was* a goddess. She walked among us for a short time and shared her love with all men."

Alma drew back slightly but didn't disagree with the statement. These people were free to choose their faith, unlike he was in his childhood home, and he wouldn't stand in their way. His energy spent, Alma settled back on the stool, taking shallow breaths.

Next, Kaman stood and reported what the village men had done so far to uncover who had been behind the fire. Alma's vision blurred, and he knew he was past exhaustion. The smoke from the fire might have left him weak, but at least he was alive, unlike Belicia.

He retied the jade necklace about his neck and traced the outline of the half-moon with his finger. The crowd swam before his eyes, the vibrant colors of the women's tunics blending together into a sunset. Next to him, Jacob grabbed his arm, steadying him. "You need to rest."

Alma nodded, trying to appear alert, but his chest felt very tight, and he felt the tickle of another coughing spasm coming on. He let Jacob lead him down the platform, and the crowd started chanting, "Alma, Alma . . ." He tried to lift his hand to wave but had to settle for a nod.

Once inside Kaman's hut, Alma succumbed to the coughing. Jacob stood by his side as Alma was able to clear out his chest and breathe almost normally again.

"Tell them I'm sorry," Alma said, his throat scratchy.

"You have nothing to apologize for," Jacob said, "You came out too early, that's all. But it did the people a lot of good to see you." He led Alma to the back bedroom and settled him on the mat. "I'll send Eden in to care for you. Once you're better, the village wants to elect you as chief."

"I can't . . . It should be one of the villagers—"

"Rest for now," Jacob said. "There will be plenty of time to argue later."

Through a tired haze, Alma heard Jacob leave the room and call for Eden. He didn't want to be chief. He wanted to be in the background, helping where he could, not seeking power. His eyes closed, and he imagined a place where a temple had been built for all people, no matter what their religious beliefs. As he walked up the polished steps, a woman stood at the top. *Cassia,* he thought, as she turned to face him. Her hair was plaited with colorful ribbons. She was laughing, her expression open and joyful, but when her eyes landed on Alma, her face changed. Her hair darkened, her face narrowed, and her eyes turned black. Tears spilled onto her pale cheeks. *Belicia,* Alma tried to say. *I'm sorry, Belicia.*

"Avenge my death, Alma," she said, weeping. "One of them must die. They must pay for what they did."

Her hands reached for him. "Promise me, my love."

"I promise."

CHAPTER 12

Is any among you afflicted? Let him pray . . .
—James 5:13

ONE WEEK LATER

Alma the Younger

Alma paced the length of the room in his hut, then turned back.

"Sit down," Kaman said, half joking. But his expression was anxious, just how Alma felt.

"Where are they?" Alma asked, mostly to himself. The others had stopped answering him over an hour ago. The sons of Mosiah were late. And the men whom Alma had sworn to secrecy were getting restless.

The wine jug went around the circle of men again—Kaman, Jacob, and two other men from the village—Muloki and Ammah. But the mood was far from jovial. The previous day, Jacob had discovered which Church group had been responsible for carrying out the order to burn the tavern.

"I say we just burn their whole village," Kaman said.

"And the retaliation will never end. Although the king is against any type of persecution, he has little control over his own emissaries," Alma said, keeping one ear tuned for the king's sons. "We need to uncover who issued the order—only then will we have the power to negotiate."

The sound of a footfall outside alerted Alma. He rushed to the door and threw it open. The four sons of the king stood there, wearing hooded robes. "What happened?"

"Another banquet at the palace," Ammon said. "It was hard to get away unnoticed."

Alma grimaced and ushered them in, and they greeted the village men one by one, all of them bearing similar scars on their palms. Alma was pleased to see the half-moon necklace hanging from the brothers' necks as well, although he knew they had to conceal them when they were at the palace.

Ammon eyed the rustic surroundings. "When are you going to get yourself a new place, Alma?"

Kaman said, "If the villagers have their way, Alma will be living in a chief's home soon."

The king's sons all looked at Alma, grins on their faces.

"No, I won't," Alma said. "I don't need to live above anyone else."

"Does that mean you'll accept the position?" Kaman said, his face eager.

"I said no such thing," Alma said. He folded his arms across his chest, indicating that the conversation topic was over. "Let's get to the real reason for our meeting. We've wasted enough time." He looked at Kaman. "Fill them in."

When the brothers were seated in the circle, Kaman stood, his hands twisting together. "The traveling shaman came to our village yesterday and told us about an interesting guest he helped about a week ago, the very day after the tavern had been burned. A young man sought his services, paying a healthy sum for a curaio salve." He relaxed his hands and paused. "The boy had no burns himself—it was for another."

Alma nodded, watching the reaction of the king's sons.

Kaman continued. "The shaman was concerned, wondering if the boy knew how to treat a burn properly, so he followed the boy. It was no easy task, since the boy moved quickly, leaving the village and running into the city of Zarahemla."

"Where did he go?" Ammon asked, rising to his feet.

Alma cut in. "To the home of a royal—a priest in the king's temple."

The brothers stared at him in astonishment, curiosity in their eyes.

"Limhi." Alma only had to say the word, and three brothers were on their feet, talking at once.

Ammon stayed silent, a thoughtful expression on his face. He looked at Alma, and it was as if they had entertained the same conclusion.

Kaman folded his arms across his chest, nodding with satisfaction. Alma had told him that the king's sons would be irate, and although Kaman had doubted, Alma knew his friends.

The noise quieted down, and Kaman said, "We suspect everyone from Limhi himself down to his most lowly gardener. It must be someone in that household, and it is only a matter of time before we find out who gave the order."

"That's why we need your help," Alma said, his frank gaze meeting that of Ammon's, then sliding to Aaron. "It will be easy for you to get closer to the family of Limhi, especially considering Aaron's betrothed . . ."

Aaron nodded in agreement even though his face had grown pale.

"Aaron," Alma said in a quiet voice. The men in the hut were completely silent, listening. "If you want out—"

"I made an oath," Aaron said, his eyes hard. "I want to discover the man behind these senseless and dangerous attacks as much as anyone." He looked around the circle of men. "I will help in any way I can."

"Me too," Ammon said, followed by Omner and Himni.

Kaman grinned. "Then it's settled." He stepped forward, slapping Ammon on the shoulder. "Are you men thirsty?"

Laughter made its rounds with the new wine.

The men were merry, their former melancholy shed. The king's sons would help them infiltrate the household of Limhi, and together the band would bring down the man ultimately responsible for the death of Belicia—one of their own. An innocent victim.

Jacob broke into song, and soon they were working their way through every ballad Alma had ever heard, and some new ones as well. Ammon made his way to Alma casually, without drawing attention from the ever watchful Kaman.

"I need to talk to you somewhere," Ammon said in a whisper.

Alma said, "Meet me out back in a few minutes." He watched Ammon slip out of the room with no one noticing. Several minutes later he made the excuse to leave for a moment. Kaman's gaze tracked him, but he made no move to follow.

The night air had cooled considerably when Alma stepped outside. Ammon's waiting figure was at the far end of the courtyard, shadowed by a sassafras tree that blocked the moonlight. He strode to his friend's side, curious about what Ammon had to say.

"I have a suspicion," Ammon said. "It might be Nehem. He's been quite vocal in his abhorrence to the practices of the unbelievers. He's been spotted in villages with the king's guard, going above his normal duties of a councilman. I wouldn't be surprised if he was the one who issued the order."

Alma stared at Ammon. "Why *this* village? Why the tavern?"

"He knows which village Jacob and Kaman came from—those who escaped the king's prison. Nehem is always flattering the king, and I can see him trying to get on my father's good side by any method, even if it means getting rid of unfavorable taverns. A dead harlot or two might even be to his advantage."

Alma blew out a breath, his body feeling weighted at the mention of Belicia. If he found out that Nehem was responsible . . .

"But that's not all."

Alma lifted his head to look at Ammon.

"I don't know if you care to hear it, but I promised to deliver a message to you."

Now Alma was more than curious. "Go on." He was surprised to see Ammon hesitate and avoid eye contact. A twinge of alarm passed through Alma. "Has something happened to my family?"

"No," Ammon said, but still he stalled. Finally, he met Alma's eyes. "It's Cassia . . . Nehem has asked for her hand in marriage."

Alma blinked several times, trying to digest the information. Nehem—that scoundrel—marrying Cassia. He'd tried to forget about her, push her from his mind, at least during the daytime. When sleep pressed against his eyes, her face was usually the first thing that came to view before the dream—the same dream night after night of the temple and of Cassia transforming into Belicia. Her tears . . . her demanding his promise to avenge her death with that of another.

He shook his head slightly and exhaled. "It doesn't surprise me, I suppose. Nehem seems to be a persistent fellow."

Ammon scoffed. "Very persistent. But if I find that Nehem is behind the arson, I'll stop the wedding myself." He waited.

Alma felt him waiting, but he couldn't come up with a response. What was he to say, anyway? That he didn't want Cassia to marry the lousy oaf? There would be other suitors if she didn't marry Nehem. She was a woman now and would have to decide soon.

"When is the wedding?" Alma asked, hoping his voice only betrayed casual politeness.

"That's what I wanted to talk to you about," Ammon said.

Alma stiffened. He didn't want any part of whatever plans Ammon had hatched up—Cassia was better out of his life now. She could never accept him for who he was anyway, especially after Belicia.

"She hasn't said yes yet," Ammon said.

"Why not?" It was a foolish question, but Alma might as well hear the answer.

"She hasn't exactly explained, but you know how a woman is—she can't do anything in a straightforward manner. Look at Ilana."

Alma smiled faintly. He didn't know who had received the rawer end of the bargain—Ammon or Aaron.

"But Cassia did say she wanted me to tell you about Nehem's proposal before she made a decision."

The pressure inside Alma's chest increased. He thought he might start coughing again, although he hadn't for a good two days. "Why me?" he croaked out, wishing he had a flask of wine.

"You know why," Ammon said. When Alma didn't respond, Ammon said, "All I know is that she relentlessly hounds me every time I see her to tell you about Nehem. I'm supposed to deliver your response to her."

Alma nodded, trying to look calm as his mind raced. But his heart sank. It was too late. She was not the same girl he used to tell his dreams too. And he was not the same man that used to be her friend—far from it. If Cassia knew about Belicia or about the blood oath he'd made, the deeds he'd done, or the promise he'd made to

Belicia's spirit, she wouldn't care if he were ordained a priest that very night. He would never meet her expectations—never be clean enough in her mind. And that didn't even account for the way her father felt about him.

"Your father approves of the union?" Alma asked.

"It seems so."

"Nehem must have the blessed life," Alma said, unable to keep the irony out of his voice. "I think your father would order me burned at a stake if I showed up in his palace—even if it were to offer my congratulations."

Ammon's gaze was protective. "I wouldn't allow him to touch you."

"I know, but you're not your father," Alma said, putting a hand on his friend's shoulder. "Nehem is a fortunate man." He paused, his chest constricting. "Tell Cass . . . tell her I hope she'll be happy."

* * *

Cassia

"What did he say?" Cassia asked Ammon.

Her oldest brother, who was normally not afraid of anything, looked extra wary. He kept fidgeting with the knife at his waistband. They stood outside in the garden, where Cassia had waited for Ammon's return all day. She'd sent him on an errand—to tell Alma about Nehem's offer. She'd made Nehem wait long enough—nearly two weeks—for her answer, since first she had to know what Alma thought, if anything, about the betrothal. Thankfully Ammon didn't pry with any questions, but did her bidding.

"You told him that Nehem wants to marry me, didn't you?" Cassia asked, squeezing his arm.

"Yes," Ammon said, looking down at her hand on his arm.

"And he said nothing? He—" Cassia bit her lip. *Alma didn't care.* That was the only answer. He didn't love her after all and didn't want to marry her.

"He knows how Father feels about him, especially now," Ammon said in a careful voice.

She let go of his arm. "Did he say that he could do nothing?"

Ammon's expression was pained. "What do you want him to do, Cassia? Show up at the palace with a box of silver and plead with Father? Alma isn't going to change his mind about the Church. He's changed more than you know—in a lot of ways. He's not the same man and doesn't feel the same about"—he waved his hand indicating the palace, then his eyes settled on his sister—"all this. He lives a different life now."

Cassia brushed at her cheeks, where stinging tears had fallen, realizing she knew Alma's answer. He wanted her to marry Nehem.

Ammon watched her closely, but her throat was too tight to speak. "I think he knows when the fight is over," he said. "He can't make everyone happy, so he's decided to follow the only path open to him now."

She shook her head, her eyes blurring with tears. "Which is a path of nothing—no family—"

"Cassia, what do you want me to say?" Ammon cut in. "Father won't let him set foot in the palace. Alma's father will demand an extensive retribution period, and that is *if* Alma wanted to return, which he doesn't. Do you want him to fight for your hand under false pretenses?"

"Why does it have to be false?" Cassia asked, hating that her voice trembled. "Why can't he just pray and find out the truth for himself? Why does he have to be so against the Church and everything about it?"

"You wouldn't be happy together." Ammon shook his head. "You'd always be fighting about the Church. He'd go one way, and you'd go the other."

Cassia wrapped her arms about her, her stomach clenched with nausea. "Tell me what he said. Exactly."

Ammon took a deep breath. "He said he hoped you would be happy."

Closing her eyes, Cassia turned away from Ammon. It was finished then. Alma had given up. He'd sacrificed his family, his home, his work, and now her, all because he couldn't accept the Church. *But it isn't just that,* she thought. *It's even bigger.* Her prayers weren't being answered. If she was really supposed to be with Alma, then why had Nehem come into her life at the very moment Alma had abandoned everything that should have been dear to him?

"It's still your choice," Ammon said.

Cassia opened her eyes in surprise. "Alma already made his choice."

"But have you made yours?"

She studied her brother. Was Nehem the only answer to Alma's rejection? She knew he wasn't, but she knew he would take care of her—love her. But would Nehem's love be enough to make her forget Alma? She shook her head, and asked, "Do you think I should leave the Church so that I can be with Alma?"

He lifted a shoulder.

"You can't possibly be suggesting that, Ammon," Cassia spat out, anger and hurt colliding in her breast. "You are the crown prince! You will be leading this country one day. You think you can be a successful ruler without following the laws of God?"

"Alma was right," he said, shaking his head. "You would never accept him unless he bowed down to everything that has to do with the Church. He knows you don't really love him—or accept him for what he is."

Cassia felt as if she'd been slapped.

Her brother continued, as if unaware that he'd just crushed her. "As for your accusations that I can't be a successful king without the Church, think about the many enemies Father has now. How long do you think this land will remain peaceful—if you can even call it peaceful now?"

"But Father has sent out edicts preventing the unbelievers from persecuting Church members."

Ammon let out a bitter laugh. "You, sister, are cloistered in a palace and have hardly stepped foot outside your precious room. Just beyond the royal plaza there is plenty of injustice, plenty of persecution. The unbelievers themselves are being persecuted as well. Offenses are not easily forgotten, no matter the law. Merchants refuse to sell their wares or goods to certain people, or they raise their prices so high that children are starving!"

Cassia flinched. Ammon's face had darkened, reminding her of Alma's fury when she'd accused him. The breath seemed to leave her body, and suddenly she was very tired. "I'm sure Father has—"

"Ha!" Ammon said. "Our father has lost control over his people. He has done nothing but protect himself with more soldiers. He sends out more and more preachers, most of whom are self-inflated and continue to berate and throw condemnation against a hard-working people who are just trying to feed their children." He turned away and left the garden.

Cassia stared after him, gripping her trembling hands together. She took several deep breaths. So Ammon agreed with Alma. Maybe not to the extent of leaving the Church, but Ammon's words still frightened her. She hurried back to the palace and made it to her bedchamber without running into anyone.

Once alone, she paced her room, keeping the tears at bay. She felt stunned but even more confused. Was marrying Nehem the path the Lord wanted her to follow? Was she being tested as to whether she'd choose the Church over Alma?

Cassia sank onto her bed and hung her head. Alma had given up on her. That was all she needed to make the decision. Still, she could refuse Nehem, making two strikes against her. She'd become known as the eternal maid, and no man would dare approach her again.

Flopping back on her bed, Cassia stared up at the ceiling. Nehem adored her, that much was clear, and he might even love her. She didn't love him, but that would probably change over time, as it did with most arranged marriages. How else could she feel about a man who treated her so well and attended to her every concern? He was also strong in the Church. He was good-looking, witty, tender . . . Cassia blew out a breath. Nehem wanted to marry her. Alma didn't. What other choice was there?

Cassia sat up, a shaky feeling moving all over her body. She knew what she had to do; she just had to put more faith in that decision.

Rising from the bed, she left her room and walked along the corridor to her father's private chambers, hoping to find him there.

When the guard saw her, he granted her entrance immediately. Cassia entered the king's room and was amazed to see Nehem with her father.

They both looked at her in anticipation, and the look of hope in Nehem's eyes was undeniable.

Nehem bowed. "I'll leave the two of you alone."

"No," Cassia said, surprising herself. "You may stay if you wish."

Both men smiled, causing her heart to start pounding harder. She took a quick breath, then said, "I've come to tell you that I'm honored to accept Nehem's proposal."

King Mosiah clapped his hands together. "Wonderful!" He crossed to her, and taking her hands, he leaned down and kissed her cheek. "Congratulations, daughter."

Warmth spread through her body as she caught Nehem's gaze. His face had flushed, and he was smiling broadly.

Her father pulled away and said, "I'll call for your mother."

When he stepped into the next room Nehem crossed to Cassia. His smile was tender as he took her hand in his. Cassia looked at him, telling herself that she'd enjoy years of happiness with this man. He pulled her hand to his lips, and this time she allowed him to kiss it.

"You have made me so happy," Nehem said. "Are *you* happy?"

She nodded, her throat too tight to speak. *It will be all right,* she told herself. Then abruptly, Nehem pulled her into a tight embrace. As the door opened, he let go and stepped back.

Cassia's parents entered the room, and Naomi hurried to her daughter's side. "Oh, my dear! Your father told me the wonderful news." She kissed Cassia's cheek, then crossed to Nehem to congratulate him. After embracing him, she said, "We must tell Ilana! And my sons!" She clasped her hands together, her eyes shining as she looked at Cassia. "Will we have a double wedding then?"

Everyone looked at Cassia expectantly. She ignored the sudden faintness that had come over her. "We will."

CHAPTER 13

. . . if thou do at all forget the Lord thy God, and walk after other gods . . . and worship them, I testify against you this day that ye shall surely perish.
—Deuteronomy 8:19

Alma the Younger

Alma hovered between the heavier set of trees and the alcove above his parents' homestead as the sun settled against the horizon. Their home sat on a large acreage of land not too far from the palace. He perched on a boulder that gave him a good view of his childhood home as well as the palace to the north and the temple to the west. It was like he was viewing the circle of influence he'd grown up in—a life where he was surrounded by people who were zealous in their beliefs and worshipful of his father and mother.

As he watched the family homestead, his two sisters came outside and moved the weaving looms to the edge of the courtyard. They each stooped several times to pick up what looked like scraps of cloth. He could well imagine his mother's scolding when she'd discovered his sisters hadn't cleaned up their work.

Then his mother appeared. Alma swallowed but found his throat dry. She had her hands on her hips, and although she was speaking to the girls, he couldn't hear her words. His sisters disappeared inside once again, but his mother remained in the courtyard.

He half expected her to walk around, looking for stray scraps of cloth, but instead, she stared at the rising hills—right in Alma's direction. He knew she couldn't see him, even if she came quite a bit closer, but it made him uncomfortable that she seemed to be looking right at him. For several long minutes, she didn't move. He assumed the supper preparations were well underway, and he was surprised she'd spend so much time just watching the hills. His father would be returning from the temple from the other direction. What was she thinking about?

Alma knew the stories. His mother had been married to the legendary King Noah, who had led his people into iniquity, then fled from the Lamanites. He'd abandoned the women and children of the city of Nephi—including his own wives. Maia had been one of those wives left behind.

His mother turned from the hills and walked slowly to the low wall surrounding the courtyard, where she sat, the wind tugging at her robe.

When they were younger, Alma's sisters had begged for more information about what it was like to be a king's wife, until his father had reprimanded them. Later, when Alma was alone with his father, he'd asked question after question. The descriptions of King Noah's temperament and what it was like to live in such a court had terrified Alma until he visualized Noah as some great dragon who sent people to their death every day.

As a scribe, Alma had read the records that his father had kept of the city of Nephi. He knew of his father's conversion. He knew of his mother's horrible life. He knew what they had sacrificed for their belief in God. And he also knew that they reviled all sinners, which now included him.

Alma's mother rose from the wall as if she'd heard something. A moment later, his father came out into the courtyard. In just a few strides, he was at her side, taking her into his embrace.

Alma felt the lump in his throat expand. His throat and chest hurt as he watched the closeness his parents shared. His father's arms were around his mother as he stroked her hair. She leaned against him, as if to draw in his strength and comfort.

Alma's eyes stung as he watched his parents. It was difficult to imagine he could ever have what the two of them had. They seemed completely happy, but if they were so happy, why was he so miserable? They were together in all things. He was alone.

And if they knew what he had done—what he was doing—they'd despise him even more. They'd wash their hands clean of him—more than they already had.

As the darkness crept down the hills into the courtyard, Alma felt as if his heart were growing darker too. Any hope of reconciliation had ended with Belicia, he knew. He could come up with no excuses, nothing that would justify his behavior when Belicia had wrapped her arms around his neck and drew him to her. He had complied, and he had crossed the threshold of no return.

But her death had washed away all traces of guilt he may have once felt. She was near-perfect in his eyes now—an innocent in a vicious circle of violence that had no end in sight. Unless . . . he went through with Belicia's request for vengeance. Alma thought of his plan to secretly infiltrate the Church with his men. It was the first step. It would only take some cunning and forged documents, supposedly signed by the high priest himself.

The idea had come to him after Ammon's news about Cassia. Alma supposed it was the final break in the thread that tied him to his former life. There would be no future for him and Cass now—their past needed to be buried once and for all. She had made her decision, and he had made his.

Alma stirred on the boulder, feeling impatient. His parents should be retiring for the night soon, then Alma could retrieve what he came for. He knew just where his father kept the high priest seal. He moved his gaze from his parents as he thought of the betrayal he was about to partake in. His mother's heart would break—again—over him. But his parents had survived worse things.

His mother had been imprisoned for standing up for her beliefs—to a king who was also her husband at the time. His father had risked his life multiple times, and then been enslaved by his greatest enemy because he'd refused to give up.

But here I am, Alma thought, *a sinner in their eyes.*

He could find a different sort of happiness—maybe not the one his parents shared, but one that could be found outside the Church.

He'd seen it in his friends and in the people of the village. They'd found plenty of joy in life.

His father led his mother inside the house, his arm around her waist and her head on his shoulder. When they'd disappeared inside, Alma realized that dark had fully fallen. Light streamed from the house, and undoubtedly his family was eating their supper, sharing their various activities of the day without a thought for him.

Alma straightened from his perch and jumped off the boulder. He did belong somewhere, he realized, just not here. In the Isidro village, an entire people revered him just as he was. They didn't want to change him. Staring at the house in the dark, he realized how much he hated the division the Church had created between him and his family. If his father could just accept his differing beliefs, he'd be at that table with his sisters . . . or perhaps he'd be the one betrothed to Cassia. But that wouldn't change the fact that Belicia had died. And his father's church was responsible. And like Belicia had told him in his dream, someone would have to pay.

He crept down the hillside, taking care so he wouldn't be spotted. He crouched behind the wall of the outer courtyard, waiting for the lamps to be extinguished and the house to quiet for the night. Ironically, Alma thought if there was a time that his father ever needed guards at his home, this was it. Perhaps his father thought he was close enough to the palace to earn some of the king's protection.

Alma rose from his cramped position. He crept across the courtyard and tried the back door. He wasn't surprised to find it unbarred, and he slipped inside, stopping to allow his eyes to adjust to the dark interior. If only he had a lamp. . . . But he knew the layout of the house by heart, so he began the slow but steady process of moving along the walls until he reached his father's document room.

The high priest often brought documents home from the temple archives to study. He also brought home baptismal records to sign and validate with the seal of the high priest. Just as Alma remembered, about a half dozen scrolls sat piled on top of the low table. He felt grateful for the moonlight streaming into the room through the double window.

Nostalgia filled his chest as he remembered shadowing his father at a young age both at home and at the temple, but Alma didn't have time for memories. He crossed the room and went to the shelves behind the table. There, in a wood box, was the seal, identical to the one in the temple. Alma picked it up and stowed it inside his waistband. He wondered how long it would be before his father discovered it missing. It might be a day, or a week, depending on the number of baptisms. Whatever the time, Alma hoped it would be enough to infiltrate Limhi's congregation.

Alma left the room, touching nothing else. As he exited the back way, he left the scene of his childhood, knowing he might never step foot in this house again. His life with his family was over for good. The innocence of his youth had long since fled, and he was now a man who neither of his parents would recognize.

* * *

Alma stood in the doorway of Kaman's home, finding him slumbering in the front room. "I'll take the position as chief," he said, bringing the sleeping Kaman to full alert.

Kaman's eyes flew open at Alma's words. He scrambled to his feet and embraced Alma.

"Steady," Alma said, pulling away from the rumpled man. It was early in the morning and dawn had just arrived. Alma hadn't slept all night, his thoughts tortuous after leaving his parents' home. But as soon as the first light paled the sky, a new fervor entered his body.

His former life was over, and this village was where he belonged. And if the people wanted him as their chief, then he would accept the assignment.

Kaman called out, "Eden! Come quick!"

"Don't wake your wife," Alma said, feeling his face heat up. "It's early yet."

But it was too late. Eden appeared at the doorway, drawing a robe around her.

"Meet the new chief of our village," Kaman said, his voice thick with pride.

Eden gasped, then threw herself against Alma. He wrapped his arms around her, if only to keep himself from being thrown off balance.

"Oh," Eden cried, pulling back and planting a kiss on each cheek. "Wait until we tell the children. They already call you chief."

Alma chuckled but shook his head. "Let them sleep."

Eden brought a hand to her chest, tears forming in her eyes. "See? He is always thinking of others, even the little children." She turned to her husband, her expression eager. "Will the feast be tonight? The women and I can start right away."

Without consulting with Alma, Kaman answered, "Yes, tonight we'll formally elect our new chief." He threw a wink in Alma's direction. "You'll meet with no dissension. You'll be voted in unanimously."

Alma smiled and clasped hands with Kaman. He left the rejoicing couple and made his way back to his isolated hut, feeling deep warmth spread through him. He would finally be validated for his beliefs—with an entire village to support him. He hurried to his hut, looking forward to getting some rest before the whole village learned of his decision. He doubted he'd get much rest once everyone found out. The thought brought another smile to his face. The excitement in Kaman's and Eden's faces could very well drown out the sorrow he'd seen on his parents' faces.

But when he reached his hut, he saw that he'd hoped for the impossible. The first thing he noticed was a woman waiting inside, the second thing, his hut had been cleaned and the table loaded with plenty of food.

"Good morning, Alma," Sara said.

"What's all this?" Alma asked, although he suspected. Sara was a cousin to Belicia, and shared her cousin's profession. Fortunately for Sara, she had escaped the burning tavern unharmed.

Sara stared at him, unblinking, the devotion in her eyes evident. "I hoped you would be returning soon." She waved her hand toward the table of food. "Are you hungry?"

He was. Alma nodded, casting a quick glance about the tidied room. It was nice to have a woman around his home—although he knew this one wouldn't stay around long, if she were like the others.

"Let me feed you, then," Sara said, her smile sweet. She crossed to him and ran a hand along his arm, still smiling. "You look as if you need to be taken care of for once."

Without a word, Alma shut the front door and let her take his hand and lead him to the table.

* * *

Hours later, Alma emerged refreshed from his hut, Sara at his side. He was newly clothed in a coat of jaguar skin Kaman had delivered as a gift from the village. Even from his hut, he could hear drums coming from the main plaza. The market had closed down early to allow time to prepare for the ceremony.

The sun had begun its late-afternoon descent by the time he and Sara reached the judgment hall. Dozens of men were feverishly working around the building. "What are they doing?"

"It's a surprise," Sara said in her soothing tone. She smiled up at Alma, and he returned it. There was nothing wrong with being nice to her, he decided. He wouldn't let himself be drawn in as he had with Belicia.

The jaguar fur felt soft and sleek against his bare shoulders. Sara had insisted that it looked better, more like a chief, if he didn't wear a tunic beneath, but only a kilt. She'd presented him with new sandals as well and wouldn't let him protest the gift. He touched her chin affectionately. "I will find a way to repay you for the sandals."

She leaned her face against his palm, closing her eyes briefly. "You already have."

He chuckled, then drew her arm into his. He was flattered by her attention but knew what she was. He would not fall for a woman of her profession again; he would not let his emotions be caught up in something that wasn't real.

The workers drew his attention again, and he led Sara along with him as he approached. Several stopped and bowed to him.

"You are already their chief," Sara whispered.

A thrill passed through Alma at the respect these men showed him. He released Sara and crossed to one of the men he knew as Muloki. "What are you doing? Shouldn't you be clearing the rest of the tavern rubble?"

The man nodded. He was a robust fellow with dark hair that fell to his shoulders. "We will be working on that shortly. But we are preparing your residence so you might sleep here your first night as our new chief."

Alma stared at the man in disbelief. *My new residence?*

"Muloki!" Sara was at Alma's side in an instant, glaring at the worker. "You weren't supposed to say anything yet."

Muloki lowered his gaze, mumbling an apology but not looking a bit sorry.

"No matter," Sara finally said, turning to Alma. "Come with me. We have prepared a special meal for you as the workers finish their tasks. At sundown, the ceremony will begin."

Alma walked with Sara to where a roof of woven palms had been erected over a platform, blocking out the simmering sun. Two men were hauling a table onto the platform. Sara led him up the steps and forced him to sit on large cushions and be waited upon.

Almost as soon as he sat, the food came, served by Sara and a few other women. Steaming dishes of cooked squash, tomatoes, chilis, maize, sliced avocado, nuts, and quail eggs were abundant. Several people joined him, including Kaman and Eden, and later Jacob. The sun was just beginning to set when Kaman stood up and pointed. "There they are."

Following the man's gaze, to Alma's surprise he saw Ammon and his brothers walking into the main plaza. They wore well-cut robes, not the usual plain clothing they dressed in when away from the palace.

Kaman clapped his hands together and rushed down the platform to greet them. Ammon embraced Kaman like an old friend, followed by Aaron and the rest.

"Isn't it fantastic?" Kaman called out to Alma, leading the king's sons to the platform. "They are here to witness your coronation."

Alma stood and welcomed his friends. Room was made at the table and more dishes of steaming food brought.

Ammon smiled at Alma, raising his goblet of wine. "To the man I always knew was smarter than me."

"What do you mean by that?"

After taking a deep swallow of his wine, Ammon said, "It's fitting—the title of chief. You belong here." He gazed across the plaza, where the workers had finished their tasks and had placed torches all around the plaza. The villagers had started arriving, wearing brightly colored shawls and tunics.

The sun set, the warm colors fading into violets and pinks. Sara climbed up on the platform. She had changed into a sleeveless tunic of turquoise green that set off her complexion. Her hair had been released from its braids and hung down her back in gentle black waves. She welcomed the king's sons, then bowed before Alma with a smile. "We are pleased your friends have joined us. We have a special dance prepared for your enjoyment."

Alma caught the king's sons staring at Sara, trying to determine who she was. "Thank you," Alma said, reaching for her hand and kissing it. *I'm just showing my gratitude,* he thought. Ammon raised his eyebrows slightly but said nothing.

Aaron's gaze followed Sara's figure as she walked down the stairs and joined a group of women in the plaza.

Alma tried to remain nonchalant as he watched Sara, but this was part of his new life. So why shouldn't he have some enjoyment? It was impossible to return to his former life—it was too late—he was too soiled. Sara proceeded to tie a brilliant red sash around her waist, then motioned for the women to get into formation.

From somewhere behind the women, the drums started. The women began to move, their dancing in perfect unison. Alma glanced over at the king's sons. All of their eyes were riveted on the dancers, Himni with a turkey leg held halfway to his mouth.

Alma leaned back, talking himself into enjoying the dancing. Sara was really quite beautiful, he thought with a bit of nostalgia. She was different from Cassia, or Belicia, but she held her own charm. Even though he knew she could never truly love just him, it didn't mean they couldn't enjoy their time together. Alma continued to drink, finding that with each swallow, his heart softened toward Sara and the other women.

The dancers swayed in sync, their movements blending together until it made Alma almost dizzy trying to keep track of which one was Sara. As the music faded and the women struck a final pose, Alma leapt to his feet, clapping and whistling. Ammon jumped up as well, joining him and the villagers in enthusiastic cheering.

Sara's glowing eyes were on Alma, seeking his approval, and he nodded, beckoning her to join him on the platform. She smiled and brought several others with her. The women promptly settled in with the king's sons. New men were an intriguing prospect in the village.

When one of Sara's friends squeezed so close to Aaron that she practically sat on his lap, Alma chuckled at his friend's flushed expression. The brothers might show surprise at these flirtations now, but he knew they would get used to the presence of these women soon enough.

Kaman rose and walked to the edge of the platform, his hands held up for silence. The villagers had filled in the main plaza, and they quieted at the sight of Kaman. "Tonight is a first for our village. Recent events have required that we need to elect a leader—a village chief—to organize our citizens and protect our interests. Will all the voting household leaders come to the platform?"

Several dozen men stepped forward, their expressions excited. Jacob left the platform and joined them.

"Raise your right hand if you are in favor of Alma being elected as our chief," Kaman said.

Almost immediately, every hand rose in the air. Alma was stunned that there was no hesitation.

After surveying the voters, Kaman said, "Are there any other names to be considered for chief?" No one responded.

Kaman turned toward Alma, a triumphant smile on his face. "Come forward and receive the symbols of your office."

Alma rose from the table and joined Kaman at the edge of the platform. Kaman bowed, then presented a feathered headdress handed over by a member of the crowd. The colors of the feathers were lighter in the center, forming a circle. "The circle shape represents the sun—for in our departed Belicia's eyes, you were like the sun, and now you are the sun to our village."

Alma dipped his head as Kaman secured the headdress on him. "We have also prepared a new home for you, a place to receive the villagers." His hand stretched toward the judgment hall that Alma had caught the workers renovating. "It is our gift to you—our gift for taking care of us."

Alma bowed his head in gratitude.

"And now," Kaman continued. "The villagers will bring you their tokens of appreciation." He extended his hand toward the crowd.

Alma's eyes widened as the crowd formed into a long line, the majority of them bearing gifts. Even the king's sons took their place in line. When Ammon reached Alma, he handed over a red-dyed leather band. "To wear on your arm and remind you of the leader I always believed you to be."

Alma took the band from his friend and studied the markings on it.

"The half-moon represents your willingness to put others' lives before your own," Ammon said. "It mirrors the half-moon necklace that Belicia gave you."

"Thank you," Alma said, tracing the pattern on the thoughtful gift.

Aaron was next, bearing a folded piece of scarlet cloth. When Alma unraveled it, he discovered a finely woven robe with an attached hood. "To honor your office as leader of this village," Aaron said, then stepped way.

Omner and Himni presented him with an elegant bow and set of arrows, similar to the ones he'd had to leave behind.

"You are all too generous," Alma murmured, accepting gift after gift, then handing them over to Kaman, who stood by his side. In a short time the platform was covered with gifts. When the line came to an end, Alma turned to the chattering crowd and raised his hands for quiet.

"Thank you all," he called out. Heads nodded. "It has been a remarkable evening, and I don't feel I deserve all of this." Several in the crowd voiced their disagreement.

"What you have given me tonight," Alma said, "I will cherish and protect. I will keep these for the appropriate time and use. This village is filled with hard workers, and most of you have fallen on hard times, and I do not take this office lightly. I am here only to serve you."

A cheer went up among the crowd. Kaman patted his shoulder, nodding vigorously.

Alma removed the band he'd tied to his arm. "This armband was given to me as a symbol of the woman Belicia and her sacrifice to our village. This band will be replicated and given to men who show uncommon heroism. It will be earned and worn with pride as a symbol of our unification."

Another shout went up.

With Kaman's help, Alma retied the band around his arm, then waited for the crowd to quiet. From the pouch tied to his kilt, Alma withdrew a small scroll. He opened the scroll and said, "I have written the names of twelve men on this scroll. They will make up the council of the village. And so that I do not wield too much power, they will have a vote on the suggestions I propose."

Scattered clapping burst out, but mostly the crowd was quiet, riveted to Alma's voice as he read the list of names.

"Kaman," Alma began. "Jacob, Ammon, Aaron." He paused as the men stepped forward. "Omner, Himni, Muloki, Ammah . . ." He continued reading from his list, watching as the men stepped forward, pride and respect in their eyes.

When the twelve men had been called, Alma said, "Each man will wear a scarlet robe as a symbol of their service to the community. Each of us will swear on our lives to protect and serve you."

The crowd burst into a roaring cheer.

Alma waited a few minutes, a smile on his face as the adrenaline shot through him. "But we ask something in return." The people hushed as he continued, "We ask for your help. We may request some hard tasks of you and your families, and sometimes we may not be able to reveal the reason, but we ask for your pledge of devotion."

"Chief Alma!" somebody started chanting, soon joined in by the others.

Alma shivered. *The title of "chief" will take some getting used to.*

As the crowd quieted, several men removed the gifts, then carried them to the judgment hall. Two men from the newly chosen council came and knelt before Alma.

One was Muloki, the man who'd been preparing the chief's home earlier. Muloki's long hair fell forward as he bowed his head. "Chief Alma," he said, "I pledge my honor and service to you. My great-grandfather was David, who was wrongly ousted by Mosiah the

First. My brother, Ammah, and I have been waiting a long time for someone to lead us to justice."

Next to Muloki, Ammah bowed his head. He was thin but strong, with tight curls cropped short on his head. "All hail, Chief Alma."

Chief Alma.

Hot pride flowed through Alma at the title. *Maybe it wouldn't take too much getting used to.* In the midst of the declarations of loyalty, another dance performance was called for, this one involving most of the women of the village. Alma took his seat at the table again and drank from his goblet. Sara was at his side almost instantly, her small hand pressing against his arm. "Tonight," she whispered in his ear, "you will sleep in a bed fit for a king."

Alma turned to see her smile, and he took her hand and kissed it. "Only if you will share it with me," he whispered back. Her eyes sparkled in response.

* * *

Drenched in perspiration, Alma sat straight up in bed. The night was still deep and Sara stirred next to him, then her breathing was steady again. He crept out of the room, not wanting to disturb her rest. After a day and night of celebrations, the house seemed so quiet. But sleep had fled Alma. Belicia had been in his dreams again, her haunting eyes staring at him, her dying voice pleading with him to never forget her, to make her vengeance complete.

Alma shivered, remembering the whispered words that had brushed his ear—as if she had been the one next to him instead of Sara.

Remember me, Belicia had pled. *Remember that you are the sun, and I am the moon.*

Alma touched the jade necklace at his throat, carved in the shape of the crescent moon. "I could never forget you," he whispered in the darkness. He made his way to the cooking room, which had been swept clean and tidied by the villagers. In the moonlight he found a stool to sit on, and he slumped against the table. Thoughts churned through his mind—*It isn't enough.* The armbands, the jade necklaces, the declarations to keep Belicia's memory alive . . . What was she trying to tell him?

He put his head in his arms, Belicia's whispers echoing in his mind. *I am the moon. You are the sun. Save my people. One of the enemies must die. They must pay for what they did. Don't forget . . .*

Alma drifted to sleep, Belicia's sad eyes, dark hair, and pale skin replacing his conscious thoughts. And then her hair was white, her eyes gray, and her skin as luminescent as the moon itself.

Her mouth pressed against his ear, whispering the sweet words of her instruction. *Bring the people to me. Teach them not to forget, and in return for vengeance, I will protect them.*

Alma was breathless thinking about it. He knew now what Belicia was asking him to do. Despite her death, he could make her live on. In death, she had become a symbol of the moon, a symbol of sacrifice. He would make her the symbol of a warrior. He would avenge her death once and for all, and there was only one place to do it. The temple.

Alma rose from the table and walked back to his bedchamber where Sara still slept peacefully. He put on his hooded robe and sandals. He knew the first place he must go to put his plan into action.

He looked at Sara's sleeping form for a moment, then, deciding not to wake her, left his new home. The village was quiet as Alma walked through the dark, empty streets. The moon hung as a half circle, lighting his way. But even if it had been cloudy, Alma would have found his way easily—the roads had become so familiar to him over the past months.

He avoided the next village, Cuello, and walked around the homes, through the crop fields. Then he joined the next road leading to another village, Piedra, but he bypassed the third village as well until he reached the path that turned uphill toward a secluded hamlet called Chiapa, which sat atop a hillside. Here lived a group of natives, a people known for mining, who had lived near Zarahemla before the Nephites arrived. They were rarely involved in the goings on in Zarahemla, although many of their women had intermarried with the Nephites. They were a quiet people, fiercely proud of their handiwork. They appeared in the city only during market day to display their jewelry and other goods. Alma had commissioned a merchant named Teoti to replicate the jade necklace that Belicia had given him on her deathbed. Each man on his council, as well as many of the villagers, now wore the half-moon necklace.

And it was here that Alma would commission an important project with Teoti—a man who had proved to be trustworthy.

The night had lessened its hold upon the land, but Alma didn't think he'd find Teoti awake quite yet. His hut was dark, and there were no signs of activity. He knew even without him arriving so early, the merchant would be up soon.

Knocking on the door, he waited only a couple of moments for the wizened man to crack open the door, a dagger in his hand.

Alma greeted him and removed his hood.

Teoti nodded, recognizing the visitor, and shuffled outside. The moonlight cast irregular shadows on the merchant's face, making him look fierce, but his eyes were welcoming and curious.

Alma towered over the small man, although Teoti was a warrior in his own right. He'd described battles fought in his youth and had pointed teeth—although they were mostly missing from one skirmish or other.

Alma put a hand on Teoti's wiry shoulder, then leaned forward, whispering his request. Alma felt that his request was almost too sacred to be spoken aloud. Teoti nodded adamantly, as if it were a natural thing to be awakened so early in the morning with a strange request. Alma handed over a pouch containing silver onties, then stepped back.

Teoti weighed the bag in his hand, then grinned. "Come back in one day. I will have the design for you."

"Thank you," Alma said with a short bow.

"Praise be to the goddess Bel," Teoti said, then raised a hand in farewell and disappeared inside.

Alma looked up at the hovering moon. The goddess Bel. It was perfect. Belicia would not be forgotten. Her words would be etched in stone and her image soon revered by all. With a sacrifice made in her memory, she would watch over him and his people.

CHAPTER 14

The Lord preserveth all them that love him: but all the wicked will he destroy.
—Psalm 145:20

Alma the Younger

"With this seal," Alma said, holding up the high priest seal stolen from his father's house, "We can infiltrate any church in any village, including the main city churches of Zarahemla."

The heads of the council members nodded in agreement.

Alma turned his pointed gaze to Kaman. The festivities of the week had wound down late the previous night, and now the council met in their first official gathering. It had been an eventful week. Gifts of all kinds had been delivered to Alma's new home hourly, sometimes several in an hour, not only from their own village, but from people in surrounding villages who wanted to join in Alma's cause of freedom from King Mosiah's religious edicts.

Alma's wardrobe was now stocked with the finest cloth in Zarahemla, ranging from robes, to fur capes, to several headdresses. He had rows of necklaces and nearly a dozen jeweled rings.

Still, Alma wore little to betray the extravagance in his wardrobe. He did not want to draw undue attention as he traveled about the land or draw notice to his high-ranking status. Wherever he went, he wore the half moon jade necklace that Belicia had given him concealed beneath his robes.

Inside the Isidro village, he let the splendor show, knowing it made the villagers proud, especially when they could pick out something they had given him. It was amazing that these poor citizens had such luxurious items, but it was mainly because they had seen better days, and now they were not able to trade in their luxury goods for food or sturdy clothing due to the tensions.

The king's sons had spent a couple of nights at Alma's new home already, now that his home was quite a bit more lavish than his old hut. The judgment hall was a two-story building with several bedchambers housed on the upper floor. The main floor consisted of a gathering room, a large cooking room, and Alma's bedchamber.

Enticing aromas drifted into the council room. Kaman had arranged for female servants to provide the food for the judgment hall, now renamed the "chief's house."

"Step one is to infiltrate their congregations and gain their trust," Alma said. "Step two will be to set the traps."

The men on the council looked at him with interest as Alma continued. "Just as I set a trap for a wild boar or a wild turkey, we must proceed with stealth. As we gain information from the congregations, we will take our final revenge for Belicia—our goddess Bel—as she has instructed."

The men knew of Alma's dream and of Belicia's wishes for the village. At the mention of her name, they all lifted the jade necklaces to their lips.

"Excellent!" Kaman declared, rubbing his hands together, a grin spreading on his face.

"Ammon has brought us sheaves of skins for writing on from the king's own temple so that nothing will be suspected." Alma held up a sheaf of skin to demonstrate. "All of you will carry your false baptism records with you to your new congregations. We will station two men per area. You will each formulate a story of how you arrived in Zarahemla and were recently baptized by the high priest into the Church. The members will be eager to fill you in on every detail about their lives and the lives of their members. Your intrusive questions about Church activity will not be suspect."

Jacob, who sat nearest Alma asked, "How will we infiltrate Limhi's congregation?"

"Aaron and Ammon will handle that area. Since Aaron is betrothed to Limhi's daughter, it will seem natural that he start attending her father's Sabbath services."

Aaron nodded, a proud smile on his face.

"Do you think Limhi ordered the tavern burned, then?" Kaman broke in.

Aaron shook his head slowly. "It's possible, but Limhi is less likely to cross the king." Chuckles echoed around the council. "But his oldest son . . . I have never cared for him."

"Nehem?" Omner and Himni spoke at once, looking at Aaron in surprise. "But Cassia—" Himni started.

"It doesn't matter his connection to our family," Aaron broke in, his tone suddenly fierce. "Alma's work is more important."

Omner fell quiet, nodding, but Himni said, "What will Cassia think?"

No one answered.

The next two hours were spent with Alma forging Church documents and making assignments for each man.

"We will meet here every three days to report our findings," Alma said. "If you have urgent news, report it immediately. We have two weeks, then we'll start the next segment. Stay careful and smart." He glanced down at the leather armband he wore. "For now, keep these hidden from public view. If you see or hear of a brave deed by a villager, award an armband. The more of the armbands we distribute, the stronger our cause will grow. Each man will begin to feel that he is part of something larger than himself."

The council adjourned, and Alma called for the supper to be brought in. He was pleased to see Sara among the servers. Although he'd chided her in the past for acting as a servant instead of a guest, he was getting used to her presence and found it comforting. Not that she spent every night at his home, and he often wondered where she went when she left, but he wouldn't worry about that now. Today she was here, with him.

Sara set a platter of steamed vegetables and maize in front of Alma, her gaze lingering on him. He smiled and she leaned close. "Tonight my ladies have a new dance to perform."

"By all means, invite them here," Alma said. "I'll have plenty of guests to entertain." He looked around at his council, and the men nodded eagerly at the suggestion.

"Very well," Sara said, slowly moving away, her flowery plumeria scent still lingering, even after she'd returned to the cooking room.

* * *

Alma woke in the dark to pounding on his door. "Come in!" he shouted, but the pounding continued. He staggered to his feet, nearly tripping over another body. For a moment he wondered if he was being robbed and wondered where his servants were. Then he remembered that the king's sons had spent the night in his home, and after the dancing, he'd sent the servants home. Conveniently, his friends were still sleeping. He wondered for an instant why they hadn't gone to bed in the other rooms but had sprawled in the main hall. It was too dark to tell, but he wouldn't be surprised if there were a few women scattered among the sleeping men.

He crossed to the door and flung it open. Moonlight lit up the man on his doorstep. "Kaman, what do you want?"

"I have news for you," Kaman said, grinning.

"I was sleeping, you fool. Save it till morning," Alma said, turning away and swinging the door shut in the man's face.

But Kaman put his foot on the threshold, stopping the door. "This can't wait."

Alma let out a sigh of frustration that turned into a yawn. "Come in."

Kaman peered inside. "Who's your company?"

"Some from the council, plus a few others—"

"This is private."

Alma's irritation rose. "All right, let's go out back." He followed Kaman outside and around the house. Alma stopped at the far side of the elaborate garden and folded his arms. "Out with it."

"We've avenged Belicia once and for all," Kaman announced in a proud voice.

Alma rubbed his neck. If he was dreaming, he'd better wake soon. "What do you mean?"

"We took Aaron's suggestion to investigate Nehem. We asked some trusted men about him. He was the one who ordered the tavern to be burned."

"Are you sure?"

"Oh yes, several have confirmed it, and we have a letter Nehem wrote with orders," Kaman said. "And there's more. He's recommended a death sentence to be placed on my and Jacob's heads. If we're caught again, no prison sentence for us. Immediate death."

Alma wasn't entirely surprised about the death sentence, but he felt angry at the thought of Nehem behind the attacks. He thought of Cassia—she certainly wouldn't approve of reacting in such a violent manner. He wondered if she knew what her betrothed was up to.

"Swear to me that you will not tell a soul what I am about to reveal."

Alma stared at Kaman's triumphant face. "What did you do?"

"Slew him."

Alma felt as if he'd been punched in the stomach. "What? Wh—who?"

"Nehem. He's gone. We won't have to worry about him anymore," Kaman said. "Our taverns are safe—his followers will be too frightened to retaliate now that we know their names. Aaron was hesitant about us having enough proof, but Nehem's letter confirmed otherwise."

Alma turned away from Kaman, trying to comprehend the horrible confession. He clenched his hands, anger and disbelief and confusion colliding in his head, then he looked at Kaman. "Tell. Me. What. Happened."

"Can you keep the secret until your grave?" Kaman asked, his face twisted into a confident smile.

Alma had to force himself not to slam his fist into the man's face. "Yes," he hissed. "Get on with it!"

Kaman looked to the left and right in darkness, then lowered his voice. "Upon my blood and your blood, you can never reveal what I am about to tell you."

Alma stared at him. "I will not."

"Jacob and I traveled to his home tonight," Kaman said in a low voice. "Jacob has a friend who used to work as a servant in

Limhi's home, so he sketched us a map of the place—the courtyards, bedchambers. As for the correct bedchamber, he had to presume a little, but he gave us a good description so that we could check before we struck. We wanted to speed things up a little—and hoped that Aaron wouldn't mind that we took care of Nehem."

Alma was dumbfounded. This was not the vengeance Belicia had asked for. It was supposed to take place at the temple . . . He wished he could stop Kaman from speaking, hoping it was a terrible dream. But the cool wind touching his skin and the steady light of the moon told him this was all too real.

"I was scared, mind you," Kaman continued, with a nervous chuckle. "I worried that he might awake and put up a fight. We both brought our daggers you gave us. You know the ones Ammon brought for every council member?" Kaman peered around Alma. "Is he inside? I need to tell him what excellent workmanship he does; I've never seen anything like—"

Alma grabbed Kaman's arm, squeezing. "Did you stab Nehem? Tell me."

Kaman's eyes widened in surprise. "We both went for him at the same time. I got his chest, and Jacob his throat—brilliant on Jacob's part, since the man might have cried out."

Alma released Kaman's arm and felt rage pump through him. Image after image pulsed through his mind as he imagined the gruesome scene, the discovery of Nehem's body by Limhi, then the news yet to be delivered to Cassia and her family. She would be devastated.

"It was unsettling to kill a man," Kaman said. "We fled the house and only set off a few dogs barking. The only problem is that Jacob dropped his dagger somewhere outside. We'll have to get his friend to search for us." When Alma didn't respond, Kaman said, "Don't worry, no one will know about this but us."

Alma shook his head, anger and reason blending together. Cassia would be heartbroken. Her betrothed had just lost his life. No doubt the king would make every effort to discover the murderer, and the dagger could easily be traced back to Ammon. More than that, Kaman had no right to act so impulsively without consulting him first. Alma clenched his right hand and drove it into Kaman's face. The man stumbled back, then hit the ground, unconscious.

Alma sprinted to the front of his home and burst through the door. "Wake up!" he shouted. "Wake up!" He shook the brothers awake, slapping Omner's face, because he was the most reluctant to stir. He shooed out the other men and women, forcing them to stumble back to their homes in the dark.

When the last house guest disappeared, he turned to the king's sons. "We need to get out of here, now!" He looked at the bleary-eyed faces and spilled out Kaman's story. Their expressions went from shock to anger, then fear.

Ammon reached for his dagger that he kept in his waistband at all times. "I'll take care of Kaman right now."

"No," Alma said. "That makes you no better than he is. He thought he was helping me—avenging Belicia's death. He has the gall to believe there would be no retaliation." His laugh was bitter. "I'll deal with him later, but for now, each of you needs to be in your own beds at the palace. When your father learns of this, he needs to know that his sons were at home asleep all night."

Aaron nodded. "Let's get out of here."

But Ammon's face was still red with anger. "Where's Kaman?"

Alma put a hand on his shoulder, restraining him. "Leave, Ammon. Now! I'll take care of Kaman. Dawn is in a few hours. Nehem's body may have already been discovered."

Aaron tugged at his brother's arm, but Ammon resisted. "You tell him . . . you tell Kaman that I want every knife back before the sun sets again. If one word is spoken of this to *anyone,* I'll personally end his life."

Alma shoved Ammon out of the door, whispering "Run!" to the brothers.

When they were gone, he turned to survey the inside of his home, the luxurious fur rugs, his prized skins, the cushions made of fine linens and intricate embroidery. Was there anything to link him to Nehem's murder? The daggers—if one was found on Limhi's property and similar ones were found in Alma's home, the link would be obvious.

But how will they know to look here? It wouldn't take but a drunken confession or two. He couldn't take the risk.

He crossed the room to the wall that housed a display of finely crafted weapons—most of them gifts but several made by Ammon's own hand.

He took all of the daggers from the shelves and dropped them into a waterskin hanging in the cooking room. Fear pulsed through his veins as he cleared them out. Anger. Grief.

Cassia—what will she think of Nehem's murder? Who will tell her? How will she find out?

The questions tumbled inside Alma's head until he could no longer stand it. He could visualize Cassia's tears, her sorrow. He leaned against the wall and sank to the floor, pulling up his knees to his chest.

There was no safety in the village of Isidro anymore for Kaman or Jacob. Alma had to get them out—hide them somewhere.

Alma scanned the room, plotting what he could use to bribe another village to hide his friends. He would have to tread carefully—ears and eyes were everywhere. He grabbed a bag of silver onties he kept hidden in a basket of grain in the cooking room, then he threw on his cloak and went into the back courtyard. Kaman was gone. Alma cursed and walked around the perimeter of his home, hurrying to Kaman's place. Even in the moonlight, the renovations on the modest hut were obvious. Since Kaman had joined the council, it seemed the villagers had treated him well.

Alma knocked on the front door as loudly as he dared. It was opened immediately by Kaman, Eden standing behind him. She scurried to the corner as Alma strode into the room. It was obvious she knew where the welt on her husband's face had come from.

"We have to get you out of here," Alma growled.

Kaman looked over at Eden, the fear in his eyes matching hers. He touched the side of his face gingerly, glancing at his wife. "Very well."

Eden covered her mouth with a small gasp. He shook his head, as if warning her, and they quickly embraced.

Her hands trembled as she released him. She whispered something to him, but he shook his head again and grabbed his outer robe. He followed Alma out the door without another word.

The two men walked to Jacob's house nearby. Again, Alma knocked as loudly as he dared, then entered the hut. Jacob was on his way out of his bedchamber by the time they bypassed the main room, his knife drawn, eyes huge.

"You're coming with us," Alma said.

Jacob disappeared into his bedchamber for a second to speak to his wife, then he was out again, following behind Alma and Kaman as they stepped outside.

The night had just begun to soften as the three men left the village and traveled along the narrow road that wound through the trees to the next village. Alma urged Kaman and Jacob faster until all three ran at a steady pace.

"Why are you so upset, Alma?" Kaman asked, his voice coming in gasps. "I thought you'd be pleased. We've had our revenge. Belicia can now rest in peace."

"You don't understand," Alma said, looking sideways at the two scruffy men. "The revenge was to take place at the temple. Killing Nehem might thwart our bigger plans. It's only a matter of time that your deed will be linked back to me."

Kaman narrowed his eyes, pushing his body to keep up with Alma's longer stride. "You know that we won't let anything happen to you."

Alma came to an abrupt stop, followed by Jacob and Kaman, confusion in both men's eyes.

"Nehem was betrothed to someone I used to know very well—in fact, we almost became betrothed ourselves."

Jacob's expression was incredulous. "But . . . Nehem is betrothed to the king's daughter—"

"Who *are* you, Alma?" Kaman said. "We have respected your privacy, but if you knew the king's daughter—and the king's sons hearken to your every request . . ."

Alma took a deep breath and looked away. These men would figure it out soon enough—and each of them owed him their very lives, especially now. If he could trust anyone, it would be them. "I am the high priest's son."

Kaman opened his mouth to speak, but nothing came out.

Jacob shook his head slowly. "That . . . that explains why you are so learned."

Alma's shoulders sagged. "Don't you see? Leaving Ammon's knife at Limhi's homestead will link the death to Ammon and then to me."

"And this girl, the king's daughter—you still care for her," Kaman said, peering into Alma's eyes.

He turned away, pain flooding through him. "It was a long time ago." He couldn't let himself drown in regret. He had comrades to hide away and a village that depended on him. And he had a movement to organize—one that would free the people of Zarahemla from religious and economic oppression.

He looked at Kaman and Jacob, seeing fierce loyalty in their eyes, and straightened his shoulders. "What's done is done. There's no turning back now. Let's go, my friends." Alma started running again, followed by the two men. With each pounding step that reverberated through his body, Alma let his heart and mind close with each beat until he was able to push all thoughts of Cassia out of his mind.

They passed along the outskirts of the next village, avoiding the homes, and only alerting a few flocks of sleepy turkeys. The path turned uphill toward a secluded village, where Alma's friend Teoti lived.

As the three men entered the village of Chiapa, the sky had just begun to lighten with the new day. Soon, Nehem's body would be discovered and the alarm would sound throughout Limhi's home. Haste mattered.

Although it was still early, Alma wasn't surprised to see smoke rising from behind the merchant's house. These people were up early and working late, day in and day out. Alma led Jacob and Kaman around the hut.

Teoti was bent over a low rock formation, fanning the flames that crackled in the center with a bellows. Even though Alma hadn't made a sound, Teoti turned abruptly, his hand at his waist as if he were about to reach for a dagger.

But when he recognized his visitor, his aged face relaxed.

Teoti hurried forward, clasping Alma's hand and bowing. "Welcome, welcome," he said, his smile showing several gaps in his teeth. He raised his thin eyebrows as he surveyed Kaman and Jacob. "Come, the tea is almost ready."

The man had a metal pot perched over the flames, not some blacksmithing instrument. The merchant busied himself with collecting wooden cups that were stacked on a nearby rock. One he shook, depositing a bug onto the ground.

"Very good," Teoti muttered as he dropped dried lemon leaves into the cups, then poured hot water over them.

As the men settled around the fire, the merchant eyed Alma eagerly, his sharp eyes taking in the jade necklace about his throat. "You came for more necklaces?"

"No," Alma said. "But my friends here wear the necklaces too."

Kaman and Jacob moved their robes so that the merchant could see their jade pieces.

Alma bid his time, taking several sips of tea before speaking again. "These are important men in my village, but there are some who wish to see them dead."

Teoti's eyes widened.

Alma leaned forward, staring at the merchant. "I need them to stay here, hidden, for a while. We will pay well."

The merchant looked up at the pale sky and muttered something that sounded like a prayer. Then he met Alma's gaze again. "How much?"

From his cloak, Alma withdrew the bag of coins and handed them over.

The merchant peered inside, then hefted the bag. "Very good." His gaze flitted over to Kaman and Jacob as if to assess them. "What did they do?"

Alma put a finger to his lips. "We need to protect you from any information. The less you know, the better off you'll be. If anyone comes to your village asking about them, you must send them away."

"Agreed," Teoti said, again weighing the bag in his hand.

"When I come to fetch them, I'll bring you another bag of coins," Alma said.

The merchant's eyes crinkled as he smiled. He rose and patted Alma on the shoulder. "Very good. This will be our secret."

Alma nodded, then looked at Kaman and Jacob, who both looked resigned to their new fate as they sipped their lemon tea.

CHAPTER 15

. . . And all these things were done in secret.
—Moses 5:30

Cassia

Cassia couldn't sleep. Her dreams were uneasy somehow, and she kept waking throughout the night. Later, she heard shuffling in the corridor. When she peeked into the hallway, she saw the disappearing forms of her brothers enter their rooms. They'd been out again.

Finally, as the night changed from black to deep purple, she gave up and climbed out of bed, pulling a robe across her shoulders. She walked to the window and peered outside. Through the copse of trees outside her bedchamber was the main plaza. It was early yet, and no one milled about. The smoke from the various cooking fires rose lazily against the sky. Most in the city of Zarahemla awoke at first light. Wives prepared meals of hot maize cakes before their husbands left for the day to work in the fields or around the city. Just beyond the plaza was the marketplace. The first vendors had likely arrived, hoping to catch the earliest customers.

Cassia propped her elbows on her windowsill and rested her chin on her hands. This afternoon Nehem would be coming to spend time with her, and they'd make some final arrangements for the wedding. Then tomorrow, she'd attend the first fitting for her wedding clothing. She and her mother had already started embroidering the veil. To anyone outside of the palace, she seemed to have a perfect life—a handsome man eagerly betrothed to her; a royal family bent on making her happy; and youthful, good health.

So why do I feel unsettled? She could no longer blame Alma for any misgivings she might have about her coming marriage—in fact, she sometimes wondered if he had really wanted to marry her at all. Wouldn't he have tried harder? It seemed that with the distance and the passage of time, she had let her memory of them together fade bit by bit. At least he didn't creep into her thoughts each moment of the day anymore, and he wasn't the last thing she thought of before falling asleep. Well, not every night.

Cassia breathed out a sigh. Working on her wedding clothing was another step in the process of fully committing herself to Nehem. She brought a hand to her lips and pressed against the warmth, thinking of saying good-bye to Nehem the night before. He had become more and more persistent in his affections, and for the most part, Cassia had resisted.

"When are you going to kiss me?" he'd asked. "The betrothal law states that we are as good as married." His eyes twinkled. "Come now, wife, kiss your husband."

She'd laughed, but the amusement turned serious in Nehem's eyes. "We'll be married soon enough," she said.

The lightheartedness returned to his gaze, and he'd taken her hand. Bringing it slowly to his lips, he said, "You are beautiful."

"I'm all angles," she protested.

"You're perfect," Nehem said, kissing her hand. "And I have a special gift for you."

"Another attempt to steal a kiss?"

He chuckled. "That would be special too, but I have something else—I'll bring it tomorrow. But we need to be alone." He reached out, touching her cheek.

"All right," she said, allowing his hand to linger on her face. "I'm available in the afternoon. My father will be in council, and my mother will be visiting with a vendor about designing my wedding clothes."

"Tomorrow then." He dropped his hand and took a step back, bowing. Then he winked. He'd left quickly after that, leaving Cassia curious about the gift. It was probably a necklace, or perhaps a pretty scarf, but still she was curious.

Without realizing it, a smile had crept to her lips as she looked out the window. Nehem was a sweet man, and his enthusiasm contagious. Maybe she could talk him into escorting her to the market today—she hadn't been recently. Her father forbade all the women of the household from traveling outside the palace grounds alone, and she and her mother weren't allowed unattended near the market. Unrest had broken out in the city once again between the Church and the unbelievers. Her father was holding another large council today to try to find more solutions.

The worry brought Alma to mind again, but Cassia quickly pushed all thoughts of him away. She knew she had loved him, but she had been a girl. As a woman, she could only allow herself to care for him as a friend of the family. If she was to be a faithfully married woman, she must let memories of Alma fade and not worry about his well-being except as a friend.

Her languishing gaze out the window was distracted by movement in the plaza below. She studied a figure hurrying across the open space, trying to decipher who it might be. Was it someone she knew? A soldier? A priest? Maybe even one of her brothers? But no, they'd been out all hours of the night, and most mornings didn't even appear for the meal. Many an argument had taken place among the men of her family, especially between Ammon and her father. But the king was so busy with quelling the unbeliever rebellions that kept cropping up, he often gave his errant sons a quick dismissal.

The figure drew closer, nearly running now. The man wore a plain robe, so he was likely not a priest, but perhaps a merchant who'd had his belongings vandalized overnight. Then Cassia recognized the woven design on the man's tunic. He was from the house of Limhi. She studied him. He seemed familiar, but she wasn't sure if he was a servant. Possibly one of Limhi's guards.

The man ascended the steps of the palace, taking them two at a time. His expression came into plain view, and Cassia was dismayed to see that he was indeed distressed. *Has something happened to Limhi?* she wondered.

The palace guards met him at the top of the steps, and Cassia wished she could overhear their rapid conversation. Seconds later, the guards turned and rushed into the palace entrance with the man.

Cassia backed away from the window, her heart pounding. To awake the king before his usual hour meant this was a serious matter indeed. She crossed the room and selected one of her robes, then pulled it on. As she slipped out her bedchamber door, her pulse quickened. This was one of the times she felt compassionate for her father's position as king of Zarahamela. He was his people's servant, and it was a constant sacrifice.

When Cassia reached the throne room, she was surprised to see it empty. The two heavy doors stood open, guards stationed on either side as usual, but no one was in the room. The guards nodded to her, but she didn't dare ask them about the early-morning visitor. Cassia made her way to her father's private quarters. If the visitor had been taken there, he must be a personal friend of her father, or something serious had happened to Limhi.

She hurried down the long hallway to her father's chambers. The guard who was posted there straightened as he saw Cassia coming toward him.

"Is someone with my father?" Cassia asked.

"Yes," the guard said. "I don't think he'll be long."

"Do you know who he is?"

"A man from Limhi's household."

"What's happened?" she asked.

The guard shook his head. "I have not yet been informed."

Cassia wanted to ask more questions, but the guard was right—he wouldn't be told anything before the king himself. Not wanting to interrupt, she waited in the hall. The guard remained quiet, and Cassia strained to listen for any inflection of voices but heard nothing.

The minutes seemed to pass agonizingly slow, and Cassia paced the hallway, staying close to the doors of her father's chamber. Then the door opened, and her mother stepped out.

"Cassia?"

She stared at her mother—the queen's face was pale, and she obviously hadn't attended to her dressing routine yet. She wore a morning robe carelessly pulled across her shoulders, and her hair hung long and unkempt over her shoulders.

"Mother, what's happened? Is it Limhi?"

The queen hurried to Cassia and took her hands. "How did you—?"

"I saw Limhi's man come into the palace."

Her mother's mouth pinched together, and Cassia rushed to explain, but the queen interrupted. "Come with me, my dear," the queen said, her voice cracking.

Cassia looked sharply at her mother, dread flooding through her. By the way her mother was acting, the news couldn't be good. "What's wrong?"

"Come," her mother whispered, her eyes filling with tears as she gripped Cassia's hand and pulled her toward the king's chambers. When she pushed open the door, the king turned, his eyes widening when he saw Cassia.

"You've told her?" he asked.

"Not yet," her mother said. "She was waiting in the hallway—she saw Magog arrive."

In response, Limhi's guard rose from his sitting position near the fireplace. His narrow face was pale and blotchy, his eyes reddened.

"Cassia," her father said, drawing her attention. "Come here."

Her legs felt weak. Why did her father's voice sound so foreboding—and why was Limhi's guard crying?

Cassia obediently walked toward her father's outstretched hands and let them grasp hers. She tried to focus on his face but found her eyes starting to blur. Why was *she* crying? She hadn't even heard any news, yet her heart knew it was grievous.

"Father?" she whispered.

Her father brought one hand to her cheek and touched it softly, his gaze tender and sad. "It's Nehem."

Cassia stopped breathing. Her body felt cold all over as alarm jolted through her.

"Nehem has . . . been found dead . . ." her father said.

In the back of her mind, Cassia heard Limhi's guard groan softly and someone else let out a quiet sob. Her mother? *Me.*

Cassia realized she had choked on a sob, and her chest started to take in another breath, but it was stuttered, gasping.

She pulled from her father and turned to look at her mother. The queen had a hand over her mouth, tears spilling onto her cheeks.

"Is this true?" Cassia said in a trembling voice, looking at Limhi's guard. The man hung his head and buried his face in his hands.

She whirled around to face her father. "What happened? *How?*"

"He . . ." The king looked away for an instant, his face twisted in pain. Then his voice fell to a whisper. "He was slain in his bed."

Cassia staggered backward, trying to comprehend. *Nehem. Slain?* Her legs crumpled beneath her, and she sank to the floor. She wrapped her arms about her torso, trying to stop the room from spinning, but it was useless. The spinning escalated, clenching her stomach, her chest, until she had to gasp for air.

Someone knelt next to her, but Cassia shook off the hands and covered her ears to block out the horrible sound that wouldn't leave her head. *Stop sobbing,* she wanted to shout at her mother. *Stop screaming!* Then she realized that it wasn't her mother.

Cassia's throat was raw in a matter of seconds, but she couldn't stop screaming. "No!" she cried out over and over. Her mother tried to hold her, but she fought against her grasp. Then stronger arms lifted her from the ground, and she struggled against them in vain. Soon she was lying in a bed, her mother next to her, holding her.

Her father's voice boomed in the background, but Cassia couldn't understand what he was saying. No matter which way she turned or how loud she screamed out, she couldn't get the words out of her mind. *Nehem. Slain in his bed.*

It couldn't be true. She wouldn't let it. She'd wake up from this horrible dream. She opened her eyes for a moment, breathing deeply, and gazed upward at the ceiling. She was in her parents' bedchamber. Her mother's cool hands were stroking her forehead, her face, her cheeks.

It wasn't true; she couldn't believe it. *Nehem is alive. He's coming for me this afternoon.* Cassia sprang away from her mother and leapt off the bed, looking around wildly. Her father was in the room, and he started for her, but she held up her hands to ward him off. "He's coming today, this afternoon. He has a gift for me," Cassia said, her voice hoarse. "He promised. He's coming this afternoon . . . with a special gift."

"Cassia," her father said, reaching her and pulling her into his arms. "I'm so sorry."

"No," she said, pushing against the king's broad chest. "He's coming today. He has a gift for me."

Her father's hold tightened around her.

"He promised!" Cassia screamed.

"I know. I know," her father said, his shoulders shaking as he joined her sobbing.

* * *

"Drink this," her mother had said, then forced the cool liquid down her throat.

From the first taste, Cassia knew the wine contained a powerful elixir. But she welcomed it and its dulling effect on the pain that wracked her whole body.

The pain hadn't lessened, but when the elixir wore off, Cassia saw that it was late afternoon. The long shadows in her parents' bedchamber told her that she'd spent the morning asleep. Her eyes were open now, but she still hadn't tried to move. She wondered what it would feel like if her body could ever experience more pain than it did right now. Every part of her felt weighed down, as if she were being slowly crushed.

Her mind was clear, though. It was as if her body were detached, experiencing physical trauma, while her thoughts raced through the past weeks. Meeting Nehem at the banquet for the first time, Nehem telling her she was beautiful, Nehem kissing her hand, Nehem tasting the honeyed delicacies she'd made for him, Nehem laughing at her, Nehem asking for her hand in marriage, Nehem telling her he loved her.

The pain increased.

But Cassia couldn't speak or make a sound. She'd screamed herself silent. After a few more minutes, she moved her hand, testing . . . The movement attracted the attention of her mother, who, Cassia just realized, was next to her on the bed.

"Oh, my dear," the queen whispered, scooting closer and touching her shoulder.

Cassia flinched at the touch, then closed her eyes. "What happened?" she croaked out.

Her mother reached for her hand. More pain. "They aren't sure yet. They are looking for . . . who might have done this to Nehem."

Her mother's voice broke off, and Cassia opened her eyes and turned her head. The queen's eyes were red and swollen as if she'd spent the past several hours weeping while Cassia slept.

Cassia pulled her hand away and sat up in the bed, her body groaning with the effort. Her stomach felt weak and nauseated, as if she'd been fasting for days, and it protested at the movement. She took a deep, shaky breath. "I must see him."

Her mother sat up in an instant, her eyes wide. "No, my dear, he—"

"Mother," Cassia said, her voice stronger now. "I must tell him . . ."

That I was ready to devote myself to you. I was ready to love you, and only you. To forsake all else for you and become your faithful wife.

"I must tell him good-bye."

Her mother's arms went around Cassia. "There will be a ceremony—"

"Today, Mother," Cassia said. "Before they take his . . . him . . . away."

The queen was silent for several minutes as she held onto Cassia tightly. Then she said, "I will come with you."

Cassia moved from the bed and stood, her legs shaky. She tried to focus on the objects in the room, but her head pounded fiercely. Regardless, she crossed the room to the basin stand. There she splashed water on her face and, with trembling hands, re-plaited her hair.

Her mother ordered a servant to bring Cassia a fresh tunic. When the servant returned, Cassia dressed and joined her mother.

They walked into the adjoining room. Several guards waited at the entrance to the hall, ready to aid the women. "We will travel to Limhi's home to pay our respects. Please inform my husband."

The two women waited as a guard took the message to the king. He returned in a few moments. "The king says he will accompany you."

A short time later, Cassia stepped out of the palace, flanked by her mother and father, surrounded by a dozen royal soldiers.

"Where are my brothers?" Cassia asked her father as they descended the steps.

"They are still in the council, making plans to capture the assassin."

"Do they have any idea who it might have been?"

King Mosiah's face was like stone. "None. It may be linked to a series of recent violent activities."

"But why would Nehem be a target?" Cassia pressed.

The king shook his head slightly, then lowered his voice. "Nehem was bold in his words of revulsion concerning the tactics of the unbelievers."

"Nehem was passionate about what he believed in," she said. "Why would he be killed for that?"

"Dear," the king said, his arm linking through hers, "there was nothing wrong with Nehem's passion. He said what most of us believed, but we fear he acted too boldly to the wrong people." He shook his head. "I should have provided more protection for Limhi's household."

"But Limhi has his own guards. How did the man get past those soldiers?"

The king let out a frustrated breath. "We are working on discovering that. All I can assume for now is that one of the guards, or a member of Limhi's household, betrayed Nehem."

Cassia fell silent. It made sense, horrible as it was. Someone within the trusted household had to have allowed the killer inside. And who outside of Nehem's inner circle of friends knew about his stringent beliefs? As they crossed the plaza in the broad daylight and passed the teeming market street, it was difficult to imagine that Nehem was truly gone. Everyone around them seemed to act no different. The citizens of Zarahemla bowed out of the way as the procession moved down the market street then along the wide river. Limhi's stately home was sprawled just across the first bridge.

Cassia kept her gaze lowered but alert for anyone who looked suspicious. For a moment she wondered if it was possible to tell by looking at someone whether they were a thief or murderer. Would it appear in their eyes, their mannerisms? Cassia could only guess, but the closer they drew to Limhi's home, the colder she felt.

They crossed the bridge, and Cassia caught sight of the river beneath. Its water looked dark and murky today, and she speculated whether the river had been a witness to the man who had taken Nehem's life.

When Limhi's home came into view, the weight returned twofold to Cassia's heart. She remembered Nehem's words—how he wanted to take her through his home. And now she would see it without him.

Several men exited the house as they approached. A couple of guards and two men she recognized—Alma the high priest and another priest named Helam. When she was a child, Helam had intimidated her with his height and the mass of scars that ran along his face, neck, and arms. But her brothers hadn't been afraid, and she took their lead, soon learning that he was a gentle man behind his frightening appearance. As she grew older, she learned that he'd been badly burned as a child. And even more poignant, his brother, the prophet Abinadi, had been put to death by fire.

Now, looking at Helam and his stoic face, Cassia took strength from his strong presence. Next to him, Alma looked as if he'd aged ten years. His usually commanding presence had faded somehow. His eyes were shadowed, and his mouth was pulled into a firm line as he walked toward them. He'd probably been awakened early this morning with the terrible news.

Alma and Helam greeted the king in hushed tones and somberly welcomed the women.

Alma's gaze moved to Cassia, and he held out a hand to her. She took a deep, stuttered breath and took his hand, finding it cool to the touch. "We are sorry for your loss," he said.

She stood there for a moment, her throat too tight to speak. Alma released her hand and motioned for her to follow him inside.

She walked behind Alma, and Helam squeezed her arm as she passed by him, his gaze deep with compassion.

It was the moment that Cassia stepped inside that she realized her grief must be but a fraction of Limhi's family's. Ilana and her parents were nowhere to be seen, but Cassia felt the emptiness and sorrow pierce her as if the stately walls were in mourning.

"This way," Alma said, steering her by the elbow along a corridor, past the main hall. Everything was so quiet. Cassia had expected people rushing around, or the sound of wailing disturbing the silence. But the quiet made the pain even deeper.

They walked, passing several chambers, when, finally, Alma slowed. They'd entered a large room that looked like an indoor garden. Small trees, plants, and even flowers grew beneath a roof. The air was moist and fragrant. It was a place that Cassia could picture Nehem showing off with flair.

But in the middle of the indoor courtyard was a table, and upon the table . . . Nehem's shrouded form. Cassia brought a hand to her mouth, staring at the linen drape that covered him. On the other side of the table, a man rose, and Cassia recognized his bearded face. He was one of the healers she'd seen at the palace from time to time. He bowed with reverence to his guests then moved away from the shroud.

The king turned to the guards. "You may wait outside now."

Noiselessly, the guards left the room, but Cassia was already walking forward. No one stopped her. She sensed her mother and father behind her, but she only saw the body that lay beneath the linen drape. Stopping close to the table, she looked down at the outline of Nehem's body. Her breathing turned rapid as she lifted her hand and placed it on the edge of his shoulder. Then her knees gave way, and she knelt next to him.

She knew her parents were hovering behind her, but no one spoke. She concentrated on his chest, waiting for it to rise and fall, waiting for this all to be declared as some horrible mistake. But there was no movement.

Cassia tried to steady her breath as she raised her other hand to lift the shroud from Nehem's face. His eyes were closed as if in sleep, his lashes fanned against his round cheekbones. His face was so tranquil that Cassia expected him to turned toward her and smile, confessing that he was only teasing her. But there was no smile, and there never would be again.

Her eyes traveled to the bandage wrapped around his neck. A shudder passed through her as she realized that the wound beneath had cost him his life. She looked again at his face then raised her fingers to his cheek. His skin was cold, rigid. The touch jolted Cassia, and she knew he was not there. This body had once held her betrothed, but the real Nehem was no longer a part of it.

Tears slid down her cheeks as she rose and bent over him. She pressed her lips against his cheek, wishing with everything she had that it was warm and that his arms would wrap around her, and he'd laugh and say, "Finally, a kiss."

Someone was quietly crying behind her, Cassia realized—her mother. Just the sound of it started waves of fresh pain coursing through her body.

"Nehem, why did this happen to you?" Cassia whispered, then kissed his other cheek. Her tears dripped onto his face. Then she laid her head against his chest, sinking to her knees again. Her tears were now hot and fast, but silent. After a moment, she felt her mother's hand on her back, and she raised her head, taking a final look at Nehem. His vibrant spirit was gone, his body but a cold shell.

She stood and with trembling hands pulled the shroud up to cover his face. "Good-bye, Nehem," she whispered.

She closed her eyes and inhaled, trying to recall the life that used to be in Nehem's eyes, the energy and his presence, so different from the too-still body beneath the shroud.

Her mother's arm went around her shoulders, and Cassia leaned into her mother's embrace, moving away from Nehem. Tears filled her eyes as her father stepped forward to pay his respects. After a moment, her mother released her and went to stand by the king's side, taking his hand. Another hand touched her shoulder. Alma was there, offering a small portion of comfort as she watched her parents.

Cassia took a deep breath, but it was as if she couldn't catch enough air. Her mother approached and held out her hand, then led

Cassia out of the room into the cooler hallway. She heard the muted voices of her father and the men as she left.

She walked with her mother to the front room, where a woman stood. "Ilana," Cassia said in a whisper. She hurried to her friend's side and embraced her.

Ilana felt soft and warm as Cassia clung to her.

The two women said nothing for a long moment. Cassia wanted to offer consoling words, but the tears were falling fast again.

After a while, Ilana released Cassia and put both her hands on her cheeks. "My dear girl, I'm so glad you came."

Cassia nodded. "I—I'm sorry about your brother." Her voice cracked, and she took a steadying breath.

"We are all sorry," Ilana said, her own eyes filling with tears. "I can hardly believe it. My mother has stayed in her bedchamber since the news, and my father is out with the guards searching the grounds for a weapon . . . or any other evidence."

Cassia took Ilana's hand in hers and squeezed. The queen stepped toward them and put an arm around Ilana.

They were standing in a protective huddle when a flurry of shouting came from the front courtyard.

"They've found something," Ilana whispered, her grip tightening on Cassia.

CHAPTER 16

Hide me from the secret counsel of the wicked;
from the insurrection of the workers of iniquity.
—Psalm 64:2

Alma the Elder

Sleep had not come easy for Alma the night before, and now as he stood in the garden room watching King Mosiah and Helam discuss the slaying of Nehem, the high priest knew why.

It wasn't that he felt he had a premonition about the death of this innocent young man, but that this senseless death was another step in the escalating events as of late. It seemed retaliation was the religion being preached throughout the streets of Zarahemla. One act of foul play was returned tenfold, until . . . what? Until the people in Zarahemla declared war on each other? Alma shook his head, the weight of sorrow mixed with fear pressing against him, muddling his mind.

He had felt numb when he had received the news early that morning. His heart had been heavy for months since the disappearance of his son, and the hope had all but faded for a repentant son to return. The ancient story of the children of Israel and their exodus had grown dear to him and his wife over the past while, and he prayed this his son would turn to the Lord again and come home. It was nearly all Alma prayed for day and night. Certainly all his wife prayed for. Even more than her own safety during her own horrific trials of danger and near-death, Maia prayed for their son with each breath she took.

"I will not give up on my son," Maia had whispered to Alma the night before. "Even if I have to bring him home myself."

Alma had wrapped his arms around her, trying to soothe her. "I know. I know it's hard to live with his decisions."

And then, like every night, she fell asleep in his arms, twisting and turning as her dreams flooded her with new worries.

It seemed that each new day brought more doom—a church burned down, a village market ransacked, a baptism disrupted, precious things gone missing—and now this. The greatest fear of all. Murder. *What will be the consequences of this action?* Alma wondered. *What else will see destruction after this event?*

Acting swiftly and decisively was what the king and Helam were discussing now. Before the rumors could spread and before the murderer had a chance to make it very far, the king had to deliver consequences. But what evidence did the king have yet?

Alma knew the theories that the council members held—including Nehem, who was now silent. A hard lump formed in Alma's throat as he remembered the last meeting, only the day before, in which Nehem had suggested a group of men infiltrate the surrounding villages, acting as unbelievers. These men would spy for the king and discover who was at the heart of the rebellions. "It would be simple," Nehem had said. "We set traps that will draw out the rebels and their leaders. The rebels won't act without their leaders' direction, so we'll have to plan small attacks to fuel a reaction."

Surprisingly, the king's oldest son, Ammon, had been against Nehem's ideas. He'd replied that it would only escalate the frenzy faster than the king could muster any control over it.

At the time, Alma thought it was drastic as well, too dangerous for those involved. But now . . . he wished he would have considered Nehem's ideas more carefully.

Or had Nehem's viewpoint reached the wrong person? Perhaps the leader of the rebellion?

Alma heard a commotion coming from the direction of the hallway. An instant later, a guard burst into the room. He bowed to the startled king, then looked at Helam and Alma. "Limhi wishes to speak to the three of you. They've found something."

Alma hurried after the men as they moved out of the room and into the hallway, until they reached the main room. The women were there, even Limhi's wife, Miriam, and their daughter.

Limhi turned as they entered, but the women stared at an object on the table in the center of the room. Trying to hold back his anxiety, Alma approached the table slowly, letting the king reach it first. When he heard Mosiah's sharp intake of breath, Alma knew something was terribly wrong.

Then Alma came into view of the object. It was a knife with an ornate hilt, one small enough to be concealed in a waistband, yet long and sharp enough to take a man's life. The room was utterly silent as Alma and the king bent over the object. Then a shudder ran through Alma as he spied the brownish-red stain, undoubtedly dried blood.

Alma blinked, hardly believing his eyes—was this the weapon that had taken Nehem's life?

Next to him, the king let out a long breath. Mosiah put a trembling hand on Alma's arm, and he looked at the king in surprise. Did the king recognize the knife? Alma looked again, studying the workmanship. Slowly, the cold seeped in through his skin. He had seen such fine workmanship before—among his son's possessions. Now he understood the king's stuttered breath and tight grip. Those knives that Alma the Younger owned had been a gift . . . from the king's eldest son, Ammon.

Alma exhaled and looked around at the gathered group. The women had turned away, quietly talking among themselves. Limhi stood with his guards, directing them to return to the location where the knife was found and to continue searching.

When the guards left the room, Limhi walked over and stood across from the men at the table. King Mosiah released his grip on Alma's arm and met Limhi's gaze.

"I have only known one man capable of this type of craftsmanship," Limhi said in a slow careful voice, his gaze boring into the king's.

King Mosiah's shoulders seemed to sag. "Ammon."

The women gasped, refocusing their attention on the king. The queen stepped forward, her eyes flitting to the bloodied knife, then to her husband.

"Who did Ammon sell this knife to? He should remember, yes?"

"Yes," the king said.

Alma froze. Ammon didn't sell his knives. To anyone. Ever. In order to obtain a prized creation from the king's son, it needed to be earned or received as a gift. Ammon should not only remember who owned the knife, but he most likely knew the man well.

It took the king a moment to speak, but when he did, his gaze was steady and his shoulders regal again. "We will call for Ammon and demand an explanation. The man who has slain Nehem must be known among us, part of our inner circles. There is no other way this knife could have been obtained."

"What if it was stolen?" Ilana said, her eyes wide with fear.

"It's a possibility," the king said, his expression troubled. "But unlikely. He keeps them secure."

Ilana turned away as if the sight of the knife were unbearable. Cassia moved next to her, putting an arm around the girl.

"I need to call all of my sons together," the king said, looking at the queen.

"They were with the council when we left," the queen said. "They are certainly waiting for news like everyone else."

The king gave an almost imperceptible nod.

"Let's wrap the . . . weapon and take it to the palace," Alma said. He made eye contact with Helam, who nodded. "We'll send a messenger before us to locate them before our arrival."

"Yes," Limhi echoed. "Let's wrap the weapon." He ordered a servant to fetch a cloth. When the servant returned, Limhi stood, holding the cloth in his hand as if he'd forgotten what he wanted to do.

Gently, Alma took the cloth out of Limhi's hands, then wrapped it around the knife into a neat bundle. Gratitude filled Limhi's expression at the small service, and he looked to his wife, Miriam. "Will you come to the palace?"

Miriam shook her head. "I don't want to leave my son—" Her voice broke, and the queen quickly put her arm around her.

"I'll stay with you," the queen offered.

"I would like to come, Father," Ilana said in a quiet voice.

Limhi looked at his daughter in surprise, then nodded. "Very well."

Ilana and Cassia followed the men out.

Once they reached the palace, Alma went directly to the throne room to await the arrival of the king's sons. Limhi and Helam accompanied him, but he was surprised when the two women followed him in.

"Father Alma," Cassia said, "Could you bestow a blessing of comfort on us?"

"Of course," Alma said. He set the wrapped knife on the large table that the king used for his council meetings. Then Alma invited Helam to join him. With the help of Helam, Alma prayed over each one in turn, first Cassia, then Ilana.

When Alma finished his prayers, he looked at Limhi. "Would you like a blessing as well?"

Limhi nodded and crossed to Alma. He sat on the stool and took a deep, trembling breath. "I pray that my son's murderer will be found," Limhi said in a low whisper. Alma nodded and closed his eyes, preparing for the blessing. While Helam anointed Limhi, Alma prayed in his heart that the questions of Nehem's death would be answered with haste and the rebellion within the city quelled.

Helam finished the anointing, and Alma prayed over Limhi, blessing him with strength to face what he must in the hours and days to come. Just before he concluded, he heard commotion at the entrance of the throne room. When the prayer was finished, he opened his eyes and raised his head.

King Mosiah stood there, his head bowed, with his four sons flanking him. Alma searched the faces of the king's sons—Ammon, Aaron, Omner, and Himni. Their appearances were ruffled, their tunics wrinkled and their hair matted, as if they'd had very little rest the night before.

Ammon looked thinner than usual—rather gaunt. Aaron's face was drawn, dark circles beneath his eyes. Omner's eyes were anxious as they looked around at everyone, and Himni was quieter than usual. Ilana rose to greet Aaron, and he crossed to take her hand. She leaned against him, closing her eyes briefly.

Alma turned to the table, reaching for the bundle. He unwrapped the weapon slowly, then laid it on the table on top of the cloth, the dried blood unmistakable. But instead of gazing again at the knife, Alma watched the reactions of the king's sons.

"It does resemble my workmanship," Ammon said immediately. There was recognition in his eyes, but Alma couldn't tell if there was more behind the man's gaze.

Ammon turned to his father. "You're sure this was used on Nehem?"

"As well as we can surmise," the king replied.

"The blood is freshly dried," Limhi said, his voice heavy with grief.

Ammon nodded, then gave a quick glance to Aaron, who wrapped an arm tightly about Ilana.

The king exhaled. "Son, do you remember who you gave this knife to?"

Silence stretched for a moment, then Ammon replied, "I do not. I'm sorry, but I can't remember every knife I've made. In fact, this may only be a close resemblance to my knives."

Alma couldn't stay quiet a moment longer. As he was wrapping the knife at Limhi's house, he'd noticed a marking at the base of the blade. Now, he reached for the knife and turned it over to reveal the etched letter in the metal.

Ammon's face flushed.

"It's your name symbol," Alma said, trying to keep his voice steady. If he discovered Ammon was lying, the consequences would be great, regardless of whose son he was.

"Yes, so it would seem," Ammon's voice was edged with harshness. His eyes glinted at Alma. "I've been making knives for years, and this could have easily been passed to almost anyone."

"But it wasn't, was it?" Alma said.

Ammon drew his brows together in disbelief.

Or is it defiance? Alma wondered. The tightness in his stomach and the dread pounding through his heart told him that the king's son was not being forthright. Ammon may or may not be innocent in his involvement in Nehem's death, but the man knew more than he was admitting.

"It might have been stolen," Ilana said, her voice soft, almost pleading. Cassia moved closer to her, taking her hand.

"Possibly," Alma said, tilting his head, gazing at the other brothers. Aaron looked especially pale, but was it from the shock of his future brother-in-law's death, or did he know who the knife belonged to? Alma's gaze trailed over Omner and Himni, who both avoided any eye contact, then it landed on Cassia. Her face was flushed a deep red as she stared at Ammon.

"What is it, Cassia?" Alma asked.

She looked at him, her expression startled, then her gaze slid back to her brother before she answered. "I—I think you know who the knife belongs to, Ammon."

He took a step back, glaring at his sister. "If I knew who the knife belonged to, don't you think I'd send the guards after him?" His already reddened face darkened. "I don't know who used this knife last night, and I don't know where they got it. Maybe you should be questioning Nehem's friends or the men on the council—what about Helam's stepson, Abe? Nehem and Abe have been arguing over the past few weeks."

The king put both hands on the table, leaning toward Ammon. "What were they arguing about?"

Ammon waved a hand. "They had different beliefs about how to stop the rebellion. It seemed they were gathering council support behind each other's backs." He looked at Ilana. "You are his sister. Had he told you anything?"

Ilana's face crumpled, and she turned her head against Aaron's shoulder.

"I still think you know who the knife belongs to, Ammon," Cassia said.

Ammon threw his hands up in frustration.

"Cassia," Alma said, focusing on the young woman. "What makes you think that Ammon might know more than he's telling?"

She looked at Alma. "I—I know my brothers, maybe even better than they think I do."

The king was more than alert now. "Explain, daughter."

Cassia took a deep breath, moving away from Ilana and Aaron. "For one thing, I know they did not sleep in their beds last night."

"We did," Himni burst out, followed by Omner's agreement.

Ammon nodded. "We were awakened just as everyone else in the palace was."

But Cassia was shaking her head. "I was awake most of the night, and I saw you creeping back into your rooms."

Ammon started to protest, but Aaron held up his hand. "I slipped into the cooking room to fetch a heel of bread. Maybe that's what you saw."

Cassia swung her gaze to Aaron, her eyes narrowing. For a heartbeat she stared at him, then looked away.

Alma followed her reaction, wishing he could speak to her without so many people around. But she fell silent, and the king looked more troubled than ever.

Mosiah looked around at those gathered at the table. "We must all take care. A nobleman has been killed, and we have yet to learn the intent of the murderer."

Everyone nodded but Cassia, who kept her steady gaze on Ammon.

"Stay close," the king admonished. "The council will reconvene in less than one hour. In the meantime, we will begin to lay plans for a funeral."

Next to the king, Limhi bowed his head.

Alma reached for the knife and rewrapped it in the linen. He would keep it close until the council meeting.

* * *

Alma the Younger

"How many armbands have been given out?" Alma asked Himni.

"Nearly four hundred so far," the fifteen-year-old said, his voice nervous. He kept looking through the trees surrounding their meeting place. It was a good distance from the road, but with the death of Nehem, they were being extra cautious.

Four hundred unbelievers have pledged their loyalty. It wasn't enough. They'd need at least twice that to make a dent against the royal soldiers and infiltrate the temple. He looked at Ammon, who stood next to Himni. They only had a few minutes to determine their plan. Aaron and Omner had remained at the palace to appease their father.

But now, with Kaman and Jacob in hiding, there were two fewer council members to help Alma. In addition, Ammon had filled him in on what was going on at the palace. The knife had been found, and Ammon could only distract the king for so long.

"How's the royal guard infiltration going?" Alma asked Ammon.

"Very well," Ammon said. "Aaron is making good progress. He estimates we have at least a third on our side now."

Alma nodded. "Did you bring the letter and sheaves?"

Ammon withdrew a few sheaves from the pack he carried, then handed them over.

Alma took them and moved to a rock that had a relatively flat top. He opened the incriminating letter written in Nehem's handwriting and read through the contents. He shook his head—Nehem had been careless. Seeing the words caused his anger to rise. It was too bad that Limhi's son had to die, but Alma was grateful that man was no longer betrothed to Cassia.

Alma spread the letter and the blank sheaf against the rock, then brought out a thin brush and a vial of prepared dye. The letter written by Nehem only hinted at his folly, so Alma's version would include more details to make the evidence more concrete.

In the heat of the day, he wrote as quickly as he dared, copying Nehem's writing style. The first letter was addressed to the priest Ben, signed by Nehem. In it, Nehem stated that he wanted the tavern burnings to be kept confidential: "This holy destruction is for the good of the believers."

In the next letter, Alma wrote to a merchant Nehem was known to do business with—whether or not he'd been involved, it would lead the trail in another direction.

When he finished, he looked up. "These letters will begin the crumbling on the inside. Tonight we will increase our recruiting efforts tenfold. Each council member will devote his time to strengthening the rebellion."

Ammon nodded, holding his hand out for the forged letters. "I should get them to Aaron immediately—he would be the best person to slip it in."

"When is the burial?"

"Tomorrow morning," Ammon said, shaking his head. "Then they will be putting their full-time attention to this matter."

"We need more recruits," Alma said. "Tell Aaron he needs to meet with the head guard tonight."

Ammon stared at him. "It will be a great risk."

"What if we're found out?" Himni asked.

"Nehem's untimely death has forced us into action," Alma explained. "If we can get the head guard on our side, a good portion of the royal guards will follow. And he'll know which ones will cross over." He put a hand over the armband concealed beneath his robe sleeve. "We must know who will stand with us in our declaration of freedom."

The brothers placed their hands on their own hidden bands. "Tonight then," Ammon said. They turned and hurried along the winding path to the main road.

* * *

Cassia

Cassia strode with Ilana, their arms linked together. They stayed on the paths through the garden, but the air was humid today, nearly stifling. "Let's walk to the pond," Cassia suggested.

Ilana nodded, her expression melancholy, but she let Cassia lead her out the back gate.

The burial of Nehem had been that morning, and earlier that afternoon, the king's council had finished their meetings. No new information had been found, only speculations made. The queen had remained with Limhi's wife for the day, and Cassia stayed with Ilana, which brought them both comfort. Cassia knew if Ilana were alone right now, left to the void of grieving, she might never leave her bedchamber again.

The afternoon sun had lost some of its heat as the women plunged into the thicker parts of the forest, following the well-worn and familiar path. Cassia had once walked to the pond with Nehem, and it was hard not to believe he'd appear around the bend at any moment. Even though she'd watched his burial, the death of her betrothed had yet to fully hit her.

"I hope it was quick and painless," Ilana said.

Cassia knew what she meant, but still she shuddered. "Do you think he knew his attacker?"

"I don't know," Ilana said in a quiet voice. "I've been trying to think of anyone he spoke of over the past few days."

"I have as well," Cassia said. She let out a sigh, feeling the grief press against her heart once again. "I—I wonder if he woke to see the attacker. What were his last thoughts?"

Ilana let out her own sigh. "I know if it were me, I'd think about Aaron."

Cassia squeezed Ilana's arm.

"Perhaps you were what he thought of last," Ilana said.

Cassia nodded, the tears building in her eyes. It was hard to believe that only two nights before Nehem had begged her for a kiss. If only she'd known. If only she'd let him kiss her. "Perhaps he didn't wake."

"Perhaps," Ilana said, falling quiet again.

As the trees thinned, they approached the meadow that opened up into a small valley. Ilana pulled Cassia to a stop.

"We're almost there," Cassia said.

"I think I heard something."

Ilana was prone to being skittish, but with Nehem's death, Cassia was extra cautious as well. Her heart began to pound. All kinds of animals frequented the pond—one reason she never came here alone. It could be anything—a deer, an antelope, a jaguar. Or a man.

Instinctively, she led Ilana off the path and into the trees where they could see both the pond and the path at the same time.

"Someone is coming," Ilana whispered.

The two women crouched, waiting in silence.

When Ammon and Himni came into view, Cassia didn't know who was more startled—she or Ilana.

"Where is he?" Ammon said as he slowed his pace, looking toward the pond. "He's late."

"What was his assignment from the king's council?" Himni asked.

"To help Limhi organize the legal documents about Nehem's death."

"Perfect," Himni replied. "He'll be able to take the letters."

"Yes—" Ammon started to say, then was interrupted by a high-pitched whistle.

Cassia's heart was thudding so loud, she worried her brothers would hear. But for some reason, she was reluctant to reveal her presence. Something didn't feel right, and she didn't want to be discovered.

"There he is," Himni said, turning.

A moment later, Aaron approached the two. At Cassia's side, Ilana made a move to rise, but Cassia pulled her back. She shook her head and mouthed, "Wait."

Ilana furrowed her brow but settled down again.

Aaron looked angry when he reached his brothers. "It was tough to get away," he said, almost growling.

"We know," Ammon said, holding out a couple of scrolls toward Aaron. "Here are the letters, just as you requested."

Aaron opened the scrolls and read through them. Then he lifted his eyes to Ammon, a smile spreading on his face. "Excellent. All I need to do is make sure Ilana is distracted while I place these letters in Nehem's chamber."

Next to Cassia, Ilana stiffened and threw a confused glance at Cassia.

It seemed that everything was suddenly quiet in the forest—not even the birds or insects made a sound.

The men chuckled. "That shouldn't be too hard," Ammon said. "She's with Cassia most of the time anyway. Does she have to know you're at her home?"

"No," Aaron said, looking thoughtful.

"Whatever you do, we must make haste. The other council members are working on their own assignments as we speak. We don't know what they'll be able to uncover. We need to erase all evidence of our knowledge of Nehem's death."

Ilana gasped, then quickly covered her mouth. The men turned in their direction. Before Cassia could stop her, Ilana sprang from their hiding place and rushed toward Aaron.

"What are you talking about? How were you involved in my brother's death?"

Aaron's face went pale, and Ammon and Himni backed away.

Cassia stared at her brothers in disbelief, staying hidden in the brush.

"I—It's not what you think," Aaron said, stumbling over his words. "There are men out there who will lie about the king's sons—do anything to bring down our father—these letters will just prove our innocence."

"That's not what Ammon said," Ilana burst out, looking at Ammon. "You said you needed to *erase* all evidence!" She turned to Aaron and shoved him in the chest. "Tell me what you did!"

"Nothing!" Aaron shouted. "Your brother died because he was trying to take away the people's agency. He was no better than a tyrant. Do you know he ordered buildings burned and people died in them?"

Ilana stared at Aaron, her chest heaving. "You know who killed him. Maybe it wasn't Ammon, but the knife belonged to him," she gasped, choking back a sob. "Who killed my brother? Tell me!"

"I—I don't know," Aaron said, his voice desperate, but his eyes were hardened. "I didn't kill your brother, Ilana."

Ilana shoved him again, and Aaron clenched his fists as if he were using every bit of willpower not to strike her back.

"You're a liar!" she screamed at him. "Maybe you didn't hold the knife in your hand, but it's as good as if you did."

"Ilana . . ."

"Stay away from me, Aaron," Ilana said, backing away. Tears streaked her face as her voice trembled. "I don't ever want to see you again. You will not come to my home today and plant your false letters." She clenched her fists together. "Your father will hear about this—the whole kingdom. You'll be ruined for what you did!"

"Ilana—"

But she turned and started running up the path.

Aaron stared after her.

"We should go after her," Himni said, his voice panicked.

"No," Ammon said. "No one will listen to her. She'll just sound like a hysterical fool." He yanked the scrolls from Aaron's hands. "But these need to be destroyed."

He tore apart the sheaves then dropped them to the ground, crouching over the torn pieces. From a leather pouch at his waist, he withdrew chert and quickly struck a flame. The others watched as the sheaves caught fire and burned to black.

After kicking dirt over the smoldering mess, Ammon said, "Come. Our plans will have to move forward more quickly now. It's not safe to return to the palace with that woman ranting about. We'll send a guard to notify Omner."

The three brothers hurried away, in the opposite direction of Ilana. They skirted the pond and climbed up the hill that led away from the palace and temple.

Cassia sat back, her breathing coming fast, her eyes burning. *I've got to find Ilana. No, I should follow my brothers.* But instead, she rose on unsteady feet and walked to the path. There she knelt on the ground and started to dig in the dirt, searching for the torn pieces. But they had disintigrated into unrecognizable ash.

CHAPTER 17

Thou shalt make no covenant with them, nor with their gods.
—Exodus 23:32

Alma the Elder

Alma stood alone in the throne room with only his thoughts and the murder weapon. He wrapped up the knife again, having shown it to the council that had broken up a short time ago. No matter how he tried to forget, the image of the dried blood upon the blade would not leave his mind, and so it was with a grimace that he tied the bundle and attached it to his waistband.

Every council member had been given an assignment to oversee specific duties that would hopefully lead to the capture of Nehem's murderer. Everyone would rest easier in their beds at night when the man was caught. Each of the priests' households had been fortified with additional guards sent by the king. Entire families now lived in fear. Limhi's household had been struck; who would be next?

It was presumptuous to think that Nehem's death was an isolated incident. That morning before the burial service, the king had received word that several carts stationed at the marketplace had been vandalized—all belonging to Church members.

Alma rose from the council table, noticing that the bright sunlight that had spilled in from the high windows had now faded. He checked to make sure the dagger he'd placed in his waistband that morning was still secured. It had been many years since he'd carried a weapon of any kind, and many years since he'd gone among the people to speak to them one by one.

Exiting the throne room, Alma found the hallway deserted except for the guards. In the air hung a degree of anticipation, mixed with trepidation. Alma could see it in the expressions of the usually composed guards. He nodded to them as he passed by, feeling his burden increase as if he'd just shouldered a bag of grain.

As he left the palace and started down the stairs, his gaze strayed in the direction of his homestead. His wife and children were under strict instructions to remain at home, and several of the king's guards had been posted there. Still, his heart ached at the situation his family had been placed in. When he brought his family and the believers to Zarahemla more than twenty years before, he'd hoped to live out the rest of his days in a peace that only a land filled with Nephites could afford.

Swallowing against the lump in his throat, he looked over at the temple and all of its stately beauty. Alma couldn't decide whether the temple was more beautiful in the early morning or the late afternoon. Shades of soft orange and yellow reflected from the stone edifice, welcoming, soothing. But today, Alma had left the conducting of the ritual sacrifices, hearing the repentants' confessions, and preparing the Sabbath's sermon to the lesser priests.

Warmth started to return to Alma's soul as he crossed the plaza and walked toward the market street. Most people called out greetings to him, and he felt their love and sympathy filling him with each acknowledgment. One man even stopped him and asked after his son.

"We've not heard from him as of yet," Alma replied.

The older man nodded, his lined face wrinkling in concern. "We're praying for him." Before Alma could respond, the man patted Alma's arm and moved on.

Alma stared after the man, a well of emotion springing inside his chest. *I am praying for him too,* he thought. *But at least I know my son lives.* In the last two days, Alma's perspective about his son's defiance had altered. He knew there were worse challenges in life than death—and some might see death as deliverance from some trials—but Alma had spent plenty of time with Limhi and his wife to know that the death of a young man who had his whole life before him was nearly inconsolable.

Alma continued to walk along the market street, soaking in the normalcy of the day among the buyers and sellers. It seemed like any other day, no gloom hanging over the heads of the people. He arrived at the first congregation structure where Church members had gathered to meet him. He greeted several by name, then walked to the front of the gathering, raising a hand for attention. The people quieted, their expressions eager to hear what he had come to say. Alma began to explain the king's admonitions for the safety of his people. "And above all else, please do not plan retaliation. The council is looking for the man who slayed Nehem, and he will be sentenced."

At one point he revealed the knife that had been used against Nehem. Gasps echoed throughout the group. Following that, several people had questions, but Alma raised his hand again for silence. "I must move on and take the message to the other congregations throughout the city, but the priest over your congregation can answer any concerns you may have."

He left as quickly as possible and walked to the next congregation building, repeating his admonition to the crowd gathered there. As he gazed over the people, he was struck by their faith, their open minds and willing hearts. They pulled their children a little closer to their bosoms and vowed not to retaliate but to let the king's guard and council handle the situation. As Alma spoke, he saw the faces of his own family in the eyes of the Church members. Their fears and concerns were the same as his. Many of them had made great sacrifices for their religious beliefs. Alma recognized several who had been part of the original party that had traveled with him from the land of Nephi to Zarahemla. Still, there were others who had come with Limhi, and Limhi's grief over his dead son was as their own—fierce and loyal.

Alma left a subdued crowd in his wake and set off for the next congregation. The shadows on the streets had become long and the air cooler. Alma pulled his indigo robe tighter about his body, feeling the exhaustion deep in his bones.

Standing in front of the third congregation, a touch of foreboding went through Alma. Several men on the front row glared at him with open hostility. As he spoke, one put a hand to his mouth and appeared to be laughing. He was the largest man of the three, with long hair to his shoulders. But when Alma focused his attention on him again, the man was looking away, a placid expression on his face.

The uncomfortable feeling wouldn't dissipate. As Alma unwrapped the knife and displayed it to the gasping crowd, one of the men actually smiled.

At the conclusion of his speech, Alma pulled aside the presiding priest over the congregation and inquired about the men.

"They come and go," the priest said, twisting his hands nervously. "They've attended Sabbath services for a few weeks now, but they aren't from this part of the city."

"I wonder if they've given any trouble to the other members of your congregation," Alma said.

"Nothing specific, although they tend to be argumentative about our teaching," the priest said in a low voice. "I try to stay out of their way when possible. When I have confronted them in the past, they become more belligerent."

Alma looked past the priest, finding one of the men watching him. "Thank you, my friend. Please keep the council informed of any . . . activities that concern you."

The priest nodded, his eyes showing relief.

Alma kept his gaze on the men as he strode up to the small group and stopped in front of them. "Tell me your names."

The men looked at him with expressions mixed with disdain and surprise. One of the men said, "Muloki." The other two kept quiet.

"Muloki," Alma began, knowing the name was familiar but he couldn't place it. "I wonder if you might be able to help me."

Muloki just stared at him, a slight smirk on his face.

Alma unwrapped the knife again and held it up. "Have you seen this before?"

The man peered at the knife, then spit into the dirt. "No." But something had flickered in his gaze.

Alma turned to the other two men. One of them looked enough like Muloki that Alma assumed they were brothers. Each of the men shook their heads in turn. The milling crowd had quieted, and several others were watching them.

"Did you ever meet Nehem?" Alma asked Muloki.

Something changed in Muloki's expression. Although it was almost imperceptible, it was there.

"I know who he is," Muloki said in a reluctant voice. He looked at his friends, who shrugged their shoulders.

"Who is he?" Alma asked.

"What do you mean?" Muloki said. "You know who he is—the son of Limhi."

"Yes," Alma said with a nod. "But how do *you* know him?"

Muloki opened his mouth, then closed it. His friends shuffled uneasily next to him. "He was known among us as a man to watch out for."

Alma rewrapped the knife, taking his time as he thought out his response. When he replaced the knife in his waistband, he looked again at Muloki. "Were you afraid of him?"

"Me?" Muloki asked, barking out a harsh laugh. "I'm not afraid of anyone."

"Of course not," Alma said, "but what about your friends?"

Muloki lifted a shoulder, then threw a glance at the two men. "They can speak for themselves."

Neither of the men offered anything, but their faces had reddened slightly.

"If . . . if you were afraid, or you knew someone afraid of Limhi's son, what did they fear?" Alma asked.

Muloki was quick to answer. "Retaliation."

"From whom?" Alma pressed.

"The king," Muloki drawled out. "Everyone knows that Nehem was in league with the king."

Alma's mind spun as he processed the statement.

"To cross Nehem was to bring the royal guard to your home or place of work."

"What would someone have to do to cross Nehem?"

Muloki composed a nonchalant expression on his face. "Nehem liked to order us around and purchase our goods at discounts. Some say he resold the goods to his father or the king at full price and kept the difference."

Alma tried not to show his surprise. "And the consequence of not giving a discount?"

Muloki lifted a thick arm and pointed toward a nearby hut. "See that roof?"

Alma followed the man's direction and saw the burnt out space where a thatch roof had once been.

"That's Nehem's retaliation," Muloki said, his voice harsh. "It seems anyone close with the king takes their power to the extreme. But of course, you'd know that, and you'd know the history of our city and how the first Mosiah came into power." He looked at the men by his side. "I've said enough. We're leaving."

Alma flinched, understanding now that Muloki was one of those disgruntled citizens—and believed the grievances handed down from generation to generation since Mosiah the First had ousted King David. He put a hand on Muloki's arm. "One more question. Who else worked with Nehem to accomplish his purchasing?"

"No one knows for certain. It was always boys off the street, paid to do one job, making the job untraceable."

As Alma watched the men leave, Muloki's final word echoed in his mind. *Untraceable.*

* * *

Alma the Younger

"We must act quickly," Alma said to the gathered group of men wearing red-dyed armbands. "We must prepare without delay." They had set up the meeting outside the city in a secluded valley. Alma noticed several new faces among the crowd—new recruits courtesy of Aaron. These men had been screened for loyalty and trustworthiness. They were the leaders in their villages and neighborhoods—men who were now inducted as captains in Alma's movement. He recognized one of the top officials of the king's royal guard, Bilshan. He locked gazes with the official, who offered a slight nod of allegiance. The recruits would multiply rapidly now.

Triumph swelled his heart as Alma looked over the sworn followers. He wore the hood up on his scarlet cape tonight. He trusted only his council with his true identity. He continued speaking, gazing out over the assembly. "Each of you has been made a captain tonight in the army of Bel. Each of you are now leaders in our movement, and others will look to you for guidance. We will form in twelve legions, in multiples of twelve. You may assign lower captains as you see fit to manage the number of recruits. You will take our instructions back to your homes and find the most trusted men to serve under your command. Tonight we will organize our forces and prepare to take back our freedom."

"Freedom!" a man toward the front of the gathering shouted, then was quickly joined by other voices. Soon the hillside seemed to reverberate with the chanting of the men.

"We will take back our villages and homes," Alma said, raising his voice over the chanting. "We will not be forced into religious rituals we don't believe in. We will not be judged on whether or not we've been baptized into the king's church. We will honor those who have fallen for our cause—specifically the woman Belicia, who we now recognize as the goddess Bel." The crowd burst into wild approval, but Alma continued to shout over them. "The goddess Bel wants us to save her people and to remember her. We will no longer give unfair discounts to priests to support their cause. Our goods will be used to help our own families. We will no longer sacrifice our animals to the king's temple. And the king will pay with his own funds to rebuild our destroyed homes and fields."

The crowd went mad, several men shouting their agreement, most of them cheering. After a few moments of noise, Alma raised his hand for silence. Almost immediately the quiet returned. "I have something to show you." He turned, looking at Muloki, who stood behind him. "Carts?"

Three carts were rolled forward, containing shrouded objects. Alma climbed up on one of the carts and withdrew the rugs, revealing a stone statue that came to Alma's waist. The men in the crowd strained to capture a good look.

"This is the goddess Bel. Note the dagger and shield she carries. She will fight with us as we move forward in our revolution." He nodded at the men who stood by the other carts to reveal the next statues. "When we infiltrate the temple grounds, we will place these statues in their rightful place—at the temple, which we will rename the temple of Bel. Then we will consecrate the altar of the temple."

Cheers erupted again, and it was several moments before Alma could speak above the noise. "You may pay homage to the goddess, but before you leave tonight to organize your legions, you will sign the edict we have prepared."

"What does it say?" a man called out. "I'm not learned."

Alma nodded to Ammon, who hovered not far away. He brought the scroll to Alma, who opened it and waited for silence to return.

"'As captains in the army of freedom, we swear to protect our own,'" he read. "'We swear to remember the wrongs against us. We swear to allow all men the right to freedom. We swear to protect our right to choose. We swear to obey our chief and his appointed council.'" When he finished he looked up at the hushed crowd. Men started clapping, until the entire crowd joined in with their thunderous response.

Alma handed the edict over to Ammon, who motioned for the captains to step forward and sign the scroll. As they passed by Alma, he gripped the hand of each man, gazing into their eyes, assessing their loyalty. Each man returned his gaze—fierce and true.

Toward the end of the line was the official from the royal guard. Alma stalled him as the rest of the men started to make the trek back to their homes. Bilshan followed Alma away from the gathering.

"Welcome to our legion," Alma said.

Bilshan bowed his head. "I'm honored to be chosen for this assignment. But I must tell you something that no one knows yet—Belicia was my sister."

Alma stared at him.

"When I learned of her death, I was angry and tried to plan vengeance on my own. I started to ask questions, and that is how I gained the attention of Aaron. I too have long wished for change."

"As do we," Alma said. "I can see that Aaron has chosen well. I'm sorry about your sister. We are of the same mind to bring your sister's wishes to all the people. How many new recruits do you think we can get from the royal guard?"

Bilshan lifted a brow but didn't miss a beat. "Several dozen, if not more."

"Enough to cripple the security at the temple?"

"More than enough. What about the palace?"

"The temple will have the largest impact on the king and his council. We are hoping to send the king into exile." Alma peered intently into Bilshan's eyes. "It's time the king and his priests realize that they can't force us to live under religious rulings and edicts that favor Church members. The citizens of Zarahemla want complete freedom. Take the message back to the recruits that they will be well compensated."

Bilshan nodded. "Thank you."

"And one more thing, my new friend," Alma said, putting a hand on Bilshan's shoulder and leaning close. "Bring your new recruits to the king's hunting lodge at midnight tomorrow. I will orient them myself . . . We have no more time to lose. Soon we'll infiltrate the temple and take back our freedom."

CHAPTER 18

. . . the hand of the Lord shall be known toward his servants,
and his indignation toward his enemies.
—Isaiah 66:14

Cassia

Cassia embraced a trembling Ilana, trying to soothe her yet again. Outside Cassia's chamber, the day was fittingly overcast, spreading its gloom around and through them. It had been two days since the funeral and Ilana's discovery of Aaron's betrayal, although nothing had been proved yet. Aaron had denied everything, but he and his brothers had disappeared. If their absence was anything to judge them by, then they were certainly guilty.

She tried to push away her fears about her brothers' dishonesty as she comforted Ilana. The girl had forced her father to announce the official dissolution of the betrothal.

"I just can't look at him as a husband," Ilana whispered, tears streaking her face.

"I know," Cassia said, for she really did know. She'd been listening to the same words for an hour now. But Ilana had no one else to talk to—her mother was still grieving over Nehem. They all were, and this made it all the more difficult for Ilana to experience.

"Even if he's telling the truth—even if Aaron had nothing to do with my brother's death . . . I don't trust him," she said, sniffling.

The now-familiar burning started again in Cassia's chest. She felt exactly what Ilana did. The anger, the fear, and the unanswered questions all combined into an uncertainty that Cassia couldn't shake. When she had looked into her brothers' eyes last, she didn't see her brothers, but men who were hiding something. Men who were deceptive.

Her heart twisted as she watched tears run down Ilana's face. Cassia's own tears threatened, although she tried to be the strong one while Ilana was with her.

"My mother wants to send me to my aunt's home for a little while."

Cassia looked at her sharply. "In the village of Piedra?"

Ilana nodded, wiping her face with a square of cloth that was already soaked with tears.

"For how long?"

Ilana lifted a shoulder and stared unseeing in front of her. "For as long as it takes to mend my heart, I suppose."

Cassia bit her lip, wanting to argue with her—persuade her that she should stay in Zarahemla. Maybe Aaron was innocent, and after the king was able to stifle the rebellions that were popping up around the city, Ilana would be able to see that too. But in her heart, Cassia doubted Aaron and her brothers as well. Ilana needed to start anew.

"Nehem used to love to visit my aunt," Ilana said in a quiet, heart-breaking voice. "She was his favorite. Did you see her at the funeral?"

"Yes. Nehem used to talk about her and her amazing garden." Cassia sighed, her heart once again feeling heavy. Why did Nehem have to die? Why did her beautiful sister-in-law have to leave? Now, Cassia wouldn't have Ilana for a sister. Not officially, at least. That grieved her even more, and she turned and embraced her.

"You must come visit," Ilana said into Cassia's hair.

"I will," Cassia said, although she doubted it would be soon. She pulled away from her friend. Right after Ilana had given her information to her father and the king, Cassia had been confined to the palace. She felt like she was living in another world or time. The usual comforts she took from creating recipes or visiting the marketplace to search for a rare ingredient were gone.

"I must go now," Ilana said in a shaky voice. "My aunt and uncle should be at my home soon, ready to take me with them."

Cassia climbed off the bed and walked around it, taking Ilana's hand. "Come, I have a special treat for you to take with you."

Ilana gave a sad smile. "You are always baking, even when everything else seems hopeless."

Cassia put on false cheer. "We have to eat whether or not our hearts are broken."

"I'm going to miss you so much," Ilana said, squeezing Cassia.

"Let's go before we start crying again," Cassia said, pulling her toward the door.

As they walked the corridor to the cooking room, Ilana gazed at their surroundings. "It's hard to believe that I'm leaving this place—when I once thought I might raise my children here—"

Cassia put an arm around her and led her into the cooking room where even the cooking area seemed somber today. The servants moved about quietly, only nodding when Cassia entered. She went straight to her set of shelves that the cooks left alone and withdrew several squares of amaranth treats.

Taking them off the shelf, she wrapped them in a bit of cloth, then tied it off with a thin rope. "Take this with you and savor them. Each small taste will remind you of me."

Ilana took the bundle, her eyes filling with tears.

"Remember, we will always be sisters—no matter what."

Ilana nodded and whispered, "Thank you."

Then they walked slowly through the palace to the front entrance. The two guards Ilana had arrived with were waiting at the palace entrance for their charge. Cassia gave her a final embrace, then stood at the top of the palace steps watching Ilana walk down the stairs and across the plaza—disappearing from her life.

Cassia lingered on the top step for a long time, knowing that the guards likely thought she was acting strangely. They probably didn't know whether to coax her inside or worry about chasing her if she fled after her friend.

But Cassia remained still, facing the direction of Limhi's homestead across the river. A half an hour passed before she sank down on the step and continued to watch the activity in the plaza. People came and went, most on their way to the temple. Her father had stopped holding hearings and grievances in the throne room at the palace. It was impossible to trust each and every person who approached the palace. The hearings were now held at the temple, with the high priest, Alma, presiding.

More and more lately, her father had turned the judgments of the people over to the high priest—for most of them dealt with matters of the Church. Cassia hadn't been informed about the extent of the conflict between the Church members and the unbelievers but knew that it was increasing at an alarming rate. And the death of Nehem had been a part of the intricate web of persecution.

The thought of Nehem brought a sigh to her lips. She had seen him buried and prayed over with her own eyes. She had heard the comforting words of Alma, who spoke of a paradise. In her heart she believed Nehem was in the presence of the Lord. He had been so kind and loving to her—so full of life.

Cassia sat and drew her knees up to her chest, knowing it wasn't exactly ladylike, but she was suddenly exhausted, having had little sleep over the past several days. Laying her head down on her knees, she exhaled, feeling a breeze move across her face and neck. The temperature was perfect with the clouds blocking the sun.

Before she knew it, her hair was damp with perspiration, and she opened her eyes. She must have fallen asleep. The clouds had parted; the afternoon sun was in full force. Cassia lifted her head, wincing at the soreness in her neck as she looked at the scene in the plaza, wondering how long she'd dozed off.

Then she realized what had awakened her. The sound of drums. A shiver went through Cassia as a slight breeze lifted the damp tendrils from her neck. *What are the drums for?* The noise was faint but unmistakable. There was no festival that Cassia knew of, plus it was still daylight. Most of the celebrations that occurred with drums took place at night when the families were together after the day's work.

Cassia stood, her legs feeling cramped after being in one position for so long. She cast a glance at the guards behind her standing alert at the palace entrance. Their expressions of confusion and curiosity mirrored her own.

And then she saw the smoke. At first, Cassia assumed someone was burning weeds in their garden, but after a few minutes, she saw a group of men run from the direction of the market square into the plaza and head for the temple. Something made her heart pound as she watched the smoke increase, spreading out in a dark, gray funnel.

The sound of the drums increased, faint at first, but now sure and strong. It seemed to be coming from the marketplace. The smoke darkened, looking out of place against the brilliant blue sky. Cassia's heart thudded as she backed her way to the entrance of the palace.

"What's happening?" she whispered mostly to herself.

One of the guards answered. "Best get inside, miss. Your father will surely want you secure."

Cassia nodded, but she couldn't take her eyes from the smoke as it twisted against the sky.

* * *

Alma the Elder

Alma stared at the man before him in the cool interior of the temple. He was a well-dressed jewelry merchant. If one didn't know his occupation, it was made obvious by the man's attire. He wore a feathered cape, several pieces of jade jewelry, and tapir-skin sandals. Alma also noticed the man's hands, smooth, without calluses. He was a man who did not mine his own jade.

"Gad." Alma repeated the man's name to hold his complete attention. "The king's law states that a merchant must sell his goods for the same price to all men, members of the Church or not."

Gad folded his soft hands together, his heavy face flushed, but his eyes were bright with conviction. "My prices are the same. Some weeks they may go up, some weeks they may be lower. It depends on my supply."

Alma nodded. He could understand that, if it was the complete truth, but he had multiple complaints against this merchant regarding price discrimination based on religion. Gad had apparently offered discounts to the unbelievers, while raising his price on a whim for Church members. When the buyers had caught on, it was easy enough to trick the merchant and catch him in his lies.

"Are not the silver onties of one man as good as another?" Alma said.

After nodding, Gad raised his gaze. "Certainly."

Alma tapped the scroll he held in his hand, then passed it along to Ben, who was acting as the court scribe today. "Let the record of the Church show that Gad must repay ten onties to each man on this list."

Dipping his brush in a vial of dye, Ben wrote on the top of the document.

Gad shuffled to the scribes table and paid his fine, his face red with anger and embarrassment. But the man demonstrated no further act of defiance. Then he was escorted out of the temple by a guard.

Alma sighed inwardly with relief. Some of these merchants were more troublesome than Gad.

A line of people stood, waiting for their judgments to be settled, all relating to a violation against a Church member. Alma's heart was heavy because the number grew each day. In fact, the other priests had started taking over some of the judgments. Alma could no longer get through them all by himself.

The progress on discovering Nehem's murderer had been frustratingly slow. Alma noticed the dejection in the king's eyes—and when Ilana accused Aaron of being part of the plot and insisted on being released from her betrothal, the king was devastated. Aaron and his brothers had disappeared—whether because they were guilty, or because they were heartbroken, Alma wasn't sure. But times had changed. The atmosphere in Zarahemla was tense, and people were keeping to themselves more, staying in at night, fearful for their own safety.

The next man stepped forward. He was elderly, his shoulders stooped, his clothing ragged. His watery gaze met Alma's.

Turning, Alma asked Ben, "What are the charges against this man?"

"This is Joseph, and he has been accused of sleeping on the temple grounds."

Alma turned back to the old man. "Where is your home, Joseph?"

The man slowly lifted a hand and pointed at the merchant, Gad, who was on his way out of the temple. "Men like him robbed me until I could no longer support my family." His voice cracked. "I lost my home, and my wife left to go live with her sister. My children refuse to help me."

"But surely your children will take you in once they learn of your state?" Alma pressed.

"No," the man said, his gaze faltering. "I—I betrayed their mother long ago. She stayed with me, but the children never forgot. And now . . . they say I deserve to die hungry."

Alma leaned over to the scribe and whispered, "Bring Joseph food and drink. Then we'll discuss what can be done."

Ben raised his eyebrows but hurried to the back of the temple where the priests kept their midday meals. Returning, he handed over a maize cake and a water skin.

The old man's eyes widened as he accepted the food. He ate the maize cake in a few bites, then guzzled the water. After wiping his mouth with a torn sleeve, he handed the water skin to Ben.

Joseph turned his gaze to Alma. "Thank you," he said in a quiet voice.

"Let's resume," Alma said. "Have you repented of your iniquities against your wife?"

Joseph hung his head. "I have not yet repented before a priest."

"Do you repent of your iniquities now?" Alma asked.

The man's shoulders sagged. "I do." He lifted his head, looking directly at Alma, remorse in his eyes. "I confess my sins before you and the Lord. With all my heart, I repent. It may already be too late, but I want my family back." He looked around at those waiting behind him for their court time. "I forgive the wrongs that have been committed against me by corrupt merchants. I forgive them as I hope that those I have wronged will forgive me of my own iniquities."

A surge of warmth passed through Alma. He knew this man was truly contrite, and even though he'd wasted years in pain from refusing to repent and forgive others, today was a turning point in his life. Alma smiled and crossed the space between him and Joseph. He clasped the old man's hand in his and said, "Joseph, your confession has been heard, and the Lord forgives those who truly repent. Your name will remain on the records of the Church. Now go and meet with your children. Ask them for forgiveness. Meet with your wife. Ask for her forgiveness."

Joseph nodded, tears standing out in his eyes.

"If your family won't take you in, you are welcome to stay in the guard bunk, and your food will be supplied, provided you are willing to work in the Church's grain building."

Joseph's countenance brightened considerably, and he bowed to Alma. "May the Lord bless you and your family," he gushed.

"Go in peace," Alma said, watching the man hurry off, moving like he was twenty years younger.

He turned to check that Ben had recorded the interchange before inviting the next person to come forward. But a shout interrupted him. Alma whirled to face the temple entrance again as a royal guard came running toward the judgment seat.

"A mob!" he shouted.

Those waiting in the court leapt to their feet, and the guards gripped their weapons, watching their charges more closely.

"There's a mob making its way to the plaza," the guard said as he came to a full stop in front of Alma. "Some say they are coming to overtake the temple."

Ben stood from his scribe table. "How close are they?"

"They've reached the marketplace and set several carts ablaze."

Alma stared at the guard, fear pounding through his heart. "Has the king sent soldiers out to stop them?"

"There are not enough inside the city to quell this mob of hundreds. The king has sent for the soldiers who guard the outlying borders of the land. But it will take hours for them to be notified and reach the center of the city," the guard said, still breathless. "The king has ordered the temple cleared. It is no longer safe."

Alma saw fear on Ben's face as well. Then he called out to the guards who held the incumbents. "Our court will resume after the mob has been dispelled. Those who came from prison will be returned, and the rest will be free to go home and check on their families."

A flurry of action broke out as the guards issued orders, and those who were freed started running for the doors of the temple. Alma helped Ben gather up the records that littered the scribe table. They carried the records to the entrance of the temple on the way to the archive room.

When Alma walked through the entrance, he came to a stop on the temple mount, overlooking the city. He froze, staring in horror at the scene below. Smoke billowed from several buildings, some he thought were homes. People were running toward the palace, and the royal soldiers were blocking their way. Dozens of soldiers were stationed between the plaza and the marketplace, swords in hand.

Something thumped in the air, and it took a moment for Alma to recognize the sound of drums. Each beat seemed to increase the tension that radiated through Alma's body. The mob wanted the citizens to know it was coming—wanted to announce its arrival to the king. Alma looked over at Ben, who shook his head, his eyes wide with amazement.

"Sir!" someone shouted, and Alma turned to see another royal guard coming toward them, hurrying up the temple steps. "A message from the king," he said, panting as he reached the platform level. "The king wants all the priests to bring their families to his hunting lodge immediately. You are to go home and fetch your families. The king is preparing to leave the palace now." He looked from Alma to Ben. "The home of Limhi has been set ablaze by the mob."

Alma recoiled in shock. "Is he . . . all right?"

The guard nodded. "Limhi's family escaped and are fleeing. There is little time. Soldiers have already been dispatched to your homes."

"Tell him we'll join him at the lodge as soon as possible," Alma said.

The guard raced back down the steps, shouting orders from the king.

Alma crossed to Ben. "Let's get the records locked up right away, and then we'll go to our families."

Ben simply nodded and hurried after Alma. The two dumped the scrolls in the archive room, not taking time to put anything back, then hurried outside again. Alma locked the door with his key, hoping that the archives would not suffer any harm.

He put a hand on Ben's shoulder. "Be safe, my friend."

"I need to secure a few more things inside the temple first," Ben said.

"I'll come with you," Alma said, although he dreaded the delay.

"No," Ben said. "You'll have to beat the mob to get across the plaza to the road that leads to your home. I can leave by the back way and avoid the commotion. Let me do it. You hurry to fetch your family."

"May the Lord protect you," Alma said, embracing Ben.

The two men drew apart, each heading in opposite directions.

* * *

Cassia

Cassia covered her ears, trying to drown out the sound of the drums, but raising her hands almost made her stumble along the sloped garden path after her parents.

It was useless to block out the thumping, so she dropped her hands and followed after her parents and several soldiers. Most of the servants had fled from the palace already, going to their homes to reunite with their families. Her father had ordered a bevy of soldiers to guard the palace and the rest to stop the mob from entering the plaza.

She still couldn't believe what was happening. One moment she was bidding farewell to Ilana, and the next she was running from her home. Had Ilana made it safely to her aunt's village? Reports had come that Limhi's home was set afire but that Limhi had escaped with his whole family. Cassia wondered if Ilana knew what had happened to her home. Now her friend would have even less reason to return to the city.

When the garden path came to an end, the king flung open the gate that led to the hunting preserve. Before leaving the garden, Cassia took the chance to turn and look over the city. This was the highest part of the garden, and through the trees she could see portions of the plaza.

People were scurrying about. Soldiers lined the edges of the plaza, stationing themselves in front of the palace and the temple steps. But it was the smoke that was the most disconcerting of all. When Cassia had awakened from dozing on the palace steps, there had been one fire, and now there were more than a dozen towers of smoke along the skyline.

"Come, my dear," her mother's voice said, and a hand wrapped around her shoulders, guiding her through the gate. "We can delay no longer."

Cassia turned to her mother. "Where are my brothers?"

"We still have no word. We hope they are not caught by the mob—anyone royal will surely be targeted." The queen visibly shuddered. "We must pray for their safety."

Cassia nodded, praying silently as the small group hurried along the path that led to the pond. Although the day was quite warm, a chill passed through her as she thought about the last time she'd been on this path—with Ilana. And the two of them had overheard her brothers' conversation about Nehem.

She wished she could shake the feeling of foreboding. It was ironic—here she was, being forced to escape her beloved palace, but in her heart, she only wished that her brothers were innocent of the wrongdoings she suspected of them. If they were proven to be honest and good, then Cassia knew her heart would be easy, no matter what destruction the mob caused.

The group passed the pond with hardly a word exchanged. King Mosiah led the procession, his expression set with grim determination. He carried a sword at his side as if he were willing to go to battle himself. Cassia hoped that would not be the case—her father's aged body was no match for a young warrior's—and an angry one, at that.

When the queen started to lag behind, the king stopped, looking at his wife. "Should we rest?"

"No," the queen managed, though she was quite out of breath. "I will be fine." She smiled grimly. "But I'm not as young as I used to be."

"Nor I," the king said, coming to his wife's side. He linked his arm through hers, and the rest of the way they walked together.

Cassia could have moved faster—after all, she spent a lot of time each day walking outdoors—but she allowed her father to set the pace. She still worried about her brothers—had they been caught up in the mob? She glanced over at her parents, noting the concern on their faces, although they spoke little. They skirted the pond and trekked through the heavier brush. The path was still perceptible, although it hadn't been used much since the king had declared the surrounding land as an animal preserve.

The lodge finally came into view, and Cassia was quite impressed. It had been years since she'd ventured this far—back when she played with her brothers and Alma. But it seemed the lodge had been kept in good repair. She was the second one inside after a soldier, and she walked around the lodge, removing wood slats that covered the windows. Letting in the afternoon light and fresh air, the place seemed brighter. One of the guards worked on building a fire on the far side of the main room. Now, if only the other families of the priests were here safely as well. She didn't let her mind wander to Alma the Younger; he wasn't even living in Zarahemla, so he'd be out of the worst of it.

Cassia left her parents discussing the others and walked into the cooking room, where she immediately took assessment of the food supplies. There were several large jugs filled with grain and sealed jars of agave wine. In the corner were two bows and a couple of sheaves of arrows. She had to do something to keep busy; she couldn't just sit and wait.

By the time the fire in the main room was warming the lodge, Cassia crossed to her mother and said, "I can prepare a meal of hotcakes for us. I'll search the surrounding area for wild vegetables or fruits."

The queen nodded, gratitude in her expression. "Take a soldier with you. We can't be too careful. It will be dark soon, so return even if you have found nothing. The men will hunt in the morning. But it would be nice to have something to eat when the others arrive at the lodge."

Cassia nodded and picked up a basket from the cooking room. As an added thought, she took one of the bows and a few arrows. Then she went outside, and a guard immediately joined her. She handed over the basket to the guard, enjoying the feel of a bow across her shoulders again. It reminded her of time spent with Alma, him teaching her to aim, but she pushed those thoughts away as soon as they came. She'd be putting all of her skills to the test while staying in the lodge. There was no reason to dwell on those who had abandoned her.

She walked through the copse of trees, keeping within sight of the lodge, the guard close behind her. In the open air, she felt as if she could breathe again. The shadows had lengthened and early evening was approaching, but she was confident she'd be able to find something to feed everyone. And just as she thought it, she saw it—a grove of guava trees. Certainly wild, but there were a half dozen trees close together, as if they'd banded in a group. She instructed the guard to start picking while she scouted the area a little farther.

Then she stopped, looking at the ground, noticing fresh rabbit droppings near a bush. The guards had raised their eyebrows when they'd seen her take a bow, but she'd return with meat. She followed the trail for a few paces, then crouched, seeing a movement through the trees. Within a few minutes, she caught sight of a furry head. Her heart thudded as she nocked the arrow against the bow string and pulled back.

Now, she told herself, and released the arrow. It twanged through the air, loud enough to alert the creature. In a flurry, it hopped away before any harm could be done. Cassia scrambled to her feet and went to retrieve her arrow, where it lay helplessly in the dirt. *Tomorrow I'll try again,* she told herself.

She returned to the guard and the guava trees, staying content to gather fruit to go with the hotcakes.

Once the basket was full, Cassia led the way back to the lodge. Dusk had settled, making the place look cozy and inviting. Limhi and his family had arrived as well as Maia and her three younger children. Helam had come with his wife, Raquel, and their children and grandchildren. Maia's parents, Jachin and Lael, stood inside. Cassia thought they must be at least one hundred years old but had the energy of twenty-year-olds. They looked no worse for the wear from traveling such a distance.

Cassia entered the main room just as Maia told the king and queen about Alma staying behind. Cassia felt ill—the high priest was in severe danger. Surely he was no match against the frenzied mob. When she heard the reason for him staying, she and her mother gasped. The mob had captured Ben.

Maia's voice trembled with her story, and the queen put an arm around her. "Your husband will be protected by the Lord," the queen said.

But still Maia looked pale. She clasped her hands together and stared into the fire, unseeing.

Cassia knew Maia still grieved over her son's whereabouts, and now her husband was in immediate danger.

The king stood after Maia's tale was finished, his face grave. "We will send for him—there are plenty of soldiers to guard the palace, but they may not know Alma is in the chaos. I'll return to the temple with the guards there myself."

"No," Maia said, snapping into focus again. "I wouldn't forgive myself if something happened to our king." Her eyes were moist, but her chin lifted in determination. "Please stay here where you are safe. My husband knew the danger he was entering into."

The king nodded, though his expression was still troubled.

Raquel mumbled something about finding healing herbs outside in case there were any injuries. Cassia turned from the group and walked to the cooking room, where she began to make preparations for the scanty meal. From the other room, she heard her father raise his voice in prayer and supplication to the Lord for the safe return of Alma and Ben. Cassia paused in her work and clasped her hands together, bowing her head.

Her father's prayer continued, asking for deliverance from the mob and safety for his sons as well, and all those who were away from home, such as Ilana. The king concluded with praying for Alma the Younger, the errant son of the high priest.

Amen, Cassia mouthed. It was good to feel concern for another's well-being instead of focusing so much on her own grief and broken heart.

The main room was very quiet as Cassia continued her work. She lit the fire in the cooking oven that vented through the wall. Then she scooped up handfuls of maize kernels and began to grind them. As she worked, she heard her father's hushed voice in discussion with Limhi. The light gradually faltered outside, and Maia's oldest daughter, Bethany, went about lighting the oil lamps. The guards had remained outside and would continue to guard the lodge throughout the night in shifts.

Then Maia appeared in the cooking room. "Give me something to do," she said.

Cassia looked up from the grinding stone. "I can do this; you should rest after your journey and with all your worries."

But Maia approached Cassia and held out her hand for the grinder. Cassia gave it to her and watched Maia attack the kernels with a ferocity.

"There is nothing I can do about my husband and oldest son right now, except pray," Maia said, wiping a tear on her cheek with her sleeve. "I must do *something* or I'll go mad."

Cassia watched her for a moment longer, then dumped the already ground maize flour into a bowl and added water from the full water skin a guard had replenished. She stirred the mixture until it formed a large, sticky ball. Then she formed small cakes and placed them next to the fire.

Maia had finished another batch of maize flour, and Cassia began to work on the second mixture.

Bethany and Dana came into the cooking room, looking hesitantly at their mother, who was still bent over the grinding stone, putting all of her strength into it. Cassia looked from Maia to her daughters. "You can slice the guavas," she said.

Bethany found a kitchen dagger and began the task, letting Dana arrange the slices on a wooden tray.

The work went very fast with the four of them, and soon the meal was ready. Cassia left to tell her parents, and then delivered the simple meal to the guards outside. With dark having fallen, she hurried back inside. Maia was sitting in front of the fire on the cushions, her two girls nestled against her side as she quietly sang.

Cassia stopped to listen for several minutes before returning to the cooking room. Maia had been a great singer in her day, but it was rare to hear her sing in public anymore. Cassia remembered listening to her performances as a youth during celebrations, but now younger women had taken to performing. Yet Maia's voice was still captivating.

Cassia walked slowly to the cooking room and picked up one of the leftover hotcakes and a few slices of guava. The room was solely dependent on the light from the oil lamps now. She sat on a stool, listening to the quiet singing coming from the next room, wondering if her brothers were safe, if Ilana were safe, and whether or not all the priests would make it to the hunting lodge alive.

CHAPTER 19

The God of my rock; in him will I trust: he is my shield . . . and my refuge, my saviour; thou savest me from violence.
—2 Samuel 22:3

Alma the Elder

With horror, Alma watched the robed men carry Ben to the sacrificial altar.

Alma's knees buckled as he gasped for breath. They can't. They won't.

"No!" Alma cried out, pushing through the frenzied crowd. The drums kept beating, drowning out his voice, and the robed men continued tying Ben to the altar as Alma plowed his way to the temple steps. He leapt up them, and no one tried to stop him this time. He was almost to the top when he was sure his son had spotted him. They locked gazes, and for an instant, Alma thought his son would come to his senses and abandon the sacrifice, but his eyes were cold, dead.

Then a man in a scarlet robe blocked Alma's way. He wore the crimson hood, his face shadowed.

But Alma recognized him. The king's oldest son—what is he doing here? Why isn't he with his family at the hunting lodge? *"Ammon?"*

"Sorry, old man," Ammon said, then shoved Alma backward down the stairs.

* * *

The drums are inside my head, pounding against my entire body. Alma brought his hands to his ears, trying to stop the sound, groaning with the movement. Everything hurt. Then he remembered. He had been fleeing with his family from their home, and he'd sent his wife and children ahead with the guards so that he could . . . *No!* It must be a nightmare. But in his mind, he saw the image of Ben beaten by the men wearing armbands, then dragged to the altar of sacrifice.

Alma remembered Ben's lifeless body as he was lifted up . . . up . . . and dumped on the altar. *I should have stayed behind with Ben, somehow protected him, somehow stopped the mob.* Alma wanted to cry out, scream for Ben, anything, but his mouth would only move; no sound would come from his throat.

Then the most horrible memory of all—his son standing on the tower of King Benjamin, wearing a red robe and hood. The hood had slipped off, and Alma recognized his son's face—his hideous grin and shaved head. *My son is the leader of the rebellion.*

The pressure in Alma's chest increased, and he gasped for breath. *How can it be?* He felt as if he had entered the very pit of hell to see his son violating every sacred trust he'd been given.

Alma tried to move, but his limbs wouldn't obey. His mind cleared just enough to hear hundreds of voices chanting in unison. *Save us! Save us!* And then before he could force his eyes open, the chants shifted to screams. Instinctively, Alma knew that Gideon and the border soldiers had arrived.

With every effort, Alma groaned and lifted his eyelids. Plants surrounded him. *I'm in a garden.* He turned his head, wincing at the pain. He was about halfway up the temple mount, having tumbled off the top tier of steps and into the garden. Now he remembered that he'd been pushed by one of those false priests. His breath left him as he remembered seeing the face of the hooded priest—Ammon. *The king's son.*

I must be in hell. This can't be happening. It can't be true.

Alma blinked in pain as his eyes focused on the plaza below, where a battle raged. The palace guards had left their posts, joining their numbers with the strength of the border soldiers. The loyal soldiers fought with swords and knives against the mob's weaker weapons of clubs and sticks.

An arrow struck a man in the chest, and he collapsed in agony. Alma rose to his elbows, nearly choking on the bile that escaped into his throat. To the east, the palace roof was lined with the king's archers, who were shooting into the mob. The archers didn't differentiate between the unbelievers and the defected soldiers, who wore red armbands, signifying their betrayal. Soldiers who had once been friends were now fighting against each other.

Alma moved carefully to his knees, but he stayed crouched, determining his next attack as he assessed the temple mount. His son had disappeared from the top of the tower—in fact, he could spot none of the men in scarlet robes. It seemed the leaders had fled the scene of battle, but a form remained on the altar. *Ben!*

Gingerly, Alma stood and hobbled to the steps. For the third time, he started up them. No one stopped him now; each man was fighting his own battle. At the platform, Alma turned and limped to the altar, passing the stone idols. In the back of his mind, he now recognized the resemblance to the moon goddess, but his focus was on the man lying on the altar.

"Ben!" he cried out in a hoarse voice as he came to a halt in front of the altar. Ben's face was bloodied, but his chest was rising. *He's alive, for now at least.* Alma searched around the altar for a knife—anything to cut the ropes. He saw nothing. The priests had scattered, either fleeing or fighting off the king's soldiers. Frantic, Alma started tearing at the tight knots that held Ben's injured body.

When Alma released the final knot, Ben stirred, moaning.

"Come on, my friend," Alma said, lifting the priest's head. He wished he had some water, but there was no time. He didn't want anyone to prevent their departure. Alma pulled Ben to a sitting position.

"Can you walk?" Alma asked when Ben's eyes flickered open.

Confusion and pain crossed Ben's expression, but he nodded.

"We have to get you out of here," Alma said, helping him stand. "Lean on me." He staggered beneath Ben's weight, but kept moving, past the tower and along the platform until they were on the side of the temple. Just before they turned the corner, Alma cast one more glance at the chaos beyond.

Zarahemla in all its beauty. *The city of cities.* A fierce sight to behold tonight. His eyes stung as he thought of his son. *How will I tell Maia?* This grief was something he could not shield her from, something that even he could not protect her from. *How will I tell King Mosiah? My closest friend, my mentor? The man who spent a lifetime building the Church in Zarahemla? The man who ordained me as high priest over all the land? How will I tell him that his oldest son, his heir, was part of the rebellion? How will I tell him about the mass number of soldiers who defected? The king has been betrayed by not only his own children but his people.*

They traveled slowly down the back side of the temple mount and into the king's hunting preserve. Ben's suffering was apparent, but Alma had to keep them moving. He wouldn't feel safe until he saw his family again and Ben could receive some care—despite the news he had to deliver.

Alma's heart wrenched as he wondered how much Ben knew about his son's role in his near-sacrifice tonight. He shook away the image of Ben upon the altar of the temple. Alma knew that his son would never serve as a priest now, never follow in his father's footprints.

Blinking rapidly against his stinging eyes, Alma's judgment as a high priest kicked in. *My son's name will be blotted out from the records of the Church.* It was like a blow to the chest, and he stumbled, pulling Ben with him.

"Are you all right?" Ben asked.

"Sorry," Alma said, then fell silent as they plodded on. He tried to shake the words from his mind, but they stayed as if etched into marble. Deep and scarring.

The sky had turned a deep purple by the time they reached the hunting lodge. Several soldiers were stationed around the perimeter, and Alma was relieved to see the guards who had been with his family there. It meant his family was safe inside.

A group of men had gathered outside the lodge, quietly talking in the impending darkness. King Mosiah stood with the priests—men who had become as close as brothers to Alma, brothers he'd never had. He knew they felt the same about him—Helam, brother of

Abinadi; Jachin, his father-in-law; Limhi, former king of the city of Nephi.

They turned as Alma and Ben approached, and Mosiah ordered several of the soldiers to help Ben and lead him inside. Without Ben to support, Alma continued toward the small group. His gait felt awkward, not only because of his limp but also because these were the final steps he'd take before delivering his horrific news.

He made his way to the small group, and Alma knew that as soon as Mosiah's gaze met his, the king would sense something was amiss. Alma crossed the last steps to reach the men.

"Are you all right? How did you free Ben?" the king said.

Before Alma could respond, he felt the king assessing him, his warm brown eyes deep with compassion and incredible knowledge—now growing dark with worry. In addition to his regal robes, Mosiah's mere presence commanded attention wherever he went, but his heart was a well of empathy. Alma and his wife had spent countless hours in counsel with the king, fretting over their son's desertion. With the king's change of expression, the other men fell into a hush, each turning toward Alma.

For an instant, he wondered how he would relay the news. Then he realized that these men loved him like family, and if they loved him, they would be the ones he'd depend on in the days to come. These were the men who had endured all manner of trials with him, including the Lamanites' grave persecutions that drove them from their homes, and watching their loved ones suffer and fall victim to death.

But the news Alma brought was one of such a terrible magnitude that it threatened the very souls and possibly lives of all those who lived in the land of Zarahamla. No, it was not a threat from an outside enemy such as the ferocious Lamanites, or of a life-crippling drought or plague, but from their own.

Mosiah was somehow by his side in an instant, silent and fluid, a hand clasping his shoulder. "What is it? Are you injured? Was your home invaded?"

The other men gathered closer, as if to add their support by forming a tight circle of concern.

Alma let out the breath he'd been holding, and his eyes started to burn, the emotion he had kept to himself while traveling here finally surfacing.

"It's my son, Alma the Younger," he said in a hoarse voice. "He is the one who breached the temple, and he has declared himself the leader of the rebellion."

Confusion flashed across King Mosiah's face as if he wondered if he'd heard correctly.

Alma couldn't pull his gaze from Mosiah, though Alma could see the understanding of the terrible truth dawn in the king's eyes.

"He's started a new church," Alma managed to say. "And your son, Ammon, was with him."

The king's face drained of all color at the mention of Ammon, but Alma had to finish what he came to say before he lost the courage. "They tried to sacrifice Ben as a symbol of the destruction of the old church and the ushering in of a new. Hundreds of your soldiers have defected and are fighting against the loyals. They have joined the cause of a new church—a church that they say will free the people from their king . . ."

***

Alma awoke in faint light. His first conscious thought was to wonder where he was. His second was of deep horror. *My son.* His son had been the one—the leader of the rebellion—the one to desecrate the holy temple of the Lord.

How did it come to this? Alma turned over onto his stomach, burying his agony in his hands, not wanting to wake his wife and children, who slept in the same room. That he had slept at all had been unexpected. He'd tried to comfort his wife long into the night until she'd finally fallen asleep, tears wet upon her face. Now his stomach twisted in pain, and he shuddered as he remembered the events from the night before.

The king and the priests had consoled him when he brought them the news at the lodge. They had wept together, prayed together, and called upon the Lord to pour out His mercy.

But how could Alma expect the Lord to have such compassion upon his son? A son who had been schooled in all things righteous, had held sacred offices of trust in the Church, and now declared himself an anti-Christ? A son who had led hundreds, if not more, astray. A son who was tearing down everything that King Benjamin, King Mosiah, and Alma had worked so hard to build.

Alma gripped his hands together, squeezing his frustration through them. But it was no use. The pain in his heart wouldn't ease. Slowly, he moved to his knees. He had been praying since he'd woken from his unconscious state on the temple mount and freed Ben. The prayer continued—never ending.

"O Lord, O God," Alma began in a fervent whisper. "The time is dire, the need is immediate. My son has been going about the city and stealing the hearts of the people. He has created much dissension, and he has become a very wicked man. Even an idolatrous man." Alma's voice wavered. The statues he had seen erected on the temple mount had left little doubt in his mind as to the reason his son had infiltrated the temple. It was to replace the one true God with a symbol of false power. "O God, bring my son to the knowledge of the truth. Teach him not to persecute the Church. Remind him of the captivity of his fathers in the land of Helam and in the land of Nephi. Remind my son how the Lord has infinite mercy for His children and how when we were in bondage, Thou didst deliver us."

Alma felt a pressure at his side and opened his eyes a slit. His wife, Maia, was kneeling next to him, her hands clasped together, her head bowed.

He continued his prayer, repeating his pleas over and over, praying as if the very salvation of his own soul depended on it.

When he finished, Maia wrapped her arms about him, and they cradled each other for several long moments. "I will fast today," he finally whispered.

"So will I," Maia said. "We will all fast for the deliverance of our son. If he can be called to repentance, Zarahemla might conquer this civil unrest at last."

Alma tightened his hold on his wife, feeling the trembling of her shoulders. "The Lord will hear our cries."

Tears streaked down Maia's cheeks as she lifted her face to his. "I am praying for nothing else." She shook her head, her eyes deep with sorrow. "When he was born on our flight to Zarahemla, I was overjoyed with the thought of raising our children in a free land where we could worship how we wished and where we could praise our Lord without hiding from a wicked king."

Alma kissed the top of her head.

"I won't let the deceiver take my son," Maia said in a fierce whisper. "I won't let the adversary lead my son away. He is *my* son. I carried him in my womb and brought him into this world. He is a gift from the Lord, and I will do anything to protect my boy." Her voice broke until she was shaking with sobs.

Alma could only bury his face in his wife's hair, rocking her back and forth.

His daughters, Bethany and Dana, were awakened by their mother's grief, and they rose from their sleeping places and wrapped their thin arms around her. Alma was grateful that Cephas continued to sleep.

Alma closed his eyes, knowing the only thing he had spared his wife from was seeing her son standing on that tower, bringing condemnation upon his soul.

* * *

Before the morning had fully bloomed, a guard had arrived to notify the king about the status of the city of Zarahemla.

Alma and Maia stood with the others, waiting for the king to bring them the news. When the guard left, the king joined them in the main room, accompanied by a tall man.

"Gideon," Alma greeted. "It's been a long time, my friend."

Gideon crossed to Alma and embraced him. Since Gideon commanded the border soldiers, he was only in the city a couple of times a year. Although he was in his fifties, his figure was still imposing, accentuated by the deep jagged scar that ran the length of his right arm. His mass of once-black hair was now a mass of grey. His beard was full and grew a bit wild, but his eyes were steady and intelligent.

"The report is not good," the king said, his voice hesitant and heavy. Deep shadows were beneath his eyes, his face pale. He looked at Gideon.

"Alma the Younger was indeed the leader of the rebellion last night," Gideon said in a raspy voice that had known years of commanding soldiers. "He has been a leader for several months now. And"—he took a deep breath—"the kings' sons have been going about in secret with him."

The room was quiet as everyone stared at Gideon and then the king in disbelief. Then a flurry of questions were called out, but the king raised his hand for silence. "We are looking for them, of course, to answer for their crimes of civil disobedience. We lost good soldiers in the fight before Gideon's legion arrived, and we know that many soldiers deserted us. But we have also arrested the dozens of rebels who had set fires on their way to the temple. We'll be returning to assess the damage today."

The king looked down for a moment, then back up, his face ashen. "The temple has been violated, but it's not just the vandalism," he continued in a quiet voice. "The mob brought in idols and were apparently about to use Ben as their sacrificial initiation." He nodded at Alma. "Every fear that we've had has been realized."

He turned to look at the rest of the group. "Today we'll hold a special fast." Heads nodded around the room. "We'll supplicate the Lord to redeem our city and return our sons to us." The king focused on Alma. "Please offer a blessing with our intent."

As a collective group, everyone sank to their knees and bowed their heads, then Alma started to pray. He repeated his earlier personal sentiments, adding prayers for the restoration of the temple and the welfare of the people and the city. When he finished, everyone stood and resolutely prepared to leave the lodge.

The king's and priests' families were somber as they traveled back to their homesteads. Guards would keep vigil outside everyone's homes, and although the mob had been completely dispersed, the king still worried it could band again within a few days. Limhi's family would be taking up temporary residence at the palace.

Maia's hand slid into Alma's, and he gripped it tightly. "I didn't think we'd be going back home so soon," Maia said.

"I didn't either," he said. They reached the hill that led up to the backside of the palace. Alma's heart was heavy as he climbed, pulling his wife along with him. He wondered what sights he would see—what damage had been done to the temple—if the archive room lay untouched. Another prayer for another detail. It seemed that nearly every word and thought was a prayer now.

They arrived at the back gardens, and Cassia rushed inside the palace, saying something about the cooking room. Alma took his family through the main hall, then out the front entrance. They paused as they exited the building. The sound of beating drums was gone, but Alma felt as if they still beat inside him. As he looked around, he remembered the chaos and confusion of the night before and marveled at the quiet of today.

Soldiers were stationed around the palace and the temple, as well as at various intervals along the plaza and the roads leading in and out of the plaza. Then Alma turned to the temple, staring. The first thing he noticed was that the building seemed unharmed, but the surrounding grounds were marred by black soot as if the grounds had been burned sporadically.

The temple steps were dotted with remains of a fierce battle, discarded weapons, bits of clothing, several helmets, a broken sword, and the telltale stains of spilt blood. Alma winced and stepped away from his wife and children. "I must look inside."

Maia nodded, and Alma walked down the palace steps. Then he made his way across the west end of the plaza where the temple stairs began. He sidestepped his way up the steps, avoiding the areas of dried blood and other debris. He paused at the top of the platform, studying the statue that had been brought in by his son. It was a replica of the moon goddess with added features. In one hand she held a dagger, in another a shield—obviously representing warfare.

With a heavy heart, Alma continued along the temple mount and stopped in front of the archive room. The door had been splintered, but not completely broken down. It appeared as if someone had started to break it but was interrupted. Alma took the key from the pouch at his waistband and inserted it into the lock. He pushed open the fractured door and stepped inside the room. Nothing had been touched—the scrolls that were scattered about the center table were just as he and Ben had dumped them in their haste the day before.

Alma's gaze strayed to the shelves of baptism records. He knew exactly which shelf contained those of his family. Hesitantly he moved to the shelf and took down a scroll with the script of his family name at the top of it. The baptisms were all recorded in neat lettering. He unrolled the record. His gaze fell on his son's name and baptismal date. The lettering blurred as Alma stared at it. He blinked against the stinging in his eyes. He had recorded his son's name and baptism himself. And now, unless his son changed, Alma would be blotting the name out.

He turned toward the broken door and exited, still clutching the scroll in his hand. Once outside, he saw that the king's guards had tied ropes around the goddess statue and were heaving it into a cart. The moon goddess, or whoever she was, had had a very short reign on the temple mount. Alma passed the guards, nodding in greeting, then entered the temple. The clean-up hadn't extended this far yet. The scribe's table was overturned; oil lamps had been shattered on the stone floor. Alma walked to the scribe's table and lifted it upright again. Then he picked up scattered sheaves that were strewn about the floor and stacked them on the table. He moved on past the judgment seats, then he parted the hanging tapestry that separated the main chamber of the temple from the Holy of Holies.

There, Alma faced the altar, and with the record still gripped in his hand, he knelt and began to pray for his son's soul.

CHAPTER 20

. . . the lamp of the wicked shall be put out.
—Proverbs13:9

Two Weeks Later

Alma the Younger

Nocking the arrow, Alma aimed at the jaguar's upper shoulder, appreciating the way the animal's fur shimmered gold in the afternoon light. It was a beautiful male, at least six years old. The cat's massive muscles seemed to ripple through its shiny coat. The beast turned its head slightly, ears cocked, but Alma remained motionless. He licked his dry lips, but no other movement came from his taut body position.

A little more patience and Alma knew he'd have himself a fine catch. He'd spent two weeks tracking this animal, playing its games, and he was ready to bring it down—two weeks since his people had been driven from the temple by the king's reinforcements.

Alma's heart still stung with the defeat. But his return would be more glorious and powerful—and more final. There was no hope for the stone statues of the goddess Bel, so Alma was having Teoti remake them.

A light breeze kicked up, ruffling the jaguar's fur. The animal's coat would rival the one given to him by the citizens of the village. One second passed, then two. The jaguar moved its gaze forward, as if he, too, were admiring the green- and gold-dappled valley spread below.

With deadly precision, Alma released the arrow. His heart seemed to stop as he waited the seconds before the arrow imbedded into the animal's flesh.

The jaguar jerked, then went rigid. Its tawny head swung around slowly, and its yellow eyes seemed to infiltrate the foliage as it searched for its predator.

Alma stood from his crouched position, the bow dangling at his side, and met the great cat's gaze. Then with an audible exhale, the jaguar slumped to the ground, eyes still open. Even in death, it was a beast of formidable power.

Alma stepped quietly through the underbrush until he reached the animal's side. There was no breath coming from it now, and he watched for any signs of movement before creeping any closer. Finally, he knelt and pried out the arrow. The tip had broken off—the arrow was no good.

But it was a worthy loss. He bent and tied the creature's front paws together with rope and repeated the action for the back paws. Then, still crouched to the ground, he heaved the great beast onto his shoulders. He staggered beneath its weight, then gained his footing and started down the hillside.

About halfway down, Alma gave out a couple of short whistles. Within moments, men appeared, armed and ready. When they saw Alma, their expressions relaxed, and two of them hefted the jaguar from his back.

Alma stretched his shoulder muscles and wiped the perspiration from his face with the back of his hand. He followed the men to where he and the council had been hiding in caves since the rebellion, waiting for the king's frenzied search to die down.

Yet each night, Alma was able to sneak back into the villages and spread the word that the rebellion was still alive. The Church of Liberty was still growing and needed its loyal members more than ever. Those who swore fidelity were given red-dyed leather armbands with the symbol of the half moon to wear concealed beneath their clothing.

In just the past two weeks, they'd nearly doubled their forces. Marching on the temple mount had made the citizens of Zarahemla wake up and understand that the revolution would not be put down.

The first week in hiding, Alma had sent a decree to the king to see if he was willing to change his laws so that the unbelievers would not be subject to the high priest's rule. The king imprisoned the messenger.

Alma slowed as the series of caves came into view.

Aaron sat in the sunshine, perched on a rock, watching Ammon and Jacob spar with swords. Ammon kept stopping Jacob and instructing him how to hold the sword at the correct angle. "One blow could sever your enemy's arm. Just one blow."

Jacob shook his head, disbelieving. "I don't believe it."

"Would you like me to demonstrate?" Ammon asked, his face quirked in a smile.

Aaron laughed at the pair. "You'll have to find someone more willing than Jacob here."

It is good to see Aaron shake his sullenness, Alma thought. Aaron turned to see Alma approaching.

"Call the council together," Alma said. "It's time to act." Moments later, the council was gathered around Alma in the largest cave, which Alma had taken over as his private quarters. The only one missing was Sara, but it was too dangerous for any women out in the wild country. The council stared at him, eyes bleary, expressions weary from nights of little sleep due to the demands of midnight recruiting.

"We must scatter the king's forces like the wind," Alma announced. "I've finally brought down the jaguar I've been chasing, and I realized something." He looked at the men—the sons of Mosiah, the other council members—each of their expressions curious. "We must draw out the king—give him no choice but to agree with our terms. If he refuses again, we'll force him into exile. I want to hear your suggestions on how to do this."

"Should we charge the temple mount again?" Kaman asked.

"No," Ammon cut in. "Their forces are well-fortified, and we'll only lose more lives."

"What about burning the king's hunting preserve?" Jacob offered.

After a moment of consideration, Alma shook his head. "It will only scare the animals away, and deplete our own food supply."

"We must take something precious from him," Kaman suggested. "Like his daughter."

Alma stared at Kaman, ready to protest, but the suggestion made strange sense.

Ammon nodded, agreeing as well. "No harm would come to her, of course, but Cassia would make an excellent bargaining piece." He looked around at the council men. "For her safe return, the king would be willing to meet our terms."

Adrenaline stirred through Alma as he thought of executing such a grand scheme. "We will put the plan into action tomorrow," he said. "Tonight we will be recruiting in Bilshan's village of Cuello. The princes will come with me. Kaman, Jacob, and the others will remain here, preparing for the abduction of the king's daughter."

* * *

These people love us, Alma thought as he turned over on the soft bed the Cuello villagers had provided for him. He reached for the nearly empty wine jug that sat next to the bed. Taking a swallow to moisten his parched mouth, he closed his eyes briefly as the sweet wine nectar slid down his throat.

They had been given lodging the night before after Alma's dynamic speech and celebratory feast. This was the village where Belicia had been born. Her parents were dead, but Alma was able to meet her siblings, one of them Bilshan, the former officer in the king's royal guard who had joined Alma's cause. The villagers had welcomed him back into their village, and in no time he was made a member of the senior council.

The entire village had come out and pledged their support and honor of the goddess Bel. Alma had donated a small replica of the larger statues of the goddess. Bilshan had become emotional when Alma revealed the stone statue.

After that, Bilshan had provided his best wine, best food. Everything. Even women. Alma turned to see a woman next to him on the vast bed. She was still sleeping quite soundly—having drunk at least as much wine as he had the night before, if not more. For a moment he stared at her dark brown hair spilling across the bedding, trying to remember her name. *Shuah.* He smiled to himself, proud that he remembered.

The Cuello villagers had brought Alma many gifts—furs, a feathered cape, and even jewels. The sons of Mosiah received equal treatment and were now sleeping in the other rooms of the two-level home. Ammon had spent time with the village blacksmith, giving him advice on fashioning the weapons for the village legion. This place contained many strong young men who were making excellent recruits.

Alma stretched in bed, relaxing for a few more moments. This morning the Cuello people would feed them early, then Alma would be on his way to take part in Kaman's plan of abducting Cassia.

In the quiet stillness, Alma let his thoughts dwell on Cassia for a few moments. She seemed to be part of another life—one that he'd left behind long ago. She was unlike the other women he'd had in his life, Belicia or Sara. Cassia had lived a privileged life and had never wanted for anything. Belicia and Sara had practically slaved in order to have food in their bellies. Yet Alma couldn't begrudge Cassia. He knew she'd experienced pain with the death of Nehem, and he regretted that. But it was no different than what the unbelievers had endured at the hand of the king.

Cassia was an innocent, *for now.* And Alma hoped she would continue to be, but her abduction was the next step in the political process of gaining the king's adherence to Alma's demands.

He rose from the bed and donned his clothing. The morning air was cool, and he pulled on the feathered cape presented to him by the village. He grabbed the wine jug and carried it with him to the main room, where he found Ammon sitting on a pile of cushions. His eyes carried dark shadows beneath them.

"Did you not sleep?" Alma asked.

Ammon shook his head slowly. "Not much. You?"

"Not much either."

"The women of Cuello are beautiful," Ammon said with a smile.

"I'll agree with that," Alma said and lifted the jug to his lips. He swallowed and wiped his mouth with the back of his hand.

Ammon was watching him with an amused expression. "I think I've devised a plan to capture Cassia."

Alma gave a short nod. "We should prepare to leave then, and deliver your plan to Kaman and Jacob."

"But that's just it," Ammon said. "I don't think those two should be involved."

"Why not?"

"They'll be too easily recognized anywhere near the palace. It needs to be someone who can be more elusive."

"Let's talk it over with Kaman when we reach the caves. Maybe he has a plan as well, and we can see which will be more effective." Then Alma hesitated as a new thought entered his mind. "What about a woman?"

Ammon raised his dark brows. "To do what?"

"To visit Cassia under false pretences. Perhaps she can bring news of her brothers—"

"That wouldn't draw my sister out."

Alma paused, thinking. "What about a secret meeting for reconciliation? A woman could get inside the palace and ask to meet with Cassia."

"Or . . ." Ammon said, nodding his head now. "She could pose as a spice merchant. Cassia is obsessive about checking the market for rare and unusual spices. My father has kept her from browsing the markets—one of her greatest loves."

For an instant, he saw an image of Cassia's head bent over a basket of vanilla seed pods in the marketplace. Alma blinked and focused on Ammon again. "We'll send Sara."

"Does she have the skills to deceive Cassia?"

"Yes," Alma said, the plan growing and forming in his mind. The more he studied it out, the better it became. On the way to the caves, he would stop in the Isidro village and fetch Sara. He hoped to find her ready and willing.

Alma asked Ammon to wake his brothers to begin the return journey, then he went to find Bilshan. He stood in the village plaza, instructing a group of workers in building a platform in front of their church house. The small statue of Bel would be set upon the platform for all to worship and remember.

Alma watched for a few minutes, pleased with the devotion of these people. Then he approached Bilshan. The men greeted each other like longtime friends by clasping each other's hands. Once someone had been initiated into the cause of freedom, it was like they immediately became close brothers.

Alma drew back. "We must leave this morning and continue our crusade. Thank you for your hospitality. We are indeed in your debt."

"You are welcome here anytime." Bilshan grinned. "There is no debt to be paid. What's ours is yours."

Alma clapped the man on the shoulder. "We can only take a few of the gifts that were presented to us last night—only what we can carry. We do not want to draw undue attention to our travels."

"I understand," Bilshan said. "We will keep the treasures for you in a safe place until you can send for them."

"No," Alma said. "If the rightful owners cannot use them for their own good, sell them for the fortification of your village, to arm your men and to recruit more freedom soldiers."

Alma left Bilshan, confidence in every step. The sons of Mosiah were ready by the time he reached the borrowed house. Alma looked over the gifts that were going to be left behind. He took a fine dagger and a pouch of inlaid gold and precious stones. Those he would give to Sara.

As the morning sun spread its warmth over the quiet village, Alma and the sons of Mosiah passed the humble huts. Several villagers came out to wave good-bye, and many of them bowed in respect. Omner and Himni returned the bows, making everyone laugh.

For once, Aaron wasn't sullen. He must have enjoyed his company the night before. Alma was glad. He'd been more cankerous than usual after nearly being turned in by Ilana.

When they'd left the village behind, Himni started singing one of the ballads they'd heard in Cuello. Omner punched him in the arm. "You're hurting my head."

"Enough," Alma said, agreeing. "We've heard the finest singers in the land perform for us, so why should we have to listen to your butchering?"

Himni laughed and continued his off-key melody.

Alma's neck grew warm as his irritation increased, and he touched the new dagger he'd taken from the village gifts. Removing it from his waistband, he turned it over, enjoying the sun's glint off the decorated hilt.

"Tell your brothers the plan," Alma said, glancing at Ammon, trying anything to get Himni to stop singing.

Ammon outlined the plan to abduct Cassia, and thankfully Himni didn't continue his song.

"Perfect," Omner said, rubbing his hands together. "A woman will draw out our sister, and our father will be forced to negotiate with Alma."

"Although I wouldn't mind some sword practice," Himni said, pulling out his dagger and making a few exaggerated lunges as if he held a sword. "Do you think I'm getting better?"

Laughing, Alma said, "You'd best leave the planning to Ammon and the village woman. We wouldn't want to have to account for your spilt blood."

Himni ignored him and continued to wave his hand wildly in the air as if he had a whole series of opponents pressing down.

Alma thought of Sara. She'd need her own protection. "Ammon," he said, looking over at him. "Sara will do well with a bit of advice on using a dagger."

"You're right," Ammon said, "although she might already have experience in defending herself."

"Indeed," Alma said as they reached a bend in the road. They veered to the right, a smaller path that was sheltered by the encroaching forest. Alma was surprised to see mist clinging to the trees. The morning was already hot, and they were above the lower valley where the mist usually burned off in the first hour of the morning. He opened his mouth to comment on the unusual mist when it thickened.

Alma's hand instinctively tightened about his dagger as an unexplained shot of dread pressed through him. He slowed, looking around furtively, noticing that the brothers had come to a stop. They stared at the mist, looking confused.

"What's happening?" Himni asked, his voice low and filled with fear.

"It's—" Alma began, then halted. The cloud had brightened as the noonday sun and formed into the shape of a man—no, there was a man *inside* the cloud. Alma's mouth fell open in astonishment. The man wore a brilliant white robe, his hair nearly the same shade. For an instant, Alma wondered if the man were alive or dead, though his eyes were open—looking straight at him.

The voice that erupted left no doubt in Alma's mind that the man was alive. It was as loud as thunder and rocked through Alma's body. "Alma, why persecutest thou the Church of God?"

Beneath Alma's feet, the ground shook. The king's sons cried out, falling to the earth. Alma lost his balance as well and fell to his knees. His hands flew out before him as he steadied himself against the ground. "Who are you?" he gasped.

Alma heard the brothers groaning. He wondered if they were hurt, but he couldn't take his eyes off the man.

"Alma, arise and stand forth." The voice shook Alma's entire body.

"What do you want?" Alma whispered, for it seemed his voice was gone. He stood, his legs quivering beneath him, and he looked at the man, wondering if he were a shaman's conjecture. The blinding white of his garments, the white of his hair, the thunderous voice that made the very ground shake. Alma swallowed, his heart pounding. Then, unbidden and unfathomable, he realized what the personage was—*an angel.*

The angel spoke again, his voice causing the ground to quake. "Why persecutest thou the Church of God? For the Lord hath said: 'This is my church, and I will establish it; and nothing shall overthrow it, save it is the transgression of my people.'"

"I—I have . . ." Alma couldn't continue as the terrible realization hit him. *I've been wrong. So wrong!*

"If thou wilt of thyself be destroyed, seek no more to destroy the Church of God."

His legs failed, and he sank to the ground. *God is real. He has sent an angel to chastise me. God will destroy me!* His fingers clutched at the dirt as he tried to steady his roiling stomach. It was as if his strength had fled his limbs and he was like a helpless child. "Please . . ." he gasped.

The angel spoke again, tearing into Alma's soul, "Behold, the Lord hath heard the prayers of his people, and also the prayers of his servant, Alma, who is thy father."

God has heard my father's prayers! His body started to tremble violently, and he brought his shaking hands to his face in astonishment.

The angel's gaze burned straight into Alma. "For he has prayed with much faith concerning thee that thou mightest be brought to the knowledge of the truth; therefore, for this purpose have I come to convince thee of the power and authority of God, that the prayers of his servants might be answered according to their faith."

I should have known that my father would be praying for me. I hardened my heart and ignored the promptings of the Spirit. I justified my wrongful actions and became blinded by my own iniquity.

"Can ye dispute the power of God?" The angel's voice seemed to gain in power, his very words piercing the air. "For behold, doth not my voice shake the earth? And can ye not also behold me before you?"

"Yes," Alma managed to say.

"I am sent from God."

I have made the most horrible mistake. Alma's body shuddered, and numbness settled over him. The angel's words echoed through his mind. Nearby, the brothers were silent, transfixed by the angel as well.

"Now I say unto thee," the angel said, his voice cutting through Alma's soul, "Go, and remember the captivity of thy fathers in the land of Helam, and in the land of Nephi; and remember how great things he has done for them; for they were in bondage, and he has delivered them."

Yes, Alma thought. *I was taught the stories as a child, before I could walk or speak. I could never forget them if I wanted to. But they were only stories to me then.*

"And now I say unto thee, Alma, go thy way, and seek to destroy the Church no more, that their prayers may be answered, and this even if thou wilt of thyself be cast off."

How can I undo my wrongs? I raised up a false idol. I desecrated the temple. I can't undo that. What will happen to me? Alma blinked rapidly. It took a moment for him to realize that his face was wet from tears.

He couldn't move, couldn't even turn his head to see if the brothers were witnessing and hearing the same message. *I have committed gross iniquities against God Himself.* A groan came from somewhere inside Alma, and his mind spun as fear encompassed him. *Only the power of God can send an angel and move the earth, and He is angry with me. I will be cast off.*

He sank lower to the ground until he was on his elbows and knees. Then his forehead pressed against the dirt, ready to collapse. The angel continued to speak to the brothers, but Alma no longer comprehended the words as he slid to the ground, his limbs useless. He blinked, tears dripping into the dirt beneath his face. *I have been a fool. I have led hundreds of people astray. I have failed.*

Then the cloud thickened, covering the angel until Alma could no longer see him. The voice of thunder quieted, and the brilliancy of the angel was gone, leaving them in the cool morning shade once again. Alma worked his mouth, trying to call out, but no words came.

If he'd had the strength, sobs would have wracked his body, but his anguish was internal, rendering him into a paralyzed state. His eyes shut as the angel's words repeated in his mind.

Panicked voices broke through the haze, and Alma felt someone rolling him over. But it was too much of an effort to open his eyes—he literally had no strength left. Someone moved his arms, touched his forehead, lifted his eyelids. He felt pressure against his chest.

I'm still alive, Alma wanted to say. *But I will be destroyed. I committed shameful acts of rebellion—went against my own family, those whom I love the most. I have brought death and condemnation to many. I have made the most awful mistake imaginable.*

He was lifted by several hands—those of the sons of Mosiah—and they started to carry him.

Oh God, I have forsaken Thee in the worst way.

The brothers' voices floated above him—worried, urgent, but they were so faint that he couldn't understand anything they were saying. And then their voices faded completely into oblivion.

CHAPTER 21

O give thanks unto the Lord; for he is good: because his mercy endureth for ever.
—Psalm 118:1

Alma the Elder

The familiar pang of hunger clenched Alma's stomach as he dressed. Another day of fasting, another day of praying for his son. Alma had told King Mosiah that he would be late today. He wanted to spend part of the morning with his wife, who had been struggling the past couple of days, more so than usual.

Maia had risen at dawn, as was her custom, to work in the herb garden, clearing the weeds and watering the flourishing plants. Alma exited through the back courtyard. His wife was bent over her task, and a stray piece of hair had escaped her plaits. Alma felt a pang in his heart, marveling how he could love her even more than the day they married so long ago.

"Do you need the water jug refilled?" Alma asked.

Maia turned her head slightly. "No, I can do it."

When he didn't move, she lifted her head and straightened. She gave him a curious look. "Are you on your way to the temple?"

"I told the king that I was going to spend the morning with you."

Maia raised her eyebrow and put a dirt-covered hand on her hip. "Oh?"

"I thought . . . that you could use some help," Alma said, studying her. Her mouth quirked in a half-smile, but instead of the rejection that he had expected, she walked toward him and put her arms around his waist. Leaning against him, Maia let out a sigh.

"Thank you," she whispered.

They stood there for a moment, then Maia drew back and looked up at Alma. Her eyes were moist, but he could see she was fighting back further emotion. "In that case," she said, "you can refill the water jug."

He smiled, leaned down, and kissed her cheek. "Right away."

When Alma returned with the jug full of well water, Maia was sitting on a nearby bench, perspiration at her hair line. She looked so young when she wore her hair down. She looked thinner this morning, more like she had when they'd first married. Alma knew she'd been fasting as much as he had. If it weren't for the vastness of their homestead and the fact that they had three children asleep inside, Alma could almost imagine they were back in the city of Helam.

Alma sat beside his wife and took her soiled hand in his. She squeezed his fingers, and they sat in silence for a while, listening to the quail and the gentle breeze ruffle the tall ceiba trees behind them.

Finally, Maia broke the silence. "I keep asking myself why."

Alma didn't need any more explanation. He understood perfectly, for he'd been asking himself the same question day and night.

"I know why our son left—and I thought it would give him the needed time to realize how important his family and the Church are . . ." Maia brought her other hand to her face and wiped at a stray tear. It left a dirty mark on her face, and Alma used the sleeve of his robe to wipe it away.

She smiled at him briefly, but it didn't reach her eyes. "Does he not know how much we love him? How much we hurt and grieve for his actions? How we would forgive him if only he would return to us?" She sighed with frustration. "I need to go to him and speak with him."

"Maia," Alma said, "He is not the same man who left our home. He has become a very wicked and idolatrous man. I don't know how he'd react to seeing you." He released her hand and put his arm around his shoulder. "I'd fear for your safety."

Maia leaned her head against his shoulder. "I can't stand this waiting, the not knowing. The worry gnaws at my very soul. I've put my trust and faith in the Lord, yet I still feel like I must do something. Even if it's just to beg and plead with him. He might laugh, he might cast me out, but I want him to know that we still love him."

Alma leaned his head against hers. "I will come with you then. We'll search every village, every hillside."

She nodded, remaining silent, and her other hand reached up to link through his. Together they watched the sun dispel the morning shadows, burning off the mist near the foothills.

"Do you think he has regrets?"

"I don't know," Alma said. "He no longer has the Spirit with him. He doesn't feel things as you and I—but has lived through many months of justifications."

"What about the king's sons? How can they all be trying to destroy the Church? Which one do you think instigated it?"

He shook his head slowly. "Our son has always been a leader with the king's sons. They seem to worship him now more than ever."

She shuddered, drawing closer to Alma. After several more minutes of quiet, Maia said, "I must begin preparations for the morning meal. The girls and Cephas should be awake soon."

Alma kissed the top of her head, then the two of them stood and slowly walked hand in hand to the house. Once at the cooking room, Maia turned to him. "You prepare for the temple. I'll be all right. Thanks for staying for a while."

"I can stay longer."

"No," she said, gently pushing on his chest. "There's no reason for all of us to be moping around."

Alma brushed a stray piece of hair from her cheek and tucked it behind her ear. "All right. I'll get ready and leave after the meal."

Before changing into his temple robes, Alma walked over to their oldest son's room. It was cool and dark, smelling of stale emptiness. He crossed to the table where a slingshot lay untouched. Alma picked it up, weighing the finely twined rope in his hands. When his son was younger, he'd carried several sizes of slings with him. He hadn't been strong enough to control distance, so he used various lengths. But as he grew older, he could use one sling for any distance, accurately and deadly.

Alma wrapped the sling around his palm, staring at the contrast of the rough twine against his smoother hands. Then he closed his fist around the rope, squeezing his eyes shut as well. Unbidden, the image of his eldest as a young eight-year-old came to his mind—running through the field toward home, excited to show his mother and father the rabbit he'd shot down with his sling. Alma could see the sun reflect off his son's dark, wavy hair and the light in his laughing brown eyes. For an instant, Alma felt as if he could reach out and touch his young son through his visualization.

But as quickly as the image had come, it was gone. Alma let the slingshot fall from his hand onto the table. He stepped away, the temporary warmth in his chest now replaced by cold barrenness.

He took several deep breaths, then walked out of the room. As he moved toward the cooking room he thought he heard someone calling outside. He paused, listening above the sounds that Maia made as she prepared the meal.

The call came again, "Father Alma!"

He strode to the door, his heart quickening. Flinging open the door, he peered out into the courtyard. Several men were coming toward him, carrying something between them. It took a moment for Alma to realize that they carried a lifeless man. Then his gaze focused on the messengers—Ammon . . . the king's sons.

Alma stiffened at the sight of them, but the expression on Ammon's face was not one of vindictive revenge but of fear.

"Father Alma!" Ammon said again, his face red with exertion.

Then Alma's gaze strayed to the limp form between the four men. "My son," he cried out and started to run. "Maia!" he called as he hurried to reach the king's sons.

Alma looked down on his son, frantically searching for wounds, blood, any serious injury, but seeing nothing, he looked up at Ammon. "Is he . . . ?"

"He's alive," Ammon said.

"Bring him inside," Alma ordered and hurried them in through the doorway. Maia had come out of the cooking room, and stood there, her hands covering her mouth.

Ammon nodded at Maia. "He's alive," he said.

Once they had placed Alma the Younger on the rug on the floor, they stood together, as if frightened.

Maia hurried to her son's side and started to examine him.

Alma straightened, eyeing the four brothers. "What happened?"

Ammon told him of the thick cloud and the angel dressed in brilliant white that had delivered a message from the Lord.

Maia's head came up, and she stared at the king's sons. Alma reached for her hand and pulled her to her feet, wrapping his arms about her. "It is the power of God," he whispered. He looked down at his son, who hadn't moved, hadn't even opened his eyes. Then Alma knelt beside him and placed a hand on his chest, reassuring himself with the rhythmic rise and fall of his son's chest.

Maia knelt next to him. "He saw an angel?" she said, astonishment in her voice.

"Yes," Ammon's voice said above them. "The angel said the Lord had heard the prayers of his people, and also the prayers of his father."

For a moment, Alma held still, letting the words wash over him. *The Lord heard my prayers.* Warmth burst through him, and he felt as if his whole being were on fire. He leaned over his son and kissed each cheek. "Praise be to the Lord our God."

He looked up at the king's sons, tears filling his eyes. "Let us rejoice! The power of God has overcome my son."

Ammon nodded, tears on his own face, joined by his three brothers. They knelt beside the body of Alma the Younger and clasped hands.

"Let us praise the Almighty Lord our God and give thanks for this miracle."

Next to him, Maia started to cry softly.

Alma offered a prayer of thanksgiving, his voice trembling with emotion. When the prayer concluded, Bethany and Dana entered the room, their long hair hanging in tangles as they walked over to their brother. A rumpled but bright-eyed Cephas followed close behind.

Maia leapt to her feet and embraced her daughters, telling them the good news. Bethany and Dana stared at the seemingly lifeless form in wonder while Cephas scrambled close to his brother and stared intently into his face.

Alma turned to his wife. "We will take our son to the palace so that everyone might witness this miracle." He looked at the king's sons. "Thank you, my friends, for bringing my son home. Our prayers have been answered. We will call a multitude together so that you might testify of all that happened to you and my son."

Ammon nodded and crossed to Alma, falling into his embrace. When the two men pulled apart, Ammon said, "We hope you can forgive us, Father Alma. Thank you for your prayers." His eyes filled with tears as he stepped back and allowed his other brothers to come forward and express their gratitude.

* * *

Cassia

Cassia woke to the sound of running footsteps outside her door. *Not another disturbance,* she thought with a grimace. Then the shell trumpets started blaring. She climbed out of bed and looked through her window. The front courtyard of the palace was filling up with people, and it looked like the priests from the temple were all present. She recognized the tall figure of Alma the Elder, dressed in his customary temple robes, and next to him stood her father.

Her heart thudding with both dread and anticipation, Cassia quickly dressed. Within minutes she was out the door, running through the corridors to the front entrance. She came to a stop at the top of the stairs. Near the bottom, through the gathering people a man lay on the ground. *Another murder!* With horror, she looked around for her mother. The queen stood in the crowd, blending with them as if she were just another observer, but there was no fear on her mother's face.

A couple of servants exited behind Cassia and scurried past, running down the steps and joining the crowd. Cassia followed them, heading toward her mother. But first, she tried to get a glimpse of the man—hoping he wasn't covered in blood or gruesomely injured.

She pushed through the whispering crowd, overhearing the word "angel" repeated several times. When she reached the front of the gathering, she stared at the man on the ground. He had been placed on a rug, his head supported with a small cushion. *Alma!* Cassia would recognize those distinguished facial features and dark eyebrows anywhere, although his wavy hair had been shorn off. She watched his face and chest and determined he was not dead. Maybe he was badly injured, although she couldn't see any immediate evidence. Why was he not at the healer's and instead laid out in the middle of a public square? And why were the trumpets blaring around the city?

Hovering near him were her four brothers, their faces concerned and awestruck. She studied them as the crowd jostled about her. She hadn't seen them for weeks, but there was something different about them. Before she could try to move toward them, her mother appeared at her side, clutching her arm.

"There you are, my dear."

"What's wrong with Alma the Younger?" Cassia asked, her throat tight. After all that Alma had done to wrong her family and the city, she found she still cared—a great deal.

Her mother leaned close and said in a quiet voice, "Alma and your brothers were visited by an angel."

A jolt sped through Cassia's entire body, and instant tears filled her eyes. She couldn't speak for several moments, but just stared at Alma's prostrate figure as her mother continued to talk.

"Heaven be praised," the queen said. "We've been praying for this day, and the Lord has seen fit to intervene." She squeezed her hand tightly. "It happened just outside the village of Cuello. Your brothers brought Alma to his father's home. It seems that Alma is in a half-slumber. He is so weak that he can't talk or move . . . or even open his eyes."

"Is he awake?" Cassia asked, her voice trembling.

"He might be able to hear us. We don't know."

Before she could ask more questions, a hush fell over the people. The high priest had positioned himself at the top of the stairs, King Mosiah next to him. Alma raised his hands for complete silence.

"I've called the priests and all of you together because early this morning we witnessed a miracle. The sons of Mosiah brought my son to my home—his strength had been taken from him by the power of the Lord."

A myriad of gasps sounded throughout the crowd.

"An angel of the Lord appeared to my son and the sons of Mosiah. As you may know, they have been secretly going about to destroy the Church."

A few in the crowd started to murmur.

"But today is a day for rejoicing and a day for redemption," the high priest said, his hands raised again for attention. "The Lord has shown His mercy to the land of Zarahemla. He has interfered with the wrongful intentions of powerful men who were bent on turning the city over to the adversary."

Cassia brought a trembling hand to her mouth, trying to comprehend all that the high priest was saying.

"My son has been left dumb, without even the strength to lift his head." He looked out over the crowd. "We will rejoice in the Lord's answer to our prayers. We will also now fast and pray to the Lord our God that He will open the mouth of Alma the Younger, so that he might speak. We will pray that the strength will be restored to his every limb."

Cassia's gaze slid over to Alma the Younger's helpless form, and she clasped her hands together, offering a silent prayer, a prayer of renewed hope, where she had lost what was there before. All around her heads bowed, and many of the people sank to their knees.

As the high priest led the people in prayer, Cassia realized she was crying. Warmth flooded her as the Spirit comforted her. She wiped the tears from her eyes, crying from the sweet assurance and also over all that Alma had gone through and was now going through.

When the public prayer was over, the people milled about, talking in hushed tones. The queen led Cassia by the hand over to Alma. Several people had knelt by his side, including his mother, sisters, and brother. Maia looked up as they approached, her face streaked with tears. She flew into the queen's arms, and the two held each other for a long moment.

The king came down the steps with the high priest and instructed the priests to carry Alma into the palace and to lay him out in the throne room on a makeshift bed. The servants hurried back to the palace to prepare the bed, and the priests lifted the body up.

As Alma was carried to the palace, Cassia's eyes caught those of Ammon, who had been kneeling on the other side of their friend. Her brother walked toward her, his eyes red from emotion. He took Cassia's hand in his own trembling one.

"I was in the dark for so long, and I hurt so many people—especially you," he said, his voice cracking. He looked down, then up again, his eyes filled with tears. "I'm so sorry about Nehem. We did not order his death, but we know who killed him. We've confessed to Father, and he will be taking action soon. But I wanted to tell you personally." He bowed his head. "We hid Nehem's murderers so that Father wouldn't find them." After a moment, he raised his gaze to meet Cassia's. "Can you ever forgive me?"

She stared into his eyes, full of grief and sorrow. Yet she felt the repentance in them. A sense of relief filled her now that she knew without a doubt that neither Alma nor her brothers had been Nehem's murderer. And now her tough brother, the one who could battle any man in Zarahemla, the one who'd almost overthrown their father's kingdom, was begging for *her* forgiveness.

Her heart swelled a fraction, and she knew it wouldn't be today, but eventually, she'd be able to completely forgive him. She stepped into his arms and held on.

When she finally released Ammon, her other brothers were waiting to speak with her, each in turn asking for forgiveness. She nodded, tears streaking her cheeks, and embraced each one.

Ammon was at her side again, taking her hand. "I want to tell you about the angel," he said in a thick voice.

Cassia wiped tears from her face. "All right," she whispered.

Brother and sister walked into the palace, but instead of following the family and priests into the throne room, they turned down the corridor to Ammon's room.

Cassia settled on a low stool by the dark fireplace and watched her brother pace the room. Finally he stopped and sat at her feet.

"It's hard to put into words," he said at last. "I've never been filled with so much fear in my life."

Cassia put a hand on his shoulder as he continued in a shaky voice. "There was a mist that thickened into a cloud. I thought it was a little strange, but it was very early in the morning. And I thought I was still drunk." He looked up at his sister, his expression filled with shame. He lowered his voice to a whisper. "But it was neither of those causes. With my own eyes I saw a man descend from that cloud. When he spoke, I knew it could be no other than an angel sent from the Lord."

Ammon exhaled, then took a tremulous breath. "His voice was as loud as thunder, piercing every bit of my body. It was like the words were resonating inside me. At the same time, the earth started shaking. We were all so astonished that we fell to the ground, but we couldn't take our eyes off of the angel."

Bumps rose on Cassia's arms as she imagined how it would be to see an angel.

Ammon looked up at her. "The angel called Alma by name. He commanded him to stand up and asked him why he was persecuting the Church of God."

Cassia brought a hand to her chest, her breathing shallow. "And what did Alma say?"

Shaking his head, he spoke quietly, "He was dumbstruck like the rest of us." Ammon took her hand. "I want you to know that Alma never intended to hurt you. He would have protected you from pain with everything he had. He was furious at our friends when he found out they'd killed Nehem. We were wrong to hide them, but now we will lead Father to them." He squeezed her hand. "You must believe that contrary to his actions against the Lord's Church, he always loved you."

She blinked back stinging tears. "You speak of Alma as if he were gone."

"He is, in a way," Ammon said. "He'll never be the same after what happened." He pressed her hand tighter. "*I'll* never be the same."

"What else did the angel say?"

Ammon released her hand and ran his fingers through his hair. "He said the Lord had heard the prayers of His people and also of his servant Alma."

"His father's prayers were heard . . ."

"The angel's final words were to tell Alma the Younger to 'seek to destroy the Church no more,'" he said.

Cassia considered this for a moment. "Do you think he'll wake up soon?" she asked.

"I don't know," Ammon said. "When the angel left, Alma fell to the ground again, and he hasn't spoken since. We tried to get him to stand, but he was deadweight. So we carried him to his father's house to report what had happened."

Cassia stayed in Ammon's room for several more minutes, then they left together to find out the state of Alma's health. At the throne room, the two guards let them pass.

The first thing Cassia noticed when she entered was the hushed atmosphere in the room. Usually the throne room was reserved for councils and individuals who'd requested a meeting with the king—which could turn into lively debates. It was also a place for official ceremonies that took place outside of the temple and for royal banquets during inclement weather.

A makeshift bed had been set up on one side of the room. Gathered around the bed were various people, sitting quietly and observing. Maia and Alma the Elder sat together, hand in hand, looking as if they were in deep contemplation or praying. Omner and Himni had their heads bowed.

Cassia recognized an older woman—Raquel, who was married to the priest Helam. She was an expert in medicinal herbs. It looked as if she had a bowl of some herbal concoction, which she kept dipping a cloth into, then placing the cloth on Alma's forehead. Cassia's eyes strayed to the throne, where her father sat. He was leaning toward Aaron, who'd brought over a stool to sit next to the king. They seemed to be whispering in earnest conversation.

Cassia didn't see her mother or Alma's sisters in the room. Only a few other priests were quietly conversing together. Ammon crossed to Aaron and the king, but Cassia hovered by the door. She was afraid to look at Alma, afraid to see him lying so still. She was curious though, wondering if he could hear what people were saying. Was he dreaming? Was he thinking about what the angel had said?

She felt torn—should she stay or leave?

Finally, she walked a little closer to where Alma lay. She was in full view of him now, seeing his flushed cheeks and his eyes moving rapidly beneath his eyelids. She stopped short of joining the circle of people. The high priest spoke to Raquel in a quiet voice, "Is there any fever?"

"No, but he does seem restless."

Cassia looked again at the sleeping face. Then she heard the faint moaning coming from him. He moved his head to the side, but still his eyes stayed closed. *Is he in pain?* Maia noticed her and motioned for her to come over. Cassia sat by the woman. "Is he any better?"

"He's the same." Maia patted Cassia's hand. "My husband thinks he might be having a vision."

The high priest leaned forward and looked at Cassia. "My son had denied the truth for so long that most likely he's being retaught by the Lord."

Maia nodded. "We must not only pray that he'll wake but also that his soul will be saved."

A shiver touched Cassia's arms. Right now, in this room, Alma the Younger was being taught by the Lord?

Maia clasped her hands together again and closed her eyes. Cassia felt compelled to do the same. Someone came and sat by her, and when Cassia looked up, she saw her father.

He put his arm around her and squeezed her shoulder. She leaned against him, drawing in his seemingly unending strength and courage.

"His countenance is already brighter," the king said in a quiet voice.

Cassia studied Alma—his face had changed. It was softer somehow, and it *did* seem brighter.

"We may have hope for him yet," the king said.

Emotion touched Cassia, and her throat tightened. After all that had happened, was it possible for Alma to be made whole again? Repentance had been taught by his father and by her father. Would Alma still be numbered among the Church? Cassia had heard the high priest's promise that whoever repented of their sins and did confess them would be numbered among the people of the Church.

She settled down for the wait, watching and praying along with the others surrounding Alma.

CHAPTER 22

. . . though your sins be as scarlet, they shall be as white as snow; though they be red like crimson, they shall be as wool.
—Isaiah 1:18

Alma the Younger

The pain was suffocating. Alma tried to move, but his body had completely disconnected, as if it had been severed from his mind and spirit. He hadn't been able to move or open his eyes since the visit of the angel.

I have seen an angel, Alma thought.

I have been struck down by the power of God.

He knew that now. He had felt the power of God to his very core and could not deny it. And feeling the fierce power of God flood through him had awakened him to the terrible, harrowing knowledge that now tormented his every thought.

His iniquities played themselves out in his mind as if he were watching them occur again. His arguments with his father, his refusal to continue in his studies of scripture, his deceitfulness in his priesthood duties . . .

Alma wanted to cry out, to twist away and block out his lecherous actions, but they were there for him to see, to remember, and to agonize over. One by one, Alma remembered the commandments he'd broken as he moved down his tormented path.

I am vile. I am an idolatrous man. I am a murderer—I have led away God's children to eternal destruction.

The dark grip of despair clutched at Alma as he thought of Belicia and Sara and the other women he'd entertained. For fleeting bouts of pleasure, he'd added damnation on their souls. And if that weren't enough, he'd dragged the sons of Mosiah—the precious heirs of the kingdom of Zarahemla—down with him.

He stood in the presence of an angel, but terror gripped him as he thought about standing before the Lord Himself. *I have betrayed Him,* Alma thought. *If I could but be banished and my body could become extinct, then I would not have to stand in the presence of my God. For I know my judgment—I will be cast out as a damned soul.*

How long he was racked with pain and memory of his sins, of leading the people astray, Alma didn't know. *I preached against the Church of God. I created and worshipped false idols . . .* All the sin sacrifices in the world would not make up for his wrongs. It would take a lifetime of repentance and time at the holy altar to make a dent in his debt.

Then a new voice entered his mind, more powerful than the angel's but as quiet as a whisper. It encompassed his heart, piercing his very soul. Alma recognized the voice of his father, who had prophesied of the coming of one Jesus Christ, a Son of God . . . to atone for the sins of the world.

Christ will come to the earth and atone for the sins of man. Alma grasped onto the memory of his father's teachings. His internal cries of agony changed to cries of mercy, and he began to pray in his heart for the first time in many months. *O Jesus, thou Son of God, have mercy on me, who am in the gall of bitterness, and am encircled about by the everlasting chains of death.*

And then slowly, the memory of his sins lessened. The pain released its grip, and he felt strength returning to his limbs. His body relaxed as the darkness faded into light. It was as if a black cape covering his eyes had been removed. The light grew stronger, but it wasn't too bright, just comforting, spreading. It was as if every part of his body were enveloped in soft warmth.

Alma breathed out, long and slow, as if the very breath were cleansing his soul. His chest expanded and joy flooded through him, strong and sure. The light increased until it had filled every part of

Alma's mind, opposing the bitterness of pain that had been there moments before.

Alma wanted to awake and share his bursting joy, but his limbs would not move. The light formed into a shape until Alma saw a throne surrounded by concourses of angels, and sitting upon the throne was God.

Just as Lehi saw Him, I am seeing Him, Alma realized. His body filled with fiery knowledge as he watched the angels singing and praising their God. And then Alma knew he would not be cast off. *I have been reborn.*

* * *

The soft voices blended above Alma the Younger, some more muted than others, but all just out of reach. He still could not move, but the heaviness had lifted. It was as if he were light, almost weightless. He wasn't sure how much time had passed since the angel had stopped him and the sons of Mosiah on the road. Days . . . weeks . . .

I have repented, Alma wanted to shout as joy surged through his chest at the knowledge. *I have suffered and been reborn.* And like a blanket warmed by the fire and spread over his entire body, the Spirit testified to him that he'd been redeemed. His heart had changed, expanded, and all of the doctrines that he'd questioned before had become clear. The Lord had spoken to him, that he was sure of. The Lord had taught him, whispering to his mind, bringing comfort and knowledge: *Marvel not that all mankind, yea, men and women, all nations, kindreds, tongues and people, must be born again.* It was as if Alma had been re-baptized. He had been changed from his carnal state, becoming redeemed. *Becoming a son of God.*

Beneath his closed eyes, tears formed. *I am a son of God. I know that now.* His greatest desire was to rise and shout it to all the people. The Lord had snatched him from everlasting burning, and now he must share the good news.

The light outside of his closed lids brightened, and he struggled to open his eyes, but they remained closed. Next, he tried to move his hands, but they were still too weak.

A voice rose above the rest—a woman's voice. Alma concentrated to hear her words, and he realized it was his mother speaking to him. What was she saying? Then he realized she was telling him a story of his youth, when he'd almost drowned in the pond. He'd been so determined to swim at the age of four that he hadn't understood he didn't have the strength to make it to the other side of the pond.

His mother's voice continued, but Alma's attention wandered as a cool, wet cloth touched his forehead, refreshing. The angel's words seemed to repeat themselves in his mind: "Go, and remember the captivity of thy fathers in the land of Helam, and in the land of Nephi . . . for they were in bondage, and He had delivered them."

Yes, Alma thought, *only the Lord can perform such miracles.* The angel's command had been clear: "Go thy way, and seek to destroy the Church no more."

I will do the opposite, Alma decided. *I will make retribution and take the true message to the people. I will end the doubt and questioning. I will teach them to repent and to accept the Lord into their hearts. I will labor without ceasing and bring the people the exceeding joy which I have found.*

A gentle hand clutched his, and he squeezed back.

Someone gasped, and Alma realized that he'd moved. He tried again. Same action, another gasp. He focused on opening his eyes. With great effort, he blinked up at the faces surrounding him. The light was bright, but not as bright as it had been when he was learning from the Lord.

He blinked several times, the faces going in and out of clarity. He saw his mother, his father, King Mosiah . . . his sisters and Cephas. Someone moved away, then it was Ammon's face, Aaron's . . . Cassia's. Alma tried to sit up. Strong hands supported him, pushing cushions against his back for support. But he felt surprisingly strong.

He looked around at those who were staring back at him, then became aware of someone clinging to his leg. He looked down at Cephas. His heart lurched at the sight of his little brother. He leaned over to kiss the top of his head. Then he realized his father was speaking. "How do you feel, son?"

Alma brought a hand to his moist forehead, then looked at his mother's tear-stained face. He held out his hand to her and she took it, pressing it against her cheek. "I feel wonderful."

Several people applauded, and Alma noticed that the room was filled with more people than he'd thought. All of the priests were there, and others were entering the doorway to the throne room. His mother held a goblet to his lips, and he drank, long and deep.

After handing back the goblet, he threw off the rug that covered him. "Be careful, son," his mother said.

"My strength has returned," he said, looking from his mother to his father. Then he stood, the men surrounding him as if to brace him up. "Be of good comfort, my friends. I can stand on my own, and I have something important to say."

His mother was at his side, clasping his hand. She drew Cephas to her. His father stood on Alma's other side, waiting to aid him in any way.

"I have been taught by the Lord." Alma's voice rose above the hushed murmurs, and the throne room fell into silence. "I have repented of my sins. The Lord has redeemed me, and I now ask forgiveness from each of you." He looked around at the small gathering, knowing how deeply his actions over the past months had hurt those he loved.

Several of them nodded, assenting to forgiveness. His mother raised up and kissed him on the cheek.

"I have been born of God," Alma said, his voice cracking. His gaze met Cassia's; she had tears running down her cheeks.

"I was living a life in which God was about to cast me off from His presence forever," he continued. He looked at Ammon and his brothers. "After wading through much tribulation, the Lord in mercy saw fit to snatch me out of an everlasting burning."

Ammon and his brothers nodded in agreement.

Alma's voice rose in conviction. "My soul has been redeemed from the gall of bitterness and bonds of iniquity." He took a deep breath and looked squarely at his father. "I was in the darkest abyss, but now . . . now, I've seen the marvelous light of God."

His father smiled through tears and drew his son into his arms. Alma held on tight for a long moment. "You were right, always right. How can you forgive me?"

"You are my son," his father said. "I forgave you from my first prayer to the Lord."

Alma drew away and wiped the tears from his cheeks. "I was so foolish. I let the adversary possess me. It grieves me to think of the pain I've caused you and Mother." His voice fell to a whisper. "And the people."

His father's hands rested on his shoulders. "Son, I know you've repented. You will find a way to make recompense."

Alma fell into his father's arms again, then he pulled away and looked at the crowd. "I am ashamed to admit that I rejected my Redeemer and denied what I have been taught by my own father."

Alma took a few steps forward. "The Lord has revealed that every knee will bow, and every tongue confess." He paused, looking at the priests. "Even at the last day, all men will stand to be judged, and they will confess that He is God. Those who live without God in the world will quake, tremble, and shrink beneath the gaze of His all-searching eye."

Alma scanned the crowd, noticing many of them had triumphant tears in their eyes. He suddenly felt their love—for him—and their faith. These people had been praying and fasting for him. His own eyes filled with tears, and he continued in a trembling voice, "I have seen God sitting upon his throne, surrounded by numberless angels."

His mother brought a hand to her mouth, and his father gazed at him in awe. The crowd was completely silent, then murmurs of praise and astonishment spread throughout the gathering. "Heaven be thanked! Praise the Lord our God!"

When they had quieted again, Alma the Younger said, "I know now that Lehi had a dream and saw the Lord. I know now that the Lord delivered our fathers out of Egypt and led them to the promised land. Just as the Lord has brought *me* out of bondage."

Alma felt his father's strong hand on his shoulder as he continued, "The Lord also brought our fathers out of the land of Jerusalem and delivered them out of bondage and captivity from their time, down to our present day." He paused, trying to control the emotion in his voice. "I now know that if we keep His commandments, we will prosper . . . The Lord has been merciful to me." He looked down for a moment, his vision unfocused. Then he raised his head. "Thank you," he said in a quiet voice. "Thank you for your prayers and fasting. Because of your faith, my soul was saved."

He held out his hand to his mother, who stepped into his arms.

* * *

"Kaman and Jacob fled before we could reach the cave where they were hiding," Ammon said as he walked with Alma the Younger toward the village of Cuello.

"And the rest of the council?" Alma asked, his heart heavy. They'd spent weeks preaching throughout the city of Zarahemla and the surrounding villages of Isidro and Piedra. For the most part, they'd been met with anger, and Alma had been viewed as a traitor as he shared his story about the angel. Few had believed. His former legions of supporters now refused to change their hearts. Regardless, he and the sons of Mosiah were committed to telling their conversion story to anyone who would listen.

"All are gone, except for two," Ammon said.

"Who?" Alma asked.

Ammon smiled. "You'll see for yourself." He turned to his brothers, who followed them. "How much farther?"

Aaron answered, "Just beyond the first bend."

Ammon turned back to Alma. "Just wait."

Picking up his pace, Alma hurried along the road. The laughter of the four brothers behind him didn't slow him down. They could tease him if they wanted, but Alma needed some good news this day.

He reached the bend in the road just as two figures stood from their perch on a large boulder. Alma hesitated as he recognized the two former men on his council: Muloki and Ammah.

They wore plain brown tunics, having done away with the scarlet robes of their former office. The two men smiled, but they weren't vengeful or malicious smiles of hatred. They were genuine.

"Muloki? Ammah?"

"We heard you preaching in Chiapa," Muloki said, throwing a glance at Ammah, who nodded. "At first we were skeptical, but then we decided there was no harm in asking for ourselves."

Alma stared at the two, hardly daring to speak. He heard the sons of Mosiah walk up behind him and stop, waiting as well.

"So we prayed," Ammah filled in. "It was—it was like nothing I ever imagined. We both felt the power of God testify that you are a true prophet."

Alma looked between the two men, his mouth open.

"We believe, Alma, and we want to serve with you."

Alma crossed to the two men and embraced them both. Muloki laughed and patted him on the back.

The sons of Mosiah started clapping.

"Come with us," Alma said to Muloki and Ammah. "We are on our way to Cuello to teach."

"Will they throw you out?" Muloki asked.

"Most likely," Alma said with a chuckle.

"We'll come," Muloki said, a broad grin on his face. "They can't be much worse than the other villages."

Once they reached the village of Cuello, it didn't take long for word to spread about the new arrivals. As Alma and the others walked toward the main plaza, they were followed by the curious villagers. A few came out of their homes and turned away in disgust, but the rest seemed interested.

By the time Alma entered the plaza, Bilshan was there to greet him. But today's greeting was quite opposite from the last time Alma saw his friend. Bilshan's face was dark with anger, and behind him stood the village council, arms crossed, expressions defiant.

Alma raised his hand in greeting, which was returned by a cold stare from Bilshan. Alma's heart sank. He knew this village would be tough—it was the home of Belicia, and the people had been ecstatic when she'd been declared a goddess.

"My friends," Alma said, and several in the crowd hissed their displeasure. "We have come to your village today to share a message—the true message of the Lord."

More hissing.

"First, I would like to ask for your forgiveness," Alma said as the crowd finally quieted. "I came here weeks ago and told many falsehoods. An important part of being a leader is being able to admit when you are wrong."

"You are no longer our leader!" a man shouted.

Alma flinched but continued. "You are right, I am no longer the leader of the rebellion or the priest of the Church of Liberty. The rebellion has been disbanded, the Church vanquished. I have been wrong—very wrong. I have now come to correct those lies. Please forgive me for leading you astray."

Several men shouted obscenities. Alma ignored the language, focusing on one woman who stood near the front of the crowd, her face open, her eyes accepting. If there were but one person he could reach today, it would be worth whatever anger the crowd threw at him.

"I have seen an angel of the Lord," Alma said, looking directly at her. "Just outside your village, the sons of Mosiah and I were stopped by a heavenly messenger."

More hissing in the crowd. Someone shouted, "You took our valuables! You promised to free us from the king!"

Alma bowed his head for a moment. "I have sent back all the valuables to your council, and I will make whatever restitution you ask. But I was wrong when I said that we needed to seek action against the king."

"Traitor!" a man said right behind Alma. He turned to see Bilshan.

The man's face was dark with fury. "You have been bribed by the king, and his sons." Bilshan waved a hand toward the sons of Mosiah. "You go wherever you are paid the highest price. And it seems that we have been outbid."

The villagers started shouting again.

"I have something for you," Alma said to Bilshan. He withdrew a jade necklace from a pouch around his waist and handed it to the man. "This belonged to your sister, Belicia. She once gave it to me, but I think it belongs with her family."

Bilshan took a few steps until he was face to face with Alma. He snatched the necklace away. "If I ever see you in my village or ever hear you speak my sister's name again, I will personally set you on fire."

Alma took a step back. "I wish no harm upon anyone. I came to share my story—please listen to what happened to me."

"We've heard enough!" Bilshan said. He motioned for the council behind him to move forward. As the dozen men closed in around

Alma, he saw several flaming torches at the back of the crowd. They were being carried closer.

"Alma," Ammon said, warning in his voice.

Alma took his eyes from the torches and looked at Bilshan again. "The angel wants us to remember the captivity of our fathers in the land of Helam and the land of Nephi."

"Enough!" Bilshan screamed, his arm swinging at Alma.

Alma felt the fist plow into his cheek, and he staggered backward. The hatred in Bilshan's eyes was unmistakable, but there were some in the crowd who would listen. He turned from Bilshan, his eyes smarting from the pain in his cheek. The flaming torches were closer now. He searched for the woman who had been listening, but Ammon gripped his arm.

"We must go now," Ammon said, tugging him.

As if to answer, the crowd started chanting, "Burn him! Burn him!"

Alma turned with Ammon and started running with the brothers, Muloki and Ammah right behind them. They pushed through the crowd on the opposite side of the torch-bearing men. Alma thought he heard Bilshan's voice shouting above the rest of the noise.

They left the main plaza, then veered off the road until they were running through the underbrush of the hillside above the village.

"That was close," Muloki panted, catching up to Alma.

Alma's chest burned with disappointment. "I hoped to at least tell my story. If they don't believe, that's their choice, but—"

Muloki shook his head. "You lasted much longer than I would have."

"It still wasn't enough," Alma said. "I'll need to return another time."

CHAPTER 23

For by grace are ye saved through faith; and that not of yourselves: it is the gift of God.
—Ephesians 2:8

Cassia

Cassia knelt on a piece of cloth spread along the edge of her garden plot. The avocados were just ripening, and she picked a few of them, intent on making paste to go with the boiled beans that afternoon. Pulling weeds or harvesting vegetables brought her peace of mind. As her hands stayed busy, she could think more clearly.

It had been several weeks since Alma the Younger's recovery, but Cassia hadn't spoken to him yet. She'd heard from her mother that Alma and her brothers were traveling throughout Zarahemla sharing the story about the angel. She'd seen Alma on a couple of occasions, but they were always surrounded by others.

Outside, encircled by the beautiful plants beneath the clear sky, Cassia wished she could speak with Alma again and tell him that she was sorry for what had happened, on both sides of their friendship. Everything had changed now. He had moved on with his life—to a better life. He was a man of God now. She was moving on too, although she wasn't quite sure what direction she was moving in. But she had her faith, and she knew that her heart would eventually heal.

Cassia dumped two more sweet potatoes into her basket, and she thought of the delicious meal it would make with the quail eggs that had been delivered to the palace.

She started to stand when she heard her mother's voice coming from the cooking rooms. "Double the recipes. My sons are home for supper."

Cassia straightened. *My brothers are home!* She grabbed the basket and ran to the cooking rooms. The servants looked up in surprise when she burst through the door. She set the basket on one of the tables; her mother stared at her.

"They're home?"

"Yes," the queen said, an amused look on her face. "I never thought you'd miss your brothers."

Cassia smiled. "Where are they?"

"In the throne room with Father, but they are not to be disturbed."

Cassia's mouth turned down. "Why not?"

"I don't know—some urgent matter—Cassia!"

She pushed past her mother and fled down the corridor, ignoring the queen calling after her. It had been at least two weeks since she'd seen her brothers. The meeting with Father could wait.

The guard stationed at the throne room raised an eyebrow when he saw Cassia hurrying toward him, but he said nothing as she opened the doors.

Her father's voice stopped mid-sentence as she rushed in, but Cassia didn't look at him. All four of her brothers were seated. Other men were with them, and they started to rise as she hurried toward them. But she didn't wait to be introduced and rushed to Ammon first, embracing him. "How are you? I heard there were terrible persecutions."

He chuckled. "We're fine. The reports were probably inflated by the time they reached you."

Cassia stepped back, studying his face, looking for cuts or bruises. "Are you sure?" He nodded, and she looked her other brothers over, assessing any damage. Seeing none, she embraced each of them in turn.

She noticed the other men watching her, two she didn't recognize, then . . . *Alma.* She met his gaze and felt her face heat. "You are well?"

"Yes, thank you," Alma said, his eyes steady, serious.

She looked quickly away from him, and still ignoring her father, she turned to Ammon. "What brings you home today? Are you going to stay for a while? Mother is already ordering the cooks around."

Ammon smiled and took her hand. "Have a seat, little sister. You can hear what we have to tell Father."

Only then did Cassia look at her father. His lips were pressed together as if he were trying to keep from smiling. He tilted his head, indicating for her to take a seat as well. Once settled, Cassia decided to take another peek at Alma. He looked so different from the man who had been listless just weeks before. He appeared older, somehow, wiser and more serious. Like her father, she realized. No, like *his* father. His eyes were kind and gentle, with a glow of new assurance. Warm.

"Father," Ammon said, and all attention was back on him. "We have shared our testimonies with the people of Zarahemla and the outlying villages. As you know, we haven't been well-received by everyone."

"Especially those we were associated with before," Aaron added. "They've been the ones who persecute us the most." He threw a glance at his sister. "But like Ammon said, it wasn't anything we couldn't handle."

Cassia smiled at him, wishing for a moment Ilana were back in their lives to see this change in Aaron. But she knew Ilana was lost to them forever. The cost of Aaron's disobedience had been high indeed.

"Sons," Mosiah said, his gaze including Alma and the other two men, "regardless of the persecutions and the refusal of some to change their hearts, you have made significant progress already."

Her brothers nodded, but Alma's gaze met with the king's. "It's not enough," Alma's voice was firm. "Teaching the Nephites and bringing them all to the truth will never be enough restitution for the damage we caused."

The king raised his hand, shaking his head in disagreement.

"Alma's right," Ammon said. "We want to go out and teach our brethren."

"But that's what you've been doing," Mosiah said, his expression confused.

"Our *Lamanite* brethren," Ammon said in a soft voice.

Cassia involuntarily gasped, then covered her mouth. She could see her reaction reflected in her father's equally surprised face.

Before her father could come up with a reply, Ammon pressed on. "If we can bring them to the knowledge of the Lord and convince them of the iniquity of their fathers, perhaps we can cure them of their hatred toward the Nephites."

Aaron leaned forward, his face eager. "Then the Nephites and Lamanites will become friendly with each other, sharing one faith, one love in the true gospel. There will be no more contentions in the land."

King Mosiah shook his head. "It's too dangerous. You will not make it across their borders alive."

Cassia let out a sigh of relief. Her brothers had completely gone from one extreme to the other. She was glad her father wouldn't let them preach to the enemy, risking their lives.

"We were the very vilest of sinners," Ammon said, his voice quiet, yet piercing. "We were about to be cast off forever before the Lord saw fit to spare us. We have been reborn, and we want to give that opportunity to every person—Nephite *or* Lamanite."

Alma placed both hands on the low table, his expression adamant. "We must declare salvation to every person. We cannot bear that any human soul should perish"—his voice trembled—"like I almost did."

Silence filled the room as Mosiah stared at the men. His gaze softened with emotion, and Cassia felt her own eyes burn.

"You have done enough, my sons. And you as well, Alma, and your friends, Muloki and Ammah," Mosiah said, his voice slow and patient, as if he were speaking to young boys. "You have had your whole lives turned around, paid penance by preaching to our people, and you continue to set a magnificent example to all." He clasped his hands together, his expression resolute. "But I cannot send you to your deaths. You have only just been found, and I refuse to lose any of you again."

Ammon's hands clenched where they rested on the table. Then he spread them wide, including all of the men in his plea. "Father, we are tormented day and night by the thought of the Lamanites dying without knowing the truth. We have the truth. We have the answers. All we have to do is share it."

The king lowered his head for a moment.

Cassia looked at Ammon, hardly daring to believe what he wanted to do. Leave Zarahemla? He was the heir to the throne. What would the people think? And what if something happened to him? She looked at Aaron, Omner, and Himni. If they all left, who would lead the kingdom? Her watery gaze landed on Alma, who was looking at the king, hope on his face.

Alma had always been in her life, either as a friend or foe. What if he left with her brothers? He didn't have responsibilities to the throne, no wife or children holding him here . . . His father would probably support him preaching outside the land of Zarahemla.

For a clarifying instant, she remembered Alma's desire to see other lands as a youth. Even then, he'd been willing to leave everything behind.

Movement from her father caught Cassia's attention. He shook his head. "I cannot give you my blessing. As my sons, you have responsibilities to this kingdom, to your own people, the Nephites." He looked at Alma. "You'll need to counsel with your father, Alma. I cannot speak for him. Muloki and Ammah, you must make this decision independent of my sons."

Alma gave a slight nod.

But Ammon jumped to his feet and cried out, "No, Father, you must reconsider! The kingdom of the Lord is more important than the confines of Zarahemla. This is *your* kingdom . . ." He looked at his brothers as his voice fell. "Not mine."

Cassia covered her mouth with her hands. She looked to her father for his response, but he said nothing. He held Ammon's gaze for a moment, then simply stood and turned away, walking out of the room.

"Father!" Ammon called after him. "Please reconsider!"

When King Mosiah had exited the throne room, everyone was quiet. Ammon sank onto the cushion next to Cassia. His deflated sigh spoke of his frustration. She looked at him, tears in her eyes, questioning if he would really leave—without their father's blessing.

Ammon took her hand and squeezed it, then he, too, rose and left the throne room.

Cassia sat helplessly as she watched her brothers leave the room one by one. No one spoke; everyone seemed deep in morose thought. The excitement and conviction that had permeated the room only moments before had been snuffed out like a lamp.

When she looked up again, she was surprised to see that Alma had remained, watching her. A sudden nervousness descended upon her as she realized that she was alone with him at last. Now was her chance to speak with him, but so much had changed in the last few minutes that she didn't know what to say anymore.

Alma broke the silence first. "Your brothers will be seeking your support."

Cassia let out a breath, feeling a burden descend at Alma's words. "Alma . . . you don't need to do this to keep repenting."

The light in his eyes changed. "It's not for *me* or for *us.* It's for *them.*"

"But the Lamanites are our enemies—is this really worth risking your life?"

"My life is no longer my own, Cass," Alma said, his voice just above a whisper. "It belongs to the Lord now."

Tears stung the back of her eyes as a sudden realization hit her. "You are just like—like that prophet who taught your father."

His eyebrows lifted. "Abinadi?"

"Yes," Cassia said. "Nothing could stop him, and he died for his preaching." She couldn't stop the flow of tears now and wiped at them furiously. She stood, shaking. "Is that what you want to do? Die?"

Alma rose and crossed to her. He looked at her for a moment, then took her hands. "Cass—don't cry. The Lord will protect us."

"But He didn't protect Abinadi," she choked out.

Alma let out a breath of air, warm on her face. He reached up and wiped away her tears. "I know this is painful, and I'm dreading my mother's reaction. I'm also sorry that you'll miss your brothers—I know how much they mean to you."

"Please don't leave," Cassia whispered. "I'll miss *you,* Alma. *You.*"

He stared at her, his expression stunned. "You'll forget about me soon enough," he finally said, looking away.

"No, I could never forget. Anything."

He moved back slightly. "Another reason that it's good for me to leave Zarahemla. You can move on with your life, without me as a reminder of the mess I made of yours."

She felt the breath leave her. He still didn't know how she really felt. "Don't you see?" Cassia said. "I don't want to move on with my life without you . . . you were right."

"About what?"

"About Nehem."

The pain in Alma's face almost caused Cassia to start crying again. But she took a deep breath and plunged on. "I could have been happy with him, yes, but I would have had to *make* myself be happy with him. He was a good and decent man; he didn't deserve to die. But I was not true in my feelings, and I feel guilty for letting him think I was."

"Cass—none of what happened to Nehem was your fault. If anything, I should be in prison and paying for hiding Kaman and Jacob."

"Kaman and Jacob are responsible for their own actions—and the Lord will see that they pay for them," she said, lowering her voice. "I don't blame you for Nehem's death. I forgive you for the decision to hide them. But it's over, Alma. I know you have repented of all of your wrongdoings. I know the Lord has forgiven you, and you are redeemed in my eyes as well." She placed her hands on Alma's cheeks, knowing there was no hiding her feelings for him once she did. "I want you to stay in Zarahemla for *me.*"

Alma stared at her for a long time without saying anything. Then he slowly shook his head, his eyes dark with pain. "I can't."

She let her hands fall to his chest, then leaned against him. "I know. And I'm sorry for asking." She buried her head against his chest and wrapped her arms around his waist, knowing that this was the last time she'd probably ever touch him.

The tears started again as Alma's arms came around her, cradling her as she cried.

* * *

It was as if the palace were in mourning. Conversations were hushed, and the servants crept quietly about the corridors, unobtrusively performing their duties. For hours each day, the king sequestered himself in his private chambers, refusing to speak with anyone.

Cassia and her mother sat together in the cooking room, alternating between fear and apprehension. It was the one place Cassia took comfort, watching the servants prepare food and assisting when they allowed her—or when her mother allowed.

This morning, the servants were preparing a dish of boiled beans and spiced mushrooms. The aroma of the cooking filled the room, enticing Cassia—who had eaten little over the past few days.

She glanced over at her mother, who stared vacantly toward the window. Cassia knew her mother would suffer with her sons gone—from worrying about the unknown. It had been a relatively peaceful era in Zarahemla, skirmishes with the Lamanites few, although ever-present, and ever-looming possibility of war. But it had been nothing like the conflict experienced by Alma the Elder and those he brought with him, nor Limhi and his people.

Cassia's eyes teared up as she thought about the internal battles fought within Zarahemla and the persecutions her brothers were now facing on a daily basis. Yet, they had a better chance of coming home at night unhurt, safe. Going into Lamanite territory was asking for conflict.

On one hand, Cassia just wanted the decision to be made and done with. On the other hand, she feared what that decision might be. She watched the high priest, Alma, enter the palace several times a day, and her father make the walk to the temple to consult with his various priests. Argument after argument occurred as Ammon and her brothers pressed the king for permission. They would not give up.

Thinking over it all, Cassia knew that her brothers could very well leave on their own, without their father's blessing, but it was most important to them to have it.

She'd seen Alma the Younger come and go from the palace, always accompanied by one of her brothers, never alone. Not that Cassia had a desire to corner him and give another embarrassing display of hysterical female emotions, but she was not ashamed of her words. They were the truest from her heart, and she had needed to tell Alma how she really felt—before she never saw him again.

Maybe it would give him added insight or strength on his mission. He would at least know that she never blamed him for Nehem, and she forgave him completely. At least she had given him that as a farewell gift.

"I must go check on Father," her mother said, patting her hand.

"I'm coming too," Cassia said, rising with her mother. The queen said nothing, so Cassia followed her along the corridors to the throne room. The guard was there, but the doors were ajar. Her mother hesitated as the conversation inside reached their ears.

The unmistakable voice of the high priest rang out. "We have debated endlessly. There is nothing left to do but take the question to the Lord."

Cassia's skin prickled as her father answered with a heavy sigh. "Yes, that is the only thing left to do, and the only way I will be at ease with this."

Then, the king was walking to the doors. When he saw his wife and daughter standing there, he took his wife's hands and kissed them. "I have more work to do," he said, his gaze moving to Cassia. "The Lord will answer our pleas once and for all. He will want our sons to stay home, and they will have to obey."

The queen nodded and let go of her husband's hands, understanding in her eyes.

Then he left the women standing at the door. Soon after that, Alma the Elder exited the room, coming to a stop when he saw the women. He bowed to the queen, then looked at Cassia. "Thank you," he said.

Her eyes widened. "I'm not sure what you mean."

He smiled in his gentle way, and Cassia noticed the lines crease on his face. The trials of his son had probably aged him a great deal. "Thank you for never giving up on my son."

Cassia nodded, her throat too tight to respond.

Alma bid farewell to Cassia's mother, then left the palace.

"Now what?" Cassia whispered.

"We wait some more," her mother said. "Let's go see about the meal." She bustled away.

"Will we be having guests?" Cassia asked.

Her mother lifted a shoulder. "It seems that all of our guests are always fasting, so it might just be us."

Cassia followed her mother back to the cooking rooms. But she couldn't stand the wait. Leaving her mother to supervise the supper preparations, Cassia decided to walk through the garden before it grew too hot. She made her way through the gardens that extended down the hillside, where she stopped at the gate that separated the private from the public gardens. People would often spend time near the gate, hoping for a chance to see a member of the royal family. Today, Cassia walked along the dividing wall, gazing out into the public garden.

"Miss," said the guard stationed by the gate. "Would you like me to accompany you?"

Cassia smiled at his offer. "No, thank you."

The guard nodded and assumed his position, but his expression didn't look convinced.

A few girls who were sitting together on a low bench on the other side of the wall looked up in surprise to see the princess. Cassia smiled at them and walked past. For a fleeting moment, she wished she had a group of friends, girls she could sit with and laugh. Girls whom she could confide in—share her worries over her brothers with.

"Cassia!" a female voice called.

She turned to see Bethany and Dana. The two girls nearly tripped down the hill, running toward her. "We've been looking for you," Bethany said. "The king just called for my father. A decision has been made. The queen told us to find you so that you could hear the news. She wants us to wait in the garden until they know what it is."

Already. The Lord had answered her father, Cassia realized. She and the girls hurried back toward the palace so that they could be ready to hear when the decision was announced.

They found a bench just outside the cooking room to sit on. Dana, the younger one, was clearly more agitated than her sister. She kept standing, then sitting, and asking endless questions. "When do you think they'll leave?"

"Shh," Bethany said. "We don't know if they'll leave yet."

"Will they really have to fight the Lamanites?"

Bethany sighed. "We hope not—"

"Alma is a pretty good fighter," Dana said. "Remember when he used to wrestle with Ammon? He almost always won."

Cassia hid a small smile. She doubted anyone could beat Ammon now—unless he was outnumbered by Lamanites. Her smile fled at the thought.

"We should make Alma something before he leaves," Dana said. "Maybe a new robe."

Cassia glanced at Bethany, who seemed to have tuned out her sister.

"Do you think they'll use swords or slingshots to fight with?" Dana asked, her eyes growing round at the thought.

"Dana!" Bethany said. "Enough! You're as exhausting as Cephas!"

Dana's shoulders fell, but the glint in her eyes remained.

"Maybe we should go in and see if our mothers know anything yet," Cassia suggested. Just as the girls rose, the door to the cooking room opened. Maia stood there holding a dancing Cephas by the hand, her eyes scanning the gardens.

"Mother, over here!" Dana shouted, waving her arm.

Cassia and the girls walked toward Maia, Cassia studying the woman's face for any sign of what had transpired.

When they were close enough to speak, Maia said, "The Lord has spoken." She looked at Cassia, then back to her daughters. "The Lord has promised that the sons of Mosiah will be safe as they travel to preach to the Lamanites."

My brothers will be safe, Cassia thought. But what about Alma the Younger?

Dana jumped in first. "Will Alma be going?"

Slowly, Maia shook her head, her eyes landing once again on Cassia. "The Lord did not specifically give His blessing for your older brother."

Cassia didn't know if she was relieved or upset. She'd seen the conviction in Alma's eyes. His heart was set on it—even if it was dangerous, he was ready to risk his life to bring his enemy the truth. Besides, the king wasn't his father, so did he need official permission?

Bethany was the first to question. "Will Alma listen to the king? What did Father say?"

"The king wants your brother to take over all the records of the Church. He's asked him to be the next high priest, after his father. The king asked him to remain in Zarahemla to take over this duty."

Cassia's mind churned, her body growing warm. Alma was to succeed his father? She looked down quickly before Maia could notice her burning eyes. That meant . . . Alma might not be leaving. She was too afraid to be happy or sad, or to feel anything.

She murmured something about going to see her mother and left Maia to answer her daughters' questions and try to corral Cephas's wiggling form. Cassia's heart was heavy, feeling the disappointment that Alma must feel, while at the same time scared for her brothers. It was comforting that the Lord had promised to protect them, but she wanted to hear more about the promise that had been given to the king.

When she entered the palace, she walked straight to the throne room. Sure enough, her brothers were all there—along with Alma the Younger, his father, her parents, and several priests.

Ammon saw her first, and she ran over and embraced him. "Isn't it wonderful?" he asked, his smile so big that Cassia didn't dare say anything else but, "Yes."

Ammon was positively radiant. Ironically, Cassia thought he'd never looked more like a king or a ruler than at this very moment—the moment he'd discovered that he'd be leaving Zarahemla.

"How long will you be gone?" she blurted out before she could restrain herself.

His face sobered a little, and he took her hands in his. "A while." He reached up and smoothed her hair back.

Cassia let the caress comfort her. She overheard her other brothers' excitement as they spoke with the priests in the room. She didn't dare steal a glance at Alma. She kept her attention on Ammon. "Do you think you'll be gone several months? A year?"

"Truthfully, Cass, it might be several years."

Her eyes widened. "How many?"

"There are a lot of Lamanites—a lot of territory to travel to."

She nodded, feeling numb. "What about the kingdom? What did the Lord say about that?"

Ammon tugged her hand and led her away from the main crowd. "I've told Father that I don't want to be king. Maybe one of our brothers will, but I've made up my mind. I don't want anyone waiting for me, and it's not fair to return after a long absence and expect to rule Zarahemla."

Cassia shook her head. "How can you walk away from your duty like this?"

"I'm not walking away from anything. I'm walking *toward* a new life. A life the Lord has laid out before me." He kept his eyes on her, watching her closely.

The emotions battled inside her, and she wanted to be alone to sort out her feelings. Like Alma had said earlier, she knew her brothers would depend on her for support. They needed her to be strong, not a sniveling sister who thought only of herself. Besides, what was she compared to the mission that the Lord had called her brothers on?

"Time will go by so fast. You'll see," Ammon said, his voice tender. "You'll marry and have children—and won't have a moment to spare to worry about us."

Cassia could only nod because she couldn't speak.

"But we'll need your prayers, sister," Ammon said.

The tears came, and she could no longer stop them. She embraced her brother again. "When do you leave?"

"Tomorrow."

She drew back, her heart feeling like it had been pierced straight through. "Tomorrow? What about your provisions?"

"We'll take only a few things since we'll be living among the Lamanites, working for our support."

"Oh, Ammon," Cassia said. "I can hardly believe that I won't see you for such a long time. Who is going to test out my new recipes?"

"I can think of one person who could take my place," Ammon said.

Cassia followed his gaze. Alma the Younger stood conversing with the king, seeming to be in deep conversation. By the expression on Alma's face, she guessed he was resigned to the change in plans. At least he didn't look angry as he listened earnestly to the king. The high priest crossed over to the pair, placing a hand on his son's shoulder.

Warm prickles touched her skin as she watched the three men together—two of them the most powerful men in the land. Even with the four sons of the king gone, the kingdom would be left in good, strong, and capable hands.

Maybe there was still a chance Ammon would return and be king. Her father was aged, but he looked healthy. Her brothers might be gone a couple of years, preach all they could, then return to rule Zarahemla.

Cassia started to feel a little better. Her brothers were happy, her father seemed pleased . . . Just then she caught her father's eye. The king walked toward her, his hands outstretched. She took his hands and kissed her father's cheek. He smiled. "At least my daughter will stay here and comfort me in my old age."

"Oh, Father, Ammon and the others will be back soon enough."

He shook his head. "They have each renounced the kingship. It is not the Lord's will for any of them to succeed the throne."

All of my brothers have turned the kingship down? Cassia's throat was tight. "What did the Lord say?"

"He said that many of the Lamanites will be converted and have eternal life. The Lord promised to deliver your brothers out of the hands of the Lamanites. They will return someday, but not to rule over Zarahemla."

"You have many years left, Father," she said. "One of my brothers might change his mind."

"We will let the people decide," Mosiah answered, his eyes studying her.

Did her father expect *her* to marry someone who would be the next king? She was relieved that he didn't mention it, but maybe it was only because they were in a public place. She should be married to Nehem right now, and he would have made a fine king. Was that what her father was thinking about?

He bent down and kissed her cheek. "Let your mother know that the farewell feast will be tonight."

CHAPTER 24

*. . . I have heard thy prayer, I have seen thy tears: behold,
I will heal thee. . . .*
—2 Kings 20:5

Alma the Younger

Alma watched Cassia speak with the servants, then disappear with them into the cooking room. She seemed to run the household more than her mother did. The farewell feast had continued late into the night—it was as if no one wanted it to end.

Alma wondered what Cassia thought now that he was staying. He'd caught her eyes several times during the meal, but she'd quickly averted her gaze each time. He was still getting used to the idea of staying in Zarahemla, but when Mosiah had talked through his impression to give the records of the Church over to Alma's care, it made more and more sense.

His father was certainly pleased, and working as a scribe for several years had given Alma familiarity with the plates of brass and the other scripture recordings. Tomorrow, after the missionaries left, he would begin the daunting task—Mosiah wanted him to start compiling the record of the people of Zarahemla.

He would miss his friends—Ammon and Aaron especially. They had been through so much together. They would be entering an incredible experience, teaching the Lamanites and bringing them the joy of being born of God, and Alma would be remaining in Zarahemla. The disappointment was still tangible, but he recognized the Lord's hand, and he had to trust in that. Alma had to trust that remaining in Zarahemla and doing his part would build the Lord's kingdom as much as leaving to teach the Lamanites.

Cassia came out of the cooking room, followed by a servant, both of them carrying trays piled with honeyed delicacies. She was smiling at something the servant said, then laughed. The two set their platters on the low table, and the servant returned to the cooking rooms.

Cassia spoke to her mother, then left through the garden. Alma wondered where she was going. The feast wasn't over yet, and her father certainly had a speech to make, if not her brothers. Regardless of why she left, he might have a chance to speak to her in private if he was able to catch her.

Alma slipped away from the banquet and entered the garden along the path that Cassia had taken, walking toward the northern portion of the gardens. It didn't take long to catch up to her as she walked slowly, her hand trailing a low bush.

She turned as she heard him approach. She didn't smile, but Alma was relieved that she didn't turn away either.

"Where are you going?" he asked, coming to a stop in front of her.

She looked up at him. "I'm sorry that you didn't get your wish."

"You are?" He hid a smile.

"Aren't *you?*"

He still felt the weight of disappointment mixed with anticipation. "Yes, a little. I don't know if I'm used to the idea yet, but I trust the king's judgment."

"I'll bet your mother is happy."

He couldn't help but grin. "Ecstatic. Although my sisters are disappointed they can't send me off. At least Cephas still wants me around."

"I heard you have your own home now, so it's not like you're there to tease them much."

He nodded slowly, soaking in her features. Even in the almost dark, he could see the faint blush on her cheeks. "No, not much."

"But you're still sad," Cassia prompted.

"I could have helped protect your brothers—Ammon is a decent hunter, but Aaron has a lot to learn still, and Omner and Himni . . . well, you know how they are. At least Muloki is a decent hunter, although I'm not sure about Ammah."

"You're too good," Cassia said, her hand touching his arm.

Warmth surged through Alma as her hand lingered. "I wish I had stayed good."

Cassia's gaze had a faraway look in it. "A lot of things might have been different." She seemed to refocus on him. "So you will stay in Zarahemla and become the next high priest?"

He nodded, watching her. "What do you think about me staying?"

"I'm pleased," she said with a laugh, then looked away as if she were embarrassed. "I mean, I'm sorry it's not exactly what you wanted to do, but now I won't have to miss you as much."

"As much?"

"Well, you'll still be very busy, spending all hours working on the records, meeting with people to get their histories, spending time in the temple learning your new duties . . ."

"It sounds like I'll be well occupied."

"Yes," she breathed.

"And what about you? What will you be busy doing?"

"Waiting," Cassia said, her eyes meeting his.

"For what?"

"For you . . ." She took a deep breath. "To propose."

He stared at her, wondering if she'd really spoken those words. Her eyes said she had. He reached for her hands and slowly pulled her toward him. "Do you think your father will approve?"

She tugged her hands away from his, taking a step back and folding her arms. "That depends . . . on whether you are going to ask him."

He reached for her hands again, this time interlacing his fingers with hers. "Don't worry, I'm going to ask."

She pulled her hands from his and reached her arms around his neck.

"Cass, someone might come—"

"I don't care if anyone sees us." She tightened her hold, and he responded, wrapping his arms around her with a laugh.

He buried his face into her neck, breathing in the scent of her. "At least I'll know who to blame."

She held on for a long moment, then pulled away, her hands still clasped behind his neck.

"Don't wait too long," she whispered.

"Is tonight too soon?"

"Not for me." She smiled. "But we should at least wait until my brothers leave, to give my parents a chance to recover a little."

He laughed and pulled her into his arms again. "Are you sure?" he whispered.

She nodded against his chest. "More than sure."

He released her and tilted her chin up with his finger. "I am not who I was . . . before I left, before I fell into iniquity. There were women—"

"You don't have to tell me," Cassia said, her gaze steady. "When I saw you after the angel visited you, I could see the change. I knew you had repented and been reborn. I could see in your expression that the Lord had forgiven you of *all* of your sins." She touched his face. "We must both let go of the past so that we can live our future together."

He gazed at her for a long moment, wondering how he deserved this good, pure woman. Then she surprised him as she raised up on her feet and pressed her lips to his. It was so light and brief that he didn't close his eyes.

She smiled as she said, "I love you, Alma."

"I love you," he said. "Thank you for trusting me with your heart." Then he leaned down for another kiss.

* * *

The overcast morning was unseasonably cool, and a slight chill pervaded Alma's robes as he stood in the main plaza. He drew his indigo priest's robe tighter about him. The group that had come to see the sons of Mosiah off was growing by the minute. Alma's parents and sisters were there already, the girls huddled together. Helam and Limhi had arrived with their families as well as the priest, Ben.

A few people started clapping as Muloki and Ammah arrived. On their backs they carried large packs. Alma was relieved that Muloki would be a part of the missionary group—the man was a fine hunter and would provide a good deal of protection.

More people from the city came, and Alma took satisfaction in seeing many new converts that had once been part of the rebellion. This brought on a sense of remorse for those who still refused to soften their hearts and listen to the truth. But Alma wouldn't give up, just as his parents hadn't given up on him.

As if he could read his thoughts, Alma's father came over to him. "The sons of Mosiah will be blessed in their work. They'll probably convince more Lamanites of the truth than we can convince Nephites here at home."

"You may be right," Alma said.

"Are you ready for this, son?" his father asked.

Alma lifted a shoulder. "It's hard to believe they're really going. And it's hard to believe I'm not going with them."

His father nodded. "You've been inseparable from Ammon since you were a young boy." He placed a hand on his shoulder. "I'm proud of you for accepting the call to compile the records of Zarahemla."

Just then, his mother came up and kissed his cheek. "Your father told me about King Mosiah's consent to marry Cassia. I couldn't be more pleased. I could die happy this morning."

"Mother, don't say that," Alma said, looking down at her. He wondered if Cassia knew yet that he'd talked to her father early that morning. It turned out that he couldn't wait until after her brothers left after all.

His mother kissed his cheek again.

Someone murmured that the king was coming, and Alma turned from his parents toward the palace to see the king and the queen start down the steps. Less than an hour before, Alma had visited King Mosiah and asked him for permission to become betrothed to Cassia.

His eyes burned with emotion as he remembered the king's response. He'd leapt up from his throne and embraced Alma. Warmth still pulsed through him as he anticipated telling Cassia the news. He looked past the king and queen, wondering where she was. Just then, the princes exited the palace. The crowd cheered as one, and the brothers hesitated at the top of the steps, broad grins on their faces.

Alma's heart lurched at the sight of his closest friends. They would be leaving, and he would be staying. He chuckled to himself as Ammon bounded down the stairs, skipping several at a time and nearly losing his balance.

The crowd moved in and greeted the king's sons, exclaiming over their departure and upcoming missionary work.

Finally, Alma saw Cassia. She hurried out of the palace as if realizing she was later than the others. Her eyes searched the crowd, then landed on Alma, who was purposely staying separate from the gathering. A smile barely touched her lips as she came down the steps. Alma met her at the base.

She reached for his hand, surprising Alma with her public display. But her eyes were bright and her expression confident. "Father told me you came this morning."

"I'm sorry I didn't wait."

Cassia laughed, squeezing his hand. "I told my brothers right away, and they approve. Look at them."

Alma looked at the crowd, his eyes meeting those of Ammon and Aaron, who were now walking toward them. "Congratulations!" Ammon called out.

Aaron elbowed Ammon and hurried ahead. "I was planning on congratulating you first."

Ammon smiled as he stopped before them. "Now I know why Alma decided to stay behind."

"I didn't—"

"We know you didn't," Aaron said with an exaggerated wink.

The brothers laughed, and Alma shook his head. "Maybe I won't miss you two so much after all."

Ammon punched Alma in the arm.

"You can't do that," Aaron chided. "He's a priest now."

"We're leaving, so he can't do anything to us," Ammon said.

Aaron's eyes were wide. "Except change our history on the records."

"I feel sorry for the Lamanites," Alma said. "They don't know what's coming."

Omner and Himni appeared, offering their congratulations. Through it all, Cassia kept hold of Alma's hand.

The crowd quieted as King Mosiah prepared to speak. He pronounced a blessing on his sons' heads and on their companions, Ammah and Muloki. Each missionary took a turn to say a few words, and many in the congregation were crying by the time they were finished.

The king's sons bid farewell to friends and family members in turn, moving through the gathering. Then Cassia and her mother said their good-byes, embracing each brother fiercely. No one knew how long they'd be gone, but they could be assured that they'd have a whole city praying for their success and safe return.

When Alma approached the brothers, he felt as if he were moving through deep water. What might they look like the next time they met? What would have happened in each of their lives? Alma embraced each of the brothers, Ammon last.

"You could stay, you know," Alma said to Ammon, a wistful smile on his face. "You could rule the kingdom."

"I know," Ammon said, "but I've made my decision." He held out something to Alma.

Alma studied the red leather armband, but instead of the half-moon symbol on it, Ammon had his name spelled across it. "To remember me by."

Alma took the armband and slipped it on. "I'll never forget." He paused as Cassia appeared beside him. "May the Lord be with you always."

"And you," Ammon said.

The two men locked hands for the final time.

In a flurry, Ammah, Muloki, and the sons of Mosiah hoisted their packs onto their backs and crossed the plaza, the crowd parting to let them through. The king's soldiers would escort them to the borders of the land of Zarahemla. But the family remained at the plaza—one good-bye was enough.

As Alma watched his friends leave, Cassia slipped her hand into his and leaned against him. Alma looked down at her tear-stained face. "Will they return?" she asked, her voice cracking.

"Yes," Alma said. "I don't know when, but I believe we'll see them again."

The new missionaries entered the market street and disappeared past the buildings. Alma stared after them for several moments, then turned to Cassia. He took her other hand in his, oblivious of the surrounding people. "It's time," he said.

"Time for what?" Cassia asked, her eyes vivid.

"To bring more souls to repentance."

"And?" she prompted.

Alma furrowed his brow. "And to teach them about the true God."

"Yes, yes," Cassia said. "But we also need to plan a wedding."

Alma brought her hand to his lips and kissed it. "That, too."

Chapter Notes

Chapter 1

Scripture referenced: Mosiah 27:8

In *Voices from the Dust,* S. Kent Brown clarifies that the sons of Mosiah left on their mission around 94 BC. This leads us to believe that events leading up to the appearance of the angel to Alma the Younger and the sons of Mosiah took place in 95 or 94 BC (see *Voices from the Dust,* Chronological Chart, 218).

Chapter 2

Scripture referenced: Mosiah 27:34; 29:2

In Mesoamerica, some animals were domesticated for food, including turkeys, and other birds such as doves, quail, duck, and pheasant. According to John L. Sorenson, deer, "the most numerous large mammals in Mesoamerica," were raised and domesticated or hunted. Other hunted animals (or in some cases caged as pets) included jaguars, foxes, wolves, and buffalo (*Images of Ancient America,* 46).

Ammon is most likely the eldest son of King Mosiah, followed by Aaron (see Mosiah 29:2). Hugh Nibley establishes Ammon as the "crown prince" of Zarahemla (*Teachings of the Book of Mormon—Semester Two,* 159). King Mosiah's next two sons are Omner and Himni. Interestingly enough, none of these four were interested in accepting the position of heir to the throne after their father.

After the conversion the four sons of Mosiah underwent (with Alma the Younger), they spent time traveling throughout the land of Zarahemla, sharing their conversion story. But in return, the unbelievers they had formerly been friends to were now against them, and the sons of Mosiah were persecuted. Nibley suggests this as a deterrent to any of them accepting the throne (159).

A definitive social structure was prevalent throughout the Book of Mormon era. From class distinctions of slaves (King Benjamin forbids it in Mosiah 2:13), to members of the poor class (Alma 32:2–3), to "those of high birth" (Alma 51:8). These examples draw an interesting parallel to the Maya society structure of slaves, commoners, aristocracy, and royalty (*Images,* 80–1).

Robert Millet presents a portrait of Sherem the anti-Christ introduced in the book of Jacob (chapter 7). This can be compared to the character of Alma the Younger as he sets out to destroy the Church and lead astray the members. As referred to in the preface, Millet describes an anti-Christ with the following characteristics: "they deny the need for Jesus Christ"; "they use flattery to win disciples"; "they accuse the brethren of teaching false doctrine"; "they have a limited view of reality"; "they have a disposition to misread and thereby misrepresent the scriptures"; and "they are sign seekers" (*The Book of Mormon: Jacob Through Words of Mormon, To Learn with Joy,* 176–82). Upon further study of Jacob 7, we find that Sherem "was *learned*, that he had a perfect knowledge of the language of the people" (v. 4, emphasis added), much how Alma the Younger is characterized in this book. In addition, Alma the Younger is described as "a man of many words, and did speak much flattery to the people" (Mosiah 27:8), just as Sherem the anti-Christ "preached many things which were flattering unto the people" (Jacob 7:2).

Chapter 3

Tortillas, tamales, squash, and boiled beans were the most common foodstuffs in Mesoamerica. Sorenson says that "bread" (as seen in Alma 8:21–22) is assumed to be a type of tortilla (*Images,* 37). Roots such as manioc, jicama, and sweet potatoes were also consumed.

Fruits such as cherries and guavas, and vegetables such as tomatoes and avocados were common as well (36). Maize was the staple of all Mesoamerican diets, although other grains were grown and consumed, e.g., wheat, barley, neas, and shem (Mosiah 9:9). Joseph L. Allen points out that all of the crops mentioned in Mosiah 9:9 are indigenous to the Guatemala region. Interestingly enough, the corn was planted first, then the beans—and the cornstalks served as beanpoles (*Sacred Sites: Searching for Book of Mormon Lands*, 32–4). In addition, fish "were consumed where it was convenient to obtain them." But the fundamental staples were corn, beans, and squash (*Images,* 36).

Cacao drink, amaranth seeds, popped corn, or peanuts were combined with honey to make delicacies for special occasions (*Images,* 45). The cacao bean was also a luxury. Sorenson says it was used as a "form of currency, [and] consumption of chocolate was mainly limited to people of wealth." The cacao tree grows in the foothills, and the seeds from the cacao fruit are ground into powder to make chocolate (42).

Chapter 4

In Sorenson's work we learn that the vineyards and wine that are named in Mosiah 11:15 refer to the agave plant from which a pulque is made. Sorenson notes that the Spaniards referred to vineyards when they spoke of where the agave cactus grew (*Images,* 45). Sorenson says that wines were also made from bananas, palm, and fermented tree bark (*An Ancient America Setting for the Book of Mormon*, 186–7). The agave nectar is harvested from a hollow that is scooped out. The nectar ferments, resulting in a sweeter and thicker juice.

According to Sorenson, "the most common musical instruments were rhythmic (drums, scrapers, rattles)," but other melodic ones included "flutes, panpipes, . . . horns, . . . and shell trumpets" (*Images,* 178–9).

Chapter 6

For thousands of years, Mesoamerica has been cultivating honey. Not only is honey used as a sweetener, but it has also been used for its health benefits since it contains various vitamins and minerals and has uses for soothing sore throats, burns, and ulcers (Karen Hursh Graber, "Honey: A Sweet Maya Legacy," http://www.mexconnect.com/articles/3286-honey-a-sweet-maya-legacy). Sorenson points out that honey was used as a delicacy since it wasn't always available in some areas (*Images,* 45).

Chapter 7

Scriptures referenced: Mosiah 25:16–18, 23

Obsidian was used extensively by the Mesoamericans for tools and decorations. Swords were made with obsidian blades mounted into a wooden base, becoming a deadly serrated weapon. Sorenson notes that in Alma 47:5, the Lamanites flee to Onidah probably because it was well-known for its obsidian outcrop (*Images*, 53).

Chapter 8

Scriptures referenced: Mosiah 27:1–2, 4–5

Throughout Mesoamerica, tributes and taxes supported governments. Sorenson notes, "Anciently there was no meaningful distinction between taxes and tribute" (*Images,* 114). The larger the city or kingdom, the greater the government requirement became. People such as priests, archivists, military leaders, clerks, and engineers received income through government taxes on the common people. Taxes, or tributes, may have been in the form of labor, food, clothing, liquor, dry goods, or precious materials (ibid).

From ancient time to modern day, the Maya have practiced a court system with judicial patterns similar to those among the Book of Mormon people. Cortez described a large building that contained ten to twelve judges who made the decisions in the cities. In the modern city of Zinacantan, a similar court still operates. Four judges sit on a bench during the day, passing judgments on civil disputes (*Images*, 116). When King Mosiah's sons refused the kingship (Mosiah 28:10), the king abolished his monarchy and instituted a kind of democracy into Nephite society as he let his people choose through the voice of the judges (Mosiah 29:25).

"One of the primary duties of a [king or other] ruler was to settle disputes among his people" (*Images*, 116). Obviously, a single ruler could not hand down all judgments, especially in a city the size of Zarahemla, and he would need judges or priests (as in Mosiah's case) to hand down judgments (ibid). Prisons and prisoners are both mentioned throughout the Book of Mormon text (see Alma 14:17 and 3 Nephi 5:4). Sorenson explains that there were also routine executions of those who were tried and convicted and therefore "executed by the law" (see Alma 2:1; 62:9). Ritual executions were also prevalent (see Alma 1:15 and Alma 14:8). Some of the ritual executions included burning, hanging from the top of a tree, or casting the victim into wild animal dens (*Images*, 117).

During King Mosiah's era, record keeping was most likely done on animal skins or tree bark. Michael D. Coe describes some of the early record-keeping methods on long strips of bark paper: "the codices had jaguar-skin covers, and were painted by scribes using brush or quill pens dipped in black or red paint contained in cut conch-shell inkpots" (*The Maya,* 211).

Chapter 9

Sorenson states that "oaths were major mechanisms for constructing loyalty networks" (Images, 110). We see the giving of oaths throughout the Book of Mormon, some of them for honest purposes, others having to do with secret combinations. Most significantly, it didn't matter if the person was part of a Nephite or Lamanite tribe; "Oaths were considered binding across the boundaries of societies" (*Images,* 123; see Mosiah 20:14 and Alma 44:8). Nibley informs us that an oath made among the ancient people is considered sacred, and in order to be binding, an oath should be made by the *life* of something (*Lehi in the Desert,* 103).

The Mesoamericans valued many items such as green jade from the Río Motagua, tail feathers of the quetzal from its habitat in the forests of Alta Verapas and the Sierra de las Minas in Guatemala. The red and white thorny oyster was considered a prize above all. In addition, conch shells were "used as trumpets in ceremonies, in warfare, and in the chase" (*The Maya*, 23).

Chapter 10

Sorenson explains that the God of Israel "had rivals throughout most of [the Lamanite and Nephite] history," which parallels the Maya culture as well (*Images,* 140). In Enos 1:20, it becomes clear that the Lamanites had idols and "beliefs and practices related to [other] gods" (ibid). Nature and animal gods and their corresponding idols among the Maya included the maize god, the sun god, the jaguar god, the moon goddess, etc.

Sorenson continues to explain that "a variety of lesser sacred beings or powers and rites connected with them were recognized among the Nephites and Lamanites" as well (ibid). Demons, devils, unclean spirits, idol gods, sorceries, witchcrafts, and magic are all mentioned throughout the text. Sorenson says, "Clearly the Nephite record gives us only glimpses of their ritual life and associated beliefs about the supernatural" (ibid). In addition, Coe notes that the creation story is outlined again and again through the "annual planting and harvest cycle of maize, the Maya staff of life" (*The Maya*, 65). He also observes, "Small wonder that many Colonial-period Maya identified the risen Christ with the Maize God" (66).

Chapter 11

Ze'ev W. Falk explains that the most common reason that a man took another wife was due to the childlessness of the first (*Hebrew Law in Biblical Times,* 127). But although concubinage existed in biblical times, the inclusion of harlots was against the law of Moses. Abinadi prophesies to King Noah's people by saying, "Wo be unto this people, for I have seen their abominations, and their wickedness, and their whoredoms" (Mosiah 11:20).

Chapter 12

Scripture referenced: Mosiah 27:8

In Mosiah 27, we learn that Alma the Younger "became a very wicked and an *idolatrous* man" (v. 8, emphasis added). A reference to idol worshipping opens the door quite wide for Alma since there were many deities to choose from. For the purposes of this novel, I settled primarily on the moon goddess, who was called Chak Chel, Ix Chel, or "Lady Rainbow" by the Maya people. The Mayans believed she helped to ensure fertility and refused to be a victim of oppression. Coe clarifies that she was the goddess of "weaving, medicine, and childbirth; . . . the snakes in her hair and the claws with which her feet and hands are tipped prove her the equivalent of . . . the Aztec mother of gods and men" (*The Maya,* 216).

Not a lot is said in the Book of Mormon about singing and dancing, but the evidence is there to at least establish the practices as part of Nephite and Lamanite society (see 1 Nephi 18:9 and Mosiah 20:1). Singing and dancing were certainly an important part of the Maya culture in which songs were sung or chanted on important occasions, such as funerals or celebrations, which "included songs of love and flirtation." Maya art and sculpture depict dancing and musical instruments. (*Images*, 178–9.)

Chapter 13

Clothing was worn according to social status in Mesoamerica since living in the tropics required little clothing. Therefore, clothing became a part of a person's identity. Materials such as quetzal feathers and jaguar skins were used only by those who had wealth and privilege. Sorenson notes, "The wealthy used sumptuous fabrics and inventive decoration to place themselves visually atop a hierarchy of prestige and privilege and to display icons that signaled their social roles" (*Images*, 88). In other words, kings, rulers, priests, or warriors could be identified just by looking at their clothing.

Chapter 14

The Mayan civilization has been present in Mesoamerica for thousands of years. According to Coe, the stages of the Mayan civilization are as follows: Archaic Period (3000 BC to 1800 BC), Preclassic Period (1800

BC to AD 250), Classic Period (AD 250 to AD 925), and the Postclassic Period (AD 925 to AD 1530) (see *The Maya,* 10). King Mosiah and his people lived during the Late Preclassic era (300 BC to AD 250).

Chapter 15

Men's work consisted mainly of farming throughout Mesoamerica. Only during the off season, "wars were fought, trading journeys were undertaken, and houses were built or repaired" (*Images*, 33). Women spent a good part of their day hand-grinding cornmeal with a flat stone, then preparing tortillas or tamales. Another meal consisted of the wet ball of dough being diluted with water and drunk. Women also wove cloth, gathered firewood, carried water, repaired household items, reared children, etc. (ibid).

Chapter 18

Scripture referenced: Mosiah 26:36

Public architecture throughout Mesoamerica included numerous temples. Sorenson explains that "there was a wide sharing of concepts throughout," although the people in the different areas developed their own specific styles (*Images,* 104). Common to the temple center were sacrificial altars, archives for priestly records, and places for events such as ceremonies (*Images,* 105). In the Book of Mormon, there are plenty of references to temples, towers, and other public buildings (see Helaman 3:11, 14; *Images,* 107).

Chapter 19

Scriptures referenced: Mosiah 27:8–9, 13–14, 16

The fictional depiction of Alma the Younger and the rebels attempting to sacrifice a human (Ben) is not to be taken lightly. Human sacrifice was part of the tradition of autosacrificing, a form of blood-letting, or sacrificing and therefore giving back life to the gods who created the sky and earth (see *The Maya,* 13; *Images,* 142). Sorenson suggests that human sacrifice might be a part of the "abominations" that Nephi prophesied of in 1 Nephi 12:23 (*Images*, 142).

Other sacrifices more familiar to us and considered routine throughout Mesoamerica included animal sacrifices (which entails removing the head or heart of the animal). The animal sacrifices were made by the priests in behalf of an individual or community. The smoke that rises from a sacrifice was believed to be sweet to the "nostrils of the gods." Quails or turkeys were typical animal sacrifices (ibid).

Chapter 20

Scriptures referenced: Mosiah 27:11–13, 16, 18–21; Alma 36:7–8, 11

Through Alma the Younger, we learn that the elite wear plenty of jewelry (Alma 31:28). Similarly, the Mesoamerican people wore jewelry or ornamentation in abundance. Gold and silver, jade and shell, feathers, and animal furs were all a part of adornment. In fact, according to Sorenson, the jadeite stone was an important symbol of living nature, such as water, maize, and vegetation, as well as was part of the burial practice in which the jadeite stone was placed "into the mouth of the dead at burial, in token of hoped-for rebirth" (*Images*, 95).

Chapter 21

Scriptures referenced: Mosiah 26:35; 27:11–14, 16, 18–19, 22; Alma 36:13–22

Chapter 22

Scriptures referenced: Mosiah 27:16–17, 23–25, 28–31; Alma 36:22–24, 28–30

Chapter 23

Scriptures referenced: Mosiah 28:1–4, 7, 20

Selected Bibliography

Allen, Joseph L. *Sacred Sites: Searching for Book of Mormon Lands.* American Fork, Utah: Covenant Communications, 2003.

Brown, S. Kent. *Voices from the Dust: Book of Mormon Insights.* American Fork, Utah: Covenant Communications, 2004.

Coe, Michael D. *The Maya*—7th ed. New York: Thames & Hudson, 2005.

Nibley, Hugh. *Lehi in the Desert.* In *The Book of Mormon*, Vol. 5 of *The Collected Works of Hugh Nibley.* Salt Lake City: Deseret Book, and Provo, Utah: FARMS, 1988.

——. *Teachings of the Book of Mormon—Semester Two.* Provo, Utah: FARMS, 2004. Licensed by Covenant Communications.

Nyman, Monte S., and Charles D. Tate, eds. *The Book of Mormon: Jacob Through Words of Mormon, To Learn With Joy.* Provo, Utah: Religious Studies Center, Brigham Young University, 1990. Distributed by Bookcraft, Inc.

Sorenson, John L. *An Ancient American Setting for the Book of Mormon.* Salt Lake City: Deseret Book, and Provo, Utah: FARMS, 1985.

——. *Images of Ancient America: Visualizing Book of Mormon Life.* Provo, Utah: Research Press/FARMS, 1998.

About the Author

H.B. Moore is the award-winning author of the Book of Mormon historical series *Out of Jerusalem.* Her next series includes *Abinadi,* which won both the 2008 Whitney Award for Best Historical Novel and the 2009 Best of State in Literary Arts; and its sequel, *Alma,* another Whitney Award finalist. She is also the author of the non-fiction book, *Women of the Book of Mormon: Insights and Inspirations,* published under Heather B. Moore. Heather loves to hear from her readers. You can contact her through her website: www.hbmoore.com.